Shadow of a Doubt

SHADOW
OF A
DOUBT

William J. Coughlin

St. Martin's Press
New York

Design by Susan Hood

FOR RUTH BRIDGET

Shadow of a Doubt

THE DAY BEGAN WITH A FUNERAL.

It wasn't much of a funeral, just a dozen assorted men and women, all looking uncomfortable, assembled at the third-rate funeral home selected by the family of the deceased, the deceased being Jimmy Ryan and the family being a nephew who wouldn't have done anything, except that a small funeral policy paid for Jimmy's sending off as well as for the grave.

It was unseasonably warm for the first week in June, but air conditioning had made the place uncomfortably—if appropriately—chilly.

The friends, myself included, were members of what we liked to call the Club, the Thursday-night meeting of A.A. held in the basement of St. Jude's.

St. Jude, the Catholics say, is the patron saint of impossible causes. Some of us were that, some of us weren't. Jimmy was.

He had, during his brief lifetime, managed to ingest a river of cheap whiskey. That liquid had boiled his blood vessels and reduced his heart muscle to mush, which was the reason he expired like a drowning swimmer, sucking for a breath that would not come, despite his having been off the stuff for over a year.

Jimmy, although he'd been Irish, had left the church, except for the weekly meetings in the St. Jude basement, so the funeral director did the honors, mouthing Bible blended with a kind of preppy psychology. Jimmy would have thought it hilarious.

1

In other years, other times, other places, we would have assembled to drink his memory in the whiskey that had killed him. But after the brief service, the body being shipped out for cremation, we gathered in a small Greek place, sopping up doughnuts with oversugared java. Coffee is the drug of choice for recovering alcoholics.

Which I am. At least I hope I am. Every day the struggle begins anew. At least it does for me, and, I'm told, each of the other members of the Club.

So, in toasts of pungent coffee, Jimmy had his memory celebrated by a strange variety of people—a doctor, a board-certified psychiatrist, a bank vice president who had been clean without a drop for thirty years but who was still only one drink away from destruction. Tinker, tailor, soldier, spy; male, female, and some who weren't quite sure—every kind of person and calling was represented by the members of the Club.

Even a lawyer.

I am that lawyer, but only by the grace of God and the benevolence of friends of influence with the bar association. Oh, I admit I was suspended—not disbarred, there is a difference—for a year. I sold real estate. But that was after the month-long clinic stay imposed on me by the court.

Still, some people might be envious. I am forty-seven years old. I figure I have made over three million dollars, although I have lost every damn penny, one way or the other. I have been married three times, each time to a gloriously beautiful woman, and each of my gloriously beautiful wives drank even more than I did. Drunks attract drunks, you see. I have a child, a daughter, nineteen, who I'm told is currently in a drug rehabilitation program somewhere in California. I haven't seen Lisa in sixteen years. Sometimes I see her in my dreams, not as she is now but as she was then, laughing and small.

Once, years ago, I had a whole floor in Detroit's Buhl Building. Five partners, twenty associates, and support troops. First cabin all the way. The money, usually from negligence lawsuits and other courtroom triumphs, seemed to flow in like an eternal river, like the whiskey. And then, for different reasons, both stopped.

Now, in a distant suburb of Detroit, I have a desk in the office

2

of a friend. His girls take my messages. I can use the conference room and the library but I have to pay for my own phone. Like the famous Blanche, I am dependent upon the kindness of strangers.

I make a living. Just.

Of course, the big house in Grosse Pointe Farms is gone, along with the servants. And the red Rolls Royce. I loved that car, I must admit, more passionately than I loved any of my wives, but the car went into the yawning maw of alimony settlements and creditors.

Now, I have a small studio. Rented furniture. No garage, just a carport. My car is an aging Ford Escort.

But I'm alive, which is more than anyone can say for Jimmy Ryan. And I have learned not to be bitter. Each day is a new life. That may sound trite to you, but it has become nothing less than the secret of life for me.

The Club members consumed too many doughnuts and too much coffee, just as we all used to consume too much liquor, and so, stuffed to the gills, we adjourned, Jimmy in our minds like a ghost.

I DROVE out to the mall parking lot next to my office in the small suburban city of Pickeral Point, located between Mount Clemens and St. Clair, both of them small Michigan cities bordering the St. Clair waterway and lying just north of Detroit, the violent, decaying giant where I made and lost my fortune.

There are no parking garages in Pickeral Point. Parking garages mean commerce and success. The only paid parking was on the street where meters waited to be fed. People usually parked free at the mall lot and walked. Pickeral Point was not exactly a hub of blossoming commerce. If you had ambition and hope, you soon left Pickeral Point for greener fields. Being somewhat short of both, I had come and I had stayed.

I pushed open the double doors to the office. They were the first leather-covered doors in the city of Pickeral Point, and they impressed the working-class clients who came through them, their mouths talking of justice but their eyes glittering with greedy dreams. The receptionist, a girl with very large breasts

3

and a very small intellect, looked up as if seeing me for the first time. Then a smile of recognition lit her dull but pretty features.

"Hey, Mr. Sloan," she said, smiling. "You got a client. At least I think she's a client. I gave her some coffee and had her wait in your office. Jeez, she must've been in there an hour or more already."

"As usual, I was delayed in church," I said as I passed. It was meant as a joke but it was wasted on the dull young woman, who nodded reverently.

SHE was waiting all right, standing in my small office and staring out the window at downtown Pickeral Point, all two blocks of it.

A dusty blonde, she had the compact build of a woman who has taken excellent care of herself. Strong legs like a runner's, a firm back and buttocks. The black suit she wore was expensive, well cut with a commanding style that reeked money.

"I'm sorry I'm late," I said as I entered the office.

She turned slowly and looked me over as if I were a piece of art, or meat, up for sale.

She exuded a quality like old wine and other precious things that grow more valuable with passing years. She wasn't young but she was an absolute beauty.

"You don't recognize me, do you, Charley?"

She was right, although there was something familiar about her, like the refrain of a half-remembered song, or an old, unidentified photo you might come across in a picture album.

"You look familiar," I responded weakly.

"Christ, I should. You used to make love to me almost every Saturday night. Have I changed that much?"

Memory is a mystery, they say: no one knows exactly how it works. I think it was her eyes that opened the rusted lock. They were green and dark, a bit like emeralds. I had known only one pair of eyes like that, ever.

"Robin?"

She grinned, displaying perfect teeth, and came over, putting her arms on my shoulders.

"Who else?" She gently kissed my lips, just a quick soft touch, but warm and unexpectedly exciting. Thirty years vanished and it was as if we were still teenagers.

4

"Surprised, Charley?"

I reached out and put my hands on her waist. I touched a strong, athletic body. "I don't know what to say."

Those eyes danced with amusement as she stepped back and looked me up and down again. "You look great, Charley. You even got rid of the pimples."

I laughed. "A triumph of modern medicine and maturity. What brings you back to your home state after all these years?"

Without responding, she turned and walked to one of my two office chairs. She sat, crossed her very good legs, and fixed those remembered eyes on me. There was a tension in that glance, as if we were strangers once again.

"It's all over the television and radio this morning," she said without emotion. "My husband was killed last night."

"Oh, Jesus! I'm sorry to hear that, Robin. What happened?"

"They say he was murdered, Charley," she replied coolly. "They've arrested our daughter. That's why I'm here. I want you to represent her."

"Where is she?"

"Here, Pickeral Point. They have her at the sheriff's office. I just came from there."

I sat behind my desk and pulled out a legal pad. "Okay, I'll get right over there. First, Robin, I don't even know your married name."

"Harwell. Mrs. Harrison Harwell."

I looked up. "Like in Harwell Boats?"

She nodded.

Harwell Boats was the county's largest employer. Harwell manufactured small, fast speedboats, cheap but well made. Harwell was the Henry Ford of pleasure boating. It was a national company. The plant in Pickeral Point was one of five around the country.

"Charley, we don't have much time for histories so I'll make this brief. I was Harrison's secretary, then his mistress, and since ten years ago, his wife."

"How old is your daughter?"

"Twenty-one." She smiled slightly as she saw my reaction. "Stepdaughter. Her mother, Harrison's second wife, died. Our daughter's name is Angel." She paused. "I consider her my

5

daughter. I raised her, Charley. I couldn't love her more if she were my own blood." The declaration was made mechanically, without any corresponding emotion.

"What happened, Robin, if you know? Was he shot?"

"Stabbed," she said calmly, but there was a tension in her now that I hadn't seen before. "One of our servants found him in his study. They called me and I called the police. He was dead, a mess, blood all over everything. The police found my daughter hiding in her bedroom; her hands and clothing were covered with his blood."

"Jesus."

She nodded slowly. "Charley, if we had more time I'd be able to put this a little more diplomatically. Angel has mental and emotional problems. She was always high-strung, but the real scary stuff started a couple of years ago when she turned eighteen. She got out of the last place just a few months ago. She's been hospitalized several times."

"Schizophrenia? I'm told it often hits in the late teens."

Robin spoke slowly, as though she wanted to make sure I understood each word. "That's what the doctors thought at first, but since then they've changed their minds and their diagnosis." Her slow smile was forced and sad. "With each new doctor we got a new diagnosis."

"What you're saying is, she killed him."

"They wouldn't let me talk to her, but they told me she admitted doing it."

"Did she give them a reason?"

She looked away. "I don't know. They didn't say." The last few words trembled, as did her lips, but for just a moment, and then she looked back at me, in control once more. "If she did do it, she was insane."

"Sounds that way."

"I want everything done for her, Charley. I don't care what it costs."

Years ago I would have taken words like that as an invitation to pry the lid off the family fortune. But things change.

"I'll get over to the jail and start the ball rolling, Robin, but I think you'll want to bring in real high-powered counsel on this case. I'll give you the names of some of the leading criminal lawyers around and you can take your pick."

6

"Why not you?"

What was I going to tell her? That I was hanging on to the earth by my sober fingernails and didn't want the emotional risk of a major case? That I didn't know if I had the grit needed for a major trial anymore and if I didn't, it was something I didn't want to find out?

Instead, I said, "I'm sort of semiretired, Robin." I gestured at my tiny, bleak office. "I handle some small matters here and there, just enough to keep my hand in. I sort of play at it now. I think you need a heavy hitter, not someone like me."

Those eyes, just like old times, could turn into two laser beams. "I have plenty of money, Charley. Enough to bring anyone out of retirement. And you're the one I want to handle my daughter's case."

I smiled. In fact, I damn near laughed. A few short years ago, the thought of turning away money would have seemed like something from a drunken nightmare. But it was natural enough now. "Well, as I say, I'll run over there, file my appearance, and get things started. But unless you're her legal guardian, she may want a lawyer she selects."

"Angel should have had a guardian appointed but my husband was against anything like that. He always thought she might get better and that having had a guardian appointed could be a stigma down the road."

Robin took up a small, expensive purse and extracted a checkbook, quickly scribbling out a check. "She is insane, Charley. Oh, she looks all right, but if you talk to her for a while, you can see she's quite ill." She handed me the check.

It was for twenty thousand dollars. I almost didn't hear the next words she spoke so confidently. "I'm sure you can get her off on a plea of insanity."

I looked up from the check. "Insanity never was an easy defense, Robin. The Michigan law was changed a few years back. No one is ever found not guilty by reason of insanity anymore. If the crime was committed and the defendant is crazy, juries will find the defendant guilty but mentally ill. It's a compromise verdict—it means the same prison term—but jurors seem to feel better about bringing it in."

Her lips parted and her eyes widened slightly. "What do you mean?"

"Someone like your daughter, someone sick and accused of a felony, unless she's baying at the moon, a jury will accept the illness but they'll use it to reach the compromise verdict, which is really the same as guilty. The prisoner is supposed to get treatment, but as a practical matter, that generally doesn't happen.

"Theoretically," I said, "they could still bring in a not guilty by reason of insanity, but they never do."

She was silent for a moment. I thought she had paled. "Do what you can for her, Charley."

THE city of Pickeral Point isn't very big, just a slice of land ending in a long picturesque boardwalk along the St. Clair River. Once our little city was the home of prosperous farmers who built large Victorian homes along the river's edge. Now, with everyone trying to get the hell out of Detroit, it's become a refuge for the rich, who buy the river homes, and the poor, who cluster in little frame houses on dirt streets, well back from the tourist-oriented main street along the riverfront.

Directly across, on the other shore of the wide St. Clair River, the connecting link in the Great Lakes, are miles of enormous Canadian chemical plants. They look like a giant set for a science fiction movie, with stainless steel forests of industrial chimneys and huge metal pipes winding around ugly expanses of long, low windowless labs and factories. This is Canada, but the shoreline looks more like a part of another planet. When the wind is right, you can smell the powerful acid odor exuded by the bubbling chemicals they brew over there.

But on the American side, at least at Pickeral Point, the shoreline resembles a calender photo. One side of the river road is occupied by an upscale shopping mall with acres of parking for patrons of its many pricey shops. Across the road is the impressive wooden river boardwalk, and beyond that are the stately Victorian mansions, sitting like fat matrons, one after another, on long wooded lots that slope down toward the busy river. Enormous ocean-going freighters bringing the world's cargo to the Great Lakes glide past, almost close enough to touch.

In the summer, when all the tourist and day visitors from Detroit flock up to enjoy the mall and the boardwalk, Pickeral Point looks prosperous. But that bustling activity is ephemeral. When winter threatens, the tourists stay home and the town's prosperity collapses like a deflating balloon.

Pickeral Point is also the county seat for Michigan's Kerry County, small in comparison with its neighboring counties and oddly shaped, like an axe head, cut that way originally to give the county farmers legal access to the river. Kerry has a sheriff, a prosecutor, a probate judge, other county officers, and three circuit judges. All occupy a cluster of new buildings set in a square just back from the river, called Featherstone Square after a dead state senator. The residents, however, call it Featherhead Square—cynical perhaps, but accurate. Featherhead Square consists of three new buildings: the county building, the court building, and the jail.

I went to the court building and filed the legal appearance form showing that I was the lawyer representing Angel Harwell, then I walked across the square to the two-story jail.

It was a modern building that doubled as the sheriff's headquarters. The stark reception area was tiled, with benches bolted to the floor. It was presided over by a sheriff's receptionist housed in a bulletproof glass cage.

The receptionist was a very fat deputy sheriff named Franklin. His uniform was tailored so the fabric didn't strain against his bulk. Franklin—he never used a first name—looked out at the world with little pig eyes, not hostile, but not friendly either. He knew me. Ironically enough, I represent a number of practicing drunks who beat up their cars or their wives. Small-time stuff, admittedly, but of sufficient volume that I'm well known to the Pickeral Point cops, guards, and court personnel.

"Hey, Charley," Franklin said into the microphone in his booth. "What can we do for you?" His voice came out the speaker with a slightly metallic quality as he stared from his cozy cocoon of thick, yellowish glass. Bonnie and Clyde couldn't have shot their way into the modern Pickeral Point jail.

"Hello, Franklin." I smiled. "I'm here to talk to a client."

"Who?"

"Angel Harwell."

The little pig eyes narrowed. He hesitated, then spoke. "I'm sorry, Charley. I have orders that no one is to see her. This morning we were ass deep in television cameras and reporters. Shit, I even got a call an hour ago from CBS in New York. Everybody wants to talk to her, even Dan Rather."

"I'm her lawyer, Franklin," I said evenly.

He frowned, screwing up his face in a manner that passed for thinking, then spoke. "I got my orders, Charley."

"Better get hold of the sheriff, then. If I have to get a court order it will complicate life."

The tiny eyes narrowed until they almost disappeared. He pursed his fat, rubbery lips, then shrugged. "Hold on. I'll call."

He switched the microphone off so I couldn't hear, then picked up the phone. He had a spirited conversation with someone, hung up, and switched the speaker back on.

"Have you filed an appearance?" he asked.

"Just now, over at court."

He raised an eyebrow. "They say I got to let you in."

"I think it's something called the Constitution, Franklin."

He chuckled, the soft flesh at his neck wiggling from the effort. "Okay."

A loud click sounded as he electronically opened the steel door leading into the bowels of the main jail.

"Go on in, Charley. Someone will take you up."

A woman deputy, looking much better in her uniform than Franklin, escorted me up the stairs to the second floor, the women's section. She moved with parade-ground precision, quick, sure, with a slightly authoritative swagger. Her uniform trousers were cut snug and she had a very nice ass.

The building was only a few months old but it had already acquired the aroma of jail: chemical disinfectant, anger, and fear. Nothing else in the world smells quite like a jail.

A woman inmate called out to me as I passed her cell. To translate into the official language of court: she offered to perform a lewd and lascivious act upon my person if I would just thrust a named body part through the bars. What she actually said in her raspy voice was far less polite but much more to the point.

"Shut up, Martha," the deputy snapped, more for show than for effect.

I was led toward an isolated small cell at the back of the jail. Another woman deputy was seated just outside the cell.

"We got her on a suicide watch," the deputy explained.

10

Inside the cell a young woman sat primly on a bolted bench. "I want to talk to her in private," I said.

Just like big-time prisons, the new jail had fancy state-of-the-art interview rooms separating lawyer and client by glass but allowing communication by microphone.

"We got orders to keep her here," the matron said. "You can talk through the bars."

"So you can listen in?"

She smirked. "Whatever you got to say, counselor, wouldn't be worth hearing." She shrugged. "It's against standing orders, but I'll let you into the cell. I'll sit over there where I can see. Unless you shout, I won't hear a thing. But don't give her anything and keep your hands where I can see them."

I opened my briefcase, although I wasn't required to do so, and let her see the contents, which weren't much.

She opened the cell door using an electronic device like a television's remote control. I stepped in. There was the narrow bench and a toilet, but that was all.

Angel watched me as I approached.

I have been in dozens of jails, sometimes as a customer, but I have never seen anyone who seemed more out of place.

Angel Harwell looked very much like her name, an angel. Her hair, stylish and short, was jet black, contrasting with perfect white ivory skin. There was a soft, almost spiritual beauty to her classic oval face, the kind of face that stares out of magazine ads for French perfume. Her eyes were blue, light blue, almost translucent. They had dressed her in a standard jail smock, blue and loose fitting, but she was tall and slender, and even in the concealing smock, she possessed a seductive feminine quality. She wore jail slippers, the paper kind that cheap bathhouses used to issue.

"My name is Charles Sloan," I said, holding out my hand. "I'm a lawyer. Your mother hired me to represent you."

Her hand was soft but her grip was sure. She moved over so I could sit down.

At a respectable distance outside, the woman deputy stared at us as if expecting us to begin to fight or make love or erupt into some other act forbidden by jail regulations.

"Can you get me out of here?" she asked. Her voice was

11

cultured, quietly assured, without the slightest hint of fear or apprehension.

"I am going to try. May I call you Angel?"

"If you like. Are you a criminal lawyer?"

"Well, I do a lot of things, criminal defense is one of them, Angel."

She fixed those appraising blue eyes on me. "Are you any good?"

"Some think I am," I said. The opposite was equally true, but that wasn't something you usually said to reassure a prospective client. I took out a yellow pad from my briefcase. "Angel, they have you here on an open charge of murder. Do you understand that?"

"I really want to get out of here. I can't urinate without one of those bull-dyke guards staring at me. Can you do something about that? It's quite humiliating."

"We'll discuss all that, Angel. But first let me tell you some things about the charge and some of the possible defenses."

"Don't you want to know what happened?"

I nodded. "Yes, but first, I want you to know your legal position."

"You'll tell me what to say, right?"

I smiled indulgently, but she had hit the nail right on the head. I couldn't come right out and tell her what to say—that would be illegal and unethical—but I could lecture and by so doing let her see the best way to go. It was a delicate technique and every criminal trial lawyer had to know where to draw the ethical line in such situations. Some occasionally went over the line, as I had in the past, but I was no longer willing to take unnecessary risks. I had lost my law license once, and if it happened again I knew I would never get it back.

"Angel," I began, ignoring her comment, "in Michigan, there are three possible charges when a felonious killing has occurred. Taking it from the top, the most serious charge is first-degree murder. They bring that when the killing was planned and maliciously carried out, or committed in the course of a felony. Second-degree murder is charged when the killing is intentional but without what the law calls malice—in other words, it wasn't planned. The least serious charge is manslaughter. That's the

12

charge when the killing is done while acting instinctively in the heat of passion. In this state, the law—"

"Cut to the chase," Angel said crisply. "What am I charged with?"

"So far, it's an open charge. A degree will be fixed by the prosecutor and he'll have to back it up in a court hearing."

"This is all terribly fascinating, but can you get me out, or can't you?"

"That's why I'm telling you this. If they charge you with first-degree murder, I can't. Bail isn't allowed in first-degree cases. But if they charge you with second-degree, the court can set bail. The same is true with the charge of manslaughter."

"Go on."

"When someone has been killed, a number of defenses may apply. For instance, self-defense. If someone is about to seriously harm another, that person has a right to defend herself, even take a life if it's a reasonable act. And then there's insanity."

She looked into my eyes. "What has Robin told you?"

"Not much. We didn't have time."

"She told you I was crazy, didn't she?"

I paused. "She said you were nervous and that you had been treated for emotional problems."

"She said I was insane." Angel paused and looked away. "Well, perhaps I am."

"Tell me what happened," I said.

"How much do you know?"

"Practically nothing."

She nodded. "We have houses all over the country, did you know that?"

"No."

"We do. Wherever Daddy built a factory he bought a house. We hardly ever came up here to Michigan, except for a few days every year. Our main place is in Florida, that's where I consider home. We came up here for a few days because Daddy had business."

"Do the three of you always travel together?"

She shrugged. "Lately we have."

"What happened last night?"

"Nothing. Well, that's hardly true, is it? Of course, something happened. My father died. I found him, did you know that?"

"As I said, I know very little."

"I was upstairs in my room. I haven't been sleeping well. I think it's this new medicine I'm taking. I went downstairs for some milk and I saw the light on in Daddy's study."

Her tone was conversational and without emotion. "I looked in. I almost didn't see him. He was lying on the floor just behind his desk. There was a knife in his chest and he was all bloody." She looked at me. "He was dead."

"What happened then?"

"At first it didn't seem real, like something on television. You see it but you know that it isn't real, it's just some actor done up by the special effects department. That's how it seemed to me."

"Unreal."

She nodded. "Of course, I realized it wasn't. I tried to help Daddy. I tried to get the knife out, but it was all slippery and I couldn't." She stopped and shook her head, then continued. "I didn't know what to do. It still seemed like a dream, a nightmare. The blood was all over everything. He was dead. I ran back to my room. I was there when the police came."

"Did you tell anybody?"

"I was too shocked. Really, I couldn't even think straight."

"I understand the police found you in your room."

"I wasn't hiding, if that's what you mean."

"What did you tell the police?"

"I said my father was dead downstairs."

"That's all?"

"They asked me how we got along, my father and I." She shrugged. "I said we got along fine."

"That's all?"

"Are you a good lawyer?"

"Pretty good. What else did you tell them?"

"You must understand I was still in shock."

"Yes, I understand. What did you tell them?"

She paused. "I'm really not sure."

"Did you tell them you killed him?"

She shook her head. "Not like that."

"Like how?"

"I'm very confused. What's your name again?"

"Sloan. You can call me Charley, if that's easier."

She nodded. "They asked me a lot of questions, Charley. I felt responsible because I had left him there all alone. I think I said something like that. That I was responsible."

"Did you say you stabbed him?"

That angel face now seemed almost serene. "I don't think so."

"But you don't know."

"If I did, they'll tell you, won't they?"

I nodded. "Yeah, they will, Angel. That you can count on."

"Can you get me out, Charley?"

I had the feeling that not even Jesse James or the Marines could get Angel Harwell out. Not now, not ever.

"Did you stab him?"

"No," she said, but blandly, with no more feeling than if declining cream and sugar.

"Angel, is there anything more I should know? Did you and your father really get along?"

"I loved my father. Will they let me go to the funeral, do you think? They should."

"I'll see what I can do."

"I suppose they'll want those damn doctors to talk to me again."

"Again?"

She sighed. "No matter whatever happens, I end up talking to doctors." She smiled slowly, but there was a sadness in it. "But they never really seem to understand."

"Do you need anything?"

She shook her head. "Not at the moment. Just some privacy."

"I don't want you to talk to anyone about the case, Angel, not the police, not the prosecutor, not anyone—not even the guards or the other prisoners or even the doctors. Not unless I'm right there with you. Do you understand that? It's important."

She nodded.

"I'll check out a few things, and then I'll come back. Don't worry. We'll do everything we can for you."

"Just get me out."

I closed the briefcase and stood up. "I'll work on that, Angel, trust me."

She looked up, her beautiful face devoid of animation.

"Do I have any other choice?"

2

THE PICKERAL POINT POLICE DEPARTMENT CONSISTS
of a dozen or so glorified traffic cops, more comic than commanding, their main job being to keep the tourist traffic flowing nicely
by mindlessly enforcing the city's parking laws. If you double-
park you have to worry about the city police, but if you're a really
serious criminal they are absolutely no threat. They wouldn't
know what to do. All serious transgressions, real felonies, are
quickly turned over to the Kerry County sheriff's office. The
sheriff has some honest-to-god cops on the payroll, mostly retired
Detroit detectives enjoying two paychecks and a view of the
river, each of them happy to be in a much gentler city than the
one that pays them their pension.

The sheriff's detectives are older, but they are very good at
their trade. They are hard-eyed professionals, and trying to get
them to tell me anything about the Harwell case at this point
would have been as productive as asking my equally hard-eyed
banker for an unsecured loan.

So I went to the county building and walked up the stairs to the
second floor and the offices of the Kerry County prosecutor, Mark
Evola. Evola could be a pompous ass at times, but basically I
liked him. He was honest and that put him a couple of notches up
on some prosecutors I've known.

Evola had proven to be something of an empire builder. His
staff now numbered twelve assistant prosecutors, who did most of

the lawyer work; a chief investigator, who was Evola's political brain; and a support staff of absolutely gorgeous women.

I always liked coming to Evola's office. It was like watching the Miss America contest; the beauties were clothed, of course, but an active imagination corrected that.

The word was out that Evola, a Republican, would challenge the district's Democratic congressman in the next election, and the common wisdom had it that he wasn't a sure thing, but had a healthy chance.

Caesar's main fault was ambition, history tells us. Mark Evola was possessed by the same kind of hunger.

He had a wife, young and pretty, and two little photogenic kids. He had a mistress, also young and pretty, who served as his personal secretary. He apparently managed to keep both women happy. Congress, I think, could use a talented man like that.

His mistress/secretary showed me into his large office. It was decorated with pictures of himself with other smiling politicians, plaques, and athletic awards from his basketball days at Michigan State University.

Mark Evola was young, thirty-five, and tall, about six feet six, blond, with blue eyes and a hint of a smile that seemed permanently painted on his smooth face. He took my hand. Evola shook hands with everyone as if he had just found out they were his long-lost cousin. If manufactured sincerity was liquid Evola would have drowned everyone he had ever met. Despite that, there was steel beneath the smile but he seldom let it show.

"Charley," he said, grinning and pumping. "Gee, it's good to see you. I'm always glad to see such a distinguished brother at the bar. You're looking especially dapper today." He managed to pat my back vigorously as he let go of my hand. It was like getting slapped by a bear.

I was relieved when he finally returned to his chair behind his big ornate desk. "Charley, is this visit social or business?" His smile exhibited perfect teeth. They didn't look false, but they were. Like many basketball players, he had had the real ones knocked out by assorted elbows under the basket during his playing days.

"Who's assigned to the Harwell case?"

The big smile retreated to the usual smaller and enigmatic one. "Why?"

"I've been retained to represent Angel Harwell."

One blond eyebrow went up like a rising bridge, slow and deliberate. "Have you filed an appearance?"

I nodded.

"Tragic case," Evola said. "She's a beautiful girl. Have you seen her?"

"I just came from the jail."

"Beautiful, but a monster." He sighed. "Charley, a lot of these crimes I can understand, but killing your own father, that's against nature."

"Also the law. Who are the detectives assigned?"

The smile turned wicked. "Morgan and Maguire."

I tried to hide my dismay. Harvey Morgan and Phil Maguire were known to defense lawyers as M and M, two gray-haired old cops, retired Detroit homicide detectives, who looked and acted like kindly grandfathers, never raising their voices or their hands in anger. Smooth, intelligent, and for the defendants in the cases they handled, absolutely deadly. They built their cases like master bricklayers putting up a wall.

"What are you going to charge her with?" I asked.

The smile became even more wicked. "First-degree, what else?"

"Aren't you overreacting, Mark? Even if she did do it, it was a family hassle, a spur of the moment thing. Where's the intent, the malice?"

He chuckled. "Charley, the next thing I know you'll ask to have the charge reduced to carving without a license. Hey, she killed her father. A very important man. Not that it makes any difference, but this is a front-page case. People all over America are reading about it as we speak. What we got here is a modern day Lizzie Borden. I'm not going to send a message that it's suddenly okay to knock off your parents. Angel—what a wonderful name— is going to have the full flame of the law's Bunsen burner applied to her cute little ass. There's going to be no deals in this one. She did it, and I'm going to see she pays for what she did."

"Are we still going to have a trial, or are you planning to bypass all that and send her directly to prison?"

18

The smile vanished, but only for a second, then it became almost oily. "Hey, Charley, there is nobody more devoted to due process than I am, you know that. You supported me in the last election."

I had bought a fifty dollar ticket to his campaign cocktail party. Every local lawyer, except the one running against Evola, did that. It was the smart political thing to do. I had gone, sipped tomato juice, and had shaken the great man's hand. It wasn't what one would consider the political act of a wild-eyed fanatic.

"It isn't first-degree, even if she did it," I repeated.

He looked solemn, but his eyes were smiling. "She confessed, Charley. Her prints were all over the knife handle. Believe me, we can make it stick."

"I want to see that so-called confession."

The mouth had formed that irritating small smile again. "It's being typed up. I'll tell Morgan and Maguire to send you a copy."

"Today?"

He shrugged. "Well, you know how these things are. God knows when one of the girls will get to it. But you'll get it as soon as it's available."

Nice comforting words, but they meant I'd have to kick, fight, and scream to see the thing.

"Who are you going to assign as the trial lawyer?"

"The best man in the office."

"Olesky?" Stash Olesky, a young guy who looked like he just got off the boat from Poland, had proved himself a wizard who had the ability to hypnotize jurors as if he were old Svengali come back to life.

Evola laughed. "Close, but no cigar. I'm going to try it myself."

I was surprised. Prosecutors avoid trying cases. If a mistake happens and the public is outraged the blame can be prudently placed on the assistant prosecutor who tried the case. Prosecutors are elected every four years, and those who have enough staff lawyers handle only the pretrial stuff that can't backfire, the stuff that looks good in print and is perfectly safe. Officeholders never gamble where their own careers are concerned.

That is, unless the stakes are high enough to make it worth the gamble.

The Harwell murder case was the kind of publicity gold mine

19

that merited betting all the chips. Mark Evola was the kind of ambitious politician who dreamed not just about being elected to Congress, but maybe someday to the White House itself.

"Angel is on a suicide watch at the jail," I said. "Is there some indication that's necessary?"

He shrugged. "It's only a routine precaution."

"I presume you people think she's insane."

"What?" No smile this time.

"Well, only insane people kill themselves. If you have put that sort of thing into operation, I think it's a fair inference that you think she may be mentally ill."

"Bullshit!"

I was amused. Evola rarely used earthy language.

"Well, it's a possible inference isn't it?"

"Like hell it is. She killed her own father, murdered him. If she has any shred of decency, she has to think about the grotesque thing she's done. She might try suicide, because of guilt."

"Shouldn't you have a psychiatrist see her? I mean, if you really think she's . . ."

The little smile came back, but it flickered like a light burning out—on again, off again. "She's perfectly fine," he said. "She's being handled the same as any other person charged with murder."

I shrugged. "Maybe. I suppose I could subpoena the sheriff's jail records to see if that's true."

"Charley, relax. Do you want the suicide watch taken off? Hey, I'm not a tough guy. I'm easy. I'll call over and take care of it." He grinned now as if he had just done me an immense favor. "Anything else you want?"

"I want to see the confession."

"That will take time. You'll get it. I promise."

That promise had the same ring as being told the check was in the mail. He stood up, indicating that our meeting was over, and walked me to the door, his arm around my shoulders.

"Actually, this should be fun, Charley. I haven't tried a jury case in a long time. And they say you used to be pretty good."

There was a condescending tone in that phrase, "used to be," and I resented it, although it reflected my own attitude to a T.

Life for me seemed to be filled with more than just one "used to be."

20

"We'll have a ball, Charley, with this case, a real ball."

I knew he wouldn't feel that way if he thought there was even the slightest possibility he might lose.

All games are great if you win.

I wondered if Angel Harwell would think it was all a game.

I know I didn't.

I TOOK another long look at Evola's ladies as I left the office. They looked back. Mine were looks of admiration. Theirs were looks of amusement, not interest. I sighed and waved good-bye. They smiled and waved back.

I took the stairs to the first floor.

"Hey, Charley!"

I turned toward the source. It was my day for walks down memory lane.

He hadn't changed. A little bulldog of a man with pocked skin and receding red hair, he wore a rumpled sport shirt and no tie. It was his uniform. He grinned, exhibiting crooked tobacco-stained teeth. I hadn't seen him since my sentencing.

His eyes were large and hooded, like a lazy reptile watching the world, looking for something choice to eat.

Those reptilian eyes flickered over me in quick appraisal. I knew what they saw. "Average" is a word I'd use to describe myself—average height, average weight, dark brown hair with a little gray around the ears, average blue eyes. But there was a difference since the last time he saw me. My face has lost the puffiness since I quit drinking and has a sort of roughness to it now, like an old car driven too long and too hard. It crinkles up like worn leather when I smile. Gone are the thousand-dollar custom suits, the gold Rolex and the fancy Italian shoes. My off-the-rack blue suit almost fits, my shoes are comfortably worn and my watch cost thirty bucks and keeps better time than the Rolex ever did. But then, maybe having the correct time isn't everything.

His name is Daniel P. Conroy. It often appears as a byline for the really hot stories exposing graft and corruption that appear in the *Detroit News*. He has the instincts of a hunting shark and, like the shark, is incapable of mercy. He is beloved by some, hated by others, but all agree that his word is his bond. He is the most respected and feared investigative reporter in Detroit.

"Hello, Danny."

He didn't offer his hand but merely walked alongside me. We left the county building as if no time had passed, as if nothing had ever changed and we were lawyer and reporter once more, just walking out of a government building together, meeting by chance.

There was a slight breeze but the air seemed even warmer. This early heat heralded the possibility of a long and simmering summer.

"I hear you got the Harwell case, Charley," he said.

"How come a hot shot like you is up here, Danny? Have you pissed off the editors at the *News* again?"

"They love me. They think I might have a chance at the Pulitzer with my series about the mayor."

"I followed that. It was good."

"Coming up here was my idea," he said. "I needed to get out of the Detroit sewer for a while. The Harwell story has potential. And it's nice up here." He sniffed the air. "What's that smell?"

I laughed. "Fresh air."

"The hell it is."

"That's the aroma from the Canadian chemical plants across the river. We only catch a whiff now and then when the wind is right. You get used to it."

He grunted. "You remember Morgan and Maguire, the homicide dicks? They're up here now. They're working for the sheriff."

"Did you talk to them?" I asked as we strolled along.

"Just now. It was like a class reunion."

"What did they say about the Harwell case?"

He grinned. "Hey, they only say what they want you to hear. Those guys are as slick as sheet ice."

"What did they want you to hear?"

"Angel—Jeez, I wish every killer was named Angel—is supposed to have confessed to chilling dear old dad. Her little angelic paw prints were all over the knife, and dear old dad's blood was all over her. Outside of planning a jail break, I can't think of anything you can do for little Angel, Charley. Or do you have other ideas?"

"For the record?"

"Whatever way you want. I'm just gathering up little nuggets of information at the moment, some for use, some for reference."

I thought before I spoke. Unless I went off the record every word I said was fair game. "I spoke with Angel briefly in the jail. She denies killing her father. She denies confessing. She found him. That's how she got the blood on her, and how her prints got on the knife. She tried to get it out."

Conroy snorted. "Jesus, Charley, you used to come up with better stories than that."

"It's what she told me."

"It's early, Charley, but how about popping in somewhere for a drink?"

"I don't drink anymore, Danny. You should know that. But I'll go with you and have a soda or something."

"Still off the stuff, huh?" Danny Conroy's laugh always came out a surprisingly high-pitched giggle. He laughed. "Jesus, they still call the ambulance entrance at Receiving Hospital the Charles Sloan memorial. That was a great photograph."

He was referring to the front-page photograph of my car sticking out of the hospital ambulance entrance, looking like the rear end of a misfired missile. The car had been wrecked, my ribs had been fractured, and what little reputation I still had then had been ruined. It had been a miracle that I hadn't killed anyone. I was arrested for drunk driving, the third time, and was sent to a substance-abuse clinic. It was the last straw in a very big bundle and my alcoholic world had come tumbling down around me.

I didn't realize it at the time, but my life had been saved.

"That's all behind you now, Charley," he said.

"Not quite. I'm existing under the first-bite doctrine as far as the bar association is concerned."

"I don't understand."

I smiled at him. "Dogs, under the common law, are allowed one bite, but if they do it again, they're destroyed. That first-bite doctrine can apply to lawyers too."

"C'mon, Charley."

"Flying my car into the hospital was just the visible tip of my iceberg, Danny. I was committing all kinds of legal sins, adjourning cases for no good reason, missing filing dates, doing everything but stealing from clients, and I'm sure I would have gotten around to that next if I hadn't ended up publicly disgraced. The bar suspended my license for a year, as you know. I have had my first bite. If I cause any additional problems the bar association will jerk my license forever. And they'll do it quickly and efficiently."

"So you're hiding out up here, is that it?"

"No. Just leading a nice quiet life, and being very careful not to get into any trouble. How about coffee, Danny? There's a little restaurant in the mall," I said.

He looked at his watch. "I'm not much on coffee, Charley, and I should be getting back to Detroit. I'll be around a lot while this thing is going on. We've known each other a long time. If you do anything in this case, you know, get a writ or stir up the pot in any way, give me a call at the paper. Maybe we can help each other out. Okay?"

"No harm in it. Okay."

Conroy nodded, started to walk away, then stopped and turned. "Just a tip, Charley. To show good faith. I'd tiptoe a little on this case until you find out more. Morgan and Maguire have questioned the Harwell servants. I think they've come up with something that may show why the adorable Angel nailed her father. They hinted at it when I talked to them."

I watched as he walked away, thinking that maybe Angel Harwell didn't need a lawyer. Maybe she needed a magician, a very, very good one.

I saw him as I walked toward my building, not that you could miss him. I saw the car first, an enormous gray limo with tinted windows parked in front. He was lounging against the car. I didn't recognize him until I got closer.

He wore an expensive cashmere sport coat tossed casually about his shoulders. His clothing sang a song of gobs of money, even at a distance. He wore his jet black hair like a lion's mane, only this mane was cut and tucked by experts, every hair a work of art. His thin ferret face was topped by tinted glasses that concealed gray fish eyes. He held a long cigarette in a hand graced by a diamond ring Elizabeth Taylor would have envied, even bigger than the ring I used to wear.

He looked like a movie star or a gangster. He was neither.

He was S. Hopkins Crane, the reigning American king of the courtroom. His picture ran in magazines alongside profiles of his latest celebrity clients, who ranged from sultans of industry to real sultans. Crane had gone far for a Detroit boy. He owned a racing stable in Kentucky and an office tower in New York. The face was the same, but everything else had changed. When I was at my zenith, I knew him as "Hoppy" Crane, the king of tarts. He represented Detroit whores then. They had been the first rung on his ladder up. He had climbed quickly.

"Hello, Sloan," he said. "I was wondering if you were going to show up. Your girl didn't know where you were."

"Hello, Hoppy." I nodded at the limo. "Nice car. Do you do weddings?"

He didn't move except to inhale on the cigarette, then he smiled without warmth. "Still the smartass, I see."

"I try, Hoppy. Why do you want to see me?"

"I want to represent the Harwell girl."

"She's already got a lawyer. Me."

He nodded. "Shall we get in the car and talk? I'll put up the glass so my driver can't hear."

"It's a nice day, Hoppy. Let's try talking right here. I don't really care if anyone's listening."

"Suit yourself, Sloan. Here's the deal. You withdraw from the case in favor of me."

"Some deal."

"Hey, I'm not done. I got ten thousand in cash to hand over as soon as you do. Nice clean profit. No strain, no pain, no taxes."

"I've been given a twenty thousand retainer. What would I do with that? Give it back?"

His expression never changed. "That's a lot of money for a broken-down drunk."

"You know how it goes, Hoppy, an apple is only worth what you can get for it. At the moment, I'm a twenty-thousand-dollar apple."

"What's your connection? The widow? The kid? I hear she's nuts."

"Nuts enough to hire a drunk, is that what you mean?"

The cold smile returned. "Don't get your hackles up, Sloan. I deal in reality. I leave romance for other people. Look, you've got the inside track so I'll make you another offer. Keep the twenty thousand. I'll still give you the ten grand. We'll be cocounsel. I'll handle the public stuff, the trial, and you can do the research."

"And what's your fee going to be?"

There was no smile now. "That's negotiable. I'll work something out. Maybe I won't even charge. It'll be a kind of public service."

"Pro bono work, even though the girl is rich?"

"Look, let's knock off the bullshit. You know exactly why I want this case. A lawyer would have to pay millions for the kind of publicity this case will produce. You used to do the same thing, Sloan."

There was that "used to do" phrase again.

"You mean, hustle a case just for the potential business it might bring in?"

"Don't tell me you didn't."

I couldn't refute it. He was right. I had done just that. Discreetly, but I did it.

"Hoppy, get lost. This is my case and I'll handle it without any help."

He tossed the cigarette to the ground and snubbed it out with shoes that cost enough to send a kid to college for a year. "Okay, let's be practical. You're a drunk, Sloan. And you damn near lost your license once. It wouldn't take much to see that it happens again, this time permanently. And I could see that it happens. I got friends, important friends. Look, I'm doing you a favor. You don't have it anymore. This is a major case and I want it. You can't play in my league, Sloan, not anymore. Why risk everything when you can sit back, make money, and enjoy life? Work with me and everything will be just fine."

"Hoppy, you were a cheap sleazy little shit when you were representing hookers. You dress better now, no taste, but more expensively. You haven't changed a bit. Go on, get out of here. I got better things to do."

I turned to go into my office building.

"You'll regret it," he snapped.

"I doubt it."

"Fuck you, Sloan."

I turned. He was climbing into the limo.

"The same to you, Hoppy. And have a nice day."

I waved as his car pulled away. I smiled, but I was shaking with anger, and maybe just a touch of fear.

26

*　*　*

THE small-brained, big-breasted receptionist actually recognized me. Her big, dull eyes were filled with dumb awe as she handed me a fistful of telephone messages.

"Jeez, I never talked to so many important people before. I think you may get invited to be on the *Manny Silver Show*. They want to talk to you."

Manny Silver was the latest star of late-night talk television. A former movie comedian, he burst upon the scene with gabby programs and experts ranging from animal sex advocates to people who claimed to collect gourmet recipes from other planets. It was a show for people with IQs of seventy or less. The receptionist more than qualified.

I thumbed through the messages. Most were from media people. A few were from lawyers. I recognized the names of most of them. They were publicity hounds, famous in their own way. Most were a cut above Hoppy Crane, the hookers' friend, but not much. They would offer more "deals." Those messages I tossed as I sought the peace of my tiny office.

Suddenly I needed a drink. It happens, not so often lately, but it happens. Without warning, usually. The overwhelming need is almost physical, as if some invisible metal claw reached out and grabbed your soul. When it happens you can't think of anything else, just that terrible desire. There are various techniques. I use time.

I looked at my watch and told myself I wouldn't drink for fifteen minutes. Just fifteen minutes, that's all I had to do. If the feeling hadn't passed by then, I'd do fifteen more minutes without a drink. Eventually, the screaming need would subside. All I had to do was concentrate on the face of the watch and hold out for the next fifteen minutes.

The telephone rang and I grabbed it. No matter who it was, talk would help ease my mind away from the clawing desire.

"Yeah," I said, snapping the word.

"Jeez," the receptionist said. She was incapable of speaking without opening with "Jeez." "The lady who was in this morning wants to talk with you."

"Mrs. Harwell?"

"That's her. You want I should put her through?"

"Please."

The phone clicked. "Charley?"

"I was about to call you," I said. It was true. As soon as the fifteen minutes had worked its magic I would have.

"Did you see Angel?"

"Yes, I did. She seemed in pretty good shape, all things considered."

"Can you get her out?"

"I'm working on it."

"Charley, the police want to talk to me."

"Which police?"

"A man named Morgan. Do you know him?"

"He's a detective here. What did you tell him?"

"I didn't know what to say. I suggested he talk to you first."

I thumbed through the messages. Morgan's call was in there, I had just missed seeing it. "I'll call him. You did the right thing, Robin. Don't talk to anyone about any of this, not unless you check with me first."

"Charley, can you come over? I think we really need to talk."

"Okay, but I have to do a few things first." Things like depositing her twenty-thousand-dollar check in my bank before she changed her mind and stopped payment. That, and call Morgan.

"I'll tell the guards to expect you," she said.

"Guards?"

"I borrowed some security men from the boat plant. We are under siege here by media people. There are remote television trucks parked out on the road and photographers by the gate. Some of them even rented boats and tried to get here by coming up the river. The security men stopped that. It's like an invasion. If you had tried to call, you couldn't have gotten through. I've had the phone bells turned off."

"I understand detectives talked to your servants. Is that true?"

"This morning they did."

"Do you know what kind of questions they asked?"

"Not specifically, no."

"I'll want to talk to them when I get there."

"Okay, Charley. I'll make sure no one leaves until they see you."

I heard a man's voice in the background.

28

"Who's with you, Robin?"

"Oh, that's Malcolm Dutton."

"Who?"

"He's the manager of Harrison's plant here. He came over to see if there was anything he could do."

Like cozying up to a rich recent widow, no doubt. "Okay, I'll be there as soon as I can. Are you okay, Robin?"

There was a pause. "Some bad moments, but generally I'm okay." She paused, then spoke, her voice just above a whisper. "Hurry, Charley. I need someone here I can trust."

3

I STILL NEEDED THE DRINK, BUT NOT AS MUCH. I
dialed the number Detective Morgan had left.

"Sheriff's office, Morgan speaking."

"This is Charley Sloan, Harvey. What's up?"

"Hey, Charley, how the hell are you? Damn if we didn't have a
visit today from Danny Conroy. Like old times, you know? You,
him, us. I looked out the window to make sure I was still in Pickeral Point and not Detroit. It's like the old Recorder's Court
gang, all together again."

"So, Harvey, you lining up an alumni dinner or what?"

"It's a thought, isn't it? Actually, Charley, this is business. I
called Mrs. Harwell to arrange to take her statement and she
asked me to check with you. She tells me you're representing
Angel Harwell."

"I am, Harvey. At the moment. I thought you talked to Robin
Harwell this morning."

"I did, Charley. Of course, things were in an uproar then. She
was naturally upset and we didn't know what we had. I'd like to
talk to her now to clear up a few things that have come up since."

"Like what?"

He chuckled. "Cm'on, Charley, this is just routine."

"So, what kind of routine questions do you have in mind?"

He paused, then spoke. "We've talked to the household staff,
Charley. We've heard a number of stories about Angel and her

30

relationship with her father. I want to get Mrs. Harwell's version."

"Mark Evola claims Angel confessed. Is that so?"

"Yeah."

"Can I see it?"

Again there was a pause. "It's being typed up."

"I'll make a deal with you, Harvey. You get me a copy of the alleged confession and I'll set up a meeting with Robin Harwell."

He laughed. "Evola told us to guard Angel's statement with our lives. If it was just me, Charley, I'd show it to you, but this is Evola's case and we have to follow his orders."

"Tell me what she said."

"I'd rather not. Things can get muddled in translation."

"Strong stuff, Harvey?"

The pause was longer. "Look, Charley, don't try to worm it out of me. You can maybe get a copy when she's arraigned."

"When's that?"

"Tomorrow morning. District Court."

"Evola said he's going to charge her with first-degree murder."

"He is," Morgan replied.

"I presume on the basis of that alleged confession?"

"That, and several other things. All will be made known to you at the proper time." He chuckled. "This is like a card game, Charley. You can't see the cards until they're dealt. Now, when can I talk to Mrs. Harwell?"

"Are you going to the arraignment?"

"I don't have much to do tomorrow, I'll be there."

"We'll talk about it then."

"We can bring her in, Charley."

"You can try, Harvey, but I hope it won't come to that."

He paused and then spoke. "Are you thinking about a plea?"

"Depends."

Morgan sighed. "Don't count on it. Evola wants to go the whole way with this one. He's got his eye on bigger things, and a circus trial beats having to buy advertising. I don't think he's open to any deals on this one. If you keep this case, Charley, I think you're going to have to try it."

"If I have to, I will."

Morgan sighed again. "It's a ballbuster, but suit yourself. Well, you never know what will happen. Nothing in this business is predictable. I'll see you tomorrow."

I hung up. The terrible urge to drink was finally gone. My mind was full of other things. Morgan's tone had held a note of genuine sympathy, plus the ghost of a suggestion that I might be wise to consider ducking what was to come. That was worrisome. Morgan was no bluffer.

Publicity can be a two-edged sword. It might be great for Mark Evola and get his name out far beyond the borders of Pickeral Point. But for me a humiliating loss might be the final nail in the almost-closed coffin that contained my career. Harvey Morgan had sounded a little sorry for me.

I THOUGHT the teller at the bank might be impressed by the amount I was depositing, but she didn't bat an eye. She stamped Robin's check, filled out my receipt, and shoved it at me while carrying on a spirited conversation with the teller at the next window. She didn't even glance in my direction. It was as if I wasn't even there. But I was, and my sparse account was suddenly fatter by twenty thousand dollars.

Money has its own seductive quality. If I didn't try the case I would have to give it all back, or most of it. I found I liked having money again. My resolve to find another lawyer for Robin remained, but it wasn't quite as strong as before.

There was no problem figuring which riverfront home was the Harwell place. Robin's description was accurate. The street in front of the entrance was lined on both sides by TV remote units with newsmen and photographers gathered in several small groups. It reminded me of pictures I had seen of newsmen flocking around the homes of presidential candidates when something was about to happen.

Two uniformed security men stood like sentries at each side of the driveway entry. I pulled in.

"Hey! This is private property," one of the guards yelled. "Get outta here!"

"My name is Sloan," I said as one of the guards advanced on me. "I'm Mrs. Harwell's lawyer."

Photographers came bounding up as if I had just announced that I had a carful of naked women. They clicked their cameras at me as the guards tried to shove them away.

The guard eyed my old Ford with obvious disdain. "What's your name again?"

"Sloan."

Some of the newsmen shouted questions at me. I pulled a Reagan, pointing at my ear as if I had suddenly gone deaf and shrugging a mute apology.

The guard frowned, not quite convinced that a Harwell lawyer would be seen in the kind of car I was driving, but he grudgingly waved me in. He and the other guard stopped the sea of newsmen trying to follow.

The Harwell place was magnificent. Queen Victoria herself would have loved it. It didn't look real, it was so well maintained. Glistening white, its three elegant stories rose to a carved roof edge. It was very big, more like a small hotel than a home. It even had an ornate widow's walk at the top of the roof facing the river.

The crushed white stone drive ended at a multicar garage at the rear of the huge house. Two Mercedes and a Cadillac, all gleaming and new, were parked in front of the garage. I pulled my car into a space next to them. The contrast was painful.

A maid admitted me. A Hispanic girl with skin the color of fine teak and haunting olive eyes, her tentative smile seemed forced, more nervous than welcoming.

"Mrs. Harwell's in the sun room." She led me through the enormous house. The ceilings were old fashioned and very high but there was nothing Victorian about the interior. The place was furnished in Park Avenue style, all elegant silks and satins. The carpeting was so thick it felt like walking across a cloud.

The "sun room" was a magnificent atrium running the entire width of the place. All glass, curving and rising, it provided a breathtaking view of the river.

I took a quick look around. At one end a huge Jacuzzi had been built in front of what looked like the cockpit of a jet plane, a stereo containing equipment that probably the Japanese didn't have yet. A person could sit in the bubbling Jacuzzi waters, listen to the stereo, sip champagne, and watch the boats on the river. It suggested a lifestyle I had almost forgotten existed.

Robin was sitting at the other end of the long room, at a table with a very tall, rather elegantly dressed man about my age.

They were sipping something as I approached; they placed their glasses on a small table in front of their chairs.

"Charley," Robin said, nodding at her companion. "This is Malcolm Dutton."

He didn't get up. He looked me over slowly and then stuck out his hand as if he could think of no way to avoid it. The hand I shook was long and bony but strong.

"Malcolm is our Pickeral Point factory manager. He came over to help. Those are his guards at the gate."

"I have some more men at the river," he said. "These newspeople are pretty innovative."

"Can I offer you a drink, Charley?" Robin asked.

"Orange juice would be fine."

She nodded to the olive-eyed maid, who scurried away.

"Robin tells me you're helping Angel. Have you had much experience in criminal matters?" Dutton spoke with the kind of supercilious tone you might use to interview a job applicant, one who had little chance of getting hired.

"Some."

"No offense, Mr. Sloan, but I called several lawyers to see who might be the best man for this kind of thing. As I told Robin, something this serious calls for an expert."

"I take it I didn't make anyone's short list?"

He frowned. "Some knew of you. It seems you've had some of trouble with the bar association."

"It happens. Even Clarence Darrow had a few problems that way."

Dutton's eyes were as cool as his manner. "I managed to come up with two names that everyone recommended. A Sylvester Drake, and a Walter Figer. Do you know them?"

I nodded.

"Good men?"

"The best. There's a saying in Detroit. If you're innocent get Drake, if you're guilty get Figer."

"Who would you recommend?"

"Charley's going to try the case," Robin said.

Dutton ignored her. "If you had a choice, Mr. Sloan, which one would you pick?"

I accepted the orange juice and took a sip. Then I smiled. "I've tried cases against both. They are excellent workmen."

"You tried cases against them?" His voice reflected his surprise. I nodded.

"I presume you lost."

"You presume wrong."

He waited for an explanation, but I merely sipped again at the orange juice.

"Look, you may have been adequate at one time, but I'll be frank. The people I talked to said you have a drinking problem."

"That's right, but it's in the wrong tense. I had a drinking problem." His manner was beginning to become more than merely irritating.

"Whatever. I don't think you're the right man for this job, Sloan."

"Malcolm," Robin said sharply. "That is my decision."

He shook his head. "Not really. The choice is Angel's."

I had come over to again urge Robin to get another lawyer, despite the allure of the big check I had just cashed. And I had planned to recommend Wally Figer. I thought I could work with Wally, maybe even keep some of the money that way. And it was his kind of case. Angel looked very guilty and guilty people were Wally's specialty. But Dutton's supreme arrogance had gotten to me. Maybe I wouldn't recommend Figer. Maybe I wouldn't recommend anybody. Maybe I would try the case.

It was a dangerous way to think.

"Angel will be arraigned tomorrow," I said, ignoring Dutton. "They're charging her with first-degree murder."

"I told you it was serious," Dutton said, looking at Robin.

But she was staring out toward the river. A huge oceangoing freighter was gliding by.

"What does that mean, exactly?" she asked, her eyes fixed on the ship.

"For openers, it means there is no bond. She has to stay in jail through the trial. If she's convicted on that charge, it carries life with no parole. There is no death penalty in Michigan."

"I'll arrange for another lawyer," Dutton said, the words crackling with authority.

Robin turned slowly, her emerald eyes fixed on me like the points of sharp steel arrows. "What can you do for her?"

"Tomorrow, nothing. It's a formality. The charge is formally presented and bond set. Of course, in this case there will be no bond. And a date for examination will be set."

"By a doctor?"

"It's not that kind of examination. This will be before a judge. The prosecution has to show that a crime was committed and there is reasonable cause to believe the defendant committed it."

"I don't understand."

"It's a way of keeping the prosecutor and the police honest. They can't run around throwing charges at people willy-nilly. They have to back them up. They have to present evidence before a judge to show they have good cause for what they've done."

"I'll have the company lawyers get someone," Dutton said.

"Shut up, Malcolm," Robin snapped, never taking her eyes off me. "What will happen, Charley?"

I finished the orange juice. "A lot depends on what Angel said to the police. If it isn't too damning, I may be able to get the charge reduced to second-degree murder at the examination. If that happens, bond will be set and she can get out pending trial."

"Suppose she's convicted of second-degree murder?" Robin asked. "Then what happens?"

Dutton was scowling.

I smiled at him, then spoke to Robin. "There are sentencing guidelines. If it's a first offense and there have been no other problems, eight years is the suggested sentence."

"Only eight years!" Dutton snapped. "For killing someone!"

"It's just a suggested sentence. It can be a lot more or a lot less. Depends on the judge. If it turned out to be manslaughter it could be much less, even probation."

"No wonder crime is rampant," Dutton said.

Robin frowned, then spoke. "Could you work something out, Charley?"

"Like what?"

"That manslaughter business, perhaps. Something where she wouldn't have to go to jail."

I shook my head. "The prosecutor wants this one to go to trial. He has the idea that this case is his yellow brick road to Washington. Unless there's a drastic change, he won't agree to a lesser plea."

"Robin, let me handle this," Dutton said. "We'll find out who has connections with this prosecutor and hire him. Everything is networking. It's merely a matter of finding the right man."

"Sometimes it is," I said, "but this prosecutor is honest. Also, this is his big chance and he's not about to do any favors for friends, not when he thinks his career is about to skyrocket."

Dutton's cold eyes showed his disdain. "Mr. Sloan here doesn't have the right connections," he said to Robin. "I'll—"

"Malcolm," she spoke sharply, cutting him off, "I appreciate everything you've done, but this is something I'll decide. Please leave now. I want to go over a few things with Charley."

He slowly nodded, but the disdain for me in his eyes had changed to loathing.

"You're making a mistake," he said quietly.

"Maybe," Robin said. "I'll call if I need you." Her words were soft, but the cool tone reminded him he was just an employee.

Dutton got up, said the usual comforting things to Robin, shot me another fierce look, and walked away with stiff-backed dignity.

"I'm sorry about that, Charley."

"No problem. He's probably right about getting someone else to try the case."

"I don't think so."

I watched a small sailboat under power, its canvas furled, as it worked its way against the strong river current. The boat, all thirty feet of it, was heading toward Lake Huron and the unknown.

Huron was sometimes tranquil, but the frequent sudden storms could quickly turn into a sailor's nightmare, the enormous waves capable of snapping the spines of steel-keeled ocean ships. Hundreds of miles of Huron's bottom were dotted with such wrecks, like underwater tombstones, each broken hull marking the place where screaming crewmen died in the tumult of crashing walls of water.

The sailboat moved resolutely on, slowly heading toward the huge watery creature that might turn like a tiger and crush it.

I felt a strange kinship with that little boat as it bobbed toward whatever fate awaited it.

"Robin," I said. "Show me where they found your husband's body."

*   *   *

HARRISON Harwell's office wasn't large but it was unusual. It was like stepping into Japanese culture. The walls were paneled in bamboo mats. Japanese prints of fierce samurai warriors brandishing long swords had been given prominent positions. An enormous samurai sword hung on the wall behind the desk. Beautiful yet deadly, its handle and scabbard were elaborately worked in vivid gold and red. Below it were brackets for something, but whatever it was was gone.

"He was lying behind the desk," Robin said. "The police cut out a piece of the rug, as you can see. I don't understand why they did that."

"Blood-soaked," I said. "They cut a piece so the lab can compare it with the blood of the deceased. These days a lot of good carpeting gets ruined that way."

Two photographs, one of a group of naval officers looking soberly out at the camera, the other of a scowling young officer, hung on either side of the sword.

"This may sound odd," Robin said, "but this office is duplicated in every home we own. Exactly. The prints, the photos, even the books in the bookcase. Harrison insisted on it. He said he wanted to feel at home no matter where he was. At least, when he was working."

I studied the photo of the young officer.

"That's Harrison," Robin said.

"World War Two, obviously," I said. The young officer was in dress blues and held a drill sword in the "present arms" position. He was a tough-looking, muscular young man with a long, almost horselike face. The eyes, hooded and prominent, looked challenging, even mean. He wore the two stripes of a full lieutenant.

"He was proud of having been in the navy," she said. "God knows why, he spent most of the time here in Pickeral Point at his father's boat works. They produced landing craft during the war. His father arranged that he be assigned here. Harrison went overseas only after Japan surrendered. But from the way he carried on, you would have thought he had been in every major battle in the war."

I looked around the office. A small, expensive-looking, and very beautiful statue of a samurai, about a foot tall, sat in the middle of the desk. "I take it he served in Japan?"

She snorted. "Yes, for all of three months."

I looked at the books in the narrow bookcase. Other than a dictionary and an atlas, the rest were slim volumes describing the best way to wage war as a samurai, a samurai who used a computer rather than a sword, but who applied the same old battle principles. No mercy, just victory whatever the cost.

"Harrison used to parade around in silk kimonos and sandals at home. But he had circulatory problems and he lost his leg hair." She chuckled softly. "I told him he looked like a pot-bellied stork in drag. After that he quit wearing the get-up."

"How old was he, Robin?"

"Seventy."

"Twenty-five years older than you, right?"

She nodded.

I looked down at the spot where the carpeting had been cut. There were still dark stains around the rim of the spot. "Did you love him, Robin?"

At first I thought she hadn't heard the question. I looked over at her, then she spoke.

"Life gets complicated, Charley."

"It sure does, but that doesn't answer the question."

She sighed. "I don't know if you can tell from those photographs, but Harrison was handsome in a rough way, very big, very, well, physical. At least he was when we, well, got together, ten years ago or so."

"Sexy?"

She smiled. "He was then."

"Age catch up with him? Impotency happens."

Robin shook her head. "Not with Harrison it didn't."

"Lucky man."

"I suppose. You men always seem to put such store on the biological side of life."

"Propagation of the race," I said. "You still haven't answered the question, Robin."

She perched her hips against the lip of the desk. She was a beautiful woman still and I felt the stirring of desire as I looked at the sensuous curve of her legs. They looked even better than when she had been a kid.

"I've never really defined love," she said quietly. "I'm not sure anyone else has, not really. In any event, if you ask that question of people who have been married for ten years or so I'm sure you'd get the usual quick, easy answer, but not the real one."

"What's the real one?"

Her smile held the shadow of sadness. "Marriage, a long one, becomes like an old shoe. It may have lost the shine, but you feel comfortable in it. It becomes more a habit than happiness. You know what's expected of you, and vice versa."

"Sounds pretty dull, frankly."

She shrugged. "It's life, Charley." She paused and studied me for a moment, then spoke. "I understand you were married."

I nodded. "Three times. Never long enough for things to get boring. For me, marriage was more like war or the prize ring."

She nodded. "The blind men and the elephant. Each senses the beast in a different way."

"Robin, I'm not prying. I'm trying to find out what really happened here. Call it love, call it anything you like, but what was your relationship with your husband?"

She seemed to focus on a print of a samurai drawing his sword, then she spoke. "At first, we were lovers, with everything that entails, the sex, the erupting emotions, everything. Then we were married and for a while it was still exciting, although reality was beginning to creep slowly into the relationship. And, there was Angel. I had to become something more, a mother, or at least a mother substitute. The realities of life do seem to have a chilling effect on romance, don't you think?"

"Maybe. What's this got to do with Angel?"

"Let's get out of here, Charley. This room gives me the creeps."

I followed her out and down a hall. The place never seemed to end. Two curving staircases with enough polished wood in the bannisters to build a house led the way to the first floor, but Robin walked me to a room at the far end of the hall.

"This is my room," she said as she led me through the doorway. "It's my own little fortress against the world."

It was large enough for a fort, bigger than most hotel lobbies and more ornate. A huge bed set on a riser dominated the room. The large windows looked out on the river.

If Harrison Harwell's den looked like Japan, Robin Harwell's bedroom looked like Paris, a very hot, very inviting Paris.

40

"Harrison's bedroom is at the other end of the hall," she said.

"You didn't sleep together?"

She sat on a small sofa and patted the seat next to her. "We never slept together, not if you mean actual sleep. Harrison couldn't sleep if anyone was in bed with him. That applied to everyone, me, his first wife, an enormous assortment of women, servants, and the occasional prostitute. He was what you might call sexually active, even at seventy." She laughed. "You remember the old description of the horny cowboy, a guy who would screw a snake, or a pile of rocks if he thought a snake was in it? That would nicely describe Harrison."

"And that didn't bother you?" I was acutely conscious of her perfume.

She shrugged. "Oh, at first it did. I knew what kind of a man Harrison was when I married him. After all, I was his mistress, wasn't I? I thought I might be able to change him. How many women think that when they marry? About ninety-nine percent I'll bet."

"What happened?"

"Oh, Harrison was faithful for maybe a month, I suppose. And that probably was a record for him. After that, he went back to his wicked ways."

"And you objected?"

She shook her head. "Token stuff. I was being territorial, I suppose. But then I started viewing the other women like a relief shift. Harrison was insatiable. Having him diverted a bit gave me a chance to rest."

"Sounds pretty chaotic to me."

Robin smiled. "How about a drink, Charley? I keep some rather good brandy up here."

"I don't drink anymore, Robin. Thanks."

"You'll have to tell me all about that sometime." She walked to a barrel cabinet and extracted a decanter and poured herself a healthy jot of the brandy. I could smell the aroma. It was distracting but my eyes were on the sensuous line of her hips and back.

Robin turned and stood, sipping from the glass. "We worked things out after a fashion, Harrison and me. He had his life, I had mine."

"No sex?"

41

She laughed, but almost sadly. "Christ, at first I was just another snake under the pile of rocks. We still made love. There was no way to avoid it, not with Harrison. Later, we only did it on rare occasions. Usually when we both were drunk. Does that shock you?"

"Very little shocks me anymore. What did Angel think about all this?"

Robin sipped again at the brandy, her eyes on me. "Angel loved her father, but it was a complicated thing even before I arrived on the scene. After Angel got sick things became even more stormy between them. Harrison couldn't accept, well, that anything was wrong with Angel."

"The cops are hinting that the servants told them something, something that might look bad for Angel."

"All families have secrets," she said, finishing the brandy. She turned and poured herself some more. "I suppose they mean the fight."

"What fight?"

Robin looked again out at the river, her face away from mine. "Last night. Harrison tried to understand Angel's illness but he couldn't. He was a fierce man and he couldn't imagine anyone who couldn't control herself. Harrison managed to control not only himself but everyone around him. At least he tried."

"What happened?"

"Angel announced she was going to New York."

"So? She's twenty-one and all that."

Robin merely nodded. "She said she was going to become an actress."

"A lot of people do that. Angel is a good-looking girl. Who knows? She might have done all right."

Robin turned slowly. She was smiling, but the smile was the kind seen on funeral directors, sad but resigned.

"Angel's done this kind of thing before," she said. "The last time she slipped the leash Harrison found her dancing in a topless joint in Manhattan, the kind of place favored by swarthy sailors and fat men with pimples. Harrison paid off some people and Angel did a few months in a rather fancy sanitarium. Against her will, of course."

"Tell me about the fight. What did she say to her father?"

Robin sipped again at the brandy. I hardly noticed. "They screamed at each other. He called her a whore and she called him a monster."

"And then what?"

"He said he'd put her back in a mental hospital."

"What did she say?"

"She said she would kill him first."

I heard the distant dreamlike clang of a jail door in my imagination.

This time it was my turn to look out at the river. The small sailboat and the ocean freighter were gone. Now there was no vessel of any kind on the water.

"Robin, I think you had better get Wally Figer. This is his kind of case."

"What can he do for Angel?"

I laughed despite myself. "Pray, I suppose. But that aside, Wally is at the top of his game. Maybe he can rattle the tree hard enough so that the prosecutor will think he might fall out. Maybe he can force a plea to a lesser offense."

"Can he do more than you?"

At the moment, no one, not Figer, not Drake, certainly not me, could do much to help Angel Harrison.

"I want you, Charley," she said, sipping again, those green eyes shinning above the rim of the glass. "I know you. I trust you."

I sighed. I wondered how much she would want me if she knew my full story. Still, it wouldn't hurt to hold on to the case for a while.

"How many servants heard Angel threaten to kill her father?"

She shrugged. "All of them, I suppose. They were screaming at the top of their lungs."

"Were you here?"

She nodded. "I heard." Which explained why Morgan wanted to talk to her.

"Why didn't you intervene?"

"Charley, fights between them weren't an unusual occurrence. I would have just made things worse."

"Can I talk to your servants? Individually?"

"Alone?"

I nodded.

Robin studied me for a moment. "You may get several different versions. There is some jealousy involved, I think. At least, with some of them."

"Like who?"

"The girl who brought you in."

I thought of the young woman with the beautiful skin and haunted eyes.

"Harrison was slipping down to her room regularly."

"Did you object?"

Robin shook her head. "No."

"And you knew?"

"Yes."

I nodded. "The rich are different."

She smiled ruefully. "Not that different, Charley. They just have more opportunities."

4

THOMAS J. MULHERN HAD BEEN FIRST APPOINTED BY
the governor, and later, elected to the post of district judge. In
Michigan, district courts handle the small claims stuff, traffic of-
fenses and the like, trials for a reasonable amount of money. The
big stuff, the heavy stuff, unreasonable money, is handled by the
circuit courts.

District courts also handle small-time crimes, felony arraignments, and examinations. Tommy Mulhern's court had jurisdiction over the good people of Pickeral Point. The city of Pickeral
Point wasn't yet big enough to merit two district judges so
Tommy ruled like a minor league prince.

Which was okay if Tommy knew you and liked you.

Tommy knew me and liked me, so it was okay by me.

Although the Honorable Thomas J. Mulhern wasn't a member
of the Club, he was eminently qualified. Like most drunks he had
his own peculiar set of rules. Judge Mulhern tried never to drink
before lunch unless it was a medical emergency. At lunch, however, he habitually belted down three or four doubles. Then, all
afternoon, he would take ten-minute breaks every half-hour to
skip into his chambers and toss down a couple more ounces of
good Irish whiskey. The local lawyers said that after three o'clock
in the afternoon, Tommy might be physically present, but not
mentally. He looked good, very judicial, and he nodded and
smiled at all the right places, but nothing registered in his
numbed Irish brain. After three o'clock Tommy was on autopilot.

45

The electors of Pickeral Point never knew that side of Tommy Mulhern. The only Mulhern they saw was the laughing, smiling politician who graced every local wedding and funeral. He always looked sober, but he seldom was.

I tactfully tried to recruit Tommy for the Club, but he wasn't ready.

He had seven grown children, each of them a success, but each a problem for him in varying degrees. Mrs. Mulhern, a dried prune of a woman, was an addict, not to booze or dope, but to faith. When you met her, her eyes seemed fixed on something only she could see, and she silently mouthed prayers even as you talked to her. I could never figure out how she had managed to descend from her spiritual plateau sufficiently often to have conceived seven children. But at the moment that puzzle for me was of a very low priority. Court was about to start.

Judge Mulhern's courtroom is in the same building as the Kerry County circuit courts, a situation the circuit judges find offensive since they consider Tommy and his jurisdiction to be a form of lesser legal and political life. Although only a few thousand dollars in salary separates them, circuit judges tend to view district judges the way French aristocrats used to view indentured peasants.

But their long-nosed attitude didn't bother Tommy. Face to face, he was civil to them, but everywhere else he consistently referred to the gentlemen as the Three Weird Sisters.

It was standing room only in Tommy's courtroom, the audience composed of ten percent curious and ninety percent reporters representing local, national, and even international print and television media. One television camera, per Michigan court rules, was set up at the side of the courtroom, its recorded product to be shared by all the electronic media.

Everyone stood as the Honorable Thomas J. Mulhern took his place on the high bench. He looked out at all of us the way a farmer might gaze out at a particularly disappointing herd.

I recognized the signs of a world-class hangover. His face was white as chalk, his eyes puffy and red. I used to look like that. I remembered, and I felt sorry for Tommy Mulhern.

Angel sat next to me. She was as much an enigma to me as before. She might be an innocent child or she might be a sinister woman, or perhaps something even more complex, something I had never encountered before. I couldn't tell. She had thanked me for having the suicide watch removed, but it was the kind of mechanical gratitude shown to waiters who bring the rolls. Robin had been allowed to visit with her for a few moments before the judge came out. I had watched to see what kind of chemistry might exist between the two women. I had expected an emotional reunion, hugging, kissing, assurances of support, the roles expected in these circumstances. They did kiss, and I thought I saw real affection, but they were both so cool and calm it was more like two friends meeting for lunch rather than the opening act in a murder case.

Robin had returned to her front-row seat. She sat with Malcolm Dutton, who scowled at me with even greater disapproval than before. Robin and Dutton were wedged between two muscular young men garbed in matching off-the-rack suits. I presumed they were Harwell plant security men. They looked exactly like Secret Service agents but without the little radio earplugs.

Mark Evola had greeted me with a solemn hello, his dignified attitude designed to conceal his jubilation at the media coverage he was about to receive. He hadn't exactly thrown on his clothes willy-nilly. Evola was as splendidly dressed as a Brooks Brothers ad. Tall, blond, with a smile exhibiting teeth that nature could only envy, he was a magnet for the attentions of the photographers and the women reporters.

I was clean and wearing my best shirt and suit but I couldn't match him. Were this a movie, Evola would be played by Cary Grant or Robert Redford, and my part would be ideal for Jack Nicholson—a wrinkled, worried Jack Nicholson.

But this wasn't a movie.

My mother, before she died, said I became a lawyer because it was like being a priest. She was talking of the ritual, not the spiritual, although I have heard more than a few confessions in my time.

She was correct about the rites of trial. In this country we get our law and ritual from ancient England. Centuries ago the English liked to run around cold castles in robes, talk of justice, do a mumbo-jumbo routine, then take the guilty defendant outside and whack off his head with an axe.

It's about the same now, with some refinements, although the axe has fallen into disfavor. The castles have become courtrooms and they are heated now in the winter and air-conditioned in the summer. But my mother was right: I am fond of the ceremonial aspects of my profession.

As his part in the ritual, Mark Evola got up, made a brief presentation to the judge, and then confronted Angel Harwell. He began to read the formal language of the charge, using archaic legal terms that old King Henry and the boys would have instantly recognized.

He ended by charging Angel Harwell with the crime of first-degree murder.

It only took a few minutes. The Honorable Thomas J. Mulhern looked out at me through pained eyes. He was anxious to get this over with, to perform his part of the ceremony, bind Angel over for examination without bond, and escape into his nice dark office. All I had to do was enter her plea—not guilty, stand mute, or guilty—then we could all go home.

I chose not to follow the script.

"If the court please," I said, "the prosecution is wrongfully withholding evidence. I cannot advise my client properly unless I know all the circumstances of the case."

Tommy arched an eyebrow over one red eye. A person with a killer hangover doesn't want to use his brain. It hurts too much.

"What do you mean?" he snapped.

"In conversations with the prosecuting attorney and the police, they allege my client has made statements detrimental to herself. I have demanded to see these so-called statements but I have been refused."

"That is untrue!" Evola was flushed. "I told Mr. Sloan his client's confession was being typed up. I told him he would get a copy when it was. I resent the implication."

Tommy Mulhern sighed and placed a hand at the side of his head, as if thinking, but his fingertips were gently massaging his aching temple. "This statement, is it typed up now?"

Evola paused. "Well, it's in the process."

"Oh? Is there something unusual or difficult about it? Is it being hand-lettered by monks?" Mulhern tried to force a smile but failed.

"Ah, it's just been completed, or so the police inform me."

Morgan and Maguire, who hadn't said a thing to him, sat there, their stoic expressions as stiff as if sculpted in stone.

"Give it to him," Judge Mulhern said, his voice barely above a rasp.

"I had planned to do so," Evola said with righteous indignation, "as soon as we had completed the arraignment."

"Now," Mulhern commanded.

His dignity bruised, Evola handed me a copy of Angel's statement.

"Take a minute," Mulhern said, getting up and stomping off the bench. He would take a hair of the dog. I used to.

I could hear Angel's soft breathing as I read. It was the usual format, question and answer. I read quickly.

Her statement was like one of those trick drawings—hold it one way you see one thing, twist it a bit, you see something else. Her words, if taken in different ways, could mean entirely different things.

"Did you tell them you were responsible for your father's death?" I whispered to Angel as I quickly read through the brief statement.

She looked at me. "I could have said that. I was very upset."

Judge Mulhern, a little more color in his face, came back into the courtroom and took his place at the bench.

He looked at me. "It's up to you, Mr. Sloan. How do you plead?"

I stood up slowly. I was conscious that the eye of the television camera was on me. If Evola was going to try the case in the glare of that public eye, I—or whoever succeeded me—would have to do so too.

"This is no confession," I said indignantly, holding the papers up as if they were emitting a terrible odor. "This is a legal outrage."

Evola popped to his feet, but the judge spoke first.

"Please, no speeches! You might be in a mood to try the case this morning, Mr. Sloan, but we cannot. We have to go by the court rules, like it or not. And those rules demand that your client enter a plea today, nothing more. Let's get on with it, shall we?"

I let my shoulders sink with studied sadness, as if he had just ordered me flogged. Put a camera on lawyers and we all become Olivier. "Ordinarily," I said, "I would stand mute in order to preserve the prosecutor's mistakes for appeal, but this charge is so rank, so patently unjust, that I've decided to advise my client to plead not guilty. And that's the plea in this case, not guilty! Period!"

There was some murmuring from the spectators. Mulhern glared out at the noise.

"Okay," he growled. "The plea of not guilty to first-degree murder will be entered. There is no bond, obviously. I shall set the examination for Friday."

Evola who had remained standing, spoke. "I would like a few more days than that to prepare, if the court please."

"For what? A homicide examination? If you aren't sure of your facts by now, you shouldn't have brought the charge." Mulhern stood up. I sensed he was anxious to get back to his chambers and another restorative ounce or two. "Friday it is. If you can't be ready, Mr. Evola, I'll dismiss the charge until you are."

"The people will be ready," Evola snapped, this time displaying real anger.

AFTER that, everything seemed like one of those old movies they speed up to produce a choppy, chaotic effect.

Out on the courthouse steps I stepped into a throng of newspeople and found myself looking into a sea of camera lenses and facing a forest of microphones. Mark Evola, who had stationed himself at the other end of the steps, seemed to be making a hell of a speech to an equally large crowd of newsmen and cameras. Whoever got off the best line would end up on the six o'clock news. I did my best to snap off a couple of zingers to give Angel at least equal time in the media wars.

After my fifteen minutes of fame, I walked to the jail and met with Angel, in the lawyer-client room, separated by glass and speaking through microphones. Although she faced the prospect of life in prison she seemed no more upset than if Gucci had sent over the wrong size shoes. Again, I was puzzled. I couldn't relate her attitude to anything I had seen before. I wondered if she might still be numbed by the death of her father, her peculiar reactions those of a genuinely confused and innocent girl. Or she might be the most emotionless killer I had ever encountered.

We went over her statement to the police. I read the questions and answers aloud.

Question: (by Evola) "Did you stab your father?"

Answer: (by Angel) "You say I did."

Q: "I'm not asking what I said, I'm asking what you did. Did you stab your father?"

A: "I might have. I'm not sure."

Q: "What do you mean, not sure?"

A: "My memory isn't clear. My father is dead. I'm not thinking clearly."

Q: "Let me put it a different way. Were you responsible for your father's death?"

A: "Yes. You could say that."

Q: "Then you did stab him?"

A: "I told you, my memory isn't clear."

Q: "Your prints are on the handle of the knife. How did they get there if you didn't stab him?"

A: "I remember trying to pull it out of him, but I couldn't."

Q: "After you stabbed him?"

A: "I told you, I don't remember that."

Q: "But you say you are responsible for his death, right?"

A: "Yes."

I went over everything with her, twice.

But I wasn't doing any better with Angel than Evola had. She was either genuinely foggy or purposely evasive as we discussed the details of her statement. She told me that she did not stab her father, but her answers became even more vague and enigmatic when I asked what she had meant when she said she had been responsible for her father's death. If she did testify, and if she gave the same answers on the witness stand, the case would be lost.

Either way, foggy or evasive, I decided to give her a day or two to think things over before I questioned her again. I told Angel I would be back and cautioned her again not to talk to anyone but me about the case.

Robin was expecting me. Her servants had talked to the police.

I wanted to find out what each of them had said, but that would have to keep. I had something to do first.

The defense of Angel Harwell wasn't my only case. In the general scheme of things, a real-estate closing isn't the equal of a front-page murder case, especially one involving wealth and fame. Unless, of course, it's your real-estate closing.

They were waiting for me at the Cruikshank Title Company. Harry Cruikshank insured the title to real estate and serviced mortgages at his small office. His place, near mine, was so convenient to realtors and bankers that he attracted most of the real-estate closings in Pickeral Point.

My clients, Donald and Myra Flint, a nice young married couple who were buying their first home, were there when I arrived. The seller, a widower named Wagner, said hello and the strong odor of alcohol floated over me like a cloud. Old Wagner was moving into a senior citizen condo and I thought he didn't look too happy about it.

The real-estate agent, a hawk-faced woman with a long neck, glared at everyone as if she suspected someone might try to rob her of her commission. Harry ran the whole thing smoothly, doing a little practiced chant with each paper, getting signatures, and conducting everything with the quick efficiency of a symphony conductor working fast before anything went wrong.

I had already checked the paperwork, Wagner's title, and the fitness reports. Everything was in good shape. Like Cruikshank, I had a little verbal routine and I performed it with solemn authority. Clients expect a little show for their money.

Robin had given me the twenty-thousand-dollar check. The fee I had set for my clients, the Flints, was a hundred-fifty bucks, which had looked big to me at the time. Now, as Donald Flint pushed his check to me, I almost regarded it as pocket money. Funny how quickly things can change.

Another thing that changed was their reaction to me. If I was lucky, I managed to get one or two real-estate closings a week. I was always treated as a kind of necessary nuisance by everyone except my clients. But now my picture had been in the newspaper, front page. And now, Harry Cruikshank deferred to me as if he owed me money. Even the hawk-faced woman's icy reserve melted slightly and I caught her sneaking peeks at me as the closing progressed.

Clearly, I was being shown a degree of respect that hadn't been forthcoming before, at least not for a long time, and never in Pickeral Point.

I liked that. Perhaps too much.

We all shook hands after the closing. Wagner watched the young married couple as they walked away arm in arm. I wondered if he was remembering other times, times when he wasn't facing an old-folks condo with two hot meals provided daily until he was carted off to the cemetery or an affiliated nursing home. But he didn't look nostalgic, just resentful.

It was past my usual time for lunch, and I felt hungry. I thought a quick sandwich and coffee would help fortify me for my afternoon inquiries of the Harwell staff.

Pickeral Point is not Paris, not even close. Restaurants are not big here. We have one good one, at the Pickeral Point Inn. It's a place for rich tourists and locals with something special to celebrate. A competing big restaurant down the shore a mile serves second-class entertainment at night and third-class food from opening to closing. There's hardly anyone there, ever. Everyone, including me, suspects it's a money-laundering front for the mob.

Other than those two ornate establishments and a few fast-food outlets there is only one other real restaurant. If it were located in a hotel it would be called a coffee shop. But it stands alone in a small one-story building near my office. It offers simple, quick meals. I eat there. Practically everyone I know eats there.

Pickeral Point isn't New York, either, and no one wastes much time at lunch. It was after one o'clock, so the main lunch time crowd had already hurried back to their stores and businesses.

Bob was sitting alone at one of the rear tables. Bob, as in, "My name is Bob and I'm an alcoholic." Bob is a member of the Club. Like me, he's a transplanted Detroiter. We sometimes drove together into the city on Thursday nights for our regular meeting.

Bob is Robert J. Williams, M.D., a psychiatrist who had a private practice in Pickeral Point and served on the staff of a number of hospitals.

What does a typical psychiatrist look like? Probably nothing like Bob Williams, who is big, trim but wide, and very tall. His brown hair was cut in a Marine-style brush cut. He once told me his great-grandmother was a Chippewa Indian. Apparently her genes skipped directly down the bloodline to him. His wide cheekbones were so high and prominent that his slate-gray eyes look slanted, almost Asian. He seldom smiled. The total effect was frightening, like looking into the eyes of an enormous threatening thug. But despite his awesome appearance, Bob Williams was a soft-hearted man, kindly, with a fast mind and a deceptive sense of humor.

He was also the closest thing to a best friend I had.

I joined him at the table. He nodded and washed the last of his hamburger down with a huge gulp of coffee.

"Still talking to us common people?" His voice was surprisingly soft, a deep baritone whisper.

"Depends on just how common they are."

"How did you land the Harwell case?" he asked.

I ordered a hamburger and coffee from my regular waitress.

"The new widow is an old girlfriend," I said.

He nodded. "Sex comes to Pickeral Point. Rumor has it that your client is guilty as hell."

"Sometimes that question gets decided by a jury. It's a novel concept, but I think it's catching on."

Those gray eyes hid his thoughts. "From what I hear, the girl confessed, left her prints on the murder weapon, and did everything but take an ad out in the paper that she had killed dear old papa. I presume you'll work out a plea eventually?"

The waitress served the burger, which had enough grease to be tasty but not enough to kill, immediately anyway.

"Mark Evola, the prosecutor, won't even consider a plea to a lesser offense. He knows a publicity cow when he sees one, and this one can be milked for buckets."

"He can't lose, can he?"

I shrugged. "You never know. Angel might have done it. It might even have been justified, self-defense. And if she didn't do it, someone else did. A servant maybe."

"Or the wife?"

"I doubt it."

He smiled. "I thought you might. How about suicide?"

"What do you mean?"

"He was stabbed only once, right?"

"As far as I know."

He sighed. "Suicide happens. Often by unusual means. I had a patient who killed himself with an electric knife. Damn near cut off his own head. When people get angry and depressed you never know what they might do."

"It's worth exploring."

"So, are you going to try it?" His tone implied an even more significant question than his words.

Part of the A.A. process is a critical self-examination. No bullshit, just truth. The truth, they say, will set you free. Occasionally, at the meetings, I had described my drinking patterns. If you hold something like that up and everyone takes a critical look, it makes it easier to spot the deadly habits and avoid them in the future.

I was a trial lawyer, and a drinker. In my case the two were intertwined like coiling snakes. Perhaps drinking was due to an underlying fear, but whatever it was, I soon found that liquor was an enormous help in trial preparation, right from the beginning of my career. As I got better in the courtroom, I drank more in the barroom.

Like most drunks, at first I could handle it. It was the pleasant fuel that sparked the intellect. But that didn't last long. The courtroom was the only place where I hadn't disgraced myself. Of course, I would have, in time, but the other parts of my life and career had collapsed first.

I had never tried an important case entirely sober. I didn't know if I could.

That was the real question his tone implied.

"I've recommended the family get another lawyer," I said, "someone who does it regularly. I'm a little rusty."

"Will they get someone else?"

I took a bite of the hamburger, chewed, swallowed, and answered. "At the moment, no, but that will probably change."

"And if not?"

"Are you worried?" I asked.

One eyebrow went up slowly. "If you're not, I'm not."

I shrugged. "We'll see what happens."

He nodded. "Well, don't lose sight of what's important."

"My sobriety."

"Another word for survival." He picked up his check and stood up. It was like watching a skyscraper rising before your eyes.

"Be careful, Charley," he said.

"I might need your help."

"We all help each other."

I smiled. "I don't mean that way, I mean professionally, as part of the case."

"Oh, well, that will cost you."

"Even for an occasional hypothetical question?"

A ghost of a smile drifted across his face. "Especially hypothetical questions. Freud said never do anything for free, especially for lawyers."

"He played with himself too much."

The doctor nodded. "Yes, but only in the interests of science."

I watched him walk down the aisle.

He was worried about me.

So was I, just a little.

DENNIS Bernard's face defied classification. It was the kind of face that blends into a crowd. His features were plain and without distinction. He was sixty but looked younger. His receding brown hair was fading into gray. He wore a dark blue blazer over a light blue shirt and tie. It wasn't a uniform but on him it seemed like one. His expression was pleasant but bland.

Robin had set me up in a small room off the main entrance in her house so I could interview the household staff. It wasn't an office—there was too much fancy furniture—but it served the purpose. Bernard sat across a coffee table from me, his wiry legs casually crossed.

"How long have you been in the Harwell's employ?"

"We came to the Harwell's just over five years ago," he said, his voice smooth and unemotional. "My wife and I work as a team, so to speak. She cooks and I serve as a houseman."

"Butler?"

He smiled, but just a bit. "Mostly, but when Mr. Harwell travels—" he paused and corrected the tense—"traveled, I serve more as a chauffeur. Of course, I do whatever the Harwells wish."

"I talked to your wife. A nice lady."

The faint smile remained fixed. "I like to think so. And, I might add, a very good cook."

"You live here, I'm told."

He nodded. "Yes. My wife and I have a room. The Harwells travel with a small staff. Besides us, there are three maids. There is a permanent houseman here year round, a kind of grounds-keeper. Each of us is assigned a room. Of course, back in Florida, our home, there are additional serving staff."

"You were here the night—"

"With my wife," he said, too quickly. "We were in our room. I'm afraid we heard and saw nothing. Of course, we were called down when they discovered Mr. Harwell."

"You heard no arguments that night?"

He shook his head. "No."

"Nothing happened out of the ordinary?"

"Nothing that I was aware of."

"That's what your wife says, too."

He nodded.

"What did you think of Mr. Harwell?"

He answered immediately. "A fine man. A very good man to work for. I shall miss him."

It was exactly what his wife had said, word for word.

His earnest pale gray eyes projected an almost palpable sincerity.

I had seen that kind of look before, many times. He was lying.

"Did you tell the police anything other than what you've told me?"

Those alert eyes narrowed just slightly. "I can assure you I told them exactly the same thing."

This time I did believe him. He was protecting his job. Hear no evil, see no evil, speak no evil—every good personal servant knows those are the only rules that really count.

"Is there anything else you think I should know? Anything about that night, or about the family?"

"They are lovely people," he said. "I can't think of anything more, Mr. Sloan, than what I've told you."

I waited, hoping the uncomfortable silence might prod him to go on, perhaps jog him into elaborating. It was a tactic that worked sometimes, but all I had managed to provoke was his faint little smile.

57

"Thanks, Mr. Bernard. I'll want to talk to you again. Now, would you please send in Miss Hernandez."

He nodded and left.

Mr. and Mrs. Bernard obviously had spent some quality time together making sure their stories matched. They were a team, but a rather odd one. Bernard was thin and wiry; his wife, the cook, was so stout that her rear end looked like a trailer following a truck. The Bernards had been with the Harwell family five years, much longer than the other servants, so I was told, and they knew a great deal. Every family has secrets. I had the feeling that not even Mafia enforcers could get the Bernards to tell all, not now anyway. Perhaps later, when I knew more, I might just find the right tool to pry open the Bernards' little horde of backstairs gossip.

Theresa Hernandez came in, looking even better than yesterday, and she had looked pretty good then.

This time I made a much more detailed appraisal. Theresa had a pretty figure, not long-legged, but nice, compact. And her legs were well shaped and sturdy, as was the rest of her, all exhibited demurely by the clinging nylon uniform she wore. Her hair, cut short, was jet black and carefully brushed. I had noticed her skin before, so smooth, like fine satin, and with the glow of pale teak.

I could see why Harrison Harwell might make nighttime excursions to see her.

But it was Theresa Hernandez's eyes that really grabbed you. Dark, and olive-colored, they had that deep, haunted look, the kind artists for centuries have painted into the brooding faces of their Madonnas and saints.

"Sit down, Ms. Hernandez, please."

She moved gracefully and sat as demurely as if she were a schoolgirl, and she wasn't much older than that.

"This is quite informal, Ms. Hernandez, so please feel at ease. What I wish to know is—"

"She did it."

"Pardon me?"

"Angel. She killed her father."

I stared at her. She had spoken the words, but they had come out with no visible change of expression.

"Did you see her do it?" I asked, using my most gentle manner.

58

She shook her head. "I didn't have to see. I know. I heard her tell her father she was going to kill him. And she did."

"Why would Angel want to kill her father?"

This time her pretty face revealed a kind of quiet satisfaction. "To keep him from marrying me. She was jealous."

"Mr. Harwell is, was, married already."

"He was going to get a divorce. He was going to marry me. His daughter couldn't stand the thought of him marrying a maid, someone she considered less than acceptable. She was jealous that he loved me."

"Did Harrison Harwell tell you all this? About getting a divorce and then marrying you?"

She nodded solemnly. "He did. Many times."

"And what about his wife, Robin Harwell?"

This time I saw a flash of anger in those dark eyes. "She is strange. He told me she was evil and she is. She didn't care about him. She only cared about his money."

I let that pass for the moment.

"You say you heard Angel threaten her father. When did that happen?"

"Just before she killed him."

"You heard this?"

"They were in his study."

"And where were you? Is your room near there?"

She shook her head. "No. But I had just left the study." She looked away shyly. "We had just, well, made love." She paused, then added, "We were going to be married so it was no sin."

"And Angel was there?"

Theresa frowned. "Of course not! She came in after I left. I saw her and I waited. I thought there might be trouble."

"You were hiding?"

"No. She just didn't see me."

"What did you hear?"

"They were arguing," she said. "They always argued. She's a sick person, you know. Her father wanted her to get treatment, more treatment. She refused. He said he would have her put into a mental hospital whether she wanted to go or not.

"They were screaming." Theresa sighed. "The other people in the house heard them. They say they didn't, but they did. It was a very loud argument."

"What happened?"

"She said she would kill him before she let him send her to a hospital again. Then she stormed out."

"What did you do?"

"I went back and asked if he was all right."

"What did he say?"

She sighed. "He didn't talk much. He seemed very sad. He told me he was going to call the doctors and have her put back in the hospital."

"What happened then?"

Theresa was getting a little teary. "We kissed good night and I went to my room. The next time I saw him, he was dead."

I sat back. "Ms. Hernandez, is this what you told the police?"

She nodded. "It's the truth."

It was my turn to sigh. Dreams are wonderful things. This pretty little girl dreamed of being the lady of the manor. But that was all gone now. Theresa Hernandez soon would be on her way back to wherever she called home, but first she would get even with the woman she believed had killed her wonderful dream.

At least Mark Evola's dream would come true.

I desperately needed a drink.

5

THIS TIME THE URGE TO DRINK WENT FAR BEYOND
mere desire. This time I sensed I needed help.

Robin wanted to talk but I had to get out of there.

I gunned the old Ford and sped toward Mount Clemens,
where I knew there was a late afternoon meeting. I had gone
several times although I really hadn't liked the people much.
A.A. meetings have their own personality. People like me tend to
shop around until they find a group where they feel comfortable,
just like we shopped around in the old days for a compatible saloon.

Comfortable group or not, I needed the stability a meeting offered, much as a drifting boat needs the strong pull of a secure
anchor.

The drive to Mount Clemens took a half-hour, but for me it was
a very long thirty minutes. Until I reached the interstate the
roadside saloons seemed to call out to me like the sirens who sang
to Ulysses, sweetly luring him to destruction, only I wasn't
strapped to a mast. I wished I were. It had been months since I'd
been afflicted by such a demonic need to drink.

But I made it. I found a space on a Mount Clemens side street,
parked, and put a coin in the meter.

The meeting was convened in a room above a downtown furniture store.

I was an alcoholic but I was no longer anonymous. Everyone

had been following the Harwell case and I was treated as a kind of minor-league celebrity, which defeated the purpose of being there. They were discussing number eight and nine of the Twelve Steps, whereby amends, whenever possible, should be made to people we had harmed. I thought of my daughter, Lisa, and wondered how I could make amends to a girl I hadn't seen in sixteen years, or if I should even try. I wondered if she ever thought about me or wondered what I was like. I stayed until the twelfth step but I didn't feel like talking, so I ducked out during the break when everyone else was gathering around the coffeepot.

But just being at the meeting had helped and the desperate addictive need had taken a step back. I knew that need would never be more than one short step behind me for the rest of my life.

I took the long way back to Pickeral Point, using the road that ran along the river rather than the interstate. It gave me time to think and provided the serenity I needed to calmly analyze why I felt so miserable. It seemed simple enough. It was the Harwell case. It was a big case, a public case, but one that looked like a sure loser. I was afraid of losing, for Angel's sake, but more for my own. I had always been afraid of losing. In other times liquor helped numb that fear. But I was in conflict. I really didn't want to give the case to someone else. The old life lured me. I liked having money again, I liked being treated with respect, and I liked the attention that celebrity seemed to command.

I had missed all that, the money, the recognition, more than I had ever suspected. That life, for me, was like the whisper of beautiful music, hauntingly remembered.

But this was one whisper I would have to ignore.

I had never really hit bottom, but I had come close enough to seeing what bottom looked like. It's true I had never had to sleep in a bus station or wash up in the men's room. I hadn't done that, but it had been only a rung or two below where I had stood on the ladder.

Nothing was worth taking that final step down, absolutely nothing.

Certainly not a murder case, or any case that raised such a risk. The price was too high to justify the wager.

I drove back to Robin Harwell's place to tell her just that.

But she wasn t there. The security men said she was at the local funeral home. I had almost forgotten that murdered men had funerals.

P. J. Anderson had a lock on all the funeral business in Pickeral Point. Anderson's was the only funeral home in town and he was clever enough to keep prices sufficiently low to discourage anyone from opening a competing establishment.

The place originally had been a large farmhouse near the center of the city. After opening up as a funeral home, Anderson kept building on wings as business improved. The front was the original two-story white frame building, but it looked like a square locomotive pulling the additions behind like a string of boxcars. The driveway was white crushed stone and the parking lot was big enough to accommodate the crowd at a shopping mall.

Like almost everything else in life, Anderson's maintained a pecking order. The famous or rich were buried from the front rooms in the old main building. Then, depending on the deceased's position a sliding economic or social scale, rites were provided on down the length of the place. The poorest were shipped from the small rooms located in the back at the most distant addition.

Harrison Harwell was both famous and rich, so I knew he would get the best suite even if Anderson had to move another customer.

Some bored photographers were standing near the entrance and one took some unenthusiastic shots of me as I approached. I tried to look fittingly solemn.

Inside, it was standing room only. As I squeezed through the crowd everyone seemed to have that grim look of people who were merely performing a chore and were thinking of places they would rather be. I suspected Malcolm Dutton had turned out all the working folk from the Harwell boat factory. I saw no smiles, sad or otherwise, nor any tears. The muted conversations made a soft buzzing sound, not unlike a distant swarm of night insects.

I was looking for Robin as I worked my way toward the front of the viewing room. I couldn't locate her but I did take a closer look at the guest of honor as he lay in Anderson's best brass casket.

Harrison Harwell wasn't much different from the photographs I had seen. A little older, a little waxy, thanks to Anderson, but

63

otherwise he had the same angry, arrogant look I had seen in the photos—even with his eyes closed. The wide mouth was set in a permanent reprimand, the bushy black eyebrows in a permanent scowl. His wide nostrils were large, almost simian. Even in death, the collar of the new shirt strained against a muscular neck. Large meaty hands were locked together over a thick, powerful chest.

I was the only person viewing the deceased. Everyone else seemed to avoid looking at Harwell as if they were afraid the eyes in that fearsome face just might open and look back.

"Charley."

I turned and saw Robin heading toward me. She wore a simple black dress with black suede shoes and black stockings. Her hair was carefully brushed back, and she wore only a hint of makeup. It shouldn't have been, but the total effect was erotic. The dress seemed to accentuate every movement. She was leading a tall, older woman, also dressed in black, by the hand.

Robin smiled, but it was a strained, nervous smile. "Charley, this is Mrs. Nancy Harwell Somerset, Harrison's sister."

Mrs. Somerset had never been a beauty. She looked like a twin to her dead brother, her mouth set in an almost identically severe expression. Expensively styled, her hair was silver; her eyes glittered like two small knives.

"This is Charley Sloan," Robin said. "He's Angel's lawyer."

People can react oddly in funeral homes, particularly toward the lawyer defending someone accused of murdering the person in the casket. Before she could shout or curse or otherwise get nasty, I spoke: "I'm very sorry about your brother, Mrs. Somerset. It's a terrible loss."

Those eyes never left mine. "I want to talk to you." She pulled away from Robin, gripped my elbow with surprising strength, and led me toward a small room behind the casket, the family room, as Anderson called it.

No one else was there and Robin didn't follow. Mrs. Somerset sat down in a chair and indicated I should sit opposite her. As I did, she pulled a cigarette from her small purse and lit up in one fluid, practiced movement. Like her brother, she had powerful meaty hands.

She produced a small silver flask and pulled on it like a sailor;

the movement exposed muscles and ligaments and made her thick throat resemble the underside of a suspension bridge.

She capped the flask and put it back in her purse. "Can you get Angel out of this?"

"It's a difficult case, Mrs. Somerset."

"Is it a matter of money?"

"Pardon me?"

She inhaled deeply on the cigarette and expelled smoke through her wide nostrils. "Money. It buys things, Mr. Sloan. Judges, for instance."

"Well, that isn't the situation here, Mrs. Somerset."

"Robin thinks she's taking care of things, but she doesn't understand the power of money. I do. It was my father's money that started the boat business. I still have my share of my father's fortune, every damn penny. Whatever is needed I can supply."

"Mrs. Somerset, I know the shock of your brother's death—"

"My niece is the only family I have left, Mr. Sloan. She has had a very difficult life and she deserves better than this sordid business."

"The state says she killed your brother."

She nodded. "Things happen, Mr. Sloan. Terrible things. But that doesn't change the flow of life. Harrison is dead and no one can change that. Angel is alive. She's the only person important to me now."

Those knifelike eyes narrowed slightly. There was a coldness in them. "I can afford the best. The very best. Tell me, Mr. Sloan, are you the best lawyer in the country?"

Her tone told me she already knew the answer.

"There is no rating system. Legal reputations come and go with the case, Mrs. Somerset. The best man today may be a has-been tomorrow. Some cases are easy, some are hard. Anyone can win the easy ones. It's the hard ones that provide the real test. Many famous trial lawyers carefully select easy ones to keep their reputations intact."

She stubbed out the cigarette. "If Angel were your daughter, who would you want to try the case?"

The thought of my daughter flashed again in my mind. I wondered what she looked like now. I wondered what I would do, if she were in Angel's situation.

"If Angel asks, I'm quite willing to step aside, if that's what's worrying you."

"Good. I'll select another attorney. I'll contact my own people and get a recommendation."

"Doesn't Angel have anything to say about that?"

She snorted. "Angel is a child."

"A twenty-one-year-old child.".

"She's emotionally immature. Angel's quite incapable of making sound judgments." Her tone was snappish, as if she were admonishing a servant who had just spilled gravy on the linen.

"As far as I know, Angel hasn't been declared mentally incompetent. No guardian has been appointed, not even Robin, your sister-in-law."

Her mouth, a lipsticked slash, twisted into a sour smile. "Former sister-in-law. Harrison's death ended that relationship, the same as divorce, only quicker and cleaner. I will be running the affairs of this family from here on, Mr. Sloan. If I think a guardian should be appointed, one will be."

She possessed the sure arrogance of someone born to wealth.

"At the moment, Angel is my client. You aren't. Robin isn't. Until Angel tells me otherwise, I will continue to act in her best interest."

"How much do you want?"

"For what?"

"To get out of the case."

"I've done a number of rotten things in my life, Mrs. Somerset, things I'm very ashamed of, but selling out a client isn't one of them."

"You're a fool, Mr. Sloan." She stood up slowly, then stared down at me. "I will be running things from here on. This case, this family, and our family business. My brother was a fool, but I'm not. I don't suffer fools or cheap chiselers, and I think you are both. And you are history."

She stalked out, leaving me sitting there like a schoolboy who'd just been scolded and expelled.

I WANTED to talk to Robin but she was busy receiving condolences from a waiting line of people. It all seemed very formal. She obviously had never met any of them and they didn't look particularly distressed. Malcolm Dutton, apparently, was stage-managing the wake and every employee had a part and played it exactly as directed.

Since she was going to be busy for a while, I decided to get some air while I waited.

It was difficult but I wiggled my way through the people to the exit. It was a lovely twilight evening, warm but pleasant. Overhead high clouds caught the last crimson rays of the disappearing sun. Two large boats signaled each other out on the river, the deep sound of their horns as soothing as the sound of a distant freight train at night. Such calming river sounds were another benefit in the peaceful life of Pickeral Point.

"You're Sloan, the kid's lawyer, right?"

I hadn't noticed him standing in the shadows near the entrance. I looked closer. I didn't know him. He was a tall, thin man with hawklike features. His suit looked expensive but it hung on him as if he had recently lost weight. It was hard to judge in the half-light but I guessed he was nearing seventy, if he hadn't already passed that mark.

"I'm Sloan," I said. "Charley Sloan."

He was smoking a cigarette and he expelled smoke as he spoke. "I saw you on television. On the news. What kind of chance do you think the kid's got?"

"Do you know her?"

He nodded. "Oh yeah. I knew Angel before she was able to walk. I used to work for Harwell."

"And your name?"

"Amos Gillespie." He spoke it as if it should mean something to me. When he got no reaction, he said, "I take it you weren't connected with Harrison's business dealings."

"No. I never met him."

I thought I saw a smile, but I wasn't sure. He had an expressionless face, the kind every poker player tries to develop.

"Can't say you missed much," he said.

"I take it you weren't one of his more ardent fans?"

He chuckled, the sound coming out like old tissue paper being crumpled. "You could say that. Of course, he hated me. I suppose I would have too, given the circumstances."

"Oh?"

"I started out with old man Harwell, the father. Hard-driving guy, but he really understood boats and business. I guess I was what you might call the old man's protégé. Anyway, he taught me the business like a son. When he brought Harrison in things got a bit dicey. Harrison resented our relationship, his old man and me. When the old man died, Harrison fired me before his father's body was cold."

"That's too bad."

"It was the best thing that ever happened to me. I moved to Alabama and started my own company. I own Three Tree Boats. You know it?"

"The bass boats?"

He nodded. "One of our lines."

"I'm surprised you came to the wake, given the history."

"I was up here anyway." He chuckled again. "I had forced Harrison to sell his company to me. The sale will go through despite this, but it would have been sweeter to see his face as he signed the papers. Now, the lawyers will do it. It won't be quite the same."

"How could you force him to sell?"

He inhaled on the cigarette then flipped it away, its red tip making an arc in the deepening night.

"Money," he said, "or more precisely the lack of it. He had borrowed heavily for expansion but the boat business took a little dip and he couldn't meet his payments."

"I thought he was rich."

"He is. Or was. But he borrowed one hell of a lot. He was always doing things on a grand scale. Don't get me wrong, I wasn't exactly destroying him. The sale will make the widow and the kid millionaires many times over, but the company will belong to me. That was driving Harrison nuts, but I call it elemental justice."

"Why didn't he get the money from his sister? I've just been told she's got it."

"I saw her here tonight. She didn't age well. She looks like Harrison in drag. Mean bitch, though. Always was. And you're right, she's got enough money to buy Fort Knox."

"Then why didn't he—"

The dry chuckle turned into a dry cackle. He lit another cigarette. "Harrison and his sister were ut from the same cloth. Both of them always wanted to run things themselves. That included the boat company. She and Harrison butted heads after the old man's death. She lost. Harrison had sufficient votes to run her right off the board, and he did. She never forgave him. She wouldn't have given him a crust of stale bread after that, not if he was starving."

"Nice family."

He shrugged. "Oh, pretty typical, I guess, if big money is involved. Of course, some might say having a kid stab daddy in the belly was carrying things a tad too far. Can you do anything for Angel?"

"I'm trying."

"Good. You see the widow?"

I nodded.

"Now that's what I'd call a prime hunk of horseflesh. That damn Harrison always did all right for himself in that department. Great hand with the ladies, always was. Wouldn't mind taking a whack at that widow myself. Of course, maybe if Harrison had paid a little more attention to profits and less to pussy, I wouldn't be taking over his company."

He fished into his breast pocket, extracted a card, and handed it to me. "If I can help the kid, let me know. I remember when she was little. Cute as a button."

"Do you have children?" I asked.

He shook his head. "Nope. Never married, either. I used to regret not having a family. But I suppose if I did, some grandchild of mine might have stabbed me in the gut."

He inhaled on the cigarette and then coughed. "Doesn't make any difference, really. These damn cigarettes will kill me anyway." He chuckled. "But what the hell, you have to die of something, right?"

I MET several people at the funeral home, people who, like Amos Gillespie, had known Harrison Harwell during his life. Each person I talked to presented a different version of the man. Some loved him, or said they did. Some expressed polite admiration although it sometimes seemed almost too polite. Others appeared to be there only to make sure Harwell was really dead.

Robin asked me to meet her back at her home after Anderson closed up.

I grabbed a quick burger and coffee at a fast-food joint, waited until I was sure things had settled down, and then drove over to the Harwell house.

The media trucks and the reporters were gone; the street lights shone down on a deserted street. The bored security guards recognized my old car and waved me through.

Dennis Bernard, the butler, met me at the door.

"Mrs. Harwell is up in her room and asks that you join her there. Do you know the way?"

"Yeah."

The house was quiet as I went up the stairs.

Her enormous bedroom was dark but I could see her silhouetted against the tall windows facing the river. She was hunched down in a chair, her stockinged feet propped up on the window ledge.

"Robin?"

"Come on in, Charley. Want a drink? I have some very good vodka." She held the bottle up as I approached. "It's chilled."

"I'm not drinking today."

"Pity, but the more for me. Sit down, Charley."

I pulled up a chair and sat next to her. Outside lights provided sufficient illumination to see her, and my eyes adjusted quickly to the darkness in the room. She looked tired.

Robin took a pull directly from the bottle.

"Is that wise?" I said.

She turned and smiled. "It's been a hell of a day and I just needed a quick boost. Generally, I use a glass." She thrust the bottle in my direction. "Are you sure?"

"I'm sure."

The black dress had crept up to midthigh. I wondered how much of the vodka she had managed to drink before I arrived.

"Robin, I think the time has come when you should start thinking about getting another lawyer for Angel."

She studied me for a moment, then spoke, this time with sharper inflection. "Did my beloved sister-in-law frighten you, Charley? She scares the hell out of most people. She told me she wanted you off the case. Is she the reason?"

70

"No."

Robin sipped from the bottle slowly, then tasted the rim with the tip of her tongue. She looked out at the river. "I talked to Angel in the courtroom. She's satisfied with you, so why talk about quitting now?"

I was tempted to tell the truth—that I was scared, in part because of the case, but mostly for myself. But that was something that wasn't easily told, especially to someone whose respect you wanted. Truth can sometimes have a bitter taste. This was one of the times. For the moment, the bitter truth was something to be avoided.

"I can handle the case through the examination on Friday. Judge Mulhern likes me. The Irish have a saying: it's better to know the judge than to know the law. I know Mulhern and he knows me. If a break can be given, he'll do it. Nothing illegal or unethical, but if the coin can fall either way, Mulhern may give it a nudge in my direction."

Out on the dark river a long ore carrier was gliding past, it's six-hundred-foot hull strung with lights like a seagoing Christmas decoration. The reflected lights danced in the dark waters. The huge silent ship sliding past seemed ominous, like a physical symbol of the unstoppable force of fate.

"After the examination, you should get a top man. I can line one up for you, if you like."

Robin didn't reply. She watched the ship until it was almost out of sight, then she turned. "I'm told you were a top man once. Why not again?"

"I'm rusty. You wouldn't want a pitcher who had been away from baseball to be throwing in the World Series. I'm flattered, Robin, but this is not an easy case. Why take an unnecessary risk?"

"Is that what you are, an unnecessary risk?"

"In this matter, that's exactly what I am."

She said nothing for a while, then spoke again. "Did you arrange it so Angel can attend the funeral?"

I had called Mark Evola. "I talked to the prosecutor, but he won't give permission. Even under guard."

"My God, it's her father's funeral!"

I nodded. "And the prosecutor says she murdered him."

"Even if she had, which she didn't, what difference would that make?"

"The prosecutor doesn't want to give Angel a shot at any favorable publicity. A few front-page photos of Angel crying over daddy's casket might cause public sympathy to swing her way. Jurors might remember those kinds of photos. Either way, security or politics, having her there is a risk, and Evola isn't taking any risks with this case."

In the dim light, Robin in profile looked exactly as she did when we were teenagers. The muted light washed away the years and she seemed magically young again.

She must have sensed what I was feeling.

"Like old times," she said, reaching across and taking my hand. Her flesh was warm, her grip sure.

"Well, this place is a touch more elegant than my old car."

She chuckled, her eyes fixed on mine. She was close. I could smell the aroma of the vodka.

"Kiss me, Charley."

"Robin, you're tired, and—"

She moved with surprising swiftness. Her lips were alive, demanding. I could taste the vodka. Her tongue darted out like a hot little snake, then she sat back, smiling.

"Remember?" she asked.

"I remember," I said, and I did. "Look, Robin, this has been a very tough day for you. I'd better go."

"Afraid of widows?"

I shrugged. "Maybe. But tomorrow is the funeral. Take it from someone who knows, the vodka may help tonight but it will only make things worse tomorrow. You need sleep more than booze right now."

"Maybe I need something even more relaxing than sleep."

"Robin—"

"Are you thinking about Harrison?" she asked quietly.

"Well, the circumstances aren't exactly propitious, are they?"

She sighed. "Charley, he was my husband in name only, for a long time. We lived together but we were estranged in every other sense."

Robin still held my hand tightly. "So, I'm not exactly your typical grieving widow, am I?"

"Still, you are the widow."

She chuckled, but it was a deep, throaty sound, born more in sex than humor. "Think of it, Charley. What a story you could tell. How many men have boffed a widow while her husband lay dead in his casket? You could dine out on a story like that for years, Charley." She lay the bottle down and in one surprisingly swift graceful motion sat on my lap. "It sounds deliciously naughty, like something out of Chaucer."

Her tongue sought my mouth again and she wiggled against my thighs.

I attempted to gently push her away but her arms held me tightly.

"Robin, are you drunk?"

She giggled. "That's not my problem."

She was just like she used to be, unpredictable, with a sudden hunger for excitement so fierce and unexpected that it blotted out reason. It did then, and it did now.

I was instantly aflame, aroused despite myself. I kissed her back and my hands searched her remembered body as if all those years had never passed. A voice seemed to whisper in my mind, a whispered warning, but my pulse was pounding and I didn't want to listen.

The trip to the bed was awkward, our two bodies locked and twisted together, moving like an uncoordinated land crab. Somehow she managed to get out of most her clothes during the graceless journey.

On the bed, the willing struggle continued, mouths, hands and moans, flesh on fire. She was more sure, more practiced, and she had learned so many more things to do.

But the taste and smell of her was the same.

Everything was the same.

We weren't teenagers anymore. But it didn't seem to matter.

DID I GO TO THE FUNERAL?

No.

Did I feel good about myself?

Same answer.

I even imagine—or perhaps it wasn't imagination—the look on the security guards' faces when I drove my car out of the Harwell's place at almost four in the morning.

The psychiatrists say the child within us never dies and the ethics and standards pounded into us in our very early years, no matter how stern or inappropriate, are never completely forgotten, but exist like reproachful ghosts in the dark recesses of our minds.

My ghost had a face and name. She had harsh eyes enlarged by thick glasses that perched upon her razor-thin nose. Her mouth was a severe line like a crack in concrete. No lips, just disapproval. My ghost's name was Marie Celeste, Sister Marie Celeste.

In the beginning she was real enough. She was the scourge of my grade school and she had resolved to save the soul of Charles Sloan, a cringing little boy, by force and violence, if necessary. She seemed to follow me from grade to grade like a black-robed fate. She still follows me.

A Catholic kid doesn't need a superego if a Sister Marie Celeste is around. Awakening thoughts of sexuality were quickly stamped

out, like the sputtering fuse to a deadly bomb. As were all devia-
tions in thought, word, or deed beyond the spiritual or behavioral
limits set by Marie Celeste. Her verbal floggings, expressed in
the form of prayer, had the force and effect of fanatical threats, or,
when she was really angry, biblical curses.

I had long ago left the church, but somehow I was never able to
escape her.

I wondered what she would think of me now. Lapsed in matters of faith, a recovering drunk, a lawyer who had eluded disbar-
ment by a chin whisker, a man hanging onto existence by his
fingertips. And worst of all, a man who had committed the "great
sin" with a widow on the eve of her dead husband's funeral.

I had heard that Marie Celeste, now in her eighties, had suffered a massive stroke and become a mindless drooler, tied to a
chair in the mother house of her order. Even if somehow I could
pose the question, she no longer had the ability to answer.

That was, of course, the Sister Marie Celeste of the flesh. The
ominous one in my mind was still fully capable of unforgiving,
furious judgment.

The sexual romp with Robin had been like a fevered dream,
half real, half delirious, a montage of taste, touch, and smell, each
animal sensation searing a memory into the consciousness. The
lovemaking had been frantic and sweaty, and only mutual exhaus-
tion had stopped it.

But those vivid memories only produced a sense of guilt that
had rolled in upon me like a heavy fog.

So I didn't go to the funeral.

Although I hadn't had much sleep and felt the effects, I decided to get some distance from my reproving ghost by occupying
myself as busily as I could.

Angel Harwell hadn't been allowed to go to the funeral. I wondered how she was feeling. Perhaps she too needed something to
occupy her thoughts.

The examination before Judge Mulhern was only one day away.
Angel wouldn't testify—it was just for prosecution witnesses—
but I thought I might be able to pry up a few more details from
her, perhaps discover something to help my cross examination.

Angel looked even better than before. Her black hair was still
wet from the jail shower, her perfect skin glowed. She was of age,

a grown woman, but there was an underlying eerie sense of the child about her, like a sprite or a beautiful innocent creature of the woodlands, someone who might appear from a morning mist. She certainly didn't have the look of a killer, yet there was something unsettling about her that provoked in me a sense of wariness. She regarded me with interest, but her pale blue expressionless eyes again gave no hint of what she might be thinking.

We sat across from each other, as before, separated by glass and speaking through microphones.

"How are you doing, Angel?"

She shrugged. "All right, I suppose. Did you go to Daddy's funeral?"

I shook my head. "No. It's going on as we speak. Are you all right?"

"About the funeral, you mean?"

"Yes."

She seemed to look past me as she spoke. "I felt bad that they wouldn't let me go. But there isn't anything I could do anyway, is there, even if they had allowed me to go? He's dead and that's all there is to it. I suppose missing some clergyman's inane sermon won't ruin my life."

"That's a good way to look at it. Are you ready for tomorrow?"

"What's to be ready? From what you told me, I won't even be able to tell my side."

"No, but they'll read the statement you gave to Evola."

"Why would they want to read it?"

"It's maybe the biggest part of their case. They'll—"

"No, I don't mean it that way. Why should they have to read it? They recorded it on videotape."

"What?"

She nodded. "They had a camera set up. Of course, they had a stenographer there too. But the cop running the camera seemed to know what he was doing. Is there some rule that they can't show that tape in court?"

It was like getting hit in the stomach. "They can show it, Angel, and they will." Evola had sandbagged me, letting me think the steno's transcript was the only thing he had. I shouldn't have let that happen. It wouldn't have happened in the old days, never. I hoped my shock didn't show. I wondered if it were only a matter of being rusty and away too long, or if I had truly lost forever the mental edge I once had. "How come you never told me about the camera?"

"You didn't ask. I didn't think it was unusual. Isn't almost everything done that way now?"

"More or less. A video will have more effect than a stenographer's dry reading."

"Will they use the first or second one?"

"What do you mean?"

She seemed annoyed that my mental processes were apparently so slow. "They shot two videos. Everything seemed to take such a long time that night. The policemen talked to me, then that tall blond man."

"Evola."

She nodded. "He talked to me several times. Sometimes a woman took down what we said, sometimes she didn't."

"Go on."

"Finally, they took me into a room with the camera. I guess I didn't answer the way he wanted, although I thought we had covered everything. So, he did the whole thing again. I suppose that's the one they're going to use."

"Angel, this is important. How many formal statements did you give the police that night?"

She pursed her lips and thought for a moment, then nodded, as if to herself. "Three. Two of them were videotaped."

"Okay, let's go over everything very carefully, Angel. That night, the night you saw your father dead, when did you first talk to the police?"

"At the house. They came to my room, two policemen in uniform. They asked me how I got the blood on me, things like that. There were only a few questions until the other ones got there."

"Detectives?"

She nodded. "I guess. Anyway, they were in civilian clothes. They kept me away from Robin and the others."

"And they asked you what happened?"

"Yes. Of course, they told me I didn't have to answer if I didn't want to, and that I had a right to an attorney. They kept telling me that over and over all night, or so it seemed."

"They brought you down to the sheriff's office. What happened then?"

"They gave me some coffee. Two of them talked to me in a small room."

"Morgan and Maguire?"

"I think those are their names. They were very nice to me."

"Think carefully, Angel. What did you tell them, exactly?"

She sighed and shrugged. "Everything seems hazy to me, really. When I think about that night, I keep seeing Daddy lying there, with the knife . . ." Her voice trailed off.

"Well, tell me what you remember telling Morgan and Maguire."

"I told them I was sorry Daddy was dead, that I felt bad because we had quarreled that night. They asked me about the blood on my clothes and my hands."

"And?"

She shrugged again. "I really can't remember what I told them. I was very upset."

"Did they question you and have a stenographer take it down?"

Angel nodded. "After a while, yes."

"Did you feel afraid?"

"No. I just felt very bad. Real bad."

"When did you first talk to Evola, the prosecutor, the tall blond man?"

"In that same small office. He came in while the police were talking to me. After they were done he asked me some questions. My memory is sort of disjointed. People kept coming and going that night."

"Did you tell the two policemen that you thought you were responsible for your father's death?"

"I don't think so."

"Why don't you think so?"

She shrugged. "I don't know, I just don't remember saying that, not then."

"Okay, you talked to Evola, then what happened?"

"They took me across a hall to the room where the camera was set up."

"And Evola questioned you there?"

"Yes. I could tell the camera was going. Those things have a little blinking red light when they record. I saw the light."

"And that happened twice? Are you sure about that?"

"It's about all I am sure of."

"What was different about the two sessions, that you can remember?"

"Really nothing," she said. "It seemed to me he asked the same questions each time."

"After the first taping, did anyone talk to you?"

"He did."

"Evola?"

She nodded.

"What did he say?"

"As I remember, he said I had to speak louder."

"And that's all?"

She shrugged. "He said I had to be more definite about what happened. I think that's when the responsibility thing first came up."

"Responsibility, was that his word or yours?"

"I'm not sure. I don't remember. Everything was so confused."

"What did you mean by responsibility?"

There was no expression. "I'm not sure, now. I certainly didn't mean that I stabbed my father. An awful thing had happened and I felt bad because we had fought earlier. I think that's why I said that, but I'm not entirely sure. I'm sorry I'm not more help. I just don't remember."

I thought for a moment. "Angel, when they asked if you wanted a lawyer, why didn't you say yes?"

"It didn't seem, well, important."

"You must have realized at some point that you were in trouble?"

For the first time I saw some emotion, maybe the beginning of tears in those startling ice-blue eyes, but she quickly looked away as she spoke.

"My father was dead. I felt terrible. What happened to me didn't seem to matter. I really didn't care, not then."

"Do you care now, Angel?"

Her eyes returned to meet mine. "Yes."

"Good. You should. I'll see you in court tomorrow morning."

"Then can you get me out of here?" For an instant only, her tone revealed real agony.

"We'll see, Angel. I'll do my very best."

She nodded. "Will Robin be there tomorrow?"

"I think so."

I tried to read her expression to see what she was thinking, but it was like looking at a mask—a beautiful one but still a mask.

"Please. Help me." She spoke the words softly, with quiet calm. Two tears rolled down from her eyes, slowly. The effect had the impact of a scream.

THE Kerry County medical examiner had come a long way from the Philippine Islands, the land of his birth—over ten thousand miles, by way of Harvard, Johns Hopkins, and Bellevue. He had worked for a while in Detroit and that's where I got to know him.

Ernesto Rey, M.D., resembled a cute little Kewpie doll, with a round baby face, so pretty that his tan features would have been better suited on a girl. He had large chocolate eyes and dark black hair that curled around his dimpled face in a tousled crown. Just an inch over five feet, he also had a doll's body, soft and cuddly. His white little teeth were perfect and he kept them exposed in an almost perpetual shy smile.

He was almost fifty, but looked thirty. Despite his size and cute persona, the word was out that he made Errol Flynn look like a Franciscan monk. Ernesto Rey, M.D., was irresistible to the ladies, and vice versa.

It was that trait that always brought him trouble. In some men a Don Juan reputation is amusing, particularly if the man looks like something that should be on top of a wedding cake. But there was a quality about Rey's single-mindedly predatory sexual nature that suggested something degenerate, even maniacal, Kewpie doll or not. Back in New York and Detroit there had been ugly rumors about orgies in the morgue, even whispers of necrophilia. Those dark whispers, true or not, combined with his unbridled tendencies had led him, a board-certified, world-famous pathologist, to seek anonymity in the quiet sanctuary of Michigan's Kerry County.

Ernesto Rey worked on contract, getting so much a body, more if he had to carve at night or on weekends. He did consulting work in other cities and made extra money by doing private pathology work for local doctors, looking at slides of tissue taken from living people to see if anything was wrong.

But he had made his reputation on the dead, and it was this work he really liked the best. He loved cops. He loved courtrooms. There was a large slice of ham in the good doctor and he enjoyed his time in the witness chair, combining an actor's easy grace with his extensive medical expertise.

He pretended to like me but I knew he didn't. In Detroit's recorders court a few years back I had nailed him to the wall, embarrassed him, on several murder cases. It had been partly luck, but his smug arrogance made him an easy target. He might have forgiven me but he hadn't forgotten. He smiled when we met but I always saw a hint of fear in those moist chocolate eyes.

Ernesto worked out of the basement lab of Dockland Hospital in Port Huron. After leaving Angel I drove up there to talk to him. He did the autopsy on Harrison Harwell and would appear as a witness.

Port Huron sits at the mouth of the river like the gatekeeper to Lake Huron, joined by the Blue Water Bridge to Canada's Sarnia. Docklands Hospital is a small private operation near the center of town. I knew it well. One of the members of the Club had died there after weeks of agony. I had visited often. I felt a shudder at that disturbing memory as I parked in the hospital's lot and walked to the basement entrance in the back.

The halls were all tile, walls, ceiling, and floor, and only a cat could have walked there without causing an echo. Rolling body carts, empty, were parked one after another in a row along one wall. The sight of them made me think of what they had been carrying.

Ernesto was lounging at a desk near the end of the hall, talking to a big-hipped nurse whose uniform was girdle tight and looked about to burst. Young, not much over twenty, she gazed down at the dapper doctor with awe and fascination. He looked at her like a starving cat might view a big, juicy mouse. He was jabbering away, smiling and vital, doing his best to charm this very big woman, so engrossed that he didn't even notice my approach.

I always wondered where he got his clothes. Everything he wore looked perfectly tailored. Even his white smock looked as if it had been made for him personally.

"Hello, Ernie."

He shot an annoyed glance my way, not recognizing me, then

returned his full attention to the large female quarry in front of him.

"Ernie, I'm here on business," I said.

The glance this time turned into wide-eyed recognition. The perpetual smile flickered out, but only for a moment. It returned instantly, even wider than before.

"Ah, Mr. Sloan. How nice to see you."

This time it was the big nurse who looked annoyed.

"Brenda," he said, "can we continue this later? Perhaps over coffee?"

She nodded, shot me an irritated glance, then walked quickly down the hall.

We both watched her. She was a big, muscular girl, and those hips moved like giant ball bearings under the tight white uniform.

"I understand her husband is a crazy son of a bitch," I whispered. "I hear he bit a guy's nose off once for just looking at her."

Ernie's eyes widened until he realized I was kidding.

"She's not married," he snapped. Then, in a gentler tone, he asked, "What do you want with me?"

"We have a date in court tomorrow morning."

He nodded. "The Harrison Harwell murder case." He stretched out the pronunciation as if he were Sherlock Holmes reminiscing about a past triumph.

"I want to look at your file."

"That's impossible."

"Ernie, nothing is impossible. I don't want to take it, alter it, or eat it, I just want to look at it. You can even watch over my shoulder if you like."

"It's not a public record," he said, his tone rising just a bit. "The only thing you're entitled to is the autopsy report."

"Are you hiding something?"

"Of course not."

I smiled. "Maybe not, but tomorrow in court I think I can make it look very much like you are. You can avoid all that by just letting me have a quick look at what you've got."

"But—"

"I give you my word I will never tell a soul, Ernie, if that's what's worrying you. This will set no precedent, believe me, and it will allow me to be a little easier on you tomorrow in the witness stand."

I could see the last part made a difference.

The loud sigh had a theatrical sound. "Well, if it's the only way I can get rid of you."

"It is."

He led me down the hall and unlocked a small office, turned on the light, and closed the door after I followed him in.

Ernie unlocked a cabinet, took out a file, and handed it to me.

"This is it. You can sit at the desk there. I can spare ten minutes, no more."

I took a chair and opened the file. He stood directly behind me.

Some things never change, and a medical examiner's file in a homicide case was one of them. There was a diary for entries, the rough notes, the audiotape made during the autopsy, copies of lab reports, and the preliminary autopsy report itself. Plus the photographs.

I quickly leafed through the autopsy report. It provided the usual details. Harrison Harwell, dead, had measured six feet one and he had been weighed in at 217 pounds. Each organ had been weighed and its condition had been noted. Aside from the damage done by the knife, the liver had been slightly enlarged and the heart showed evidence of a previous coronary problem, but nothing really life-threatening. So except for one hell of a stab wound in the chest, Harrison Harwell had been in relatively good shape for his age. The cause of death was shown as homicide with a short statement that sounded as if one of the cops had written it for Ernie, but I had expected that.

The photos were better than average, and there were more than usual.

Most were of the body, naked if you didn't count the knife sticking out of the hairy chest. Some shots showed the whole body exhibited, others were close-ups catching the knife in all its hideous invasion. Harrison Harwell's eyes were open, which made the grisly color photos even more gruesome. When they were shown to a jury, those dead staring eyes would give the photos real show-biz punch.

Several shots showed the knife after it had been extracted. One displaying the knife next to the puckered wound was especially dramatic. Others merely showed the knife against a measure. The curved handle and the blade were stained. But despite the blood, it was a beautiful thing, and a perfect match for the big sword hanging in Harwell's study.

"Who took the snapshots?" I asked.

"Some were done by the police photographer. Most of them I did. I have several cameras."

"You're pretty good, Ernie. You've missed your calling. You got any around of the nurses? Maybe some of big Brenda? You know, art studies."

"Your time is up."

I looked at the photos again. "Is this how they brought him in, with the knife still in the chest?"

"Yes."

"I mean, didn't they bring him in with the knife out and you stuck it back in to take these pictures?"

"I did like hell. What you see is what I saw. He was dead when they found him, so they left the knife in."

"Was he found naked?"

"No. He had clothes. They're here, marked as evidence."

"But he came in naked?"

"No. I took off his clothes before taking the pictures."

"But the knife?"

He sighed in exasperation. "I was able to get the damn shirt off. It's just routine. I often just cut the clothes off unless it's important to the case. The shirt was a kind of silk pajama top. It was already open when his daughter stabbed him."

"Even Pickeral Point takes photos of homicide scenes, Ernie. I can check the cop's pictures taken at the scene. If that knife is in the wrong way it will be your ass in court, you do understand that?"

"Check all you want. That's how he came in here."

"I see you got a copying machine over there." It was a desk-top model. "Let me copy a few of these pictures."

"No way."

"Ah, then you did doctor up the body, didn't you?"

"Damn it, I did not."

"Then you should have no objection to my making a couple copies."

"Look—"

"It will be our secret, Ernie. We both know you shouldn't have

84

even let me in here. Just a copy of a few shots. And then I'll leave." I made my tone innocent but he understood the implied threat.

The smile had really gone for good this time. He stalked over to the table and flicked the copier's switch. An electrical hum filled the room.

I quickly made a copy of each photograph. They were black and white and grainy but they would serve my purpose. I could almost feel Dr. Rey's growing anger.

"You got an envelope I can put these in, Ernie?"

"Get the fuck out of here!"

"I'll see you tomorrow," I said as I left. "And watch out for Brenda. She looks like the kind who might get carried away with passion and do you serious bodily harm. The living ones can do that sometimes, you know."

When he slammed the office door, the noise echoed down the empty corridor like a cannon shot.

I DROVE back to Pickeral Point, my mind working on possible strategies for court in the morning. Guilt continued to gnaw away at me, but not quite as violently as before. I knew I would have to call Robin. I wondered how she felt and how the funeral had gone. I wondered if she would want to see me. In a way, I hoped she would, but simultaneously I hoped she wouldn't. I tried to put all that out of my mind; it wasn't that important now. What was important was to get prepared for the morning. Much of what would happen to Angel Harwell in the future would depend on what I could do for her in the morning. Her softly spoken plea for help echoed in my mind.

As I pulled into the mall parking lot near my office a large red Rolls Royce was pulling out. Rollses are a rarity in Pickeral Point. The blood-red finish glinted as if it had just been oiled. The windows were tinted so I couldn't see the passengers. When I owned my Rolls I wanted everyone to see whose car it was. But to each his own.

Our big-breasted receptionist was almost glad to see me. "Some guys were here looking for you," she said, "but they left. You just missed them."

"What were their names?"

She shrugged. "They wouldn't give names. There were three of them, black guys. Scary-looking. Street guys, but they were wearing really expensive jewelry. I don't know much, but I do know jewelry. The guy who I think was the boss they called Little Mike, although he was tall. Maybe it was a joke, you think?"

"Did they leave a message, a phone number?"

She shook her head. "No. They just said to tell you they would be back. They didn't want to make an appointment. They didn't seem the kind that would. I think they want you for their lawyer, anyway I kinda got that from the way they were talking." She handed me a pack of messages. "These people called. Oh yeah, and Mitch would like to see you."

"Thanks."

As I walked toward Mitch's office I looked through the messages. Most were from reporters and media people, although a few were from local people who I didn't know, and one call was from Robin.

Mitch Johnson was talking on the phone when I stuck my head in his door. He smiled and motioned me to come in and sit down.

The furnishings in his office were very much like Mitch himself, plain but of very good quality. Mitch Johnson was my benefactor. We had been law students together, and while I had pursued fame and fortune in Detroit's criminal courts, he had come up to Pickeral Point. He had not found fame but he had done all right in the fortune department. Mitch ran a three-man partnership that represented most of the local banks, so the firm got much of the big-money trust and estate work in the county.

Mitch was talking to a banker about a trust question as I sat down.

Despite the disastrous publicity resulting from my conviction and my subsequent brush with the bar association, Mitch had extended the hand of friendship when I needed it. It was the only one offered at the time, and I appreciated it. He let me use an office, rent-free. I heard later that the other two partners had been upset, but Mitch had insisted. His help had been like a lifeline to a drowning swimmer.

Mitch had lost most of the thick brown hair he had when we were students. His dark eyes, large and friendly, now peered out from behind thick steel-rimmed glasses. He had put on weight to

86

the point of being pudgy and his conservative clothes always looked a size too small despite being carefully tailored. He smiled a lot and had an excellent sense of humor. He resembled a small-town banker and maybe that's why he got their business.

Mitch completed the call and hung up.

"You're becoming quite a celebrity. The whole town is talking about the Harwell case. Pretty exciting stuff for you, I'll bet."

I thought I detected a strained quality in his voice, the tone a person uses in a conversation he really doesn't want to have.

"It's my fifteen minutes of fame, Mitch."

He nodded. "Well, this certainly marks a new start for you, Charley. Back to the big time, eh? I suppose you'll be leaving this stodgy old firm now."

"What's the problem, Mitch?"

"What I mean, Charley, is you'll be raking in the big fees again. You'll need more space than we have and now you'll need your own clerical staff."

"Hey, Mitch, relax. You can talk straight with me. What's the trouble?"

He slowly shook his head. "God, I hate to do this, but I have to ask you to leave our offices."

"Sure, Mitch. No problem."

"Don't you want to know why?"

"Mitch, you were the only one who helped me when I needed it. You, of all people, don't need to give me a reason."

"Ah, Jesus, Charley, you make me feel even worse. Look, it's a business problem, mostly. You know what we do here, a nice quiet probate practice. Most of our clients, the important ones, are gray-haired old widows who have us look after their estates. This isn't exactly *L.A. Law* around here, as you know."

I smiled. "I know."

"You're back on the front pages, Charley, and in a very good way. The publicity's great for you, but not for a quiet probate firm like this. Murder, criminal law, that sort of thing frightens our kind of clients."

"I understand."

"The other guys pitched a bitch when they heard you took on the Harwell case. They were afraid the firm might get hurt by the association. And today kind of finished things off."

"What happened today?"

"Your prospective clients."

"You do mean the three street dudes waiting to see me? I missed them."

"You're lucky. They looked like a rerun of a *Miami Vice* episode. One of our widows, an old gal worth about forty million, came by to see me while they were out there in the reception room. Jesus, Charley, the sight of them scared her away. She called from the drugstore, very upset."

"Nothing to worry about. I'll be packed and gone tomorrow. And I certainly understand, believe me." There was no point in telling Mitch that I would be out of the Harwell case after tomorrow.

"Who were those guys, Charley?"

It was my turn to sigh. "From what I can learn you saw a gentlemen called Little Mike, an old client of mine, from Detroit. His name is Michael Tyler. He's a businessman primarily."

"He didn't look it."

"Mitch, his business is drugs. And, to help business, murder, if he thinks it's necessary. I guess he reads the papers and thinks I'm back full-time in criminal practice. I represented him a couple of times in Detroit, always with good results. He always liked me. Little Mike must be doing all right. I think I saw his car, a Rolls. When I knew him all he could afford was a Mercedes. Of course, he was only seventeen then. He has to be twenty-one, maybe twenty-two now. That's old in his line of work."

"I feel terrible about this, Charley. I wish you didn't have to move."

"Mitch, you've been more than a friend to me. Don't get silly."

"Do you have anyplace to go?"

"Obviously, I hadn't thought about it. I suppose I can find an office somewhere around here."

"Maybe I can help you out."

"Thanks, but you've done enough."

A relieved smile crept across his face. "Well, maybe it's more like you helping me."

"What do you mean?"

"I'm executor of Simon Matthews's estate. He was a tax lawyer up here. I don't think you knew him. He was dead a year or so before you came up. Anyway, I run one of his buildings, maybe you've seen it, an ugly-looking thing up by Windsong Marina, looks like a concrete fortress."

"The marine insurance place?"

"Yeah, that's it. But that outfit only rents the first floor. Simon had an office suite on the second floor. It's just a one-room office with a reception room. There's an outside stairway up to the place. He owned the building so I guess he decided to locate his office there. Anyway, I've been trying to sell the whole place since he died. His heirs are a couple of greedy nephews in Florida. The place doesn't have many uses so I haven't had even one offer. I tried to rent the law office but nobody wants it, it's too out of the way."

"And you're offering it to me."

"Well, as a stopgap only. I'd have to charge you real rent since I have to account to the court, but you can have it as long as you want or until I sell the building."

"I don't have any furniture, Mitch."

"Old Simon's is still in there. It's not exactly what you'd call high fashion, but feel free to use it. You can have the telephone company transfer your number there. There's a phone, unconnected now, of course."

"What's the rent?"

Mitch shrugged. "Like I say, I have to account to the court so I can't even give you much of a bargain. Those nephews watch every nickel. It's a thousand a month. I'd make it no lease, just month to month. Can you handle that?"

"I can. For a while."

"Then it's a deal?"

I stood up and we shook hands. "I will never forget your kindness, Mitch."

He sighed, then smiled sadly. "Sure you will, Charley. Everyone forgets kindness. The only thing anyone really remembers is when they get kicked in the ass."

He pulled open a drawer, hunted around, and pulled out a small envelope.

"Here's the key. Let's hope it opens a whole new life for you."

WHAT's that old line—I've been thrown out of better places than this.

Still, I couldn't put aside a sad, nagging sense of rejection.

I didn't feel like talking to Robin, at least not yet, and I didn't feel like answering the other messages, either. So I drove out to take a look at my new office.

The Windsong Marina can only handle small powerboats since its sole access to the river is a canal under a bridge. But it is home to a hundred or so boats small enough to clear the bridge even if their owners have to duck.

The marine insurance office was closed when I got there. I had often driven past the building and the only memory I had of it was that whoever had built it had taken his architectural degree in advanced ugly. Square, squat, concrete, with only a few small windows, it looked like a place where small animals were put to death. It was located across the road from the Windsong Marina, on the river side.

The outside stairway, which looked more like a fire escape, was located on the side of the place, rising up from the small parking lot. I wouldn't be getting too many old lady clients—it was quite a climb to the top.

There really was no second floor. The office seemed like an afterthought, another small squat building set on top of the flat roof like a hat.

The office door still had Simon Matthews's name on it, although the glass was so dirty it was hard to see it. I used the key and went in.

The place had the musty atmosphere of an ancient tomb. I flipped on the light and took a look.

The reception room was small, with a desk and chair for the secretary and a large, very worn black leather couch. There was a matching chair, equally old and equally worn. The carpet looked older than I am.

I stepped into the office proper. The desk looked like something out of Charles Dickens, a piece Ebenezer Scrooge might have used, so old that it was probably extremely valuable. Behind it was a high-back leather chair, worn and listing a bit to one side. The dust on the desk was as thick as a first snowfall. Three walls were filled with bookcases, all full and very dusty. The fourth wall was mostly window.

I looked out the window. At least Simon Matthews hadn't

cheated himself on the view. It was the same river, and almost the same vista seen from millionaires' row.

A cramped phone booth–sized bathroom, with a toilet and a washbowl, was tucked away near in a corner, its door almost hidden by the bookcases.

I took a look at the law books. Every set ended with 1988. I figured that was probably the year Matthews died.

The dusty, archaic office was something out of another century. I loved it.

7

THE ALARM, SOUNDING LIKE THE WAIL OF A SCOUT car, melded into my dream, becoming for a moment part of the drama elaborately scripted and directed by my sleeping mind. But then the nightmare evaporated as the incessant ringing propelled me back into the real world. I reached over and shut the damn thing off.

I was awake but not rested. The night had been a series of tension-inspired dreams interspersed with long periods of sleeplessness. I regretted having passed on my usual Thursday night meeting of the Club, something I hadn't done in months. I had told myself I would need that time to prepare for the preliminary examination. But I should have gone—most of my preparation time had been wasted, used up struggling against that old nagging urge for just one quick drink.

After the court hearing I planned to move my few belongings to my new place of business, but I still had a key to Mitch's office so, after everyone had left for the night, I had gone back, let myself in, and used the firm's small library, concentrating on cases dealing with the exclusion of confessions. I found many but somehow I just couldn't seem to focus on the key cases I needed to read and understand.

I had telephoned Robin from there, wondering if someone like the ghostly Sister Marie Celeste might not have found another conscience to bother. If Robin was feeling guilty, she didn't sound it. But she did sound tired, and I was not invited back for a rematch, which prompted in me a surprising conflict-ridden sense of relief and irritation. Robin had described the funeral. It had been no different than any other. Harrison Harwell now lay in a grave next to his father. Robin seemed pleased that a plot had been reserved for Harrison's sister, her sharp tone implying she hoped that the vacant·space wouldn't go unused for long.

She said she would see me in court in the morning.

And now it was the morning.

I sat up, but my legs seemed heavy. It was a chore to move. It was as though I were the one being charged, not my client.

A drink would have done it, just a small one, just enough to ease the increasing grip of galloping anxiety.

It felt like I was about to go on trial.

And, in a way, I was.

TOMMY Mulhern looked in pretty good shape, although his puffy cheeks had a deep rosy blush, the tint seen in sunsets and on the faces of people with very high blood pressure. But Judge Mulhern exhibited no signs of hangover, and he seemed to enjoy meeting with me and Evola in his chambers, briskly setting rules for the conduct of the preliminary examination like a director telling his actors what to say and where to stand. Mulhern had already met with the television people, and a single camera, set back by the empty jury box, was manned and ready.

"Let's do a nice, quick, workmanlike job," Mulhern said to both of us, though it was clear he was aiming his remarks at Evola. "They got everything out there but the elephants and the tent, but I'm not going to let this thing get turned into a circus. If either of you should be tempted to get a bit theatrical, I will perform some stagecraft myself and the offender will end up looking like a prime asshole. And I think you both know I can do just that, right?"

I nodded, but Mark Evola looked irritated.

"This is a routine murder examination," the judge continued. "The reporters, cameras, and all the rest of it don't change that. I want this run like any other case. Murder is just a fatal assault and battery, nothing more. Get the witnesses on, get 'em off, and remember that damn television camera isn't going to make the decisions here, I am. So play to me, not the lens or the crowd."

Evola smiled, but it was forced. "Judge, we have no control over what the media do. But I assure you I'm going to conduct this case just like any other."

Mulhern snorted. "Oh yeah? If that's so, then how come you're doing the court work yourself and not one of your usual lackeys?"

"This is—"

Mulhern raised a beefy hand. "Enough. I got things to do this afternoon, so let's not drag this thing out. Unless you boys got something else to discuss, let's get the show on the road."

Evola composed his features so that his handsome face seemed almost angelic as we marched out from the judge's chambers.

The crush of spectators did resemble a circus crowd, expectant and impatient to be entertained. Every available seat held human flesh, so packed together that breath and movement looked impossible. Local attorneys were jammed shoulder to shoulder with famous writers. High-paid media types snuggled next to low-paid court workers who, like kids wiggling under a circus tent, had snuck away from their own duties to peek at the legal wonders to come. The crowd, their combined whispered conversations producing an electrical buzzing, seemed to me for a moment like a many-headed monster, all eyes and moving mouths.

Evola took his place at his side of the counsel table, sitting in front of Morgan and Maguire. The two detectives had assumed the solemn expressions of monks at prayer.

Angel seemed equally composed. She sat directly behind my chair, a uniformed court officer behind her.

Robin sat in the first row of spectator seats. I recognized the man seated next to her. Every attorney in Michigan knew him.

I walked back. "Good morning," I said. Robin seemed tense, uncomfortable.

She nodded in response, then spoke quietly. "Charley, this is Nate Golden. He's handling the sale of the boat company for us, for Angel and me."

I nodded and he nodded. Nate Golden was a past president of

the state bar. If anyone had to name the number-one attorney in our state, Golden would make everyone's short list. I knew he was at least seventy although he looked much younger, his skin tan and almost wrinkle-free. Nate Golden reminded me of that little Esquire man of years ago, the short round guy with the big eyes and the white mustache. His bulging blue eyes and a carefully trimmed white mustache were those of the Esquire man, but Golden was whippet-thin and very tall, his hair full and so white it looked like a stage prop.

"Might I have a brief word, Mr. Sloan?" Golden's voice was deep and soothing.

He stood up, moved gracefully past the others in the spectator row, then passed through the opening in the hip-high polished wood barricade. He took my elbow and guided me to a spot just in front of the judge's still-empty bench, the only place where we could talk in some privacy.

"You know me?" he asked quietly.

"Yes."

"Robin tells me you're stepping aside in this matter as soon as this hearing is done."

"It's been discussed."

He smiled, an expression that was almost spiritual. "I recently had my gallbladder out," he said. "I've recovered nicely."

"That's good."

"It's not exactly brain surgery, having a gallbladder removed. The operation is performed every day in every hospital all over the world."

I kept an eye out for the judge, who had not yet appeared.

"Still," he continued in a voice that was just above a whisper, "routine or not, it was of concern to me."

"I don't—"

"Mr. Sloan," he said, even more softly, "would I have selected a surgeon who hadn't done a major operation in four years, one who had almost lost his license because of alcoholism? Obviously, I wouldn't, not if other competent surgeons were available."

He patted my arm. "I'm describing you, am I not? And certainly a murder charge is a much more serious situation than nipping out a mere gallbladder, isn't it?"

His manner was still friendly, but his words had the effect of an unexpected slap. I felt the anger rising and he sensed it.

"Come now, Mr. Sloan, don't take offense. I'm dealing in facts. Your last major case was the successful defense of the Carter brothers, two young gentlemen who decapitated several competitors. A very impressive win, but that was almost four long years ago, before your . . . ah . . . problem led you into all that difficulty."

"I am a fully licensed attorney," I said. "And criminal law is my primary field."

"It was," he said, "and I'm sure it will be again. But this is far too important a case to use as a practice run, Mr. Sloan. We're both lawyers. I know how difficult it must be for you to re-establish yourself. I will propose a new lawyer and suggest to Robin that you work with him as a kind of consultant. I'll see that your fee is protected. You won't be hurt financially by stepping aside."

I was looking up at him. His benign expression was like that of a favorite uncle who was explaining why he couldn't let you drive his Mercedes. Those bulging blue eyes glistened with benevolence.

"Mr. Golden, I told Robin that I—"

The clerk rapped the gavel and the crowd produced a rumbling noise as they struggled to their feet.

"I'm sure you're a reasonable man," he said, patting my arm again, "and I know you'll do the right thing."

He returned, as gracefully as before, to his place next to Robin. He was smiling at me, a knowing little smirk, as if we shared a juicy little secret.

I felt a wave of revulsion. I would step aside, I had already told Robin that I would. That didn't bother me. But Nate Golden would think I had folded because of his power and the promise of easy money. That did bother me. A lot.

"Come on, let's get this thing going," Judge Mulhern rasped.

"The people are ready," Evola said, standing.

I walked back to my chair. I was conscious of Angel's eyes on me. Her expression was as inscrutable as before, but her eyes were not. They were filled with fear.

That made two of us.

"The people are ready," Evola said once more, his voice echoing in the sudden silence of the packed courtroom.

JUDGE Thomas J. Mulhern, who had cautioned us against the bite of the publicity bug, demonstrated that he was not immune to it himself, giving a long-winded lecture at the beginning, glancing occasionally at the crowd but mostly speaking directly into the glass eye of the TV camera. He explained that a preliminary hearing was a judicial investigation, that guilt or innocence didn't have to be proven, only that a crime had been committed and that there were reasonable grounds to believe the defendant had done it. It sounded to me as if he might have rehearsed the speech. His phrases were just a little too smooth and finely articulated to have come trippingly off the judicial cuff.

To my surprise, Evola was as good as his word, quickly and efficiently questioning the policemen who had answered the call that night to the Harwell house and demonstrating that he knew his way around a courtroom. Next on the stand were Dennis Bernard and his wife, the two Harwell servants who had identified the body.

The policemen told Evola what time they had first questioned Angel, which was the only thing I wanted to establish, so I had no questions for them or the Bernards.

To someone not familiar with court technique it might have appeared that I wasn't doing my job. But I was only waiting for the right opportunity, which presented itself in the small, dapper person of Dr. Ernesto Rey.

For the first time I began to enjoy myself. Evola began by having the doctor identify himself. He asked me if I would stipulate to the doctor's qualifications, a usual courtroom courtesy.

It was time to rattle the cage. I stood up.

"If the court please, I wonder if I might ask just one question about the doctor's qualifications?"

"I have no objections," Evola said.

"Go on," Mulhern commanded.

"Dr. Rey, would you be able to estimate for us the number of abortions you've performed?"

The spectators gasped in unison and Rey's brown eyes opened wide in surprise and alarm. Even his tan seemed to fade.

"Oh, I'm sorry," I said before Evola could protest, "did I say abortions? I meant autopsies. These medical terms can be so confusing. Oh well, I suppose it doesn't really matter. For the purposes of this hearing only, I will stipulate to Dr. Rey's qualifications."

It was a cheap trick admittedly, but it worked. It had unsettled the doctor. From that point on Rey watched me like a bird might eye a prowling snake. He answered Evola's standard questions hesitantly, since his mind was more on me than what he was saying. I objected to his conclusions that Angel had done the stabbing. Judge Mulhern sustained that objection, although he let stand Rey's statement that murder had been the cause of death, reminding me from the bench that this was only the preliminary examination and not the trial.

I didn't ask Rey about the possibility of suicide. If it proved to be worth presenting I wanted to keep that for the trial itself, although I reluctantly had to remind myself that I would not be the lawyer trying the case.

The knife was admitted into evidence with no objection from me, which seemed to surprise Evola. There was no way to keep the knife out, and I hoped to turn it to my own benefit later.

Angel had sat behind me quietly, never asking a question. I had glanced back at her several times. It was as though she were not involved, three feet outside herself, in a world of her own. I wondered if her attitude was born of fear, or perhaps from something much more complicated.

Evola called Detective Morgan to the stand. He was about to put the confession into evidence. I waited while he took Morgan up to the point when he had first questioned Angel.

Show time, as they say.

I stood up. "If the court please, I object to anything said by my client to this police officer, Mr. Evola, or any other investigator connected with this case."

Mulhern looked annoyed. "Why? Didn't they read her her rights?"

"Oh, they did, they certainly did. Over and over again."

"Well, then, what's the problem?" Mulhern said.

"The problem is they badgered this young woman for over five long hours, taking statement after statement from her. She denied stabbing her father but that wasn't sufficient for the prosecuting attorney. He worked her over with a kind of mental rubber hose until she finally gave up and used the words he told her to say."

This time Evola was really angry. He was yelling and his face was flushed. For a moment I thought he was going to punch me, which would have been good for the case, but, given his size and athletic ability, very bad for me.

"Hold it!" Mulhern cracked his gavel and glared at Mark Evola. "This isn't a barroom. One at a time. Sloan is making an objection. When he's done, Mr. Evola, you can have your say, not before. Sit down."

The judge then directed his attention to me with an equally unpleasant glare. "Save the rhetoric and make this brief."

"Judge, I was led to believe that only one statement was made by my client, a statement that was taken down and typed up by a stenographer. And I wouldn't have even gotten that if you hadn't made them give it to me. Now, I'm informed that Miss Harwell was interrogated by a number of policemen that night, by detectives Morgan and Maguire, and finally by the prosecuting attorney himself. She made several statements to the police in the presence of a stenographer. She made a videotaped statement to Mr. Evola. When she again stated her innocence, Mr. Evola persisted in questioning her off camera, and after she caved in to his suggestions, took the final statement, also videotaped, which they will now try to present to you. I object to the statement as having been given under duress. They badgered Miss Harwell over and over again for hours until she was too exhausted to think straight. The statement she gave was about as free and voluntary as those given by people having their toenails extracted. It violates every provision of due process and I object to its introduction."

Evola was standing only a few feet away, glaring at me.

"Your turn," Mulhern said to him.

"First of all, I deeply resent the untrue and unfounded allegations made by Mr. Sloan. He has a rather odious reputation and he's doing his best to live up to it."

"Come on," Mulhern growled, "save that stuff for a jury. Get on with it."

"We do plan to introduce a statement made by the defendant.

It is more than a mere statement, it is a confession to murder. We did film it, so everyone can see it was made completely voluntarily and free from duress. It was made by the defendant after having been fully informed of every constitutional right available to her. We will show that Angel Harwell confessed to killing her father, a murder that resulted from an earlier quarrel. We will show that she planned to kill and that it was done with premeditation and malice. We will show—"

"Hold it," Mulhern said. He looked over at me. "Are you planning to ask for a Walker hearing on this?"

"If it comes to that, yes."

He nodded, then smiled toward the camera. "In this state, a defendant can ask for a hearing before trial to determine if a confession was voluntarily made. It's called a Walker hearing, and it's held for that sole purpose." He sounded like a TV anchorman explaining an item on the evening news.

He again turned his attention to me. "This is not the trial, Mr. Sloan, and this is not even the Walker hearing. So, unless something else presents itself I'm going to allow this statement."

"But—"

"Butts are something to stick in ashtrays, Mr. Sloan. Your objection is a bit premature anyway. I'm overruling it for the present." He nodded to Evola. "Let's cut to the chase. If you have something on videotape, let's have a look at it."

Evola tried to set up the equipment so that the television camera could catch it but the angle wouldn't allow it. Reluctantly, Evola had the screen set so the judge could see it. I walked up to the bench to have a look.

As soon as it started to run, I objected again, asking that the other statements be produced, but I was quickly overruled. I think Mulhern was more curious than anything else. So was I.

The tape had the date and time at the bottom. That would prove useful later. Taped confessions are no novelty anymore, but this one had a strange, almost eerie feeling. The camera was trained on Angel's face, the only thing on the screen. Evola could not be seen, but his voice could be heard.

She looked childlike, those marvelous eyes seldom blinking. If she was tired, she didn't look it, which was unsettling. She spoke evenly, without any emotion, not robotlike, but like she were tell-

100

ing a story she didn't find particularly interesting. A jury would not be very sympathetic to Angel's cold and detached screen image.

I objected again when Evola asked her on the tape about killing her father. The tape was stopped while the judge heard me out. But he ruled against me and the tape continued.

The people in the courtroom couldn't see the screen but they could hear the questions and answers. There was a hushed quiet as everyone strained to listen.

Finally, it was over.

At the risk of making Mulhern angry I again asked that the statement be stricken. I talked of the hours that Angel had been held in custody, the incessant questioning, the horror of her father's death, and the terrible effect that had upon her mental state. I did not mention her emotional illness. That card would be held until later—to be played by whomever ended up trying the case.

Evola summed up, asking that she be bound over on a charge of first-degree murder.

I was given my turn. I did my best. Mulhern, for all his bluster, was an emotional man, and he held the police in no special esteem. That was the man I spoke to.

For me, it was like old times. I was doing what I had done so many times before. It felt comfortable, like taking a nap in an unmade bed. I attacked the confession again, along with every other aspect of Evola's case.

Mulhern looked like a piece of sculpture, sitting motionless through both of our speeches.

When I had returned to my seat I reached back and took Angel's hand. I was surprised at the strength of her grip. It was the desperate grip of someone slipping off a ledge. I tried not to think of how she might feel. To do a good job, a professional must remain objective. A lawyer tries to distance himself emotionally from his clients. Often, that is not an easy thing to do.

Thomas J. Mulhern, like the good showman he was, leaned back in his big leather chair and studied the ceiling for a moment, letting the suspense build. Solomon probably looked like that just before he proposed carving up the kid.

Cameras doth make Barrymores of us all.

Mulhern began with a long-winded explanation of the varying degrees of murder and the elements that must be shown. Without the camera and the attention, his decision would have been one or two sentences long. Now, it was beginning to sound like the Gettysburg Address, only longer.

Mulhern finally moved toward the meat of the matter. "I find that the crime of murder has been shown, and, although I have some questions about the alleged confession, there is sufficient evidence to establish probable cause that the defendant committed it."

I thought Angel might crush my hand.

"However," he continued, "the prosecution has failed to show the element of premeditation required by law. I therefore require the defendant, Angel Harwell, to answer to the lesser charge of second-degree murder."

Evola was on his feet, charging toward the bench. "I must protest this decision."

Mulhern raised an eyebrow. "Not to me you won't. I've decided. You can protest to the court of appeals if you want, although I doubt you'd get anywhere with it." He looked over at me. "Now, the question of bail."

I pried my hand away from the trembling Angel and joined Evola before the bench.

"I would ask that my client be released on her personal recognizance, if the court please."

"I object to bail of any kind," Evola said.

Mulhern smiled icily. "I said this was going to be treated like any other case, and I meant it. Bond will be set at two hundred and fifty thousand." He stood up. "Okay, that's it."

The clerk rapped the gavel and Mulhern left the bench as majestically as a cruise ship sailing toward port.

MY request that Angel not be returned to jail but be kept in the courtroom until bail was arranged was granted. Judge Mulhern permitted me to use his office and telephone. The judge was gone, seeking his usual lunch, one sandwich and enough whiskey to drown a small dog.

It had taken a number of phone calls and almost two hours before it was done. Arrangements were finally completed and the necessary papers signed. The media people had gone off like a cloud of locusts seeking new crops to devour.

Robin, Angel, Nate Golden, and I were alone, seated around the counsel table.

"Everything is all set," I said. "You're free to go, Angel."

She nodded.

No one got up.

"We need to get this business about new counsel straightened out," Golden said, his voice full of smiles and authority. "We've been talking about it."

I didn't say anything. I noticed Robin had looked away.

"I explained to Angel," Golden continued, "that you had done an excellent job so far but that we would bring in a lawyer, more specialized, to try the actual case."

"I want you," Angel said quietly, looking up at me.

"I explained to Angel that it was your idea to bring someone else in," Golden said. "Also, she understands you will be working right along with whomever we select, so it's not as if you are abandoning her." He spoke as if Angel were a young child being persuaded to go to school. Golden's tone was mild, but parental nevertheless.

"I don't want another lawyer," Angel said.

I pulled over a chair so I could face her and sat down. "I appreciate your confidence, Angel," I said, taking her hand. Again, she gripped like a five-fingered vise. "But I think you'd do better with someone else. You asked me once if I was any good. I am, I think, but I've been away from this kind of work for a long time. I'm rusty, and you need someone who isn't. I'll be part of the team, I can assure you of that. It's just that we want you to have the very best."

Her grip just grew tighter. Those hypnotic eyes were fixed on mine. I had let a number of people down in my lifetime. Now, it seemed in my imagination that they were all looking at me through those clear blue eyes.

"The judge reduced the charge," I said, "but second-degree murder can carry a life sentence, Angel. The prosecutor is ambitious and he's going to pull out all the stops to get a conviction. You saw all the press coverage—this is not a case where a reasonable settlement can be made. It is going to be all or nothing, for everybody. Most people can't afford the very best, Angel. You can. It's only smart that you take it."

"It makes sense," Robin said quietly.

Angel never looked away from me. "No," she said, so softly I could barely hear. "I don't want anyone else, I want you, Charley."

I heard Nate Golden clear his throat, the way people do when they want attention and plan to say something unpleasant.

"Angel," he said. His smooth tone had taken on a definite edge. "There is more to this than you know. Mr. Sloan has had some personal problems. I regret to have to bring this up, but Mr. Sloan has had a drinking problem, a problem that has adversely affected his professional life in the past. He hasn't tried a major case in years. So you see, our concern isn't exactly unfounded."

She never changed, her face was as noncommittal as before, her eyes as intense, her grip as strong. It was as if she hadn't heard what he said.

I tried to laugh, but it came out bitter. "Basically, what he said is true, Angel. I don't drink anymore but I haven't done any major trial work in a long time. To be honest, I'm not sure I'm up to something like this."

"Is it a matter of money?" Angel asked. "If it is, I have money. I have a right to have the attorney I want. I can pay whatever it costs."

"Mr. Sloan has been well paid," Golden said. "Robin paid him, probably more than she should have, but money isn't the core of this problem. We have to insure you have the best trial lawyer around. Unfortunately, this is not going to be an easy case."

"I'll plead guilty unless Charley defends me," Angel said.

"Angel, don't be ridiculous," Robin said.

"I'm not being ridiculous. I will not be treated like some brain-damaged child. It's my life that's on the line here. I'll make my own decisions."

"It's been a very difficult day," Golden said, the old silky tone operative again. "Let's drop this for now. We can all go back to the house, have something to eat and drink, relax a bit. Then we'll be in a better frame of mind to discuss all of this."

Robin stood up. "That sounds good to me."

104

Angel shook her head slowly. "This is going to be settled here and now. Charley, I want you to be my lawyer, no one else."

Her grip was strong but her hand was trembling.

"Angel, you heard what he said about me. Under those circumstances, can you give me one good reason why you'd want me?"

There was a pause, but then her answer came quietly, with the force of a blow.

"Because I trust you."

ANGEL drove off with Robin. Nate Golden followed me to my car. He glanced at it with open disdain.

"I realize you were in a bind back there, Sloan. Humor the girl for a day or two. Then we'll arrange for a substitution of trial counsel."

"I'm not very big on lying to clients."

He shrugged. "Look, this is a major case. You are a sole practitioneer. Whoever tries this will need a team, legal support, investigators, the works. You don't have any of that. She's entitled by the Constitution to adequate counsel. I told both of them just that. Under those circumstances, your continuing in her defense just isn't practical, I'm afraid."

Golden sighed. "I represented her father for years. I know Angel's problems, they're of long standing, let me assure you. Today, you may be her knight in shining armor, but tomorrow she may consider you her enemy. She has mood swings, that girl, bad enough to have resulted in several hospitalizations. In other words, Sloan, she isn't competent to make major decisions."

"You're handling the sale of the business for Robin and Angel, right?"

"Now, yes."

"Are you going to have a guardian appointed for Angel?"

"What do you mean?"

"If she isn't competent, then she should have a guardian to look after her interests in the sale."

"She's competent enough for that. And I'll be looking after her interests."

"If she's competent enough for a multimillion-dollar deal she's competent enough to protect herself in a criminal case." It was his manner that infuriated me, not his logic.

"Sloan, let me make this crystal clear. If you should carry this through to trial I shall make it my personal business to see that you are disbarred. The bar is no place for fools." He quickly added. "Or drunks."

"If I'm that bad, shouldn't I be disbarred now? I represent other people besides Angel Harwell. Or doesn't competency count where only poor people are involved?"

The smile was frosty and superior. He spoke firmly. "Withdraw, Sloan, and you'll be unharmed, perhaps even rewarded. We can always throw some work your way. If you don't, the trouble you've seen in the past will be nothing compared to what will come."

"I take it that's a threat?"

"You're goddamned right it is."

8

MY CLIENT WAS ON THE STREET, NOT HOME FREE perhaps, but not looking at life in prison without parole, either. Angel Harwell, even if convicted, would realistically face no more than eight years behind bars because of the reduced charge.

If I didn't do another thing for her, I had earned my money.

In the old days when I'd scored a pretty good courtroom win I'd celebrate, and the boozy celebration might have lasted several days, depending on my trial schedule. Of course, when I lost a big one I didn't call it a celebration, but I did exactly the same thing. Alcoholics have a universal method for marking all occasions, good and bad.

This was a good occasion, although I didn't really feel elated. For some people eight long years in prison could be worse punishment than death.

They expected me at the Harwell place, but that would expose me to more crocodile smiles and whispered harassment from Nate Golden. I needed time to think before facing that, so I drove out to my new office.

It was a pleasant day, the sunny afternoon perfect for sipping Scotch while watching the boats sail up and down the river. I decided I would do exactly that, only I would skip the Scotch.

I climbed the outside staircase and used my key to open the office. I found two cardboard boxes that hadn't been there before. A letter from Mitch was attached. In it he explained that he had

had his girls package up my few belongings. He hoped I didn't mind. He hoped I would do well in court, and he asked that I mail back the key to his office. The letter was cordial, but his anxiety that I might somehow return to the firm's quiet chambers wafted through the written words like urgent background music.

The drapes were already open. I sat in the slightly lopsided desk chair and swiveled around. The clouds over Canada had a wet, pregnant look. Our sunny weather was about to change.

A Japanese freighter glided by, presumably coming from Chicago on the way to Detroit and eventually the Atlantic. Its huge white superstructure looked like a moving skyscraper.

I wished I was on it.

The phone rang. I turned and stared at it as if observing a miracle. Then I realized Mitch had probably had my number transferred to completely sever any lingering connection between me and his dignified place of business.

"Sloan," I said, noticing that the receiver mouthpiece was dusty.

"Where are you?"

"Who is this?"

"Angel. I'm home. You said you were coming here."

"I am, Angel, eventually. I have a few things to do first."

"Can I come there?"

"That's not a good idea. I think you should plan on staying out of sight for a while. Besides, I just rented a new office and it's a mess. This is my first day here."

"Where's here?" she asked.

I told her. She knew the place.

"I'll be right over." She hung up before I could protest.

I debated trying to clean the place up, but it was a job that would need more than a few minutes, probably more than a few days. I sighed aloud. Once Angel saw my decrepit surroundings, she wouldn't need much persuasion to look for a new lawyer. For that reason her visit might be in her best interests.

I turned away from the river and cleaned off the desk, using some scrap paper to dust it off. I got up and cleared some old books off the office sofa. The leather was so old it was brittle.

It was a matter of minutes when down below, I heard a car door slam and quick steps coming up the stairway. She tapped on the door and entered before I could respond.

It was as if I were seeing her for the first time. She was just as beautiful, but this time she looked much more like a woman than a child. She had changed into tailored trousers and a soft silk top that was both demure and revealing. Around her throat, she had casually tied a fire-engine-red scarf.

Angel's expensive perfume filled the old room, driving out the musty odor the way springtime drives out winter. She stood in the doorway for a moment, then walked quickly to me and kissed me softly on the lips.

"Thank you, Charley," she said, still standing close. She said my name in an intimate, provocative way, but as before her perfect face was expressionless.

I stepped back. "You don't need to thank me. It's all part of the job," I said. "Have a seat, Angel. I warned you, this place isn't much to look at." I returned to my lopsided chair.

She turned, surveyed the office, walked around it for a moment, and took a seat across the desk from me.

"Why did you move here?"

"The rent's cheap and I like the view."

"Are you going to stay? It's so small."

"I sort of like that."

"Where's your secretary?" she asked.

"I just left a law firm. I used their people. I haven't hired a secretary for myself yet. I haven't had time."

"I'll be your secretary."

"I appreciate the offer, but that wouldn't be such a good idea."

"Why?"

She stared at me. I wondered if something might be wrong with her facial muscles. It was like talking to a mask.

"You're my client, Angel, at least for the moment. It's not a good idea to mix things in this business." I didn't want to tell her that there wasn't anything for a secretary to do except answer a phone that seldom rang.

"I could fix this place up. I could be a real help to you."

"I'm sure you could, but it's out of the question."

"Don't you like me, Charley?"

"Sure I do. But that has nothing to do with it."

"Are you so sure?" She stood up, looked around, then seated herself again, this time on the old sofa. She crossed her long legs,

109

which, like everything else about her, seemed so perfect they looked sculpted.

"We could have fun, you and I," she said, her eyes as intense as twin laser beams. "Suppose I wasn't your client? Would that change things?"

"We should talk about that, Angel."

"They want me to dump you. That's not news, obviously. But I'm not going to do that." She looked around the office. "Do you have anything to drink here?"

"I'm afraid not."

"Oh, yeah. I forgot. You don't drink."

"That's right."

"Nate Golden said you almost lost your license because of drunkenness. He said you got in a lot of trouble."

I nodded. "He's right about that. Wives, a kid, a fortune, and a reputation. I managed to drink all of that away."

"He thinks you still drink."

"Finally, the great man's wrong about something. Anyway, that's not the reason you should get someone else."

"I don't want someone else."

"Angel, this isn't some little two-bit case where everybody shows up on trial day, tells the jury all about it, and waits for the verdict. A small army of investigators is working away, looking into every aspect of your life from the kind of diapers you used as a child to what type of cake you had for your twenty-first birthday, digging up every unkind word you ever said to your father and anything he might have said to you. The prosecutor will have a team of lawyers sorting out every scrap of information, planning every step of their case, looking up every legal decision that might help them to stick you in prison. Clerks, stenos, messengers, computers, whatever's needed they have and will use. Sort of overwhelming, isn't it?"

She shrugged. "So?"

I gestured at my dusty office. "This is what you've got. A recovering alcoholic, who doesn't even have a secretary, alone in an old office that hasn't been used in years and looks it."

I was almost becoming accustomed to her unreadable face.

"You can hire whoever you need," she said.

"Maybe yes, maybe no. Look, Angel, I got retained in an

emergency. I used to know Robin a long time ago when we were in high school together. You had just been arrested for murder and she was desperate to find an attorney, any attorney, who might be able to help. I was, as they say, in the right place at the right time, that's all. I did what had to be done. Now, you need somebody else."

"Could anyone have done better than you have?"

The question had caught me like an unexpected punch, and I hesitated. Actually, no one could have done any better. I thought of how to avoid saying that.

"Everything so far has just been preliminary. From here on in it gets rough. You're going to need someone who has the expertise, the staff, and the equipment to match what the prosecutor is going to throw against you."

"What's the real reason you don't want to continue?" she asked.

"I just told you."

She shook her head. "No. You told me why I should get someone else. You didn't tell me why you want out."

I nodded. She was right, of course. It was another answer I wanted to avoid. Perhaps I wanted to avoid it because I really did want to continue, to enjoy again the feeling of being on top, of being a player, to answer the challenge like an old athlete returning to the arena. But that wasn't the real reason, the one I didn't want anyone to know.

But she was the client and her future was at stake. She was entitled.

"I don't think I've got the nerve for this sort of thing anymore," I said. My words hung in the air, heavy, as though they had assumed physical dimensions. "I've been away too long and I've been making mistakes that never would have happened years ago."

"What mistakes? You did everything you promised to do."

"You wanted the reason, Angel, and you've got it. Now, let's talk about the lawyer who will try the case."

"His name is still Charley Sloan," she said quietly.

"What's Robin say about that? She's the one who paid the money."

Her eyes narrowed almost imperceptibly, the first sign of animation in that fabulous facade. "It's my decision, not hers."

"She agrees with Nate Golden, I assume."

"We haven't talked. We haven't had time."

"But you do listen to her. She is your stepmother, after all."

For a moment I wondered if she had heard the question; there was a long pause, then she spoke. "I've never considered Robin a mother substitute, if that's what you mean," she said evenly. "She has been, perhaps, more like a friend, a best friend. I do listen to what she says, but I make up my own mind."

"Do you know who Nate Golden is?"

"My father's lawyer, at least in matters of business."

"More than that," I said. "Nate Golden is a former president of the state bar. A legal powerhouse. He's interested in what happens to you, Angel. He wants you to have a different lawyer, the best money can buy."

"So what?"

I laughed. "Kid, this Golden is what you might call connected. If I don't get out of this case he'll have me for breakfast. If I so much as burp, the state bar will use that as an excuse to disbar me. You wouldn't want that to happen, would you?"

Her glance took in the office once again. "It doesn't look as if you'd be losing very much."

"Maybe not, but like they say, it's a living. Not much, maybe, but better than a lot of other things I could end up doing."

"Golden goes with whoever has the money," she said.

I nodded. "I can't argue that."

"My father's dead. I have the money now, or at least half of it. Nate Golden will do what I tell him to do."

"Angel," I said, "there's an old rule of law. A person can't profit from murder. If you end up convicted, you won't get a cent from your father's estate. Those are the rules. So if that misfortune should happen, you'd have no hold over Golden, would you?"

She didn't bat an eyelash. "I think it might be good to have a lawyer who would be ruined if he lost."

I sighed. "That's the old gladiator rule: win or die."

"I have money left by my mother. I'll pay Robin back so you'll have only one loyalty. Hire whoever you need, Charley, to get the job done. I'll pay whatever's needed."

"Angel, think this over for a few days. Talk to Robin."

"Robin expects you for dinner, by the way. I forgot to tell you."

"Will Golden be there?"

"No. He's going back to Detroit. The boat company sale is about to happen and he has to work on that."

"Okay, I'll come for dinner. We can discuss this further then."

"There's nothing to discuss. You're my lawyer, I'm your client."

"We'll see."

She studied me, again with no change of expression. When she spoke the words came out in the same even way, although I hardly expected the question.

"Would you like to fuck me, Charley?"

"Pardon?"

"Would you like to fuck me?"

How do ya answer that? She was young and beautiful and there was a surprising sexuality about her. Still, she was a client, and since she had just experienced things usually confronted only in nightmares, she was more than vulnerable. Besides, sex with clients was far more dangerous professionally than smoking around gasoline, an ethical consideration I had conveniently ignored with Robin.

Old Izzy Goldstein popped into my mind. Izzy, who had been Detroit's leading divorce lawyer before he died. Izzy looked gay, wore a fresh flower in his lapel, and didn't consider a woman to be his client until he had bedded her. Izzy had minced his way through more women than Casanova, had violated every canon in the lawyers' code, but he had gotten away with it.

It must have been the flower.

"Angel, it's common for women clients to see their male lawyers as some kind of savior, a knight come to rescue them. Lawyers know that and are careful not to take advantage. You're a lovely, attractive young woman, but what you're feeling is—"

She stood up, those ice-blue eyes fixed on mine. "Do you want to fuck me, or not?"

"Angel, as I said, I—"

She walked to the door. "Maybe not now," she said, with no change of expression or voice, "but before this is all over, Charley, you'll change your mind."

And then she was gone.

LIKE a mystic studying a rock in the desert, I kept staring at the door long after Angel Harwell had left, as if somehow an explanation for everything might be found in the sooty window glass still bearing the name of Simon Matthews. Perhaps a rock held answers, but the window glass did not. Except it did arouse in me a curiosity about Simon Matthews.

He had sat in the chair I occupied so much that it leaned to one side. He had no family. This office had probably been his life, from what little Mitch had told me.

I had a lot of serious problems to think about. The least perplexing of which was what kind of life a long-dead tax lawyer might have lived. And perhaps that was what made it so appealing, since everything else seemed to arouse my anxiety.

Mitch, a very thorough, probate lawyer, would have made a careful inventory of everything in the office when the old man died. It was unlikely that he'd have missed anything of great value—old stocks, coins, anything like that. If they existed they would have been gathered and sold long ago.

But I wasn't interested in coins or old stocks, just what kind of man had inhabited the place before me.

The old desk was pretty standard, with a middle drawer, three more on one side, two on the other.

The middle drawer held no secrets. It contained a jumble of old pens and paper clips, a few business cards, and the schedule of the 1987 Tigers with the date of each televised game circled in red. Apparently Simon Matthews had at least one other interest in addition to taxation.

I opened and surveyed the other drawers, finding mostly collections of ancient receipts, bills, and the other junk of life, bundled up and bound by rubber bands.

There was only one photograph. It was an old black-and-white, slightly out of focus, showing a young woman leaning against the fender of a big prewar Buick. It wasn't provocative, just a pleasant memory of someone who had once been important. She was blonde, a little flat-chested and a bit big in the hip. Not my type, but obviously his. I wondered if she had been his girlfriend, or just someone he wished had been his girlfriend. The photo was one of those nostalgic little mysteries, the kind where you construct a story to match it. There was nothing on the back to identify the subject or the reason it was taken or the year.

The deep drawer on the left-hand side held some old bank records and letters. I glanced through the accounts. Judging from the amounts, Simon had carefully marshaled his money, and while he wasn't rich, he hadn't been exactly scratching around for his next meal either.

The drawer looked deeper on the outside than it seemed to be inside. I used a ruler to measure the inner space against the outer depth. There was a false bottom.

Like every kid, I used to dream of finding hidden treasure. Suddenly, that old boyish excitement returned. I wondered if Simon had hidden away jewels or gold or something even better under the false bottom of the drawer. I cleared out the bank statements and papers and looked for an easy way to pry up the false bottom.

It was there, a small metal loop near the front of the drawer. I hooked a finger through and gently pried it up.

It was treasure, after a fashion. A pint of very expensive French brandy, nearly full. Next to it was a small .25 caliber chrome automatic, the kind of pistol called a purse gun. And at the back of the drawer were several glossy magazines.

The magazines were foreign and to characterize them as merely dirty would be a gross understatement. Old Simon Matthews, even at eighty, apparently had a taste for the perverse.

I flipped through the pages, which looked well worn. The pictures were not provocative, not to any person with normal appetites. The sex in several of the magazines was between humans and animals. It was like picking up a rock and finding twisting, writhing maggots. I tossed the magazines back where I had found them.

The automatic looked as if it had never been fired. I checked the clip. It was loaded. It was the kind of weapon described as a ladies' gun, with imitation pearl panels inlaid along the small handle. You could hold the thing in the palm of one hand.

If Matthews had been a drunk he had had expensive tastes. The brandy bottle was capped with a little silver cup. I presumed Simon had taken a nip now and then as he flipped through the pages and fantasized about owning his own kennel.

I replaced everything quickly, as if somehow he might come back and catch me looking.

I wondered if burglars ever found such guilty little secrets

115

when searching for loot. I had represented a number of burglars, but it was something that had never come up in conversation.

Old Judge Flynn, the Detroit scourge of criminal court, who had befriended me when I was just starting out, once told me that you could know everything about a person: his family, income, prejudices, medical problems. Everything except his sex life. Flynn said everyone had peculiar little sexual secrets, either in fantasy or in fact. His theory had proved true often enough. And it was certainly true of the late Mr. Matthews, Pickeral Point's leading tax lawyer, baseball fan, and animal fancier.

I wonder how often he had sat where I was now, sipping from that small silver cup and poring over the magazines.

That thought propelled me from the lopsided chair. I would get rid of the brandy—I didn't need the temptation. The little pistol was of no use and I could toss it in the river some night when I had nothing better to do. The magazines couldn't be put out with the trash. I wouldn't want someone thinking they belonged to me. I'd have to find someplace to burn them.

But that could keep. I put everything back the way I had found it.

I had other problems, much more pressing.

The situation with Angel would have to be resolved, if not at dinner, soon.

As I closed the office door to go to the Harwell place, I looked again at the name on the glass.

I wondered if Harrison Harwell had had a secret life. It might have been something as harmless as Matthews's, who was just a toothless old geezer secretly slobbering over bestiality photographs, or possibly something much darker, much more sinister, something to do with why he died.

Monday I would call people to have Simon Matthews's name scraped off the glass. Then I'd get rid of the crap in that old desk, maybe even the desk itself.

I felt like I needed to wash my hands.

FAME, as the poet said, is fleeting. It's especially true in the electronic age. The big story had been the morning's courtroom struggle and the release on bail of Angel Harwell, which had attracted enough newspeople to fill a small stadium. The film clips and interviews would play all weekend on the tube and the region's newspaper pages. But that was the morning, and now, since there was nothing more to photograph, no more participants to shout questions at, the tumultuous parade had moved on.

The street in front of the Harwell place was as empty as an after-hours joint following a police raid. The two bored security men remained at their post at the entrance to the driveway. They waved me in with a show of stony indifference.

Robin met me at the door. She wore a loose, silky smock like an Arab caftan. I vividly pictured the body beneath that flowing cloth and experienced a jolt of sudden desire. She led me into the glass atrium, the place with the Jacuzzi.

"I know you don't drink, Charley. Does that apply to wine, too?"

"Yeah, it does."

"Just one glass?"

"I'll be frank, Robin. I'm not the kind of drunk who goes into a feeding frenzy after one drink. If I had one glass of wine it wouldn't hurt me. But then tonight I would probably have another. Tomorrow, a couple more, plus maybe an after-dinner martini, and then before a week was out, I'd be back in business at the same old stand, slopping that stuff down until my brain was fried."

"You make it sound as if that has happened."

I nodded. "Among us it's called a slip. 'Slip' is a nice little word that can cover anything from one beer on a hot day to a ten-day binge."

"And you've done that? Slip?"

"Once. It started almost the way I described. I had been dry for months, and I convinced myself that meant I could handle the stuff. And I could. Just wine, a glass now and then. Of course, since I could handle that so well I had an occasional real drink, or a beer or two at lunch. And then, boom. Drunk for three days, really ripped. The cops picked me up on a golden-rule arrest, held me until I sobered up, and then let me go. I was on probation in Detroit, so if it had happened there I would have been in real trouble. Luckily for me, my downfall culminated in Cleveland."

"What were you doing in Cleveland?"

117

I smiled. "I haven't the foggiest idea. Does that give you some idea of the problem? Anyway, that's the story of my one little slip."

"How about a lemonade?"

"Sounds good. Where's Angel?"

"She'll be down." There was a small bar set up in the atrium with its own compact refrigerator. Robin poured out my lemonade and a white wine for herself.

We sat facing the river.

"Nate Golden is quite adamant that you not try the case," she said.

"He talked to me."

Robin sipped the wine. "He doesn't believe you really want out. He thinks you're pretending."

"What do you think?"

She smiled. "I don't agree with him, if that's what you mean. You've been up front with me from the start, Charley. Of course, the more I told him that, the more he seemed to believe you were up to something sneaky."

"Has he lined up a lawyer?"

She nodded. "Several. Angel refuses to even see them."

"She will."

"I don't think so. Once Angel's made up her mind, dynamite can't change it."

"Your friend Golden suggested that he bring in someone to try the case and that I stick around just to keep Angel happy. Maybe something like that can be worked out."

Robin shook her head. "Sometimes Angel acts like a child, but she doesn't think like one. Harrison was convinced she's mentally ill, but even if she is, her intelligence is somewhere near genius level. You might be able to fool somebody else with a ruse like that, but not Angel."

The lemonade was tart. "Something has to be settled quickly," I said. "These cases take on a life of their own. Whoever tries this has to start now. There's a tremendous amount of groundwork to be done."

"And if Angel won't accept anyone but you, what then?"

"Lincoln freed the slaves, as you recall. I can't be forced to try the case."

"Can you do that, just step aside?"

"Sometimes it's a violation of ethics, if you've taken a fee to see a case all the way through. But I only agreed to handle things through the preliminary examination, so I can withdraw."

"What about Angel?"

"Golden will get the best there is and that will be that."

Robin sipped again at the wine. "She's says that if you don't try it she'll plead guilty."

"She just wants to get her way. She'd never do that."

"I'm not so sure. She used to frighten me, even when she was growing up. She will do whatever she says she will, even if it's foolish or dangerous. She will never back down. Harrison claimed it's all part of her illness."

I was about to ask about the illness when I noticed Robin's eyes shift to a point behind me.

"Is that how you girls dressed for dinner in jail?" Robin smiled, but there was an cutting edge to her words.

I turned and almost dropped the lemonade.

Angel stood there. She wasn't naked, but she was close. She had a small yellow towel draped over her shoulders. She wore a bathing suit, if it could be called that. If you cut your finger you'd want a bigger bandage than what she was wearing, just three little crimson patches held together with scarlet string.

"I was sunbathing," she said as she walked past us to the bar.

Angel had a truly remarkable figure, the kind New York model agencies would recognize as the source of instant riches. But she was so perfect it was like looking at a statue in a museum, so coldly beautiful and so aesthetically pure that lust was not evoked, only awe.

Robin called to the maid. "Get Angel a robe."

Angel didn't protest. She fixed herself a mixture of vodka and some kind of juice I didn't recognize.

The maid brought a thin silk garment and Angel slipped into it. Sexuality is a mystery to us all. Naked, she wasn't provocative. Now, with the red silk clinging to every concealed curve, I felt an impulse statues wouldn't evoke.

"That's somewhat more civilized, Angel. We want Charley to be able to concentrate on dinner after all."

I had hoped Angel might smile, or frown, or do anything that might give a clue to what she was thinking, but the mask remained in place. She sat down and sipped her drink.

"We were talking about who should try the case," Robin said.

"That's all settled," Angel answered. "Charley will do it."

Robin looked at me.

"In a few days we'll know what judge will be assigned to hear the case," I said. "There are three circuit judges here. One of them will get it. I'm not really popular with any of them. What you need, Angel, is a lawyer who either knows the judge or who has such a heavyweight reputation that the judge will be awestruck. It's no guarantee of victory, but it can help on the close calls."

"I thought this was going to be a jury trial," she said.

I nodded. "Under the circumstances, it has to be. These three judges aren't known to be easy. A jury trial is an absolute necessity."

Angel didn't reply, but she looked at her watch. "I'd like to see the six o'clock news," she said. "I'd like to hear what they're saying about me."

The atrium had a television set. We shifted our chairs around and Robin used a remote to switch it on.

The first segment of the local news was devoted to a Detroit school board incident. A board member had taken a shot at the chairman, but had missed. The drama in the commentator's voice seemed to place it on par with the assassination of Lincoln.

The second segment concerned a highway accident and showed a car mangled by a big truck. They would have shown the bodies but they had been removed before the camera crew had got there.

We were number three.

It was a national story, and the local guy gave it the kind of emphasis an important story demands. He sounded incredulous when he reported that the charge had been reduced. They showed footage of Angel coming into the courtroom. I even got on for a few seconds out in the hall. I said Angel was innocent. Although his bit was edited for brevity, they gave Evola much more air time, piecing together several high points of his statement. They had got to him just after the ruling and he was obviously still upset, his actor's face stern with outrage. He vowed

120

that justice would triumph despite the setback. Then, in response to a question, he said Charles Sloan, the local attorney, would not try the case. Angel was a rich girl, he said, and a really competent attorney would be brought in, but no matter who they imported, he, Evola, guaranteed a conviction.

The anchorman promised the viewers that his station would keep them up to date with every juicy development in the murder trial. Then they went to a commercial.

"That wasn't very nice, was it," Robin said quietly.

"It was edited," I said. "I know Evola. He's not a bad guy. They probably took that business about me out of context. That happens."

"He did everything but call you an incompetent asshole," Angel said.

It was true. Anyone seeing that segment would think I was some kind of boob, possibly brain-damaged, just a local hanger-on who bumbled his way through something he didn't fully comprehend. Evola's segment was edited, but he was probably angry enough to let some of his rage slip my way during the interview. No one likes to lose, especially a competitor like Mark Evola.

I silently downed the lemonade.

Robin switched to another local channel in time to catch the story there. This station didn't give me any air time, but they used the same filmed statement by Evola. This anchorman told his audience that a really big legal gun would be brought in to try the case. He mentioned several names, big names, hinting that he really knew the answer but couldn't go public just yet.

I was steaming.

It was the guy substituting for Dan Rather on CBS who really did it. This was national, but they too used Evola's courthouse-steps speech. Evola was photogenic. The Dan Rather substitute elaborated on the different qualities of representation in American justice, saying that a really good lawyer would be brought in now and things would reflect that change. Money talks, he said.

Robin looked embarrassed. "I'm sorry, Charley," she said. "That was just awful. Especially since you did so well today."

Angel had finished her drink and had made another, standing now by the bar.

"Well, does that change things?" she asked, looking directly at me.

I shook my head. "Not really."

"The world thinks you're some kind of idiot. Do you like that, Charley?"

"I'm not thrilled, but nothing's changed."

Her cold, intense blue eyes never left mine. "If you don't know what will happen," she said, "I'll tell you. If you withdraw, they'll bring in whoever is king of the courtroom nowadays. He'll strut and fuss, use the television like he owned the network, milk the case for a billion dollars' worth of publicity, put on a great act, and then the shitkicker jury up here will still send me to prison. That's what will happen, and you know it."

There was some truth in what she said.

"Angel, Nate Golden and others will see that doesn't happen."

She shook her head. "No. You see, no one really cares whether I go to jail or not. They really don't. They care only about themselves, that's all. I don't trust any of them, not one of them."

She stared at me. "The only one who cares is you, Charley. I sense that. I know it. I trust you."

"Angel, I—"

"If you don't try the case, I'll plead guilty and try to get the best deal I can. Maybe a few years can be shaved off that way. If someone else tries the case, it will become a circus and the judge will be the ringmaster. When it's all done, he'll be able to look wonderful to the public by giving me the toughest sentence he can. He'll love seeing his name in all the editorials saying the little rich girl got what she deserved for killing her father. People do things like that, Charley, they're human."

"Did you kill your father, Angel?" I asked.

"No."

"Then you shouldn't even think about pleading guilty."

For a moment I saw the beginnings of a wry smile, but it faded. "I refuse to become a circus animal. And I'm not going to gamble on someone I don't trust. I'll make the best deal I can."

"Angel, that's—"

"Unless you try the case."

"I told you I can get into a lot of trouble."

This time she did smile. It was like an unexpected sunrise, although there was no real warmth in it.

122

"That's all the better, from my point of view," she said. "That way, we both have a lot to lose."

"Angel—"

"And, maybe, when you show what you can do, they'll stop referring to you as an incompetent asshole. That has to be worth some risk, Charley."

Robin had only listened. I looked over at her, but she looked away.

"Make up your mind now, Charley," Angel said sharply. "Right now."

I believed she meant what she said. It was a little like being caught in a dangerous whirlpool, being swirled around faster and faster, being drawn toward the center and whatever waited there.

"Will you do exactly as I tell you?" I asked.

She nodded, slowly and deliberately.

She was right, I didn't much like anyone thinking of me as an incompetent asshole.

"Okay," I said, feeling like I had just been sucked into the vortex of the whirlpool, "I'll do it."

9

THE SOUND OF RAIN WOKE ME. IT WAS NO LONGER
night. A squint at my cheap but accurate watch informed me it
was just after seven o'clock, and it was Saturday.

Sometimes, in the mornings, just like when I used to drink, I
can't remember what happened the night before. This was one of
those mornings. I had to concentrate hard to kick my memory
into life.

The phenomenon occurred often enough that I had developed
a method for retrieval. I rolled my consciousness back like a film
until I hit something I remembered, then I worked forward.

I remembered the courtroom. And I remembered getting Angel out on bail, and her provocative behavior in my office. And I
recalled going to the Harwell place for dinner.

Then, nothing. For a moment I wondered if I might have been
drinking, but suddenly it all began to come back, as if some inner
lens brought everything into sharp focus.

I wished it hadn't.

I had agreed to try the case, I remembered that clearly
enough. And I remembered that I had lost my appetite for dinner
because of that dangerous decision. I recalled that it had
provoked a feeling like walking into a dark alley in the worst part
of town. There wasn't much hope of anything good happening,
and there was a near-certainty that any number of very bad things
probably would happen.

I realized Angel had maneuvered me into it, but I still wondered at my own motivations.

It was a foolish decision. Even if Angel carried out her threat to plead guilty, what was that to me? I had known her only a few days, and even in that short time I had found her strangely remote, prompting me to suspect that perhaps a psychosis was being artfully concealed beneath that beautiful but emotionless face. So it wasn't as if I was absolutely convinced of her innocence.

And it wasn't as if the prosecutor had a weak case. Defeat was almost assured. And if I lost, even if I was able to keep myself sober and together, I'd be defenseless against Nate Golden and others who would see the courtroom loss as the ultimate proof of my incompetence. I'd be disbarred with the speed of an executioner's axe.

But I had agreed to do it. My reasons for trying the case were many and complex, but pride was woven through all of them. Pride, as Sister Marie Celeste always reminded us in school, was the deadliest of all the deadly sins. Why I had agreed no longer mattered. It was done. Someone had to defend Angel Harwell, and the defense had to begin at once. I was committed.

I sat up and put my feet on the worn carpeting. The rain beat a steady tattoo against the window.

There hadn't been even a hint of an invitation by Robin to stay the night. If anything, I felt like a guest whose departure would be welcome. Following dinner the conversation between the three of us had seemed formal and strained, but despite that, Angel and Robin demonstrated an easy ability to communicate with each other silently. Again, I sensed they were sincerely fond of each other. Given the circumstances, I had found that touching. Both Women had been drinking. Robin knocked back imported vodka with a sure hand. Angel sipped, consuming substantial amounts of brandy. I drank diet soda, but I had watched their glasses going up and down the way a hungry man might watch other people wolf down a steak.

I excused myself early, saying I had a lot to think about. I did, but when I got home I couldn't concentrate on anything for long. I had gone to bed anticipating a wakeful night but sleep had come quickly and unexpectedly.

I got up and padded into my tiny kitchen. The milk in my refrigerator was about to go sour, but it was probably good enough for one more bowl of cereal. I was out of regular coffee, so I heated water for instant.

I flipped on the television as I gulped down the murky-looking coffee. The networks were providing their usual Saturday-morning fare, hours of screaming cartoons with more violence than a major war. I used the remote to click around the stations until I got to a cable news service.

It was just past the half-hour mark and I came in at the middle of the lead news item, showing policemen in some foreign country beating the hell out of fleeing protesters. I wondered sometimes if they used the same footage over and over, since no matter which country the protest occurred in, the nightstick-swingers and their victims always looked the same.

That item was followed by a clip of our president's speech about farms and farm produce. He emphasized the importance of increasing production without the character-sapping help of federal money. From the distressed look of his audience of farmers, it appeared that they might not object to having their character sapped a little.

The third item was the Harwell murder case. I saw myself briefly in some courtroom footage as the commentator rattled on about crime and the rich. Then they replayed the same Evola segment I had seen the night before. I knew it was my imagination, but Mark Evola appeared to get better each time I saw the thing. He reminded me of a young blond Jimmy Stewart, better looking maybe, but just as sincere and intense. If this kind of coverage kept up, Mark Evola would sneer at a mere seat in Congress. He might catch the big wave and end up having a shot on the national ticket.

But the conclusion to be drawn from Evola's speech didn't change. Anyone seeing it would know that the evil Angel Harwell had been defended by a local bumbler who got lucky but who would be quickly replaced by someone competent.

The incompetent local bumbler resented it as much as he had when he had first seen it.

I turned off the television. The rain rattled even louder outside. It was a perfect day to go back to bed. But I couldn't, not now. My decision to try the case, whether foolish or self-destructive, had changed everything.

I was the general in charge, and it was time for me to set about gathering an army.

By the time I had showered and dressed, it wasn't raining so hard. I drove the rain-slick road to my new office. I was surprised to see small boats moving out from the marina across the road, braving the probable thunderstorms and the possibility of being instantly microwaved by a bolt of lightning. It was Saturday, by God, and the boat owners were going to enjoy their investment, even if it killed them. Apparently I wasn't the only one who made potentially dangerous decisions.

I opened the office door and discovered why the place had such a constantly musty odor. The roof leaked in one corner, and water dripped slowly down on an out-of-date set of tax manuals whose pages must have contained more mold than a penicillin factory. I'd have to call Mitch and ask that the leak be fixed.

In another age a person's history and life could be traced from entries recorded in family Bibles or in diaries. But Bibles and diaries had gone out of style. Now the history of a person's life can be reconstructed by looking through his Rolodex. I retrieved mine from the boxes Mitch's girls had packed. A thousand years from now maybe some archaeologist will dig up my Rolodex and study it, flipping it around and around, wondering at the possible significance of all those little cards attached to the center wheel. He might think it is some kind of primitive religious artifact. Mine damn near is.

My cards contained the phone numbers and addresses of hundreds of cops, lawyers, judges, medical doctors, investigators, experts of all kinds, and clients, including thieves, killers, con men, and call girls. Then there are my friends, many of whom are cross-referenced since they qualify for a number of those same categories.

I flipped to the S section of cards.

He was there. Sidney Sherman, complete with his Penobscot Building phone number in downtown Detroit, and his unlisted residence phone.

It was Saturday, so I called his home.

A boy answered the phone with that peculiar voice that male children develop as their hormones propel them through puberty, alternating between a squeaking soprano and baritone.

"This is Charley Sloan," I said. "Is Sidney Sherman there?"

"Who is this again?"

"Charley Sloan."

"Hang on," he said to me, then I heard him yell, "Pa!"

Pa was Sidney Sherman, one of the more interesting creatures to inhabit the planet. He was my age, midforties, a slim man with protruding watery eyes set above sallow sunken cheeks. He wore a perpetual smile on his skinny face, an apologetic smile, as if he had done something stupid and was sheepishly sorry about it. His mop of washed-out brown hair looked like a bad wig, but it was all his.

Frederico Fellini would have loved Sidney Sherman's face.

He had once been a Detroit cop, a detective who had specialized in undercover work since he looked like anything but a cop. And he was good at it. Sidney had been approaching legend status when a suspect with a shotgun blew away half of his intestines, an injury so extensive Sidney said it left him able to eat nothing spicier than boiled carrots, while crapping only rabbit pellets.

The rabbit analogy was enhanced by the fact that Sidney was married and had fathered seven children by last count. The gunshot blast hadn't affected that function.

After taking a disability pension Sidney became a private investigator, specializing in workmen's compensation and other business cases. He had done very well; he lived in an expensive Grosse Pointe home, drove a Cadillac, and sent his children to the best Eastern universities.

But Sidney never did criminal work. Except for me, in the old days.

"Yeah," he said, his tone friendly. I could almost see that well-remembered smile.

"Hey, Sidney, it's Charley Sloan."

"Not *the* Charley Sloan, the defender of little rich girls who pop their fathers?"

"The very same."

"Hey, Charley! I saw you on the tube." He paused. "You looked like shit." Then he laughed.

"That's my usual way of looking, pal. How have you been?"

"You mean in addition to the excruciating pain and the lingering sense of dread due to my trauma-induced depression?"

I had represented Sidney before the pension board and I had used those words, among others, to get him benefits.

"Yeah, besides that."

"Couldn't be better. Ford Motor is outraged over the amount they pay out in workmen's comp, so they are investigating everybody on their rolls to see if anyone is working someplace else. Lots of people, lots of investigation. Bad for them, good for me. My work has tripled and the checks are coming in like snow in a blizzard. On the downside, my wife is a nympho who wants it at least once or twice a year, and my kids are ungrateful little farts who think I'm made out of money. Other than that, life is just great."

"Sidney, I want you to do some work for me."

"Whoa, didn't you just hear me? I got more on my plate than I can handle. I appreciate you thinking of me, but I got too much to do now."

I paused for effect. It seemed to work.

"Wait a minute, Charley," he said, "if you're thinking of bringing up that business with the pension board or my kid, forget it."

I didn't reply.

"Not that I'm not ungrateful. I know you didn't charge me for getting me the pension. And, hey, that business with the kid was a big deal, I know that. You got the little shit off clean. Maybe smoking a little dope is no big thing, eh? Of course, a conviction would have kept him out of Yale. He's doing good there, by the way."

It was his turn to pause.

It was a long pause. He sighed, then spoke again. "Okay, Charley, what the fuck is it you want me to do?"

"It's this Harwell case, Sid. I'm going to need a major effort. I'll need a background check of all the leading players, plus hospital records, financial stuff, not only here but probably in several other states. In other words, I'm going to need the works."

"I'll have to hire people, Charley."

"Okay. There's an open checkbook on this one. These people have money and are willing to spend it."

There was another pause before he spoke. "No offense,

129

Charley, but I'll need something up front if I have to bring in other people."

He knew I didn't have money; if something went awry, he wasn't about to risk his own cash.

"What are we talking about here, Sid?"

"For what I think you want, very heavy money."

"Like what?"

"Ten thousand retainer. After that's used up, payment on presentment of bills. I'm honest, Charley, you know that. I'm not going to clip your client, but I don't want to run up big fees and find the bag has suddenly gone empty."

"Sounds reasonable. You've got a deal."

"You going to handle this yourself, Charley, or what?"

"Angel Harwell wants me to try it. She insists on it."

Again, the pause.

"You don't sound like you share her enthusiasm," he said.

"I haven't tried a major jury case in a long time, Sid."

"You still off the stuff?"

"Yeah."

"A lot of us used to think you were the best around, Charley. That kind of talent just doesn't go away. You got nothing to worry about. You'll do fine."

He chuckled. "Of course, a lot of your brethren at the bar will smell that Harwell money and try to grab the case away from you."

"That's been tried already. I anticipate a whole lot more of the same."

"Fuck 'em. Don't let them screw you out of it, Charley. How do you want to handle this?"

"Can you come up here, say, Monday?"

"Jesus. I've got—"

"It's important we get started quickly, Sid. I'll need to go over a lot of things with you."

"Up there?"

"Pickeral Point isn't all that far."

Sid Sherman chuckled. "No, it isn't. What is it, an hour's drive, maybe less? We used to drive the kids up years ago. It's swell up there. You can get an ice cream, stroll the boardwalk, and watch the big boats go by."

130

"I'll buy the ice cream."

He sighed. "I don't think this is one of the smartest things I ever did, but I'll be there."

I CONTINUED to skip through the Rolodex. It was a few years out of date. Some of the people were dead. I'd have to toss those cards. Some were in prison, or on the run for various reasons. Some addresses had changed. Those with good luck went upscale economically. Those with bad luck drifted out of sight.

Robin and Angel had agreed to my proposal to hire a public relations expert. A celebrated case is often decided before it ever gets to the courtroom. Jurors may say they aren't influenced by pretrial publicity, but a phrase, a word, can set an impression in their minds as permanently as a footstep in cement. We needed an expert to make sure there were no such damaging footsteps.

I looked for the home phone of the Owl. No one ever called him Owl anymore. Millionaires usually inspire awe and not nicknames. He was no exception. Harry Richmond had been a reporter for the *Free Press*. He had been known there as the Owl for two reasons. One, he possessed an uncanny wisdom about what was news and what wasn't. Two, he looked like one.

Harry had left the *Free Press*, started his own public relations firm, and magically attracted big-time clients the way the Pied Piper gathered rats. In only a few years his billings looked like the national debt and a German firm had bought him out for millions, allowing him to continue as the head man. Then, after a bitter disagreement, they fired him.

I hoped for Angel's sake that he was available.

Harry was at home and for a while we did the usual routine that people do when they haven't talked for years. Half gossip, half history. Then we got down to business.

"I'm sorry to hear about the thing with the Germans," I said.

"Screw them. They'll run the agency into the ground and in five years I'll buy it back for peanuts." There was a momentary pause. "I saw your client on television. I presume that's why you're calling. I don't know what you can do for her legally, but she's going to be convicted in the great court of public opinion unless things change drastically."

"Will you help?"

"Does this vile murderess really have money, or is that just an illusion?"

"She has money. Lots of it."

"Under those circumstances, and at my usual rates, I shall be glad to help." His chuckle was dry, mirthless. "When can I talk with this poor innocent child?"

"Is Monday all right?"

"As the actors say, I am at liberty. Monday will be fine."

I HAD heard the tapping while I was on the phone with Harry but I thought it was just another effect of rain and wind.

As I hung up, the door opened and a tiny person concealed in a huge raincoat stepped in.

"Christ, didn't you hear me?" a voice demanded from somewhere within the wet folds of plastic. The figure reached up and pulled off the large rain hat, exposing a mop of clipped blonde hair and two very large and indignant blue eyes set in a pleasant, round little face. For a moment I thought she was a young schoolgirl but on closer examination, I saw she was a mature woman. Maybe forty, maybe fifty, it was hard to tell.

The wet raincoat was whipped off. She was a cute little thing, a well-formed miniature woman, dressed in a sensible sports dress but adorned with a spectacular display of bangles, belts, and bracelets.

"Where can I hang these?"

"Just drop them right there. Whatever could happen to this carpet has."

She cocked her head toward the door. "Who is Simon Matthews?"

"The former tenant. What can I do for you?"

She walked over, pulled a chair up close to my desk, and sat down. Those big eyes remained fixed on me.

She produced a cigarette from her purse and lit it with a small lighter, all in one swift and graceful motion. "Do you mind?" she asked, blowing smoke at the same time.

"No."

"Some people equate smoking with pederasty. I'm glad you don't." She again inhaled deeply, paused for a moment, and blew out a stream of smoke from her pursed lips, which showed age in the adjacent crinkling skin.

132

"The question," she said, "to paraphrase the late president, isn't what you can do for me, but what I can do for you."

"If you're selling something—"

She shook her head as if trying to dry her hair. "I'm not." She shrugged. "Well, perhaps in a way I am. Do you know me?"

"Should I?"

She nodded. "Do you read?"

"If the words aren't too big."

She smiled wryly. "Books, magazines?" She gestured at the shelves of law books. "I'll bet you don't read that junk for relaxation." She took another quick pull from the cigarette. "How about last week's *People*? Did you read that?"

"Look, if you're selling magazines, I'm—"

"I'm featured in that issue," she snapped. "I'm Mary Beth Needham."

When it became obvious that I didn't know the name, her eyes narrowed.

"*People* calls me the blonde pit bull," she said.

"Do you consider that a compliment?"

"In my line of work, yes."

"What's your line of work?"

"I write books. My last one, *The Queen from Colorado*, was on the *Times* best-seller list for almost four months."

"I'm not much on women's fiction, to tell you the truth. I like mysteries, that sort of thing."

She sighed and shook her head in disgust. "I do nonfiction books," she said crisply. "The queen in that title is Hector Farber, the actor, the guy some people think is the new John Wayne. My book straightened out a few things about Hector, so to speak. If you hadn't just dropped in off the moon, you'd know that. I'm here to do a book on the Harwell murder."

Now her name and that of the actor evoked a foggy memory of headlines and accusations.

"I'm afraid I can't help you, Miss Needham. Lawyers can't talk about their clients, as you may know. It's a confidential relationship."

"Unless the client agrees, right?"

"Well, sometimes even—"

"Angel sent me over here," she said. "Does that tell you anything? You can call her if you like."

"I just arranged for someone to handle press relations. As soon as he's set up, I'll have him contact—"

She interrupted again, with easy arrogance. "I'm not interested in talking to some spin-control expert. I need access to the players themselves." One eyebrow rose slowly like a bridge going up. "Sloan, you got two ways to go here. You can cooperate with me and everyone in America will read about what a smart, clever, and honest lawyer you are. Or, if you go the other way, you'll come across as the country's greatest asshole. People believe what they read. The choice, pal, is entirely up to you." She looked around the office. "I know you're an ex-drunk, but do you have anything to drink around here?"

"Have you ever thought about a career as a diplomat? I really think you have the touch."

The smile was completely unexpected. She laughed. "I have a fearsome reputation. Sometimes it helps if I live up to it." Then she shrugged. "But, sometimes, it doesn't. Are you sure you have nothing to drink around here?"

I thought about the French brandy concealed in the old desk but I said nothing, since producing it would have sent the wrong signal.

"Here's the way this goes," she said. "This trial, like any other big newsy courtroom circus, is money in the bank for people like me. I'm small. You probably didn't see me in the courtroom yesterday, but I was there. Not only me, but Jacky Cannon and J. Booth Smith. Do those names ring a bell?"

They did sound vaguely familiar.

She grimaced. "They write the same kind of thing I do. Not as successfully, but they do all right. Sloan, this is going to be a horse race. Cannon, Smith, and me are here to gather material for books about the murder. Whoever gets to the printer and out to the stores first will win the race. It's not a small-stakes race either, pal, we're talking at least half a million here. It's a race I plan to win."

"Good luck."

She snorted. "Jesus, Sloan, I want more from you than best wishes. I want cooperation. And it's not a one-way street, either."

"Miss—"

She waved a miniature hand. "Call me Mary Beth."

134

"Mary Beth, I can't cooperate, not without risking my license."

She shrugged. "How about a teaser?"

"What do you mean?"

"You help me, I help you. I'll give you a small taste. What do you know about the happy Harwell family?"

"A little."

"I just came from their home base in Florida. Pal, I dig up gossip the way dogs dig up bones. I know where to sniff and where to dig. As soon as I heard about the killing I hopped on the first plane to Sarasota. The Harwell's have more palaces than the Queen of England, but the main one is on Sheridan Key. Ever been there?"

"No."

"It's a spit of very expensive land set out in the Gulf of Mexico. Pretty, a palm-tree paradise for millionaires, but it looks as if a good storm could wash the place away. Anyway, the Harwells have a boat factory in Sarasota and a house on this little tropic isle a couple of miles away. I went there and dished with the neighbors. Lots of wonderfully sordid things go on out there on balmy Sheridan Key. Kinky stuff. The kind of things that sells books. It's where you go if you're rich and so twisted that you've been thrown out of Palm Beach. You end up on Sheridan Key. They have a regular cozy colony out there, a bunch of wealthy outcasts. I heard some really hot stories."

"Like what?"

"Do we have a deal?"

"Not yet. I thought you were going to treat me to a teaser?"

She nodded. "I did say that, didn't I?"

"Yes."

"Okay. Here's a sample. It seems that Harrison Harwell had been getting somewhat physical. Hey, violence begets violence, right? Even murder sometimes. They say he was knocking mama and the kid around pretty good. And it wasn't all one-sided."

"There's always that kind of talk in a case like this. You should know that, in your business."

"Hey, I have to sift through tons of crap to get one nugget of gold. I know crap. This isn't crap."

"Oh?"

She grinned like a tennis player about to smash an easy lob.

"This is more than idle chitchat, Sloan. I checked it out. The cops were called twice last month because Harrison was raising hell."

"That happens. People drink."

"You'd know about that, wouldn't you?"

I shrugged. "As a matter of fact, yeah."

"Well, I vamped a couple of the local cops into telling me a few details. Cops treat rich people differently, especially the ones who pay the taxes that pay their salaries. Poor people would end up in jail. Not so in Sheridan Key. The cops give warnings and let it go at that. Of course, they said they basically considered the Harwell problems a civil matter."

"Civil matter?"

"Whoa," she said, smiling. "Do we have a deal yet?"

"Not yet."

"I don't know if I should give you anymore free samples, Sloan. A lot of people don't trust lawyers."

"I'm different. What civil matter?"

She hesitated, then spoke. "Divorce. The cops were told there was a divorce in the works. I suppose that gave the police the excuse to back off. On the books it would be treated as just another family dispute."

"This divorce, has it been filed? Do you know?"

"The papers were being prepared, that's what the cops were told."

"But they weren't filed?"

"I checked the local court. No case. I talked to the lawyer who the cops were told to contact. Like you, he turned wimpy and wouldn't tell me a thing."

"He'd have to clear it with Robin Harwell."

Her smile was triumphant. "Why? The guy was Harrison's lawyer. From what I could get, Harrison was about to tie the can to his little wifey, not the other way around. Surprised?"

"Where did you get that?"

"Do we have a deal?"

"Not yet. Com'on, what's your source?"

"I showed you a little leg, pal, but that's as far as it goes until you cooperate." She crushed out the cigarette in an empty paperclip glass. "I'll be around, Sloan."

She stood up and retrieved her rain gear. "Talk to Angel. She's not dumb. She'll tell you to help me. I can be a good person to have in your corner. We can help each other, a lot more than you even realize."

She slipped into the rain hat and coat. "Think about it," she said as she let herself out the door.

10

THE DIVORCE RUMOR HAD TO BE CHECKED OUT. I called the Harwell place and I recognized the smooth voice of Dennis Bernard, the houseman.

"This is Charley Sloan. I'd like to speak to Mrs. Harwell."

"Oh, Mr. Sloan. This is Bernard. I'm afraid Mrs. Harwell isn't here."

"When will she be back?"

"Monday evening, I believe."

"Is Angel there?"

"She went with Mrs. Harwell," he said.

"Where?"

"New York. To do a little shopping, to sort of get away from things for awhile, I think."

"Jesus! Angel's out on bail. She isn't supposed to leave the state without permission."

"Was she aware of that?" His tone implied that I hadn't done my job.

"She certainly was. I told Angel and Mrs. Harwell."

He sighed. "Well, perhaps they misunderstood. In any event, they'll both be back Monday. I hope this isn't going to cause any trouble?"

"It won't if she gets back and there aren't any incidents. You'd think Mrs. Harwell would know better."

"This has been quite a strain on all of us, Mr. Sloan. She probably just forgot about the bail-bond restrictions."

"Maybe."

So that the phone call wouldn't be a total waste I thought I'd try again to pry some inside information out of good old Bernard. He had been cleverly tightlipped so far, but it wouldn't hurt to try again.

"Mr. Bernard, I—"

"Please. Call me Bernard. It's customary to use a butler's last name. I'm more comfortable with that."

"Okay, Bernard. Did you know that Mr. Harwell was planning to divorce Mrs. Harwell?"

"No. I'm wasn't aware of anything like that," he replied evenly. "And I'd know if such a thing were true."

The lie detector needle would have jerked wildly on that answer. His manner was so positive it was phony.

Theresa Hernandez, the maid who claimed Harwell was boffing her, had told me he talked of getting a divorce. I had doubted her story then. Now I wondered.

"Is that young maid, Theresa Hernandez, working today?"

"She's no longer here," he said.

"She's been fired?"

"No." He dragged the word out slowly to give it emphasis, as if he thought she should have been fired. "She's been assigned back to the main house staff in Florida," he said.

"Sheridan Key?"

"Yes. However, Theresa isn't there now. I understand there's a serious illness in her family. Mrs. Harwell was kind enough to give her several weeks off."

"Do you have an address or phone number where I could reach her?"

"She's in Puerto Rico. I don't have the address. Perhaps Mrs. Harwell does. You can ask her when she gets back." He sounded sure that I would believe him. I didn't. A butler would know details like that since it was his job to run the staff.

"Bernard, there's talk that Mr. Harwell occasionally knocked Mrs. Harwell and Angel around. Is that true?"

"Certainly not."

"There are official Florida police reports to that effect."

"Well, if something like that happened, I didn't know about it." He paused, then spoke again. "Married people do get into shouting matches, Mr. Sloan. It happens in many families. Perhaps

139

someone misunderstood something like that and called the police."

If nothing else, Bernard was a consistent liar.

"What time do you expect Mrs. Harwell and Angel back on Monday?"

"I'm not really sure. Early evening, I believe."

"Isn't anyone picking them up at the airport?"

"No. Mrs. Harwell drove to the airport. She said it was less complicated that way."

"Where are they staying in New York?" I asked.

"Usually, Mrs. Harwell stays at the Plaza, but I understand this time they're staying with friends."

"Which friends?"

"I don't believe she said."

"Did she leave a number where you could reach her?"

"I'm afraid not."

"Don't you think that's strange, Bernard?"

"No," he replied easily. "The trip was a spur-of-the-moment thing. She really didn't have time for any kind of planning. If I knew where she was, sir, I would tell you."

I had a mental image of Bernard's nose growing inches longer with every easy answer.

"Have her call me when she gets in."

"Certainly, Mr. Sloan."

"You've been a great help, Bernard."

"I try to be."

THE rain had become one of those steady all-day downpours. My view of the river was distorted by rivulets of water trickling down the office window glass.

Nothing moved out on the water now. A sense of loneliness settled on me, so strong it was almost physical. It was Saturday. I had nowhere to go and no one to see. Loneliness is a common condition among alcoholics, recovering or not. Go into any bar on any afternoon. There's always a couple of people sitting by themselves, staring straight ahead as if they expect the answer to life's puzzle to appear from behind the bottles in front of the mirror.

Those of us who no longer sit at bars all too often feel that same gnawing emptiness.

140

The telephone rang and I was grateful.

"Sloan," I said.

"It's Bob Williams, Charley. I just got through seeing my last patient for the day. How about lunch?"

"Fine. Where?"

"Let's go upscale. I'll meet you at the Inn. This rain will keep the tourists away so we can get a table."

"Ten minutes?"

"Good. I'll see you there."

THE Inn at Pickeral Point isn't as posh or as famous as the St. Clair Inn a few miles up the river, but it's more casual and comfortable, although the prices are about the same.

The rain was keeping people away, leaving the Inn's restaurant only half full. In good weather the place is usually packed on weekends.

Bob Williams sat at a table near the windows, looking like he'd been there forever. A massive man, he was framed in the dull light from the river, his high cheekbones making his impassive features look more like metal than flesh. He could have been a model for Sitting Bull or Crazy Horse, a chief staring out at the future, or perhaps the past.

Those slate-gray eyes turned my way as I came up to the table. "We missed you Thursday night," he said, referring to the regular meeting of our Club.

"I couldn't make it. You know what I had waiting for me in court Friday morning."

"I saw you on television. How's it going?"

"So far, so good. I'm going to try the case."

He studied me for a moment. "Are you sure that's wise?"

"Are you asking as a psychiatrist, a friend, or a fellow drunk?"

"All three."

"To be frank, I'm not sure. I guess there's only one way to find out, isn't there?"

He nodded. "So long as you remember what's really important. Don't get so busy you can't make the meetings."

"Is this a lecture, Doctor?"

A small smile flickered tentatively across his lips. "In my profession, we don't lecture. We just sit there and let people lecture themselves."

"At a price."

"Everything has a price tag on it, one way or another, Counselor."

"Speaking of professions, I'm going to have to hire some of your colleagues, even you, if you're interested."

"To what purpose?"

"My cute little client gave a statement to the police in which she says she may have been responsible for her father's death. They say it's a confession, and a jury might agree. She said this after many hours of interrogation. Angel Harwell in the past has been hospitalized for emotional problems. I want to keep that alleged confession out of the trial, obviously. One way is to show that she wasn't competent when she made it."

"Are you planning an insanity defense?"

"That's a sure ticket to a conviction, given the new verdict of guilty but mentally ill. No, we're defending on the basis that she didn't do it. But there'll be a separate hearing on the confession. It's nonjury. It's called a Walker hearing. If Angel is fragile emotionally, it's only logical that the long, incessant interrogation by the police would cause her to finally break and say something they wanted to hear just to get them to stop."

"Stretching things, aren't we?"

"Not really. That argument's worked in other cases. Anyway, I'll need someone to test her and to testify."

He nodded slowly. "What do you think about her?"

"She's bright, as far as I can tell. But vulnerable, I think. Besides, there's something about her that strikes me as odd."

"Like what?"

"I really can't put my finger on it. She doesn't seem to show any emotional response. Fear, anger, frustration, whatever, if she does feel them it's not obvious. Not to me, anyway."

I could see he was becoming interested.

"Do you know why she was hospitalized, specifically?"

"No, but I plan to find out."

We both ordered. The place was famous for its fish. Then he spoke as he looked out at the river. "I could evaluate her, if you like, but I've never been especially good on the stand. There are psychiatrists who specialize in testifying in these cases, as you know."

"Forensic psychiatrists," I said. "The woods are full of those guys. I can always find one who will take my point of view and run with it."

"So why would you need me?" he asked.

"I need to get an honest reading on her, if that's possible, so I can know exactly what I'm dealing with."

"Curiosity?"

"More than that. If she's really nuts, my whole strategy changes. Eventually I'll have to decide if she can be risked on the stand without sinking the case. I have to know what's she's like to make that kind of decision."

He sat back and thought for a moment. "I can have all the psychological tests administered. Some are pretty good, some not so good. None of them is infallible. We try to get a cross-sampling to develop some kind of reasonably accurate emotional or mental profile. After that, I can examine her in light of those tests. The garden variety stuff, schizophrenia, dementia, is evident right off the bat. But usually it's not that easy. Nothing on earth is as complex as the human mind. I can probably get a handle on what kind of personality you're dealing with. But you'd have to call in one of the hired guns to do the court work."

"Timewise, what are we talking about?"

"A day, maybe two. Usually, if we give the standard tests, the old ink blot and draw-a-stick-figure-of-your-mother stuff, plus the multiple-choice exams and others, it takes up the better part of a day."

"How long would your examination take?"

He shrugged. "Depends. If she tells me she's hearing voices or seeing things, it won't take long at all. The condition of people who are desperately sick is usually quite apparent. However, those who are just as ill but look and talk normally can take much longer. Especially if they're clever. I'd like an hour, maybe two. I should be able to come up with a reasonably accurate appraisal."

"How accurate?"

He smiled. "As close as I can make it. But if you're looking for a wizard you should seek someone with a funny hat and a stick with a star at the end. I'm generally pretty much on the mark in diagnosing what's wrong with patients. That's not the big problem."

"What is?"

"Curing them. But since I won't have to worry about that with your young lady, I should do all right."

He looked out at the river. "Did she do it?"

"I thought she did, but now I'm not so certain."

The waitress brought our food and served it.

She smiled in a friendly way. "Are you sure I can't get you gentlemen something from the bar?"

I noticed that we both paused for a telltale instant before saying no.

WHEN I left the Inn, it was still raining, but not as hard. I had a choice of activities. I could go back to my little apartment, sit around, and look out the window. Or I could go back to my office, sit around, and look out the window. My office had a better view, so that's where I went.

I pulled into the lot next to the building. A battered pickup was the only other vehicle. It was parked near my stairway.

As I hurried past the truck, a man got out and followed me up the stairs.

"Mr. Sloan, can I talk to you?" he asked.

"Let's get out of this rain." I opened the door and let him in.

He wore faded work clothes, laundered so many times it was impossible to tell their original colors. His skin had the leathered look of a farmer. There were still a few farmers in Kerry County.

"I saw you on television," he said.

I nodded.

"I don't know many lawyers."

"Some people might envy you."

"My name's Wagner," he said, extending a hand that was as hard as concrete and just as rough. "David Wagner."

He sat in the chair I indicated as I took my place behind the desk. "What can I do for you, Mr. Wagner?"

"You do criminal law, right? I mean, I saw you on the television."

"That's right. What's the problem?"

"It's not me," he said, smiling nervously, showing a gap where a bottom tooth used to be. "It's my son."

144

"Tell me about it."

He shifted as if he was not used to sitting very much. Then he spoke. "Christopher is nineteen," he said. "I have six children, three girls, three boys."

"Big family," I said. "You're blessed."

He sighed. "I've never looked at it quite that way. Anyway, Chris is my youngest. They're all problems, one way or the other, but Chris holds the family championship."

"It happens sometimes with the youngest in a big family."

"Perhaps. Chris is being held over at the jail."

"What's the charge?"

"Breaking and entering, they told me. A felony."

"Do you know what he's accused of?"

His smile was sad. "They caught him inside the Pointeside Gallery about four this morning."

"The place with all the paintings of ships?"

He nodded. "Some of those paintings are quite valuable, as you probably know. Chris was after the paintings and any cash he could find."

"Who said?"

He shrugged. "Chris. I talked to him at the jail."

"Has he ever been in trouble before?"

"He got caught a couple times as a juvenile. Once as an adult, but they dropped the charge for lack of evidence."

"What was that charge?"

"The same as this, breaking and entering." He shook his head slowly. "The police seem to think Chris is a burglar, not without cause. I'd like you to defend him."

"It sounds as if they have a very good case."

"They do. I'm hoping you can work something out, probation or something like that. Chris is small and scrawny. I'd hate to think of what might happen to him in prison."

"Mr. Wagner, the fees in this sort of thing can run into some pretty serious money. The county has a public defender. They work free of charge in cases like this."

"You have to be poor, right?"

I shook my head. "Not poor, exactly. A working man with a big family, they'd take that into consideration."

"I have money," he said quietly.

He was a proud man, obviously. "Mr. Wagner, even if this

145

doesn't go to trial, a lawyer has to spend a great deal of time talking with police, witnesses, working out a deal, if that's possible. The fee can add up, maybe a thousand or two, maybe more."

"Will you take the case?"

"This Harwell case is keeping me pretty busy. Why don't you try the public defender?"

He looked even sadder. "I have three hundred and sixty acres in Orion township. I had more land but I sold it. They're starting to develop there because it's so close to the freeway."

"I wouldn't want you to put up your farm."

"I wouldn't. The land there is going for ten thousand an acre. How's your arithmetic?"

"You're a millionaire. A couple or three times over."

He nodded. "Even the public defender can figure that out.' He pulled a checkbook from his shirt pocket and quickly scribbled out a check. "How about a thousand as a retainer?"

"How about two thousand?"

He looked up at me for a moment, then wrote out the figure. He handed me the check.

"I don't care what you do, Mr. Sloan. I don't care what kind of deal you have to make, just so long as you keep Chris out of jail."

"I can't guarantee anything."

"I know."

"How come Chris is into stealing?"

"You mean, because I've got so much?"

"Something like that."

He stood up. "I'm not a hard man. But I'm careful with my money. Chris never lacks for essentials. He has two flaws, and the way I see it, that's the cause of his problem."

"And those are?"

"He likes excitement. I think he likes the thrill of being a burglar, that's one flaw. The second flaw is he's stupid."

"I'll go over to the jail and talk to him. He'll be arraigned Monday morning at the courthouse. It isn't necessary that you be there."

"Maybe not. But I'd feel better if I was. I'll meet you there." He got up and left the office without another word.

I looked at the check. Fame, however fleeting, has a dynamic all its own. The only reason Wagner sought me out was because he saw me on television. The Harwell case was changing my life.

146

Last week I would have been excited to get a nice easy burglary case. Last week I would have charged only two hundred dollars and I would have been damned grateful for that.

Fame. It tends to make the price of everything go up.

I tucked the check into my wallet and went over to the jail to see my newest client.

THE Wagner kid knew as much about the practical aspects of criminal law as I did. Maybe more.

He had an ideal build for a burglar. He was about as thick as a snake, with the kind of rail-thin body that could wiggle through even the smallest opening. He had long hair and a terminal case of pimples.

The true mark of any real professional is a comprehensive knowledge in his chosen field of endeavor. He had that. Chris Wagner told me which assistant prosecutors were tough on B-and-E artists like himself, and which were easy. He told me what the going sentences were from each of the three circuit judges. He knew his one arrest would work against him at sentencing, but he thought I should be able to work around that if we got the right judge. He was a treasure-trove of practical information.

He did most of the talking at the jail. It was almost as if our roles had been reversed.

Chris Wagner, only nineteen, understood the criminal justice system a lot better than most Supreme Court justices. He knew my function in these circumstances was more that of an agent than an advocate. If he had been a rock star I'd be bargaining for a percentage of the gate and playdates. But he was a burglar, so I'd bargain to see he didn't play state prison, and to get the shortest probation and the lowest fine.

Chris Wagner knew a lot about the law but not enough about alarm systems. He had efficiently shut off one without knowing the gallery had a backup, a silent alarm, the one the police had answered.

He was guilty as hell and admitted it. The threat of going to trial could be used only as a nuisance tactic with the prosecutor, something to negotiate with, the prospect of tying up a courtroom, jury, judge, and officers for maybe a day. It wasn't much of a bargaining chip, but the courts were busy, and it was the only one I had.

I told Chris I would appear with him at court on Monday morning. I'd know then who Evola would have handling the case. If we couldn't make a deal, bail would be set. It would be up to his father to decide whether to post it.

I left the jail in a much better mood than the day I had first seen Angel Harwell there.

Chris Wagner was different from Angel. He was a businessman. True, his business was burglary, but there was meaning and purpose in it. He understood the risks, the rewards, the dangers. He understood the legal system. It was almost refreshing.

It was good being busy again. In the old days I had handled a steady parade of criminal and civil cases, juggling court dates, keeping occupied, making money. It had been hectic and stressful but I had managed it all by drinking my way through.

It wouldn't be half bad if clients came streaming in again. I wondered if I could really handle that kind of life sober. If I could, it would be very much like a dream come true.

TO ANYONE BUT A LAWYER, THE MORNING ACTIVITY in a courthouse looks as chaotic as a bread riot. Lawyers, witnesses, clients, cops, and other officials mill about like anxious cattle waiting to enter the killing pens.

But to the attorney the morning melee is as predictable and recognizable as an oft-performed ballet. There is a flowing tide of humanity swirling around clumps of bargaining lawyers, and collections of witnesses huddled about lawyers who, like coaches, whisper last-minute instructions to players about to go into the big game.

By Monday morning the weekend rain had ended. The Kerry County courthouse bustled as usual on this bright, beautiful morning. Usually no new trials were scheduled for Monday morning, which was reserved for other court work. The courthouse was a busy legal factory, and it was more concerned with quantity than quality.

I looked for David Wagner, my client's father, in the mob outside Judge Mulhern's courtroom. As district judge, Mulhern handled arraignments as well as a parade of misdemeanor cases. Wagner wasn't inside the courtroom either.

The three circuit judges had courtrooms on the second floor. I thought he might have gone up there by mistake so I went looking for him.

Judge Theodore Brown was hearing miscellaneous motions. His

courtroom and the hallway outside his door contained a mob consisting mostly of lawyers. Some would be asking for various kinds of temporary relief in all kinds of civil cases. Other lawyers, their opponents, were doing everything in their power to see that the relief requested wasn't granted.

The area around Judge Phillip Swanson's courtroom was so crowded it looked like he was running a sale. He had the morning's divorce docket. Michigan is a so-called no-fault divorce state, so the only real contests anymore are over property and kids. The divorce procedure itself is now as cut and dried as getting a driver's license renewed. Judge Swanson's part of the hallway was jammed by sympathetic lawyers and their clients, mostly women, who were waiting for the five-minute ceremony, complete with testimony, that would officially snip the legal ties of marriage. Judges can marry people and they can divorce them. Both ceremonies take about the same amount of time.

My destination was the far courtroom of Judge Kevin Collins, who had the morning criminal docket, his chief business being sentencing those previously found guilty.

The benches outside his courtroom door were filled with a mixed crowd. Most were defendants, some were their friends, some were their victims. Nobody looked very happy to be there.

Inside the jammed courtroom, Judge Collins, a squat, bald man, presided with the patience and sympathy of someone who would rather be in Philadelphia, snarling out sentences and dispositions as the morning parade slowly passed before him.

Wagner was there, seated with other spectators, dressed exactly as he had been in my office. A worn-looking woman, as faded as her print dress, sat next to him. I presumed she was Mrs. Wagner. I extracted them from that mob, escorted them down to the mob below, and found a seat for them in Mulhern's courtroom.

Attorneys who had never acknowledged my existence before nodded and smiled as I worked my way forward to the clerk handling arraignments. For a while, at least, thanks to the Harwells, I was a star.

Chris Wagner sat with other prisoners, jammed together on a long bench at the side of the courtroom, watched over by two bored court officers. I nodded when I made eye contact with my client.

The clerk directed me to the assistant prosecutor assigned to the case. The prosecutor was a tiny thing, pretty in a tough way. She conducted some business with two other attorneys before she got around to me.

"Sloan, right?" Her voice was as flinty as her eyes. She spoke low, harshly penetrating the noise of the courtroom without disturbing it.

I nodded.

"My name's Stepanek. Who do you represent?"

"Christopher Wagner."

She picked through the files she carried until she found my client's. "The burglar," she said.

"Alleged."

"Alleged, my ass. They caught him inside the joint. What do you want to do here?"

Judge Mulhern was scolding some lawyer for something but both the prosecutor and I ignored everything except the negotiation we were conducting.

"He has no convictions," I said.

"One arrest."

"Have you talked to him?" I asked.

"No." She gestured at the files she had. "He's just one of many on the list this morning."

I pointed Chris out to her. "That's him. The kid. He looks like he should be in grade school rather than here."

"Skinny," she said, but I saw that her eyes softened as she looked at him.

"Our only shot is to go to trial and hope the jury feels sorry for him. Like you say, you people have a pretty good case."

"It's a perfect case. And it's one where we aren't going to accept a plea to anything less than the main charge."

I shrugged. "I can appreciate that. I'm more interested in the sentence than the charge."

She cocked an interested eyebrow. "Plead on the nose. We can run him upstairs and have Collins accept the plea this morning. Judge Collins will do whatever we agree to. How about two years probation, first six months in jail?"

"Look at him. He wouldn't last fifteen minutes before he became someone's bride. How about probation with the provision that he return to school? He still has a year to go to finish high school."

She started to shake her head, but then she looked at Chris again and that seemed to change her mind. "Okay. But if he doesn't go to school, he goes to jail. School is an absolute condition of the probation."

"It's a deal. Are you sure the judge will go along?"

"The school thing will sell him. Collins talks tough, but he's the softest judge in this building, at least with kids. He likes to think he can help young criminals."

"Maybe he's right."

"Bullshit. Most of the little bastards come right back." She glowered up at me. "Okay, Sloan, we'll give your man a last chance. It'll be probation and school. I'll have the officers take him up to Judge Collins. You'll have to wait your turn to plead him guilty. It's busy up there this morning. The judge won't sentence him today, he always requires a probation report, and that takes two weeks."

"Suppose he changes his mind after he reads it?"

"He won't. When you talk to the kid, tell him this isn't some sham. If he drops out of school, he'll drop right into Jackson Prison."

"I'll tell him."

She studied me for a moment. "He's lucky. It's a good thing kindly old Judge Brown doesn't have the criminal docket this morning. Everybody goes to jail. That's Brown's rule."

"That's what they say. I always try to stay away from him."

The eyebrow darted up again. "Then I guess Angel Harwell's luck isn't running too good, is it, if that's the way you feel."

That fleeting sympathy that I had seen in her eyes when she looked at Chris Wagner was now directed my way.

"The Harwell case," she said in a whisper just loud enough to hear, "has been assigned to Judge Brown for trial."

"What!"

She sighed. "I heard about it at the office before I came over here. My condolences."

The noise and bustle in the courtroom seemed almost distant.

Drawing judges was like shooting dice. If you rolled a seven, you won. If you rolled snake eyes, a two, you lost.

Theodore Brown was the judicial equivalent of snake eyes.

CHRIS Wagner liked getting probation, but he did not like having to go back to school, not until I suggested he take some electronics courses since burglar alarms were electronic devices. That appealed to his practical nature.

Getting through the plea had taken a while. I talked to his parents to explain what we were doing. Then we waited until his case was called. My part was brief, telling the judge that after careful consultation and explanation of all legal rights, Christopher Wagner, seeing the error of his youthful ways, had decided to plead guilty to the main charge.

Ms. Stepanek, my client, me, and Judge Collins knew the deal had been cut. But for the benefit of his courtroom audience, Collins rambled on as if no agreement had been struck. Like a preacher, he gave a long moralistic sermon about the evils of crime and the promise of earned redemption before he formally accepted the plea.

I had to make arrangements for Chris's release on bail until sentencing.

Everything had taken longer than I had anticipated, so I got back to my office later than I had expected. The sun was shining, but my mood—after learning that Judge Brown would hear the Harwell case—was dismal. I drove back to my office and pulled into the parking lot next to my building.

"Well, I was beginning to think you stood me up," Sidney Sherman said as he emerged from his big Cadillac. He hadn't changed a bit. Still as thin, perhaps even thinner, with the same apologetic smile. "Whose name is that on your office door?"

"The last tenant. I'm going to have that changed." We shook hands and I led the way up the outside stairway and into my office.

He sat down opposite the desk. "This place smells like an old sock, Charley. You should toss everything out and start fresh. And you should have a secretary. Jeez, this place doesn't exactly inspire client confidence."

"At the moment I have only one client. Whoops, make that two. They seem confident enough. Number two is why I was late.

153

I was making arrangements with the local authorities for his future. Have you lost more weight, Sid?"

"Maybe. Who knows? What I'm able to eat wouldn't keep a gerbil alive. But I'm not here for nutritional advice, am I?"

"No."

"It's not like when I was a cop, Charley. I didn't mind sitting around then and chewing the fat on city time. But it's my time now, and I do mind. Let's get right to it, okay? I have things to do back in Detroit. First off, let me know what you know about this Harwell thing." He took out a small notebook. "Shoot."

I told him the story as factually as I could. He occasionally interrupted with a question but otherwise just listened and made notes. Just telling the story helped me organize things better in my own mind. I told Sid that having Brown as the trial judge would make a bad situation worse.

When I had finished, he sat quietly for a moment before saying anything. "Okay. I'm in the picture now. You're going to want Angel Harwell checked out from cradle to present, right? School grades, who her friends are, what kind of trouble she's been in, official and unofficial, correct?"

"And especially anything about her relationship with her father."

Sid nodded his agreement. "That's a given. We'll look into her old man too, at least as far as his relationship with the kid's concerned."

"More than just that," I said.

"Like what?"

"Sid, I think there's a chance this was a suicide."

He snickered. "C'mon."

"No. I'm serious. I know he was having some major trouble in business. Maybe enough to kill himself. See what you can come up with on that, okay? Also, anything else that might have spelled big trouble for him. Girlfriends, maybe. Even boyfriends. Who knows in these times? Gambling, drugs, booze. See if he was having any problems with things like that."

"It will cost more if you want this done properly. I'll have to hire people in Florida, and maybe other places too."

"Money, for once, is no object. And all this is a job that has to be done."

154

Again, he nodded, then closed the notebook and stuck it back in his pocket.

"I saw Angel on television," he said. "Gorgeous broad. What's she like?"

"She's either scared to death or she's really nuts."

"Do you like her?"

I shrugged. "I don't know. She seems, well, childlike in a way. I'm beginning to feel very protective."

"Be careful. You wouldn't be the first lawyer who fell for a client."

"That won't happen, Sid. She's young enough to be my daughter."

"Funny, that's what those other guys said too. You know how it goes, Charley. You get an erection and the blood drains out of the brain and you can't think right."

"Not this time, Sid. I'm treating Angel as just another client."

"Sure." He laughed. "Say, it's something, isn't it, Morgan and Maguire working up here, and on this case? I never thought I'd see those two again. We're old pals. I used to work vice with Morgan. A standup guy. While I'm up here I might as well hop over to your police department and see if they're around. Maybe I'll dig up something about the Harwells from them."

"They won't so much as burp when you tell them you're working for me."

The smile developed into a full-scale grin. "Maybe yes, maybe no. You forget, I'm pretty good at this sort of thing. If I get anything juicy, I'll let you know." The grin faded. "By the way, you got the ten thousand advance we discussed?"

I wrote him a check. He took it and examined it with a skeptical eye. "I don't lay out cash for anything until this thing clears the bank. You do understand that?"

"The check's good, Sid."

"We'll see." Then he grinned again. "If it is, you just bought yourself a shitload of detective work."

He tucked the check away and started to leave but stopped at the door. "You're not a bad guy, Charley. It's good to see you back in the game."

And then he was gone.

*   *   *

I WAS going to miss lunch. Everything was running late and I heard Harry Hickham coming up the stairs. I glanced at my watch. It was one o'clock. Punctuality was almost a religion with him, and, as usual, he was precisely on time.

Hickham opened the door, squinted at me through his thick glasses, then glanced around the office. He looked more like an owl than ever.

"This place is like something out of Charles Dickens," he said, walking across the worn carpet.

He didn't even offer to shake hands as he gingerly lowered his plump body into one of my old chairs, obviously expecting it to collapse beneath him. "You need a decorator more than a public-relations expert. This joint would scare away starving alley cats. God, you used to have such flair, Charley."

"I still do, I just hide it better now."

"I saw Sid Sherman driving away. Is he going to work for you on this Harwell thing?"

"Yes," I said. "How about lunch, Harry?"

He shook his head. "I just had mine. Besides, I don't approve of doing business while eating. It's a distraction. Now, where's our young lady defendant?"

"Not here. She's in New York. She's scheduled to get back tonight."

His large eyes blinked rapidly, a sign of annoyance. He ran a hand over his bald pate. "I presumed she'd be here. How can I set up a publicity campaign without talking to her? It's like trying to do Romeo and Juliet without Juliet. I'm disappointed in you, Charley. You might have called and saved me the trip up here."

"We don't need her, Harry. I don't think Angel is necessary at this point."

"Oh? She's the star in this drama. Let me tell you what's going to happen. Every magazine, television commentator, and talk-show host is going to do a piece on this case. It's a natural. It's got everything—murder, beautiful women, decadent rich people, the conflict between children and parents, maybe even sex. This case has everything but Donald Trump and the Pope. Angel Harwell's photo will be on the cover of every tabloid and magazine in America. Your little Angel is going to be tried and convicted for murder every day of the week unless we can get her out on the circuit and counter all the crap that's sure to come."

"We can't put her out there, Harry."

The blinking increased. "Are you going to pull the usual lawyer crap?" He scowled. "This is one time when silence isn't golden. You think it's too risky because the Harwell girl might say something they could use against her at trial, right?"

"That's a big part of it, Harry, but that's not the main reason, not this time."

"Oh?"

"She's a beautiful girl, dynamite figure, good voice."

"Perfect."

"Perfect, except that she's apparently incapable of registering any emotion, good or bad. Talking to her is a little like speaking with a robot, or maybe an alien."

"That's just a matter of technique. I can teach her. When I'm through with her she'll be so goddamned good she'll be able to go on the stage."

"Angel's been in mental hospitals, Harry. I'm having some experts examine her in depth. I can't risk putting any pressure on her until I know exactly what she can take. So, for now, anyway, she can't take an active roll."

Hickham slowly shook his head. "The kid is cooked in the media if she just sits on her ass."

"You're the expert, Harry. I'm sure you can figure a way—"

"Nobody is that expert," he interrupted. "She's going to be a sitting duck unless her side of the story is effectively pumped out to the world, and repeatedly."

"Can't you do that?"

"Charley, the story is the kid, not me, not you. We couldn't buy time, but the media people will fall all over themselves to get her on camera. People want to see the tears in the eyes, the lower lip trembling, the tremulous voice when she talks about lately departed, dear old dad. And if the media moguls can't have her, they won't accept anybody else."

"There's got to be some other way."

He shook his head. "Oh, we can put out press releases, maybe line up an expert or two that the talk shows might go for, but without her it would be an almost impossible sell."

He started to get up.

"Where are you going?"

"Home," he said. "There's not a thing I can do for Angel Harwell. Not under these circumstances."

"Are you sure?"

"Absolutely. I'm being honest with you."

"There must be something."

He shook his head. "Without her it would be like trying to put out a forest fire with a squirt gun, a no-win situation. I can't afford to be connected with something that's doomed from the start. I'm sorry, Charley, but that's how it is."

"What do I owe you, Harry?"

He smiled wryly. "I suppose I should charge you for my time, but what the hell. If you decide to let her out into the sunshine, let me know. But you had better do it quickly. The more time goes by, the worse it'll be. People get tried and convicted in the press. Sometimes that's a lot worse than anything that could happen to them in court."

He walked to the door, then stopped and turned back to me.

"You might think about diving out of this thing before it's too late, Charley. If the girl is as ditsy as you suspect, she might be your ruin. All I know is what I read in the papers, but this whole thing sounds like something that could really blow up on you. If I were you, I'd approach all of this with extreme caution. Crazy people. You can't trust them. You could end up holding the proverbial bag."

HARRY's dour words lingered in my consciousness like a ghostly warning. I jumped when the phone rang.

"Mr. Sloan?" The female voice had a commanding quality, brisk bordering on unfriendly."

"Yes."

"This is Clarice Taylor, Judge Brown's law clerk. The judge would like to see you in his chambers before court tomorrow morning. He suggests eight-thirty."

"What's this about?"

"The Harwell case. The file indicates you are still the attorney of record." Her tone indicated she disapproved.

"I'm Angel Harwell's lawyer," I said. "What does the judge want to discuss?"

"I'm sure he'll tell you tomorrow."

"Just me?"

"Mr. Evola will be there. I've already called him."

"Can I talk to the judge for a minute?"

"No, you can't. I presume you'll be here tomorrow?"

I laughed. "Do I have a choice?"

"This is entirely informal," she snapped. "Is there some reason you can't make it?"

"Oh, I'll be there. But no one likes surprises. Can't you give me a hint?"

"I'm just the judge's law clerk," she said, but the tone indicated that she considered herself much more important than that. "He asked me to call, that's all."

"I understand Judge Brown is assigned to try the case."

"Yes."

"Is he about to recuse himself perhaps?"

She snorted. "Of course not! There's no reason why he should step aside."

"Then what is this going to be, just a review of the ground rules?"

"I told you," she said, this time sharply, "I don't know what he wants. Just be there."

She hung up abruptly.

Lawyers try to ingratiate themselves with law clerks, knowing the clerk's opinion might be sought on key issues. It didn't sound like Clarice Taylor was yearning to be my adoring fan.

I dialed Mark Evola's office and eventually was put through to him.

"Charley! I was just thinking about you. You did one hell of a fine job the other day. I don't know if I told you that."

"You didn't."

"Well, you were just marvelous."

"Are you priming me for a campaign contribution, or what?"

He laughed without embarrassment, the typical hearty politician's laugh, full of good will and enthusiasm.

"I'm being sincere, Charley. Can't you tell?"

"Not really. I understand we have an appointment with Judge Brown tomorrow morning. His law clerk called."

"Did you ever see her?" Evola asked.

"Not that I remember."

The laugh this time was more of a snicker. "Hey, you'd have remembered. There's three things about her you can't forget—two of the best jugs this side of Dolly Parton, balanced by a disposition worse than a wounded lion's."

"Just your type, I take it."

"Hey, not this one." I could almost see the toothy smile. "I'm a brave man, but not that brave. I don't think anyone scores with Clarice, not even the judge."

"I can't wait to meet her. What's this conference about?"

"Have you done much work before Brown?"

"Not much. Is he going to try to force a plea?"

Evola chuckled. "That's not his style. He just wants to establish that he's the boss. He sets up rigid schedules and expects attorneys to toe the mark. He's a tough old guy. This is his last year on the bench. He can't run for reelection because of his age. I think that's making him even nastier than usual. He's one of those old ducks who loves the job. They'll probably have to pry him off the bench when the time comes."

"Did you have anything to do with him getting the case?"

"You know I'd never do anything like that." Evola's laugh was distinctly less hearty. "But if I had, Charley, the case would have gone to one of the other black robes over there. Old Brown is just too unpredictable for my taste. Sometimes he likes us, sometimes he doesn't. If I'm going to fix something, I'll do a proper job of it. Brown wouldn't be my choice."

"Are you still going to try the Harwell case yourself?"

"Didn't you see me on television? I looked terrific. Of course I'm going to try it. You couldn't buy publicity like that."

"Suppose you lose, Mark?"

This time there wasn't even a trace of good humor. "I won't lose," he said flatly.

"Maybe. Maybe not. Are you sending someone over tomorrow or are you coming yourself?"

"I wouldn't miss it, Charley." He paused. "Look, you and I are friends, but I hope you realize the gloves are off on this one. Brown isn't Mulhern. I don't think you're going to do so well from here on, frankly."

"My heart is pure and my cause is just."

This time he laughed out loud. "Okay, Sir Lancelot. I'll see you

160

tomorrow. But bring along your shield, buddy, and keep it over your ass. You may need it."

I CALLED the Harwell place. Dennis Bernard answered. Robin and Angel had not yet returned. He reminded me that they were scheduled to arrive later in the evening—gently, so it didn't sound so much like the rebuke it was.

I said I would call later.

Then I sat there needing a drink.

The bottle of brandy was still concealed in the desk. I regretted I hadn't poured it out. But now the need for a drink made it too risky to think of handling the bottle, even with the good intention of tossing the stuff down the drain.

What I did was leave. A cheeseburger was about to become a substitute for a bourbon and water. It wouldn't be the same. It never was.

They were waiting in the parking lot.

The Rolls was parked so the occupants could see both the street and the building.

Little Mike climbed out of the passenger side as I came down the stairs.

"Let's walk down by the river," he said, talking as usual in a very soft, almost feminine voice.

Another young man got out and leaned up against the car. He looked like a sentry, and he was.

We strolled down the grass to a rotting dock. The river gurgled below as it flowed past the old wooden posts.

Little Mike hadn't changed. He seemed even taller than I remembered. He was dressed in black leather that looked as soft as butter. A small gold necklace dangled from his black silk shirt. A diamond the size of a walnut swung at the end. That, except for one small ring, was his only jewelry. In his profession, he was woefully underdressed, but it was his trademark outfit.

"How'd you know I'd be here?"

"Just took the chance. It's a nice day for a drive. You're looking good," he said. "Thinner."

"What's up?"

"I got some work for you."

161

"Bell invented the telephone. It's a great invention. You ought to try it out sometime."

He looked down the river at a small boat moving with the current.

"Man, the feds have more wires aimed at me than a NASA rocket. When I pick up a phone, a dzen FBI agents automatically listen in. I like to do business in the great outdoors. They can still pick up what you say but it makes it more difficult for them." He turned and looked at me. He had dark brown eyes, large and docile like a deer's. If I didn't know who he was I wouldn't have been afraid. But I did know.

"I got a murder case in Detroit I want you to take," he said.

"Detroit's a little far for me now. Why don't you get one of the local recorder's court guys?"

He smiled. "I need someone with a special knack. I always said you were the best, Sloan."

"What do they have you charged with? Second-degree, manslaughter?"

"It's not me," he said. "It's one of my associates. Rick Allen. Do you remember him?"

"Ferrari Rick? Sure, I remember him. I'm surprised he's still alive."

He nodded slowly. "They got him on first-degree. It's not a really good case, you know. I thought maybe you could get the charge knocked down to second or something. We would like to get Rick out on bail. Maybe you could do for him what you did for the little girl up here."

"The Harwell girl has no record. You could paper a small house with Rick's."

"We just want him out. If anyone can do it, you can."

"Rick used to be a rival of yours, as I recall. How come all of a sudden you've become such great pals?"

He shrugged his shoulders. "Business. We got together on a few things. It was not a wise thing to do on my part."

"You're worried that he might turn on you?"

"He's just a friend, a business friend. I'm interested in getting my friend out, that's all."

I shook my head. "And how long would he last on the street? An hour, a day? As I remember you have a pretty direct way of dealing with potential witnesses."

162

His smile flickered. "Name your price. Cash. Easy money and it can't be traced."

Now it was my turn to watch the small boat. "I'm a lawyer, not a bird dog. I'm not going to flush him, even if I could, just so your people can blow him away. You're trying to use me."

"Everyone uses everyone else," he said quietly. "Lawyers, accountants, bankers, they're all tools to be used by the businessman."

"This tool has got his hands full up here. I couldn't help you even if I wanted to. Get whoever is hot back in the city. I don't even know the key people there anymore."

"Money's awfully good," he said. "Just give me a figure."

"I can't do it."

He nodded slowly, then reached equally slowly into the folds of his leather jacket. I felt my heart pound.

When his hand came out it wasn't holding a gun or a knife, but a crisp hundred-dollar bill. He handed it to me.

"That's okay," I said. "You don't owe me anything. This is on the house."

"Take the money. It's a fee. If you take money, I'm a client and you can't testify about any of this." Little Mike wasn't smiling now, and the effect was chilling, like a dangerous thunder cloud suddenly blotting out the sun. "The money's for my protection. Have dinner tonight on me, Sloan."

I took the bill and pocketed it.

He turned and walked with a kind of quick animal grace back to the Rolls. The sleek car was beginning to move as he got in.

Then it was gone.

If he had life insurance, Ferrari Rick's beneficiaries were about to collect. Rick had a terminal disease, and it had just driven away.

12

MY QUICK LUNCH OF CHEESEBURGERS AND FRIES SAT at the bottom of my stomach like a bowling ball. I tried to work it off by doing some shopping. I bought a telephone-answering machine, a cost I would charge against the Harwell case. Then I returned to my office.

The answering machine was easy enough to install. I listened to my own voice after I recorded the little opening message. "Hello, this is Charles Sloan. My secretary and I are away from the office right now, but if you'll leave your name and number at the sound of the beep we'll get back to you as soon as possible."

The secretary bit was stretching things, but I didn't want to sound like a shoestring operation, which, of course, I was.

That chore done, I went to my magic Rolodex and found the name of a New York insurance attorney who had worked with me on a personal injury case. Five years had passed since then.

His name was Jack Flynn and he had prospered. He was now vice president and general counsel of his insurance company. Luckily, he remembered me, and we spent a few minutes rehashing that old case we had done together.

Then I got down to business.

"Jack, I'm defending a murder case and I need to get the name of a good pathologist."

"The Harwell case, right? I read about it. Doesn't sound like you have much of a chance."

164

"Don't believe everything you read in the newspapers, Jack." I then explained the possibility that the death might have been a suicide.

"So, what you need is a doctor who will say death was self-inflicted, right?"

"I'll need someone who is legitimate. A medical whore won't do it for this kind of case. Obviously, it wouldn't hurt if the doctor were inclined to rule on the side of suicide."

"We have a list of both kinds of experts. As you know, Charley, insurance policies have suicide clauses that can go both ways. Sometimes we want to show a death was a suicide to escape paying on an accidental death provision. Sometimes we need to show it wasn't a suicide for similar reasons. Anyway, we have a raft of pathologists. Who we pick depends on which way we want to go. Some will say Abraham Lincoln was a suicide. Some will say Socrates didn't know hemlock was poison. These guys are real specialists. You'll want someone who will say Harrison Harwell jumped on the knife all by himself, I presume?"

I laughed. "That, and the ability to handle himself on the witness stand. For obvious reasons I'd prefer a qualified export who honestly believes what he says, based on the evidence."

"Right. I think I can suggest the exact guy for you. Hans Voltz. The good doctor worked as a pathologist in major cities, taught in medical schools, and even wrote a textbook on pathology. He has credentials up the wazoo. Good-looking older guy, tall, thin. A German with just enough accent to sound authoritative. And, for your purposes, he thinks damn near every death is a suicide. Usually, he does a pretty good job of proving it. We use him a lot."

"Sounds like the man I'm looking for. Where can I contact him?"

"I'll have my girl get the number for you. There is one problem with Doctor Voltz."

"What's that?"

"He's nuts."

"How bad?"

"Not too bad. It's more of a word-of-mouth thing among pathologists. No reputable medical examiner will hire him anymore, or any medical school either. He makes most of his money by testifying. He stands up pretty good on cross-examination. But look out if religion is mentioned. That's when the lunacy emerges."

"And you still think he's the best?"

"I don't think it. He is. Hold on. I'll get his number for you."

On the telephone Dr. Voltz had a deep, soothing voice. His accent was hardly evident. I described the problem. If he was crazy he didn't sound it when he discussed his fee, which was enormous.

After a bit of unsuccessful haggling I agreed to the money and the advance he required. I said I would send a copy of the autopsy report. From my brief description he said the death might well have been suicide. He asked the right questions and he sounded legitimate. Dr. Voltz said he would study the report, prepare a written opinion, and testify at the trial.

Then he asked if Harrison Harwell had been a religious man. The question was gently put, but his tone rose slightly, and his words seemed suddenly strained. It was the sound of a man who had cut up one body too many. He asked if Harwell had had a deep personal relationship with God.

I told him I didn't know and quickly ended our conversation.

Fortunately, questions about religion, since it would not be an issue, could be excluded at trial. My witness might be a bit quirky, but I could make sure the jury would never see that side of him. If I used him.

The rest of the day went slowly, although I did receive calls from two prospective clients, more spillover from the Harwell case publicity. I set up appointments.

As time dragged I could vividly recall the quiet solace offered in dark saloons. Too vividly. Several times I had to resort to my fifteen-minute drill until the urge to drink passed.

The cheeseburger was still with me so I skipped dinner.

The third time I called the Harwell place, just before nine, Dennis Bernard told me Robin and Angel had just arrived. He offered to call Robin to the phone, but I told him I would be there in minutes and hung up.

There were no security guards anymore at the Harwell place. They were no longer needed. The media people who had been camped out on the street had moved on to more exciting things.

A high wind whipped the trees above the darkened house, and the moon was obscured behind dense clouds in the night sky. A storm, a big one, was beginning to move in.

Bernard admitted me and led me to the darkened atrium. A small dim lamp at the far end of the glass-enclosed room was the only illumination.

Angel and Robin were seated close together at the other end. In the shadows they looked like ghosts.

"Bernard, bring Mr. Sloan an orange juice," Robin said. "Do sit down, Charley."

They were drinking but I couldn't tell what.

Angel and Robin were both dressed in jeans and blouses. Angel had her shoes off, her long legs stretched before her. Her eyes, catching the light from the distant lamp, looked like two shining diamonds.

"You realize you violated the provisions of Angel's bond by going to New York," I said to Robin. "I told you she couldn't leave the state without permission."

"It was only a few days. We both needed to get away, Charley."

"You should have told me. I would have made arrangements."

Angel spoke softly. "And what if they had said I couldn't go? Why even ask?" She sipped her drink. "What they don't know can't hurt them."

"It could hurt you," I said. "Unless you've fallen madly in love with our jail. They're keeping a room over there in your name, just in case."

"Let's not overreact," Robin said sharply. "My God, we've had Harrison's death, the funeral, this horrible court business. Too much. We just had to get away for a while. We had to. We needed some time alone, just the two of us."

"I'm not arguing that. But understand they can pop Angel back into jail in a wink of an eye if they're given a chance. From now on let's play everything by the book. There's just too much at risk here to do otherwise."

Bernard returned with my orange juice. He left us alone again as I sipped.

"We did have a marvelous time, Charley," Angel said. "It's a shame you weren't with us. I can never get enough of New York. The shopping, the shows, the people. I love it."

167

"But it was exhausting," Robin said. "We're both about to hit the hay."

It was her polite way of telling me to leave. But I wasn't about to go, not yet.

"I need to find out some things. This will only take a few minutes."

"Oh, Charley," Angel said. "You work too hard. Relax and smell the roses."

My eyes had adjusted to the dimness. Her face, expressionless as usual, was even more beautiful in the half-light.

"I understand Harrison was about to serve you with divorce papers in Florida." I watched Robin to see what kind of reaction my words had caused.

She sighed and rolled her eyes. "My God, we were always yelling about divorce at one another. It was that kind of marriage, right from the beginning. But we never did it. Never intended to."

"Harrison is supposed to have retained a Florida law firm for that purpose. Everything was ready to roll, the court papers, the works, according to my information."

"That's just talk. I must admit we did come close to splitting up several times over the years. What married couple doesn't? I doubt that Harrison ever thought seriously about it."

"You're sure?"

She shrugged. "I suppose nothing's ever sure, is it? But Harrison was hardly the kind to keep something like that to himself. He would have gone around bellowing about what he was going to do. That was his style."

"I never heard anything about a divorce," Angel said quietly. "Nothing serious, anyway."

She took Robin's hand. I was struck again at the mother-daughter relationship—there was a nice, comfortable affection between them.

"What happened to Theresa Hernandez?" I asked.

"Who?" Angel asked.

"Theresa, the maid. The small, cute one," Robin prompted.

"Oh, her."

She looked at Robin. I saw no obvious reaction, just Angel's usual mask.

168

"I talked to Theresa," I said. "The detectives did too. She told me she was having an affair with Harrison. She said he told her he was getting a divorce."

Robin shook her head. "As I told you, Harrison had a few problem areas. Women were one," she said. She looked at Angel. "This isn't going to embarrass you, is it?"

Angel sipped her drink. "Of course not."

"Look, Harrison could never keep that damn thing in his pants, especially with the hired help. We have lost an army of maids over the years because of that. He would tell them anything to get them into bed. He was quite shameless about it. Of course, he tired of them quickly, so we would pay them off and get rid of each in her turn. It was a shame. Some were quite competent and good help is so hard to get. But I told you all this, Charley. It's not as if we were trying to conceal anything."

"So, where is little Theresa?"

Robin sighed. "Like the others, she accepted everything Harrison told her as gospel. If you look at it from her point of view, this was a terrible personal tragedy. Here she was, a poor girl about to become the wife of a rich and powerful man. And then he dies. Talk about broken dreams."

"Where is she?"

Robin chuckled. "Do you think I've done away with her, Charley? Is that it?"

"No. I just want to know where she is."

"She was quite useless around here," Robin said. "When she wasn't sobbing she was openly hostile. Not exactly a soothing circumstance, given everything else that's happened. I sent her home to Puerto Rico. I have the address somewhere around here. If it's important I can get it for you in the morning. I just couldn't bear to search for it now."

"Tomorrow's fine. Is she still on your payroll?"

"Yes. I send the checks to her mother. I thought it would be wise to continue her on salary. We don't need any extra trouble at the moment." Robin cocked an inquisitive eyebrow. "Charley, you can't believe that Harrison actually planned on marrying that—"

"If she told her story to me," I said, "she told it to the police too. What *I* believe isn't important. What they might believe is.

169

Theresa is what they call a loose end. The detectives handling this case aren't fools. She's a loose end that will be all tied up before this is over."

Angel, who had been looking out at the dark river, now turned toward me.

"Do I need permission to go back home to Florida?"

"It's out of state," I said. "So the answer is yes."

"Well, then, talk to whomever you must. Robin and I want to go Wednesday."

I looked at Robin.

"I think it's a good idea, Charley. We need to get some distance from things for a while. Besides, this place, after what happened here, isn't very comfortable for either of us."

They both looked comfortable enough, and if they were grief-stricken they didn't show it. Their reaction didn't seem to match those of women who had lost someone close. But appearances could be deceiving.

"I'm to meet with the trial judge tomorrow morning. I'll ask permission. But before you go I want to have Angel examined by a doctor."

"What kind of doctor?" Angel snapped.

"A psychiatrist. A friend of mine. He will do some psychological tests in addition to talking to you."

"Why?" I thought I detected fear in her voice.

"I'm going to try to keep your statement out of evidence. I may need expert opinion to do that. That's the reason for the testing."

"Are you going to say I was insane?"

I thought this time I might see a definite reaction, but her face remained impassive.

"Angel, I'm going to say that your mental state that night wasn't stable, given the shocking death of your father, and that the continuous questioning over hours reduced your ability to make a statement voluntarily. It's a standard tactic in this kind of case."

Angel was about to speak again, but Robin cut her off.

"How long will these tests take?"

"A couple of days."

"So that means we can't leave Wednesday, I presume?"

"It would put things off for a few days."

170

"Why can't the testing be done in Florida?" Angel asked calmly.

"Because I want to use my own expert, someone I know and trust."

"She'll be happy to do it, Charley," Robin interjected. "But try to arrange it as quickly as possible, if you can. We desperately need to get out of here for a while."

"I'll do my best." I spoke to Angel. "I'll need a list of the hospitals and doctors who have treated you so I can get their reports. I'll have some medical release forms prepared for you to sign."

"Release forms?" Angel asked.

"The doctors can't legally release any medical information unless you give approval in writing. It's all confidential information. I can't get it without your okay."

Angel thought for a moment, then spoke. "The police can't get it, I assume."

"That's right."

"Then why even bother with it?" Angel said, finishing her drink.

"I need it to evaluate the case and build a defense. No one will ever see the reports besides myself and the doctor I'm having examine you. You have nothing to worry about."

She looked at Robin.

Robin nodded. "We can get a list up, Charley. But not tonight, all right? We're both exhausted."

"Okay. I'll check back with you after I see the judge tomorrow."

"Who is this judge? The same one as before?" Angel asked.

"No. I wish he was, but this one is a circuit judge. They have jurisdiction over felony cases. His name is Brown."

"What's he like?" Robin asked.

"Frankly, I wish the case had gone to someone else," I said. "But so does the prosecutor. So I suppose we're both starting out even."

"You don't think you'll do well with this new judge?" Robin asked.

"I wish I could answer that. I can't, not now anyway." I looked at Angel. "You might want to consider getting another lawyer. Someone else might do better with this judge."

"You're my lawyer, Charley," Angel said sharply. "That's been settled once and for all, no matter what happens."

I looked at Robin.

She smiled. But I thought something in her expression was less than enthusiastic.

"We have to get to bed, Charley," Robin said as she stood up. "I hope you won't think ill of us for that."

Angel laughed softly.

I wondered why, but her lovely expressionless face gave no clue.

EVOLA and I were escorted into Judge Brown's spacious chambers by the court officer.

Judge Theodore Brown did not look seventy-one. Nor did he look fierce, but that also was an illusion.

He was a touch over six feet tall and stringy thin except for a potbelly, usually hidden beneath his judicial robe.

Brown's eyes were pale green and his hair had grayed to an attractive blend of salt and pepper. His flesh had sagged a bit over the years but he still looked good. He was one of those people who had been handsome in youth and who became craggy and distinguished in age.

The tip of a small hearing aid peeked out of his left ear and he wore half glasses perched near the tip of his nose.

I recognized the young woman sitting on the judge's couch from Evola's description. She was Clarice Taylor, the judge's law clerk. She wore no makeup and had her blonde hair tied back. And Evola was right. Even with a loose-fitting top, she was magnificently endowed. Also, in keeping with Evola's appraisal of her attitude toward the world, she scowled at both of us as if we were trespassers.

The walls of the judge's chamber were decorated with framed photographs, all of the judge, mostly with local and national political figures. An enlarged photograph of himself hung modestly behind his large desk. The photo was him all right but without the sagging flesh, half glasses, or hearing aid, and given its placement, it was obviously his favorite. He was very young then and had his air force pilot's cap cocked rakishly over his eyes. He had posed in front of a World War II fighter plane. It reminded me of the similar picture Harrison Harwell had of himself.

Brown sat behind the desk in shirt-sleeves, a cup of coffee in front of him. He didn't stand or offer his hand, just watched sternly as we approached.

"Sit down." His voice was crisp and commanding.

We took chairs across the desk from him.

"You may consider this little get-together, gentlemen, as an informal pretrial conference. I intend to try this Harwell case like any other. There will be no special considerations or accommodations to either side. And I will not allow it to be turned into a media carnival. I trust I'm making myself clear?"

I nodded. I could sense that Evola was becoming uncomfortable.

"I presume there will be no plea?"

"That's correct," I said.

The judge peered over the little reading glasses, the green eyes as cold as agates. "Mr. Evola, how long do you think you'll need to put in your case, exclusive of the jury selection?"

Evola shifted in his chair. "Well, that's difficult to estimate at this point, judge. It could be a couple of days. It could be a week."

"For our purposes this morning, we'll say a week. And you, Mr. Sloan? How long do you expect to take?"

I wondered if I was seeing challenge or frank hostility in those green eyes.

"I'm in the same boat as the prosecutor. It's difficult to estimate at this time. Two days, maybe three. But it could be longer."

The judge looked at Evola and then back to me. "I would allow a day for jury selection, a day for argument and the charge. As a rough estimate, special circumstances aside, we appear to be talking about a trial of approximately two weeks."

"Judge, this is all conjecture at this point," the prosecutor said.

Those eyes swung toward Evola. "That's obvious, isn't it," he snapped. "But I have to get some idea of what kind of time we're talking about in order to arrange my docket. I had planned to take a vacation during the month of August, but I can change that. I will schedule this matter for trial to begin Tuesday, August first."

"Judge, that doesn't give my office enough time to prepare," Evola protested.

"Me, too," I added. "There is a considerable amount of investigative work to be done. This is an extremely complex case, your honor."

The eyes flashed my way once again. "Oh? The charge is murder, is it not? I've tried hundreds of murder cases over the years, gentlemen. In my opinion, murder may be the stuff of high drama, but legally it's one of the simplest issues to come before a court. Somebody's dead. Somebody's accused of making him that way. The only thing a jury has to decide is whether that's true or not. Simple."

"But, your Honor, this case—" Evola began to speak but was cut off as the judge raised a restraining hand.

"I said this case would be tried the same as any other, Mr. Evola, and it will be. I don't give a damn about how the press treats it. I will treat it exactly the same as any other murder case I have ever presided over. The trial is set for August first."

"But, judge—"

Brown glared Evola into silence and then spoke to me. "I understand there is a confession in this matter. Do you plan to ask for a Walker hearing on the admissibility?"

"We dispute that the statement is in fact a confession, but yes, we are going to ask for a hearing."

"That is your right," he said, but his tone implied that he found that distasteful. "I propose to set the hearing for July fifth."

"I need more time," I said. "I have expert witnesses who need to review the evidence. Psychiatrists, psychologists, among others."

"Are you going to plead insanity?" the judge asked.

"No. The testimony will address my client's mental state when the statement was given."

He stared at me for an uncomfortable moment, then referred to the pages of a date book on his desk. "All right, Mr. Sloan. I have the morning of July twenty-sixth free. We'll schedule the Walker hearing then."

"Judge, that's less than a week before the start of the trial," Evola protested. "On the outside chance that your honor might disallow the admission of the confession, we would need time to appeal. It would change the whole thrust of our case."

The judge's smile was frosty. "It allows plenty of time for an emergency appeal, Mr. Evola. That's not a valid objection." He wrote in his date book. "The Walker hearing is set for Wednesday, July twenty-sixth."

"Now, is there anything else?" the judge asked, but it was spoken as a form of dismissal.

"My client wishes to go to her home in Florida," I said. "It's a condition of bail that she not leave the state without obtaining permission."

"We object to that," Evola said quickly. "She should be sitting in a jail cell now. Florida is out of the question. She has money. She could leave the country. She should stay here where we can keep an eye on her."

The judge pursed his lips, then looked at me. "Does she have a passport?"

"I'm not sure. I think she probably does."

He nodded. "All right. She can return to her home in Florida, but no other place, until trial. However, she must turn over her passport to the sheriff before she leaves. All other conditions of bond will remain the same."

"Thank you, your honor," I said.

He leaned back in his leather chair and studied the two of us for a moment. "I have a reputation for punctuality, gentlemen. It is something I insist upon. Attorneys seem to have a built-in clock that perpetually runs late. But that clock is not tolerated in my courtroom. Also, I insist on professional decorum at all times. Should there be any deviation to that rule, I shall deal with it quickly, and in a way neither of you will like very much."

He paused. "If you have any questions before trial, feel free to contact Miss Taylor, here. Unless I note otherwise, she speaks for me in procedural matters."

The green eyes focused on me. "I hesitate to bring this up, Mr. Sloan, at this time, but I suppose I must."

He studied me for a moment, then continued. "The Sixth Amendment to the Constitution provides that persons accused of crime shall have the right to be represented by counsel. The courts, both federal and state, have interpreted that to mean adequate counsel. Anything less may be grounds for appeal."

I nodded.

"This may be painful, but I must address the issue. You have had the reputation of being, how shall I say it, Mr. Sloan, a heavy drinker. I presume you agree?"

"I'm a recovering alcoholic," I said, feeling both anger and fear blossom.

He smiled, again as cold as ice. "Yes, that's how it's put nowadays, isn't it? Well, let me make this absolutely clear. I don't think people under the influence of alcohol should fly airplanes, drive cars, perform surgery, or," he paused, "try lawsuits."

"I don't drink now," I said, knowing I was coloring.

"Yes," he said, his tone disbelieving. "However, if you did, and you tried this case, it could allow an appellate court to find that your client really wasn't represented by adequate counsel. That is something that isn't going to happen, Mr. Sloan."

"I don't understand. Are you saying I can't defend my client?"

The eyes seemed even colder. "No. However, if you run into any of your old difficulties, or if I think you've been drinking, even the odor of alcohol will be sufficient, I will declare a mistrial and personally move for your disbarrment. Your client will be tried again since jeopardy under that circumstance won't attach. However, the consequences for you will be devastating. I hope this is sufficiently clear to you?"

"I don't drink," I repeated.

His smile was more of a smirk. "Yes. I'm just telling you what will happen if you do."

I could almost see the headlines.

176

13

JUDGE BROWN'S WARNING TO ME WASN'T THE BEST
way to start the day.

Evola walked out of chambers with me, but with no show of
fraternal affection. It was as if he had just learned I had a particularly loathsome disease. Polite, but no longer convivial, he moved
quickly away in case what I had might be extremely contagious.

The Kerry County courthouse was relatively new and had a pod
with three pay phones in the lobby, identical to the modern
phone pods in most airports.

One was free. Getting Dr. Williams on the line was about as
easy as getting through to the president. I went through a succes-
sion of nurses, being put on hold for a few minutes each time,
which gave me some opportunity to observe my fellow tele-
phoners.

In theory, the small plastic barriers at the side of each phone
provide privacy. That's only in theory. We stood almost elbow to
elbow. The caller on my right was a young man in a very expensive suit, sporting an equally expensive haircut. His gold Rolex
flashed as he gestured. From his conversation I gathered he was a
lawyer waiting to go to trial. He was talking to his stockbroker,
demanding information and giving crisp buy and sell orders. He
was oblivious of the world around him. As far as he was concerned he was the center of the universe. I saw in him an echo of
what I had once been.

The other caller, a bondsman, shaped like a pumpkin and sweating like a fountain, wore an ill-fitting sports jacket over a rumpled shirt and stained tie. He was talking to someone about a customer who hadn't shown up for sentencing. His grating voice had a singsong quality as he whined about how hard it was for an honest man to make a living anymore. I got the impression that his defaulting customer was about to find the world a very dangerous place. The bondsman was stand-up comedian and menace, mixed about half and half. He looked shabby but I figured he could probably buy and sell the kid lawyer at the other phone.

Both conversations were interesting and I almost regretted it when Bob Williams finally came on my line.

He had set everything up as I had asked. Angel was scheduled to see the clinical psychologist on Thursday. Williams had set aside an hour to talk to her on Friday morning. I thanked him for his fast action and hung up.

My partners at the pod were still at it, the bondsman complaining about the cost of doing business and the lawyer snapping commands about some obscure stock.

It was nice being back in a courthouse again. A busy courthouse has a life of its own. Like the bottom of the sea, there is always a lot going on that isn't visible from the surface.

I was going to call and see if Angel and Robin were up yet, then I decided to just go over. My visit wasn't social.

They were up and they weren't alone. Apparently the atrium was the gathering spot of choice for the Harwell women. Angel and Robin were still in robes, sitting with Mary Beth Needham, the writer, who was dressed in casual jeans and a sweater. I was reminded of photos of suburban housewives sitting around morning coffee. The kind of women who might be gossiping of milkmen, but not about murder.

But there were no milkmen anymore in Pickeral Point. And they weren't housewives.

The presence of the writer alarmed me. I had warned both Robin and Angel to avoid journalists and writers. My instructions about that were being as carefully obeyed as those about not leaving the state.

I accepted coffee, then asked if I could see Angel and Robin privately.

178

"Com'on, Charley," Mary Beth Needham said. "We're all pals here. You have nothing to fear from me. If this is off the record, my lips are sealed."

"No offense, but a lot of lawyers prefer to see their clients alone. A little like priests and doctors."

She didn't appear offended. "Priests examine the soul. Doctors the body. What do you examine?"

"Evil and the appearance of evil."

She laughed. "That must be fun. I'll go, but first, I understand you talked to the trial judge this morning. Has a trial date been set?"

I nodded.

"Tell me and save me a phone call. Surely, there can be no risk in that?"

"Trial is set for August first."

"That soon," Robin said in surprise.

"This isn't a big city. There are fewer cases. Besides, the judge is canceling his vacation so he can bring this to trial."

"That's very accommodating," Needham said. "Why would he do a thing like that?"

"Everybody likes to be a star. The judge is retiring the end of this year, so I suppose ending his career by presiding over a nationally covered murder trial isn't the worst way to say adieu."

"Can we go to Florida?" Angel asked, as unconcerned as if the trial involved someone else.

"Yes. You have to surrender your passport, though."

"Why?" Angel demanded.

"So you won't take your trust fund and run off to Brazil or some other place where it would be tough to get you back. It's a standard provision in cases like this," I said. "You do have a passport?"

She nodded. "Yes."

"Then Florida will be no problem."

"And we only have to come back for the trial?" Angel asked.

I wondered if she really understood what was at stake. She seemed to regard her trial for murder as if it were some minor bureaucratic exercise. Something that really wouldn't significantly affect her.

"You'll have to come back for the Walker hearing. That's set for July twenty-sixth."

"What's a Walker hearing?" Needham asked.

I didn't like discussing the case with her, but it was public information so it could do no harm.

"When a defendant has made a statement that the prosecution intends to introduce at trial, the defense can ask for a separate hearing on whether that statement is admissible or not."

"I've never heard of that," Needham said.

"It's something we have in Michigan. A few other states have similar procedures."

"When you say statement, you really mean confession, don't you?" Needham smiled at me with what she hoped was wide-eyed innocence.

"Look, I know this isn't polite, but I do have to talk to my clients."

"Do you represent both these ladies?" Needham asked, with the same pretended innocence. "I thought Angel was your client?"

"Technically, you're right," I said. "Now, if you don't mind . . ."

Needham showed no irritation. She finished the last of her coffee, kissed both women on the cheek, promised to visit them in Florida, and then was gone.

"I thought I told you to avoid the press." I spoke to both of them but I looked at Robin.

"Mary Beth is a friend," she said.

"That friend intends to write a book about all of this. If it's cutesy and bland she won't make a cent. But if it's packed with juicy personal tidbits, the spicy kind picked up over girl talk and coffee, the book can make her a millionaire. Friends like that you don't need."

Angel said nothing, just gazed out at the river and sipped her coffee.

"She's different," Robin said, dismissing my advice.

"There's a lot of people sitting in jail who made the same assumption about other writers. If you must see her, at least watch what you say. She has a reputation for getting harmful admissions out of people."

180

This time Robin joined Angel in staring out at the river. I wasn't making much of a sale.

So I went on to something else. "We've set up the psychological tests for this Thursday, Angel. Friday morning you'll see Doctor Williams."

Angel looked over at Robin and cocked an eyebrow when I mentioned Friday.

"Bernard can take you," Robin said, then looked at me. "I have to be in Detroit for a court hearing on Friday morning."

"Oh?"

"Harrison's sister is trying to block the sale of the boat company. Nate Golden is having her suit thrown out on Friday. He said it won't be any problem, and Amos Gillespie asked that I be there. Amos is buying the company."

"Why is the sister bringing legal action?" I asked.

"Oh, just to make a pest of herself," Robin said. "She doesn't want the boat company owned by anyone who isn't a Harwell. That, plus she hates the idea that I'll get any money from the sale."

"How much will you get?"

She shrugged. "Since Harrison got the company into so much financial difficulty, not much. A little over four million."

"Some people would think that could be defined as much."

Robin laughed. "If Harrison hadn't become so overextended, it would have been ten or twenty times that. We're lucky to get out with anything at all, frankly."

"We?"

"Angel gets the same amount. We split everything equally, so Nate Golden says."

"Under the will?"

She shook her head. "No. Actually. Harrison changed his will several months ago. It all has to do with my status as widow, something Nate called the 'widow's election.'" She looked at me. "Do you know what that is?"

"Yes. The widow is entitled to assets even if her husband cut her out of the will. You get half?"

"We agreed, Angel and I."

I looked over at Angel. She nodded.

The amounts they spoke of made my other task a bit easier.

"Speaking of money, Angel, I'm going to need some more before you take off for Florida. I had to advance ten thousand for an investigator and there'll be some similar expenses coming up."

"Bill me," Angel said.

Robin smiled. "Charley will need the money up front."

She knew I didn't have that kind of cash.

"I'd prefer it," I said. "It keeps things a bit more businesslike."

Angel sighed as if an enormous task had been asked of her. "I suppose I'll have to write a check," she said. "How much?"

Robin looked at me. "Will another twenty thousand do it, Charley?"

I nodded. "I'm keeping track of every penny. Everything will be accounted for when this is done."

"Write a check for that amount," Robin said to Angel. "If you don't have that in your account, I'll cover it."

Angel shrugged, stood up, and walked off. Her moements were those of an athlete—easy, powerful, and extremely sexy.

"Don't step on your tongue," Robin said, observing my gaze. "I thought you only looked at me like that?"

I felt myself coloring.

She laughed. "Don't worry about it, Charley. If I were a man I'd react the same way. Angel is absolutely breathtaking."

She paused for a moment, then spoke in a soft voice, almost a conspiratorial whisper. "What do you think these psychological tests might show?"

"I hope I can use them to show she is fragile emotionally and the strain of that night caused her to say things she didn't mean."

"Suppose they show something else, something worse?"

"Insanity?"

She looked out at the river. "I'm asking what you think."

"I don't think anything, Robin, not at this point. Those evaluations are up to the experts."

"Experts can be wrong. Suppose she says something detrimental?"

"Fortunately, these are my experts. If I don't like what they find, I don't have to use it."

"Can you do that?"

"It's not evidence, not in the usual sense. This is being done just for my benefit. I can use it or not. So if I elect not to use it I'm not obstructing justice."

She raised that eyebrow again. "Oh?"

"It can be a fine line, I admit, but I'm on the right side of it this time."

She turned and studied the river, her face solemn. "Suppose the tests reveal something that might make you feel differently about her?"

"Like what?"

She shrugged. "Oh, I don't know. It might be anything. Who knows? But if it was something, well, terrible, could you still defend her, knowing it?"

It was my turn to shrug. "I've defended child molesters, mass murderers, and pimps, Robin. I haven't exactly been in love with any of them but I did the job I was paid to do."

"But—"

"Attorneys have to be objective, like doctors. An appendix is an appendix. A surgeon does the best job he can no matter who the appendix belongs to. It's the same with lawyers. No lawyer takes a case based on whether he likes the client or not."

"A pretty speech, Charley," she said. "Although I'm not sure anyone can be that objective about anything."

Angel came back and handed me a check.

I tucked it away.

"Will you come to visit us in Florida?" Angel asked.

"I'm going to be pretty busy."

Angel smiled that odd little enigmatic smile. "You'll come. You'll find a reason."

She sounded as if she really knew.

I HAD driven by the Harwell boat plant at least a dozen times before but I had never really looked at it. It was just another factory. But not anymore. The boat works had become very interesting.

Pickeral Creek isn't even shown on some maps, although on others it's designated a river. It trickles down through the farm country and drains into the big St. Clair River. Pickeral Creek is more of a ditch, at least in some places, and the only time it looks like a real river is when it floods during the spring rains. Even then it's a kind of half-hearted flood. It's a half-hearted river generally.

I followed the winding road that borders Pickeral Creek. Little farmhouses were scattered along it, like sentinels watching over their planted fields. Coming from town, the road turned past a heavy clump of ancient oaks, and then the sprawling boat plant came into view, looking huge and incongruous in contrast to the flat farmland surrounding it.

The modern plant building, two stories high and with few windows, seems to stretch on forever. It was surrounded by acres of parking for the workers. Sleek boats, stacked one after another, sat on caravans of trucks, waiting for shipment.

The little river delivered just enough water to supply a small manmade lake just behind the factory. The factory and all the other buildings had been painted a light industrial blue.

I parked by a sign saying VISITORS and walked into the administration building, a structure that was nearly all windows. The walls were also painted that peculiar shade of blue.

Inside, the reception area was done up in the same blue, including the modern furniture. Enlarged photos of Harwell boats took up the little wall space that wasn't ceiling-to-floor glass.

The receptionist, a young brunette, the only thing in the room not painted blue, smiled a professional smile—wide, gleaming, and insincere.

"How may I help you?" she asked. The enamel of her teeth reflected the room's bright lights.

"My name is Sloan," I said. "I'm the lawyer for Angel Harwell. I'd like to look around Harrison Harwell's office, if that's possible."

The smile flickered out so quickly it seemed as if a plug had been pulled. "I'm afraid I don't have the authority to approve anything like that," she said.

"How about Malcolm Dutton? Is he here?"

The name seemed to reassure her and the smile came back, but not as enthusiastic as before.

"I'll call him," she said.

I waited while she announced me. I could see she was surprised by the telephoned reaction she got from Dutton. The smile melted into a nervous frown. "He'll be right here," she said to me, then made herself visibly busy so that any further conversation was impossible.

Dutton charged through a door like a fighting bull entering the arena.

His eyes glittered with hostility. "What is it that you want, Sloan?" he demanded.

"It's good to see you again, too," I replied, using my own professional smile, though it had no effect on him. "I'd like to look around Harrison Harwell's office."

"Why?"

"I have my reasons."

"This is a business office. Unless you have a court order, I—"

"I don't, but if you like I can call Robin. Until this place is sold I presume she's still the boss."

His eyes narrowed and the muscles around his jaw twitched. Then he spoke, with icy control. "That won't be necessary. I can let you in there for a few minutes, I suppose, but you can't take anything, not without a court order."

"Fair enough."

He turned to the receptionist, who was looking extremely uncomfortable.

"Have Max Webster take him there."

He bolted back through the door without a word. If I'm ever cold and hungry, I won't expect to be rescued by Malcolm Dutton. He still considered me an obstacle between himself and the Widow Harwell.

I was, of course.

The receptionist made another call and after a few minutes an elderly man, rail thin, with a weather-roughened face, came through the same door Dutton had used. His light blue sports jacket, the same color as the factory, looked as if it had been intended for a much larger person.

"I'm Max Webster," he said, extending his left hand. I glanced at his right. It couldn't be called a hand. All that was left was a battered thumb sticking out from a scarred ball that had once had fingers.

I shook his left hand as I introduced myself. He had a very strong grip.

"Come on with me," he said, holding the door to the inner offices open.

"How's Angel and Mrs. Harwell doing?" he asked as he led me down a long hall past rows of small identical offices. The people inside had no privacy since the offices were almost all glass.

"Do you know them?"

He nodded. "Oh yeah. I've been here a very long time. I knew Angel's mother better than I do the new wife. I suppose I should say widow now, eh?"

"Did Angel come here often?"

"Sure, but not lately. I mean, not for the last ten years or so, I guess. She used to come here as a kid. Her grandfather liked having her around." He stopped at the end of the hall. Like the others, the office was almost all glass, only it was much larger. He opened the door and stood aside as I entered.

The desk was a duplicate of the one Harrison Harwell had in his house. There was no wall space to hang pictures. However, a very small, expensive-looking Japanese knife lay on a wooden tray on top of the desk. There was one picture in a silver frame, a smaller duplicate of the photo in his home office—Harwell in naval uniform, glaring out at the world.

"What was he like?" I asked, nodding toward the photo.

He hesitated, then smiled. "Oh, like most of us, he had his good points and his bad. I liked him."

"What were his bad points, Mr. Webster?"

"Call me Max. Everyone does. I'm head of security here. I been doing security work here for I guess almost twenty years, ever since I sawed off my fool hand."

"What happened?"

He shrugged and examined the stump as if he had just discovered it was there. "We used a lot of hand-held power saws in the old days. Most everything is stamped out by machines now. But then we usually cut and shaped wood and fiberglass by hand. A man had to be careful. I wasn't and ended up seeing my fingers on the floor.

"Old man Harwell, Harrison's father, was running things then. He didn't relish paying me workmen's compensation for the rest of my life, so he offered to hire me as a security guard. Wasn't much a one-handed man could do then, at least one without much education, so I jumped at the offer. I've been doing it ever since. I'll retire as soon as this takeover gets done. I don't think working here will be the same under the new people."

"Tell me about Harrison Harwell, Max."

He sat down on the blue leather couch. I perched myself on the desk.

"I always felt a little sorry for Harrison. He lived in his father's shadow even after the old man died. Maybe it's that way whenever a son takes over a business the father built. Everybody measures the boy against the man. Anyway, it was that way with Harrison. He knew it."

"Did he get along with his father? I understand he worked here for years before his father died."

Max shrugged again. "He got along as well as anyone could. The old man was hell on wheels. He could do every job in this plant and do it better than anyone else. He was a rough-cut old guy. He never finished the eighth grade but it never bothered him." He smiled. "They used to call him the Henry Ford of the Waterways, and I guess he was. Like old Henry, he sometimes got a little odd, but he built this and other factories from nothing but scratch and sweat. The old man was tough, and he could be bone mean. Harrison never inherited that toughness or that streak of hard meanness, although he tried to imitate it. Harrison was cut from different cloth, so he never quite brought it off."

"You said you liked Harrison."

"I did. I think I understood him better than most. He tried to be something he wasn't. He would swagger around and try to give the impression he was a tough guy like his father. Mostly, it was just bluff. He was one of those men who probably would have done better at something else. He probably should have sold the business after his father died. He would have been happier. He didn't have much of a head for business. Too much bluff and not enough brains, I'm afraid. At least no business sense like his old man."

I smiled. "Harrison doesn't sound very lovable to me."

Max laughed. "Well, I suppose he doesn't. But we became sort of work friends, he and I. After hours we'd sit around here and talk. Could be anything—sports, hunting, whatever interested him at the moment. I don't think he talked to many people like that. He didn't have many friends."

"You said he tried to be mean. Did you ever hear of him hitting his wife?"

His eyebrows shot up in surprise. "Harrison!" Then he chuckled. "Not him. He might have strutted around like John Wayne but I don't think there was much violence in the man. At least, I never saw any. Besides, he loved the Japanese and tried to live like he thought they did. He would have considered hitting a woman dishonorable, I think. Even when he was drinking."

"Did he have a problem?"

"Depends on your definition. It's tough being daddy's boy. We used to sit in this office after everyone left and have a few belts. He got stiff once in a while. But he was more of a crying drunk than a fighting drunk, if you've had any experience with people who drink."

I smiled. "A little. How about his daughter? How did he get along with her?"

"All right, I guess. Angel was more the blessed granddaughter, to tell you the truth. The old man thought the sun rose and set on her. I don't think Harrison understood the father business any too well, either. He tried, but he was the kind of man who had problems establishing relationships, even with Angel. Anyway, that's how it looked from my point of view."

"How was his mental attitude after he got into business difficulty?"

Max sighed. "He was always in business difficulty. He wanted to expand for the sake of expanding, to build something bigger and better than daddy did. It caught up to him in the end. He borrowed too much and couldn't raise enough to pay back in time. He really began to drink when he knew he'd have to sell the business or go belly-up. I saw him one night in here crying his eyes out. He didn't see me so I just slipped out of the building."

"Do you think he was capable of suicide?"

Max paused. "I don't know. Maybe. God knows, he talked about it often enough."

"He did?"

"He loved the Japanese ways, you know. He would have run around in sandals and a silk robe if he thought he could have gotten away with it. Japanese people, if they fail and lose face, have a way of knocking themselves off. It's a matter of pride. He spoke of that. He admired it."

"And he said this to you."

Max nodded. "Yes."

"Would you consider being a witness at Angel's trial? To testify to what he said to you about suicide?"

188

Max Webster frowned. "Do you really think he might have killed himself?"

"I think it's a good possibility."

He paused, thinking, then he spoke. "That's about all I could testify to, is what he told me about his ideas on suicide."

"When was the last time you talked to him about it?"

"That night."

"What night?"

"The night he died. I was the last one around here when he left. He talked about it then, before he went home."

14

I RETURNED TO MY CAR IN THE PARKING LOT OUTSIDE the administration building. A big Cadillac pulled in next to my old Ford. The driver hopped out, glanced my way, then at the Ford. He was about my age, blond but tan as an old walnut. He wore white sailor's jeans and a tailored pullover with one of those little decorator animals over the left breast. I could read the frank appraisal in his eyes. He instantly dismissed me as someone not worth his attention.

His passenger climbed out of the Cadillac, but much more slowly. I recognized Amos Gillespie, the man who was about to become the owner of the Harwell Company.

He looked even thinner than he had at the funeral home. He flipped away the stub of a cigarette and smiled.

"Well, we meet again. You're Angel's lawyer, right?"

"Charley Sloan," I said.

He turned to the driver. "Go on in, Cecil," he said to the driver. "I'll be there in a minute."

Then he looked at me. "That's Cecil Benton, the current king of boat racing. I use him as a spokesman for our product, and," he chuckled, "as a part-time chauffeur."

Gillespie lit another cigarette. "How's it going with little Angel? She got a chance now?"

"I think so."

He nodded. "What brings you out here?"

"Just checking a few things."

"Like what?"

"Mr. Gillespie, how did Harrison Harwell seem to you when you were negotiating to buy his company?"

"How do you mean?"

"Mentally. I think he may have committed suicide."

Gillespie took a deep drag on the cigarette, his eyes fixed on mine. Then he spoke, smoke wisping out with each word.

"Mostly the lawyers handled things. Harwell and I had very little personal contact. When we did, he was so pissed he could hardly talk. He was enraged about having to sell to me, like I told you at the funeral home, but I don't think he was the kind to kill himself over something like that. He liked himself too much."

"So you observed nothing unusual?"

He shrugged. "Harwell was a pompous pain in the neck, just like always. Same as his damn sister."

"She's suing you, I'm told."

"Until Friday, then both she and her lawsuit are going out on their ass."

"You sound very sure about that."

"It's strictly a nuisance thing. The woman has no legal standing. She owns a few shares of stock but that's all. She's asked for an injunction to stop the sale. She's not being hurt, nor is anyone else, so our lawyers say the court will toss her case out as soon as the motion is heard."

"If she's not hurt, why is she trying to stop the sale?"

The American Cancer Society's warnings hadn't made much of an impression on Amos Gillespie. He inhaled deeply enough on the cigarette to suck smoke down into his toes. Then he smiled.

"She hated Harrison while he was alive, and I think she hates him even more now that he's dead. It's like his dying robbed her of her revenge for being tossed out of the company. She'd dig him up and knock hell out of his corpse if she could. This lawsuit is a substitute for that. She wants the world to know what a jackass Harrison really was."

"That's her only reason?"

"Mostly. She hates Harrison's widow. I think she hates Angel too, although she makes a lot of mouth music about looking out for the kid's interests."

He flipped this cigarette away too. "She's a lot like Harrison, all puffed up with herself. That kind of misplaced pride can get you into big trouble if you aren't careful."

"Mr. Gillespie, would you like to help Angel?"

He shrugged. "I suppose I would if I could. Why?"

"Your testimony about Harrison Harwell's inflated sense of pride and how the sale was a crushing defeat for him might help convince the jury he did kill himself."

"I don't like to go to court, son. Even when you win, you get hurt."

"This would be just as a witness."

"When's the trial?"

"August."

"I really don't think you want me as a witness."

"Why?"

He chuckled. "Oh, I sure can lay it on about the crushing defeat stuff. Hell, I loved that. But if anyone asks me, I'd have to say I don't think Harrison killed himself. I doubt if you'd want that."

He was right. Still, it might be a good thing to have him in reserve. Just in case Max Webster wasn't enough.

"If it came down to it, would you testify?"

"Maybe. I'd have to check it out with my lawyers first."

"I could subpoena you. Then you'd have to."

"Don't you have enough enemies now?"

"What do you mean?"

"Robin Harwell's lawyer, for one. What's his name?"

"Nate Golden?"

He nodded. "Yeah, him. He's handling this injunction business. I've talked with him a few times. I gather he isn't your greatest fan."

"That's a pretty safe bet."

Gillespie laughed. "Yeah, it is. In fact, if I were you, I'd stick a pie plate over my ass. I don't know why, but this Golden really wants to carve you up. He will, if he gets the chance. Does that worry you?"

"Some."

He lit yet another cigarette. "That shows you got some smarts. A man should know who his enemies are so he can keep an eye on them. Well, I've got to tend to business."

"Thanks for your time."

He smiled. "I hope you can do something for Angel."

"So do I."

THERE were some messages on my answering machine when I got back to my office. One was from an insurance agent selling malpractice insurance. In the few seconds allowed on the tape for a recorded message he managed to squeeze in all the dreadful things that might happen to me if I was left without the protection of his company. I didn't call him back.

Two calls were from reporters. I jotted down the numbers.

Mary Beth Needham had called. Her recorded voice didn't sound as if it was anything urgent so I presumed it was just another attempt to enlist me as a secret source for her book. That was another call I didn't plan to return.

Mixed among the other messages were two from the same person, a young woman who sounded nervous and unsure, perhaps afraid. "I'm not any place where you can call me back," she said the first time. "I'll call again." She didn't leave a name. I didn't recognize the voice. Her second message was identical. Her tone had a haunting quality, the sound of someone who really needed help but was reluctant to ask.

A Mrs. Magdelan Freeman called. She said she wanted to retain me as her lawyer. Her I called immediately.

She answered and judging from her voice she was a very dignified older lady.

"This is Charles Sloan," I said. "What can I do for you, Mrs. Freeman?"

"Are you the lawyer on the television? The one defending the Harwell girl?"

"Yes."

"I saw you. I was very impressed. I need someone intelligent who knows how to handle himself in court."

"I try, Mrs. Freeman. What's this all about?"

"I know Angel Harwell. A very nice young lady. I'm sure she'd have the very best lawyer. That's why I picked you."

"You know Angel?"

"Yes. Mr. Sloan, I presume you know who Howard Hughes was?"

"Howard Hughes, the millionaire?"

"Billionaire," she corrected me.

"I know of him."

"He's very famous."

"Yes he is, or was."

"I'm his daughter," she said.

"I didn't know he had children."

"Just one. Me. But that's the problem."

"What is?"

"The people handling my father's estate deny that I'm his daughter. They don't want me to have the money, you see. Very greedy, don't you agree?"

"Sounds that way. Mrs. Freeman, how do you happen to know Angel Harwell?"

"Angel is a lovely girl. So pretty."

"Yes. But how do you know her?"

"We met at the hospital."

That figured.

"What hospital?"

"Buckingham. It's a lovely place. One of the nicest around. Very expensive. Of course we were on different floors."

"Buckingham." I was almost about to say mental hospital but I realized that would be a mistake. "They treat nervous disorders there, isn't that right?"

"Yes. Very nice people."

"Angel was a patient there when you met?"

"Yes. So was I. I've become a bit nervous since my husband died. He was president of Freeman Cement. Did you know him?"

"No. When did he pass away?"

"Twenty-five years ago, this coming November."

It was a long time to be nervous.

"I was on the second floor at Buckingham. I'm almost a regular there. Angel was up on four. Anyway, will you be able to take my case?"

"As you can imagine, Mrs. Freeman, I'm very busy with Angel's matter. I'm not taking any outside work at the moment."

194

"Oh, what a pity. Who should I go to?"

I had been so long away from a full-time law practice that I had forgotten the crazies. They were as much a part of life as lunch.

"Have you tried other lawyers?"

"Yes. Hundreds. None of them were able to do a thing."

"How about the attorney general?"

"Oh, yes, I tried there, but I don't think they believe me. I'm desperate, Mr. Sloan. I want this settled once and for all."

"How about the prosecutor?"

"The tall blond man who was on television, too?"

I smiled but tried to keep it out of my voice. "Yes, him. Mark Evola. Odd coincidence here, Mrs. Freeman. Evola is a leading Howard Hughes expert."

"Really? That's wonderful. Will he talk to me?"

"It will be difficult to get through to him, but just keep trying."

"Shall I say you told me to call?"

"No, Mrs. Freeman. He and I are opponents in this Harwell case and it would be unethical for me to recommend him. I'm doing this because I like you, but it will have to be our little secret, okay?"

It was a harmless prank. And it would give her something to do, something to nurture the delusion that apparently kept her going. She would probably drive Evola bananas. She was the kind who wouldn't take no for an answer. I tried to keep from laughing.

"You're a wonderful man, Mr. Sloan. I shall tell Angel that if I ever see her. Of course, we never saw the people on four much, so I don't know if she'd even remember me."

"What was up on four, Mrs. Freeman?"

"Oh, I would have thought you knew. That's where they kept the violent people. I heard Angel stabbed someone, or tried to. I didn't believe it, of course. She is just too pretty and too delicate to do something like that."

I no longer felt the urge to laugh.

MRS. Freeman's call reminded me that I had to prepare medical releases for Angel's signature.

The old typewriter in the reception area worked well enough, although it needed a new ribbon. I found some paper and began preparing a release form. It was tough going. I could remember the language, but my typing was two-fingered and not very accurate. I did it three times before I came up with something that looked reasonably professional.

Mitch's office had had everything necessary for running a modern law office: a copy machine, word processors, a fax, plus secretaries to run them. He had allowed me to use his equipment and people.

Now I had only the old typewriter.

I took the single-page form I had prepared down to the marine insurance office below me to beg some copies. It was our first formal meeting. If I had become a minor celebrity they didn't appear very impressed. The reception seemed a trifle chilly.

The office manager, a woman who looked like she'd been frozen in aspic, reluctantly made copies for me on their machine, but she let me know it was a one-time thing. She made it perfectly clear that the insurance office was not about to become my unofficial branch. She suggested that in the future I buy or rent any equipment I might need.

But at least I had the copies I needed. And she did have a point. I decided I would call an office-supply firm and arrange to rent some things. I climbed the outside steps back to my office.

I smelled her before I saw her. I hadn't locked the office; there was nothing worth stealing anyway. In the few brief minutes I had spent in the insurance office she had come up.

She was alone. Her perfume was expensive and it filled the air as if she had bathed in the stuff. She sat in an old chair in the reception room, as relaxed as if she owned the place.

"Do you remember me?" she asked.

"I always remember people who threaten me. You're Harrison Harwell's sister."

She nodded. "Nancy Harwell Somerset."

She was dressed in the best by the best, but those solid features, so much like her brother's, suggested an origin more peasant than patrician.

"Would you like to come into my office, Mrs. Somerset?"

If she was appalled by my drab surroundings she didn't show it.

"I may have been a bit harsh in the funeral home, Mr. Sloan. I was upset. Harrison was my only sibling." She didn't look or sound apologetic. "I presume you are still Angel's lawyer?"

"Yes."

"One of the reasons I'm here is to discuss Angel's case."

"Angel would appreciate your interest, Mrs. Somerset, but there isn't much I can tell you."

"You mean, there isn't much you will *tell* me."

I smiled. "Ethically I'm in no position to discuss very much, not even with Angel's relatives."

"She only has one blood relative," she said. "Me."

Nancy Harwell Somerset's features slowly took on the expression I remembered from Harwell's navy picture of himself, stern and challenging.

"I may be able to help," she said firmly.

"How?"

"I have brought suit to stop the sale of my father's company," she said.

"So I've heard. But how will that help Angel?"

"I'll come to that. It's important that I stop the sale. I want to preserve the company, Mr. Sloan, as much for Angel as for myself. I don't want it sold. That's the other reason I'm here. I want you to become my lawyer for that purpose."

"Who is representing you now?"

"The firm of Gallagher, Kalt, and Blum."

"High-priced and powerful," I said.

"High-priced," she said. "I'm not so sure about the power. They have been less than enthusiastic. I've been passed through the partners and turned over to a young associate. I don't think they have much confidence in what I've asked them to do."

She tried to smile, but apparently she did so so rarely that she couldn't remember how. The result was a kind of a constricted grimace. "I want you to take over the case. I think I have a proposition that will be advantageous to everyone concerned."

"Oh?"

"I have money, Mr. Sloan, more than enough to purchase the company."

"Have you made an offer?"

Her eyes were unique. They reminded me of the eyes of a snake looking for prey.

"I attempted to make an offer to buy the company, but only after my brother's death. Harrison never would have sold to me. When I did make the offer I was told the deal with Amos Gillespie had been approved by both corporate boards and the only thing needed to complete it was the signature of the parties. They refused to consider my bid."

"It's almost impossible to set aside a valid contract agreement, Mrs. Somerset, unless you can show fraud or something similar."

I leaned back in my tipsy chair. "Why are you so intent on buying the company?"

"It is my father's business."

"And that's your only interest, a sentimental one?"

The eyes narrowed slightly. "I wish to protect Angel."

"How would that help her?"

"What happens if she's convicted?"

I sighed. "The usual sentence, given all the circumstances, figured in time actually served, would be about eight years."

"No one can profit from murder. So, if Angel is convicted, that whore my brother married will get everything, and Angel nothing."

"So? If you bought the company, that wouldn't change anything. That law would apply to your purchase money the same as Gillespie's or anyone else's."

"I'd make arrangements. I'd keep the business away from that whore. I'd make a gift of it to Angel when she gets out."

"She's not in yet."

Those snakelike eyes glittered. "She will be."

"What makes you so sure?"

"She's been set up from the beginning. Her wonderful stepmother has orchestrated everything to make sure Angel will be convicted."

"I think you've got things backward. Robin Harwell has done everything in her power to protect Angel's interest."

"Like hiring you?"

The tone was intended to be insulting. It was.

"Am I mistaken? Didn't you just ask me to take your case?"

"Only because you are in a unique position. You have influence with my brother's widow. Use it. If she calls off the sale now, you'll be well paid."

"Mrs. Somerset, I think you've—"

"You aren't about to tell me what an honest and ethical lawyer you are, are you?" Her chuckle had a brittle, cutting sound, like breaking glass. "Frankly, I can't think of anyone with a law license who has a reputation as bad as yours. However, that doesn't matter. I'm a realist. Money talks, Mr. Sloan. You'll find I have a rather loud voice. You fix this with Robin Harwell and I'll make you rich."

"Fix it?"

"If she backs out of the sale now, it will collapse."

"Even if that were true, why would Robin Harwell want to do such a thing?"

"To keep my mouth shut."

"About what?"

Her expressionless mask reminded me of Angel for a moment. Then she spoke. "Family secrets."

"Like what?"

"Things my brother told me," she said.

"Mrs. Somerset, you and your brother were absolute enemies and had been for years. That's hardly the kind of relationship to foster secret-sharing, is it?"

"I know some rather surprising things." Those eyes didn't blink. "Mr. Sloan, I've asked you to become my lawyer. What is your answer?"

I smiled. "There's a rather obvious conflict of interest, between you and Angel. The answer is no."

"Do you know how much money is at stake in my father's business? Millions. You would be paid proportionally. I said you would be rich, and so you will, if you do as I ask."

"And fix the sale?"

"That is one way of putting it. You wouldn't have to represent me formally. It could be our little secret."

"You're fond of secrets. I'm sorry. No."

For a moment, the impression of a hunting snake seemed even stronger. "You are a fool, Mr. Sloan."

"Perhaps."

"You don't know Robin as I do. She will see that Angel is convicted. You weren't selected at random, you know. I'm sure you're part of her plan. Perhaps you're in it with her. If you aren't, I'd be quite worried if I were you."

"Why?"

"If Angel didn't kill Harrison, then who?"

"Robin? Do you have any proof?"

"Will you do as I ask?"

"No."

She stood up and looked down at me. "You are indeed a fool, Mr. Sloan. And you are in way over your head. I can't pity a fool but I do pity poor Angel."

She walked quickly out but with surprising athletic grace.

The slithering was only in my imagination.

I BROUGHT the release forms to Angel to sign. She and Robin had been sun-bathing.

At forty-seven I don't consider myself an old geezer, but today's bathing suits aren't anything like I remember as a boy, and I lived in a pretty advanced neighborhood.

The amount of cloth used for either Robin's or Angel's suit wouldn't have been enough to make a pocket handkerchief. I tried not to look, or to look like I wasn't looking.

Angel's body was like polished marble, perfect. Robin was different, but not bad different. Hers had an earthy suggestion of ripeness not found in statues. The two of them, nearly naked, were like the difference between perfection and reality. A smart person would choose reality, since perfection is often nothing more than a tormenting illusion.

I tried not to look.

We were once again in the atrium. A table had been brought by the maid so Angel could sign the forms.

"Why so many?" she asked, thumbing through.

"It's always best to have more than you need. You never know when you'll need an extra one."

She began to sign. Her signature was slow and deliberate, not the usual scrawl most of us use.

"I'll need that list of doctors and hospitals where you've been treated. I'm chiefly interested in anyone who might have treated you for emotional problems."

"I'm not insane." Angel spoke in a conversational tone as she continued signing.

"Of course you aren't," Robin said. "Charley just wants to know the names of the doctors who've seen you.

"It began," Robin said, "when Angel went off to New York."

"My father said I ran away," Angel said evenly. "I was old enough to vote but he still considered me a child."

I thought Robin was beginning to look uncomfortable. "Angel was arrested by the police there," she said.

"Arrested?"

Robin looked at Angel, then me. "The arrest was for performing as a nude dancer. Harrison saw to it that it was dropped."

"It was for prostitution," Angel said, again without emotion. "I worked for a Forty-second–Street place. Some of the girls did more than dance for the freaks who came to see us. I didn't but the police said I did. Anyway, there was general hell to pay when my father came up to New York."

"Angel was put into a New York hospital until she agreed to go to a youth center in Hawaii," Robin said quietly.

"It was called Island Clouds, the place. It was mostly for kids who had drug problems, mostly rich kids who had been shipped out by their parents. I was there a couple of months. It wasn't bad but it was still a hospital," Angel said as she continued to sign. "It's on Maui. If it's still there. They were about to sell it to a Japanese firm as a vacation spot for their workers."

"And after Hawaii?" I asked.

Angel began a recitation of doctors she had seen. She seemed to remember everything, including dates and addresses. I wrote it all down as she talked.

"You forgot the place in Georgia," Robin prompted.

"The Brooke Center in Macon, Georgia," Angel said. "It's a glorified drunk tank for rich people."

I knew about drunk tanks.

"Were you having problems with drugs or alcohol?"

She shook her head. "I was the only person in the place who wasn't. They put me there to get me away from"—she paused, looked at Robin—"from family."

"Things were getting a bit hectic," Robin said. "The doctor thought it might help if Angel got away for a while."

"Did it?" I looked at Angel.

Those icy blue eyes held no clue to her thoughts. We might as well have been talking about last year's fashions. "I spent six weeks at the place. It was like prison, only with waiters and physical fitness advisors. There was only one other young person there, a girl from Chicago who was coming off cocaine. She followed me around like a puppy, although I really didn't like her. I didn't like the place. If it did me any good, I wasn't aware of it."

Robin smiled nervously. "Harrison wasn't pleased at her progress so he took Angel out."

"And after that?" I asked.

Robin smiled. "That's all the hospitals."

I looked at Angel. She nodded her assent.

They hadn't mentioned Buckingham, the local mental health farm. I wondered if Mrs. Freeman might have had the same kind of delusion about Angel that she had about being the daughter of Howard Hughes. If not, they were lying to me.

"No other hospitals? Even up here in Michigan?"

They both nodded.

If they were lying it would be easy enough to find out. One of the release forms would go to Buckingham.

I looked at my notes. The information was skimpy but it was enough to start with.

"That's all of it," Robin said. "Oh, there were a few other doctors, but for sore throats, colds, that sort of thing."

Neither of them had specified the problem that caused Angel to be hospitalized and treated by the psychiatrists.

I decided not to ask. The information I needed would be in the reports.

"I'll contact the places I can," I said. "After I get everything together, plus the results of the testing to be done here, I'll be in a position to go over it with you, Angel."

"We'll be leaving Friday for Sheridan Key," Angel said. "As soon as I've talked to this psychiatrist you want me to see." She paused. "I really think all this is unnecessary, Charley."

"It may be," I said. "But we want to cover every base."

Robin reached over and tenderly stroked her stepdaughter's arm. Despite her beauty and stony poise, Angel reacted to the touching like an affection-starved child. I wondered what her life had really been like. She looked at me with those startling blue eyes. "Do you think you'll really come down and visit us, Charley? I'd like that," she said.

202

Robin, I noted, said nothing.

"We'll see." I got up to leave.

I had almost become used to their lack of clothing, but not quite.

If they were lying to me I would find out.

And if they were, I wondered why.

15

MY LIFE WAS CHANGING. WHEN I CAME HOME A MOV-
ing van was pulled up in front of one of the corner apartments and
furniture was being carted out. I had no idea who was moving. I
didn't know any of my neighbors in the small apartment complex.
I did know that corner apartments were much larger than mine,
had two bedrooms, but cost a hundred and a half per month more
than my place.

I was in the bucks now so I called the mean old woman who ran
the place and asked to rent the apartment being vacated.

If I had asked to ravage her daughter I'm sure she wouldn't
have been half as nasty. She tried to work me for more than the
usual rent, but I held firm. Finally, reluctantly, she agreed to let
me have the place. But she let me know the apartment company
wasn't going to waste any money on new paint, not for me, not at
those prices.

I didn't have much furniture, so moving everything a few yards
down wouldn't be much of a job. I would need to buy a few more
things. It wouldn't be a big change, the view would be the same,
but I thought having a larger place might be good for my morale.

I thought about getting rid of my old Ford for the same reason,
but a new car could wait. The make and model I might buy could
be upgraded considerably if the Harwell case went well. If it
didn't, the Ford would have to do.

I had been sober now for a very long stretch. But after all that time the end of the day was still the worst. I even found myself nostalgic about it, remembering how it felt then to go home to the wife or girlfriend of the moment, kick off the Gucci shoes, and sip icy martinis or margaritas.

But I had to content myself with diet soda. I poured some into a plastic kitchen glass over ice, stuck a frozen dinner in the oven, and flipped on the television to catch the news.

The Harwell case wasn't mentioned. A minor movie star had killed himself. Clips of his old movies and a shot of a morgue wagon driving away from the crowd gathered in front of his Hollywood home had apparently replaced any need for an update on the *people* versus *Angel Harwell*. Oddly, I felt a tinge of disappointment.

The phone rang while I was dipping the cardboardlike veal patty into the cottonlike mashed potatoes. Everything was hot on the outside, but still frozen in places on the inside. I had not yet mastered the mysteries of the microwave.

I swallowed as best I could, sipped the soda to wash it down, and answered the phone.

"Hey, Charley, it's Sidney Sherman. Did I catch you at a bad time?"

"I'm here in bed with a beautiful naked woman who was about to demonstrate how remarkably imaginative her lips could be. Thank God you called, Sid. What's up?"

He chuckled, but he was only being polite. "Nothing dramatic, but I thought you should know what we've come up with so far. I tried your office but all I got was the machine."

"So?"

"Little Angel's no dummy. We got her grades from the time she was in kindergarten up through high school. Thirteen years of school and almost nothing but straight A's. At least until her last year in high school. She transferred from a tony private place to a local Florida school for that last year. She dropped down to a few B grades. She started missing classes then. Maybe she got too interested in the beach and boys. Who knows?"

"How about college?"

"Never went, as far as we can find out. The records show she applied and was accepted by a number of colleges, good ones, but she must have changed her mind."

205

"How about behavior problems in school?"

He paused. "There were some, I think."

"You think?"

"Charley, I do a lot of this stuff, and I know from school records. We search them for a number of reasons. Something is very screwy with your Angel. All the records are straight arrow until she hits high school. Then, after a year or so, pages turn up missing. Her grades are okay, except for missed tests, but I think someone got rid of the records of something they considered detrimental."

"Are you sure?"

His sigh carried an offended tone, as if I had just insulted his competence. "Nothing's ever sure, Charley. But it looks that way to me. People do that sometimes, you know. Edit school records."

"Why?"

"Mostly to clear something that might cause a college to turn someone down, or the army. Or maybe an incident that could screw up employment later. You know, like being caught smoking dope in the john, things like that."

"Did your people find anything of that kind?"

"No. Just the missing places where the pages used to be. We tried to cross-check to see if any copies existed. They don't."

"It could be something trivial, Sid."

"If it was, why do it? But whoever did it did a good job," he said. "On another front, my people down in Florida are getting everything concerning that divorce that was supposed to be in the works."

"And?"

"I'll have more for you, but it does look like everything was about to be filed. We'll find out, but we have to sort of work around the lawyer down there. I don't think you need to know how, okay?"

"Try to stay out of jail, Sid."

"Always," he laughed. "By the way, I think the Harwells may have entered into a prenuptial agreement?"

"In Michigan?"

"As far as I can find out so far, no. The damn things are nearly worthless in Michigan, as we both know. Apparently, Harwell had

206

the new bride sign one in Florida, where it's done daily. They're enforceable there. Those old folks down in the Sunshine State want to keep everything for their own kids before they climb into the sack with another surviving ancient "

"So, what's in this agreement?"

"I don't know. We can find out, eventually, but it'll cost. Why don't you just ask the widow for a copy of the thing, if there is one? It might be her most treasured possession."

I thought about it for a moment. "I'll ask, Sid, but to be safe, see if your people can get a copy."

"Don't you trust her?"

"This is going to trial, Sid. Everyone always tries to present his best side. I've learned you can't trust anyone completely in these circumstances. Some have even been known to lie."

"Even private investigators?"

"Especially them."

IT had been a typical evening at home for me. First, I watched a little television. I like flicking around the cable channels with the remote control. It's like fishing: occasionally you hook into something good. But I found nothing to my liking.

Books, thank God for them. I read a little, but my concentration wandered. I was working on three at once, a mystery, a thriller, and a biography. I sampled them all, but none provided the usual magic.

Finally I went to bed.

The call came at a few minutes after one.

In the old days I would never have had a listed home phone number. I was above that then. But not now. Now I welcomed the business, no matter what the hour. Mostly, I got the drunk drivers who had been locked up after turning the wrong way into a one-way street or doing one of the other erratic things drunks do with their vehicles, sometimes fatally.

Something in his voice blew sleep away. I guessed him to be fifty or sixty from the sound. Speaking as if he was on the lip of anger, he said he was Dominick Farley, a foreman in the Harwell plant, a man of substance. He said he associated my name with the defense of murder.

Sounding barely under control, he told me his daughter, Mary

207

Zekia, a married woman of twenty-nine, had just killed her two children, a boy and girl, ages six and three. Her husband had come home from work—he worked the afternoon shift at a small local factory—and discovered the bodies. The woman was being held by police. Her father asked me to do what I could for her.

I drove over to the home where the killings had occurred. It was a typical Pickeral Point house, a small one-storey frame ranch, a little seedy, with some junk lying around the garage and a snowmobile propped up and covered.

The outside lights were on so I could see everything. Numerous police cars, both city and sheriff, were parked at angles in front of the small house. One car, a sheriff's patrol car, was empty but its rotating overhead lights were on, painting the night with pulsating slashes of strobe-light red.

Neighbors, some in pajamas, stood in little groups, silently watching the house. Every light in the house was on.

I walked up. A squat man in running pants and a sports jacket was sitting on the porch smoking a cigarette. He watched my approach.

I recognized him as I got closer. He was Stash Olesky, Evola's number-one murder prosecutor. The outside lights cast shadows on his wide cheekbones and deep-set eyes, making him look like a sinister actor in an old Russian movie.

"What's up, Sloan?"

"The woman's father called me," I said.

He nodded slowly, as if I had just told him the true meaning of life.

He stood up and flicked the cigarette away. It made a red arc against the night sky. "C'mon."

Inside, the place was awash with cops.

"They just took the bodies away," he said. He led me past a tiny kitchen. It looked as if someone had dropped a can of red paint, but, of course, it wasn't paint. Someone had chalked the outline of a small body on the linoleum.

"She chased the little boy in here," he said quietly. "Slashed and stabbed the kid. Ugly stuff."

Then he led me to a bathroom. Here, it looked like red spray paint.

"The little girl, the baby, got it here. It wasn't quick." He nod-

208

ded toward one small red hand print on the wall. I felt my stomach churn.

"We got the husband in the back bedroom. His brother is on the way from Lansing."

"Any chance that the husband was in on it?" I asked.

He shook his head. "None."

The husband was small, thin, with worn hands. He clearly earned his bread with those hands. He looked at me as if he was embarrassed, as if the house needed straightening, or the yard. He talked as if he had been in an accident, lucid but stunned. His wife had wanted him to get a different job, he said. She wanted to move. She was afraid of being alone at night, and she had become increasingly nervous. But, there had been no warning. . . .

I walked out of the place with Olesky.

"We have the woman at Buckingham Hospital. They'll move her to the Port Huron psychiatric unit in the morning. I talked to her, she's crazy as hell."

"I assume you won't prosecute."

Stash smiled wryly. "We have to, Sloan. The doctors will pump the poor creature full of narcotics, say she's better, and let her go. We have to go through the charade of a formal charge just to keep her in custody."

"But . . ."

He sighed and lit another cigarette. "Hey, this is one you can't lose. She is absolutely insane. All we want to do is make sure she doesn't get out until she really recovers. If such a thing is possible."

"It was terrible in there," I said.

He grunted. "You should have seen the bodies."

"Can I talk to her?"

"It won't do much good. She's living in some other world, but I'll call over there and clear the way if you like."

"I'd appreciate it."

"You know, I wish I hadn't come out here tonight," he said. "Sometimes you see things no human was ever meant to see."

BUCKINGHAM Hospital had almost completely shut down for the night, but they let me in and led me to the floor and the room where my new client was being held.

A young uniformed sheriff's deputy nodded as I went in.

She wasn't alone. A nurse sat next to the bed in the half-darkened room. I stood close by.

"She has enough stuff in her to knock down an elephant," the nurse whispered. "But she's as bright as a penny."

The rails of her bed had been raised and her wrists had been tied to the rails with bandage. She half-smiled up at me. Only one word is needed to describe her condition: madness.

She was twenty-nine but she looked fifteen. Like her husband, she was thin and small. She seemed almost lost in the hospital gown they had tied around her. Her face was almost beautiful, with large eyes and a wide, full-lipped mouth. In the dim light I thought her hair was either light brown or blonde. She wore it short and it was disheveled.

"Mrs. Zekia," I said, speaking softly, "My name is Charley Sloan. I'm a lawyer. Your father asked me to represent you. Do you know why you're here?"

The smile broadened. "I put my dollies to sleep," she said in a quiet voice.

Her eyes were fixed on mine with a kind of childish interest.

"Mrs. Zekia, are you feeling all right?"

"Oh, yes."

The bland smile, so coyly innocent, annoyed me. I suppose that's why I asked the question.

"Mrs. Zekia, you said you put your dollies to sleep. Do you remember exactly what happened?"

At first I thought she hadn't heard me, then those two eyes grew even larger. It seemed like slow motion. As her eyes widened, her mouth formed into a perfectly round O, enlarging, like her eyes, until her lips were drawn white and her eyeballs seemed like they might pop from her head.

Then the sound began.

It started low and deep, like a rumble of distant thunder, but it increased in sound and scale until it filled the room and then the hospital with a shriek that seemed to come from hell itself.

She strained against the restraints as she continued screaming; her bed was shaking violently when the nurse shoved me out of the room.

A doctor, very young, very self-important, hurried down the hall toward the screaming. I stopped him.

"That's my client, Mrs. Zekia," I said.

He scowled at me, his eyes stern and unfriendly.

"You had better take further precautions," I said. "She killed her children. I'm afraid she might try to kill herself."

"You mind your business," he snapped, "we'll mind ours."

He pushed past me.

I walked away. The scream followed me down the hall, down the stairs. It seemed to follow me out into the parking lot.

I drove away. I couldn't get the sound out of my head. And I couldn't believe Angel Harwell might once have been a patient at such a place.

If there was ever a time I needed a drink, this was it. I slowed as I approached a bar. It was almost closing time but a few cars were still parked in front.

My hands were shaking. I think that's why I didn't stop. I didn't want anyone to see me in that condition. Vanity can sometimes be a virtue.

I didn't go into my apartment when I got home but sat in the darkened car for a minute. The screams continued to echo in my imagination.

Tomorrow I would go through the formality of filing an appearance as her defense attorney. Olesky was right, handling the case wouldn't be difficult. Still, I wished her father had called someone else.

I couldn't help conjuring up what the last minutes had been like for those two children. I tried to push the thought out of my mind and think of something else. I tried imagining the last few minutes of Harrison Harwell's life. If he had been a suicide, did he think about what might happen when they found him? If his daughter had killed him, what did he think as the sharp blade sliced into him? A child killing a parent. Was that so different from a parent killing a child?

Madness.

SLEEP wouldn't come. Every time I closed my eyes I saw that blood-stained kitchen and bath. I would visualize those widening eyes and hear that terrible never-ending scream.

I got up and watched an old movie on television for a while, but it didn't calm my restlessness. I tried reading but that too was impossible.

I was tired so I lay down again and tried to occupy my mind with other things. I left the light on. It made me feel less alone.

Even summoning up fond memories didn't help much. I thought about the beach in Hawaii, alcohol-drenched honeymoon number three, as much of it as I could recall. Sex and booze seemed to have formed the core of my early life. Now, I had sworn off one and saw very little of the other.

The memory of those screams kept creeping back into my consciousness.

So I went back to something I seldom thought of anymore—past courtroom battles, including triumphs and defeats. I could remember my first jury trial in such detail that the faces of the twelve jurors emerged like characters in a Rembrandt painting, every feature clear, their eyes on me.

Even the sounds of that courtroom came flooding back, the muted coughing, the scrape of chairs, the squeaking of the judge's chair as he rocked slowly back and forth.

And the waiting for the verdict. You always remember that. I could recall vividly the sound of the courtroom clock. I suppose that's when I finally fell asleep.

I WAS already half awake when the phone rang. I glanced at the clock radio. It was a few minutes before seven.

I rolled over and picked up the phone. "Hello," I said.

For a moment there was no response. I thought it was just a misdial. Then he spoke.

"This is Dominick Farley," he said. "I called last night, about my daughter, Mary."

"Yes, Mr. Farley. I went over to the hospital and talked briefly with your daughter. I talked with the assistant prosecutor who will be in charge of the case. I'll know more later today."

"That won't be necessary," he said.

I assumed he had reconsidered his choice of attorneys.

"No problem, Mr. Farley," I said.

"She's dead."

"Pardon me?"

"She's dead," he repeated in a flat tone, drained of all emotion. "The hospital just called."

"How did it happen?"

212

"They say she hung herself." This time his voice trembled as he spoke the words. "She was left unattended to take a shower, they said. Just for a minute. She made a noose of a hospital gown and hung herself in the shower." His voice trailed off.

"Do you want me to look into it, Mr. Farley?"

"I don't understand?"

"If the hospital was negligent, there might be a cause for action. The cases are called wrongful death actions and they—"

"No." The single word was spoken with a quiet firmness. "No, this has to stop somewhere." I heard him breathe deeply, then he continued. "You talked to Mary last night?"

"Yes."

"I called the hospital last night but they said I couldn't see her." He paused. "How did she seem to you?"

I knew what he wanted, so I gave it to him.

"To be brutally frank, Mr. Farley, she was completely insane. She didn't know who she was or what had happened. How she managed to hang herself, I don't know. It might even have been an accident. She was completely out of her mind. She wasn't responsible, Mr. Farley. It's terrible but it happens to people sometimes. It's like getting hit by lightning. There's just no explaining it."

I could hear his labored breathing. "She was such a good daughter, never any trouble. She loved her children—" And then he started to cry.

"There was no help for it, Mr. Farley. Something snapped. It wasn't her fault."

"You may be right," he said slowly, trying to control himself. "I appreciate your help, Mr. Sloan. What do I owe you?"

"Nothing, Mr. Farley. I didn't do anything."

"But you went to the hospital last night—"

"There's no charge, Mr. Farley."

"Will you come to her funeral?" he asked quietly. "I don't think many people will, not after what happened."

"I'll be there." I thought about telling him how sorry I was, but that seemed unnecessary.

His breathing sounded even louder. "You're a good man, Mr. Sloan."

I hadn't heard that for a while.

16

IT WAS THURSDAY NIGHT. THURSDAY NIGHT MEANT the meeting of the Club. No one had to tell me how important the weekly meeting was. It was an anchor in the stream. Lately my stream had become much more turbulent, so I knew it was time to set my anchor firmly.

I had missed the last two meetings and I was determined not to miss another.

I was late so I pushed the old Ford harder than it deserved up the main northeast artery in and out of Detroit. I kept an eye peeled for the state cops who patrolled I-94 for road crazies.

The meeting had started by the time I made my way down the stairs to the church basement. I smiled a greeting to those who looked my way. The usual suspects were in attendance, plus some people I didn't recognize. Like most newcomers, they looked nervous, ashamed, and ready to run for the door.

Nobody likes to admit he's an alcoholic, but that's what you eventually have to do.

Our group, the regular Club members, were comfortable with each other the way old loose clothes are comfortable. The reading of the twelve steps progressed. The meeting was like church for me, although the members were usually as boisterous and contentious in this basement as they had been long ago in saloons. Despite the easy rowdiness, I always felt an inward calm, both physical and spiritual. I drew strength from the others present, knowing that here, at least, I was in control of myself.

As usual, after the meeting everyone gathered around the big coffee urn and knocked back the liquid caffeine as if it was vodka.

Bob Williams, looking like a well-tailored mountain, stood talking to a small elderly woman who could have stepped out of a Norman Rockwell painting. Mary Ricci had that serene face, that placid air that Rockwell liked to evoke for holiday illustrations—grandma bringing in the turkey.

Mary was a white-haired grandmother, but the similarities stopped there. She ran one of the toughest bars in Detroit, a place where even a Hell's Angel would get nervous. She took it over after her fourth husband died following a fight in the joint. She ran it even after she quit drinking. Mary admitted that she had worked her way up to two quarts of the hard stuff a day by then. But her past didn't show in her gentle face. She would have stumped any panel on the old *What's My Line* show.

Mary giggled at something Bob Williams said, then waved good night and made her way out. Thursday night was always a busy one at her bar. Every night was.

I grabbed a cup of coffee and walked over to Williams.

"Were you hitting on Mary just now?" I asked.

"Widows are known to be mad for sex," he replied evenly. "And that's not just my opinion. Ask any of my fellow psychiatrists. However, I was not hitting on Mary, for two very good reasons."

Playing straight man for the doctor, I asked, "And they are?"

"First, she's twenty years older than I am. Despite Ben Franklin's advice, older women don't move me. At least not when they are that much older."

He came as close to a smile as he ever did. "Second, she's tougher than I am, a lot tougher. If I said stop, how do I know she would?"

"Good point. Speaking of the ladies. How did Angel do today?"

The look he gave me was inscrutable. His eyes, emotionless, peered down at me. For a moment, he reminded me of Angel.

"She performed all the tests," he said. "The psychologist brought the results over just before I came down here. I glanced through them."

"So?"

"There are some surprises, Charley. I hope I'll know more after I talk to her tomorrow."

"What kind of surprises?"

"Let's hold off until I have a chance to see her. Now, she's just a bunch of test results to me. I prefer to see the lady herself before I start interpreting what those results might show."

"How accurate are these tests?"

He paused for a moment. "Ever take them, Charley?"

I laughed. "Sure. When the court sent me in to dry out they ran me through everything before assigning me a bed. I don't remember much. It was all a jumble then, to tell you the truth."

"There are three main areas of testing," he said, as if lecturing a child. "We test the subject's intelligence. When appropriate, we may test for aptitude. We didn't do that with Angel, just the standard IQ test. We call that an objective test."

He nodded to a member of the Club who was leaving, then directed his attention back to me. "When the clinic took you in, they probably had you do a test called the Minnesota Multiphasic Personality Inventory, the old MMPI. It's multiple-choice questions. You mark the answer you think is closest to the truth for you. We use it to test personality and behavior. It's one of a group we call subjective tests. Actually, it's my personal favorite.

"The last area is projective testing, stick-figure drawings and the like. Depending on how these tests are given, you can tell a great deal about how a patient's mind works."

"How did Angel do?"

One eyebrow raised up in a silent objection. "Tomorrow, Charley. I'll tell you tomorrow. But don't be misled, these tests are only tools. Sometimes they work well, sometimes not at all. The results can vary with how a patient is feeling at the time, or sometimes even with how the examiner is feeling."

"Whatever happened to the feathers and bones you guys used to use for diagnostics?"

There wasn't a flicker of a reaction, none. "Most physicians don't use those methods anymore," he said sternly. He paused, then continued in a whisper. "Of course, I still do, but don't tell anyone. People have odd ideas about psychiatrists as it is."

He chuckled, amused at his own joke.

"By the way," I said. "I sent a medical release to Buckingham Hospital. It's not on the list of places Angel gave me, but I think there's a chance she might have spent some time there recently."

216

"For what?"

"I don't know. Perhaps Angel will tell you."

He shook his head. "Charley, let's be clear on my function. You want my opinion as to the state of Angel Harwell's mental health. That's what you'll get. But it would defeat that purpose if you expected me to act as some kind of back-door investigator for you."

"Well, it may come up. Buckingham, I mean."

"We'll see," he said. "You drove down?"

I nodded.

"Do you think that decrepit old car will make it all the way back or would you like me to drive behind you?"

"I'll take my chances. Call you tomorrow."

He left. I stayed behind to talk with some of the other Club members who like me, seemed reluctant to leave.

We talked, laughed, joked. None of us talked about the problem that had brought us all together. We stood around the coffee urn. Most of the lights in the basement had been turned off. Only the light above the coffee table remained. Everything else was in deep shadow.

I was reminded of paintings of cowboys gathered around the comfort and protection of a campfire, a light that kept the lurking dangers of the night at bay.

This really wasn't all that different.

FRIDAY morning was as humid as the tropics. The air was sticky the way it usually is before a bank of thunderstorms rolls in. Until the storms hit, everyone moved slowly, even in air-conditioned buildings.

My new office had an ancient window air conditioner. It worked surprisingly well, although it was loud as an outboard motor. I had to cup my free hand over my exposed ear to hear telephone conversations.

Dan Conroy called from the *Detroit News*. He was their number-one reporter and he asked me some questions about the case, but I got the impression that wasn't the real reason he was calling.

"Charley, I take it you know who Mary Beth Needham is?"

217

"I've met the lady. She tells me she's doing a book about the Harwell case."

"She's pretty good at what she does. She really digs into things."

"So?"

"I thought I'd tip you off, she's been doing some digging here in Detroit about you."

"Since I'm the defense lawyer, I suppose that's to be expected."

"Maybe, maybe not. She's been nosing around, looking at old clips about you. Talking to people, lots of people."

I could hear him lighting a cigarette. "And she's been hanging around the courts, too. From what I hear, she's been talking to a lot of people who aren't your greatest fans."

"Like who?"

"Judge Regan, for instance."

"Oh, shit!"

Judge Arthur Regan hated me. It had begun when he was an assistant prosecutor and I had beaten him in several high-profile cases. It continued after his election to Detroit's recorder's court, and later when he was appointed to the federal bench. I had tried cases before him in both courts. If hostility was liquid I would have drowned. Regan liked to think he was on the inside of things. He was the type who whispered about the scandalous "real" facts, which he usually had wrong. I could imagine what he had whispered in Needham's eager little ear.

"She's talked to one of your ex-partners," Conroy said.

"Wiener?"

Conroy chuckled. "He likes to tell people you were responsible for him doing time and being disbarred."

"I had nothing to do with that. His problem was trying to cheat the IRS, not to mention our clients, and me. He got caught. I tried to help him but the case they had on him was airtight. He's nuts if he says it was my fault. How come you know all this, Dan?"

"The little lady talked to me, too. Hey, she's got a few miles on her but she's still kind of cute. She uses her allure rather well, I thought. Anyway, based on what she said and what I found out it looks like she's going to try and nail your ass in that book of hers. I thought you should know."

218

"Thanks."

"Why don't you take her out and give her a jump, Charley? Then, if she rips into you, you can scream that she's a disenchanted lover, something like that." He chuckled. "Of course, she's probably too smart for that, but you could give it a shot."

"When you went to school, Dan, what kind of marks did you get in your journalism ethics class?"

"I flunked." I could hear him suck on the cigarette. "Anyway, when this Harwell thing starts to heat up keep me in mind, eh?"

"Did she talk to Squint Kelley?"

Conroy sighed. "He was among the first. Take care, Charley." He hung up.

Squint owned Harp's, the bar where I used to hang out and regularly disgrace myself. Squint loved me, the way drunks love drunks, and he kept enlarging those old stories about my escapades and polishing them until they gleamed.

I could just imagine how he loved having Mary Beth Needham's full attention. Squint, who never drew a sober breath, wouldn't have even noticed that her little tape recorder was running.

I DROVE over to the Harwell place. My next car would definitely have to have air conditioning. Even with the windows open my Ford felt like an oven and my body was soon as hot as a roasting squab. There were few cars on the road; not even the tourists were out.

The Harwell home was pleasantly air-conditioned. My wet shirt clung like gooey plaster as Dennis Bernard guided me into a small sitting room near the front door.

Robin and Angel were there, bags packed and dressed to travel, both attired in light summer dresses that seemed more like colored clouds than fabric. The women could have been models about to go on a photo shoot.

"I'm so glad you came, Charley," Robin said. "We wanted to say good-bye but things got so busy we just couldn't find time."

"You could come with us if you wanted to," Angel said.

"I have things to do here," I said, "mostly to do with you. How did things go with Doctor Williams?"

"What's his problem?" Angel asked, one eyebrow rising over her expressionless features.

"What do you mean?"

"Christ, it was like talking to a rock. You didn't tell me he was so big."

"Big psychiatrist, small psychiatrist, I don't think that makes a difference, do you?"

"I found him intimidating. I don't think you're going to like whatever he has to say about me."

"Why not?"

She looked at Robin and then again at me. "He doesn't like me."

"How do you figure that?"

"He was cold, right from the start. He didn't believe me most of the time. I could tell by the way he asked his questions."

I sighed. "Angel, his purpose was to test you, not charm you."

"He's a pedophile," she said.

"What do you mean?"

"He gets his sexual kicks from little kids. He kept asking me about my childhood. He always came back to that, no matter what else we were talking about. I mean, really. I think if I had showed up in a little girl's dress and pigtails he would have raped me."

Robin laughed.

"Did he talk about the psychological tests you took yesterday?"

"Not directly, except he showed me the drawings I had made and asked me to explain them. Again, he loved it when I talked about little girls. I think he probably hangs around school yards. He's that type, Charley. Where did you find this guy?"

I decided that telling them we met at an Alcoholics Anonymous meeting wouldn't do much to bolster their confidence in my selection of an expert.

"He's a leader in his field," I said. "How long did he spend with you?"

"About two hours. I think he even canceled another appointment to continue. He did some of that whispering doctors do with their secretaries. Anyway, it was a long two hours for me. I certainly hope that's the end of that kind of thing."

"Did he go over the times you were hospitalized?"

Angel nodded. "It's easier to talk about what he didn't go over." She smiled that peculiar emotionless smile. "Charley, you need a vacation. Come with us, at least for a week or two."

Robin smiled too, but I thought hers lacked enthusiasm. "You'd be more than welcome," she said politely.

"I can't," I said.

I wondered if I imagined that Robin seemed relieved.

"We're going to have Bernard and his wife stay up here since we'll be coming back for the trial," Robin said. "I've instructed him to make this place available to you whenever you need it. I've left the numbers where we can be reached with him."

"Numbers?"

She smiled. "Our house down in Sheridan Key, obviously. But we belong to clubs there, too. Bernard has those numbers, just in case."

"Will you visit us?" Angel asked.

"Maybe. It depends on how things go here."

"It's different down there," Angel said quietly. "You make your own rules, Charley. Nobody cares what you do. Doesn't that sound appealing?"

It did, but I didn't want to admit it. "What happened with the court case?" I asked Robin.

She shrugged. "I don't know why Nate Golden wanted me there. It took all of ten minutes. Just as Nate said, the lawyers for both sides spoke and then the judge threw Nancy's case out."

"Was she angry?"

"She wasn't even there. I think she knew what was going to happen anyway."

"How's my greatest living fan?"

"Nate?"

"He loves me."

Robin chuckled. "Nothing's changed there. He still insists that Angel get another lawyer."

"He can go to hell," Angel said evenly.

"Nate was a great help," Robin said. "There were a number of reporters there. I suppose because of the case up here. Anyway, Nate talked to them and kept them away from me."

"So, the sale to Gillespie is still on?"

Robin nodded. "Yes. It's just paper-shuffling from here on, according to Nate. The payment will be made later, probably in September. Gillespie is doing that for some tax reason. Nate says it has to do with an accounting period. He tried to explain but I really didn't understand the details."

"We're going to miss our plane," Angel said.

"We do have to leave, Charley." Robin turned to Angel. "Honey, I think I left our tickets on my bed. Could you run up and get them?"

Angel nodded and hurried out.

Robin waited until she was out of earshot, then spoke. "I'm sorry we haven't had any time together. I've thought about it a lot, though. I hope you realize that."

"Me too."

She smiled. "Good thoughts?"

"Depends. If you count erotic, yes."

"Me too." She paused. "Will you come to see us?"

"That depends, too. I'm working hard on Angel's case. These cases sometimes assume a life of their own. It's like wrestling Jell-O. There's just no place to grab hold."

"Will you need money?"

"Maybe. If I do, I'll let you know."

Angel came back in.

"I couldn't find the tickets," she said.

Robin took up a purse and opened it. "Oh, here they are. Sorry."

Angel as usual showed no reaction.

"We have to go, Charley. I'm having Bernard drive us to the airport. Would you like to come along for the ride?"

"Thanks, no. I have a few appointments."

"With that pedophile?" Angel asked.

I laughed. "Among others, yes."

"Don't forget us, Charley." Robin kissed me, a quick chaste kiss, barely touching my lips.

Angel kissed me too, but with surprising passion, her tongue flicking between my lips.

"Angel, let's go," Robin said sharply.

I wondered if she was jealous.

I WENT out with them and watched Robin and Angel climb into the big Mercedes. Bernard put their bags in the trunk and waved to me as he climbed in behind the wheel. And then they were gone.

It was a nice little scene, two beautiful women off on a nice relaxing trip with no cares in the world. That's how it looked. You would never guess that one of them was about to be tried for murder. If Angel was nervous about it or even thought about it, she didn't show it. That in itself seemed odd.

Outside, the still air was even warmer than before. The river was as smooth as glass, its surface disturbed only by the criss-crossing wakes of the flotilla of small boats filled with people trying to beat the heat. In the trees above, the leaves were motionless.

A distant rumbling, barely audible, warned of an approaching thunderstorm, but the sky remained clear and the relief offered by rain squalls was still miles away.

I had made the mistake of parking the Ford in the sun. The steering wheel was as hot as new steel and I had to drive with one hand wrapped in a handkerchief to protect my tender flesh. Traffic was becoming heavy now. People from Detroit were flocking up, heat or no heat, some for the weekend and some just for a Friday-night outing.

The old air conditioner back at my office could be heard a block away, but it still worked efficiently and my office was blissfully cool.

I stripped off my sweat-soaked shirt and hung it near the window unit so it flapped like a breeze-driven flag. Then I checked my messages. There was only one, from Bob Williams.

I called. His girl said he was with a patient but would call me back when he was through.

I turned my tippy chair and watched the action out on the river. A big freighter had just passed, leaving mountainous waves behind it. Small motorboats popped around on the waves like surfers. A few came within inches of colliding.

I was pondering this aquatic gridlock when Bob Williams returned my call.

"I saw your client today," he said.

"I heard."

"I think we should talk, Charley."

"How about dinner?"

He grunted. "Not tonight, I'm afraid. I've been invited out. How about tomorrow afternoon?"

"My curiosity is killing me. What about right now?"

"If you can hop right over. I won't have much time, though. I have to go home and change before dinner."

"I'll be there in minutes."

My shirt hadn't dried, but it had gotten cold. I sniffed and decided I, too, should consider changing clothes before too long. I gingerly put it on. It was like sliding into ice.

I had parked the Ford in the shady part of the parking lot so I didn't have to put anything around my hands to drive this time.

The rumble of thunder was closer and the sky had begun to darken in the west. It wouldn't be long now.

Dr. Robert Williams was one of three psychiatrists who shared office space in a modern two-story building near the shopping mall. The building catered to medical tenants exclusively—internists, surgeons, psychologists, and dentists. Theoretically, you could have your mind and body, including molars, attended to in one stop.

Bob Williams and the other shrinks shared a reception room. The decorator had tried to make it different from the usual doctors' offices, using pastel colors, cheerful prints, and stuffed soft chairs and sofas. The magazines were still the same, only a little more mangled than usual.

It was almost closing time and the receptionist, a small woman with reading glasses propped on her nose, glanced up at me as if I was an intruder. I had never seen her before.

"Mr. Sloan to see Doctor Williams," I said.

She frowned. "Are you a regular patient? I don't see your name on the appointment list."

"It's a personal matter. I just spoke to him and he told me to come over."

"What kind of insurance do you have?"

"I'm not a patient," I said. "I'm an attorney. I'm consulting Doctor Williams on a legal matter."

Her eyes blinked up at me. I could see the disbelief. She was used to dealing with mental patients, and she had definitely placed me in that category.

"Have a seat," she said, her tone edged with firmness. "I'll let him know you're here."

I took a seat as instructed. The only other person in the room was a young man dressed in a three-piece wool suit, despite the weather outside. He sported an institutional haircut, the kind that looks like it was done with a bowl.

He smiled shyly. I nodded.

"Mr. Sloan," the woman called from her spot at the reception slot, "Doctor Williams will see you now. Go through the door over there." Her tone had changed. She sounded friendly now that my identity had been verified.

Bob Williams, his shirt-sleeves rolled up, was waiting for me in the hall outside his office. We shook hands and he escorted me into his very spartan office.

"Where's the couch? I thought all you guys used one."

He sat down behind the desk. It was bare except for a note pad and a telephone. Like the office itself, the desk indicated that the doctor employed a simple, no-nonsense approach.

"That's only in the movies. They like the Freudian symbolism of a couch. Care for a drink?"

"Scotch, if you have it."

He chuckled softly and padded over to a small refrigerator set on a matching dark brown cabinet. He extracted two cans of a diet cola and handed one to me, then perched himself on one corner of the desk. It was like looking up at Mount Rushmore.

"Angel Harwell is quite a package," he said as he sipped the cola.

"So, what do you think? Is she a mental case?"

Outside, the muted sound of thunder sounded closer.

"We all are mental cases at some time or another. You are, I am, everybody. It's usually a matter of frequency, severity, and timing."

"That's not telling me a whole hell of a lot."

"How bright do you think Angel is?" he asked.

I shrugged. "I know she got almost straight A's in school. But she didn't go to college. Maybe she's no genius but she seems bright enough to me."

"She just might be a genius, at least based on her IQ level. She tested out at one forty-five. Genius, to use that term, is arbitrarily set at one fifty in the standard test. She's close enough. She's in the top one percent of the population as far as intellectual testing goes. What do you think of that?"

"I'm impressed. But what does it mean?"

"It means she's bright enough to manipulate the other tests we gave her." He chuckled. "We use the projective tests, the so-called stick drawings and others, to get a picture of how people view their world. Angel did one of those, drawing nice little flowers and birds on one side of the paper and hands holding bloody knives on the other side."

"So?"

He finished up his cola and tossed the can into a wastebasket. "The flowers and birds are standard for someone who sees the world as a pleasant friendly place. The bloody knives usually indicate a kind of paranoid fear. The point is, the two cannot coexist, not in such a stark contrast. Your little Angel was having fun, fooling the doctors, playing with us, so to speak. Somehow she knew about the drawings and what they indicated. Perhaps she did a bit of reading during one of her hospital stays. In any event, she was having a little joke."

"That sounds pretty sane to me."

"Me too, if that's as far as it went. But it wasn't. All the tests generally show a superior mind, but the mind of someone who is making every possible effort to hide something."

He got off the desk and took his usual chair behind it. Angel was right, his size and manner were intimidating.

"Charley, to make this quick, a personality is nothing more than the sum of how we function, the things we do to get what we need. It's our basic structure. It's how we perceive the world and, to a lesser extent, how the world perceives us. When there is a significant flaw in the techniques we use to manage our lives, we call that a personality disorder."

"Fascinating, but what are you getting at?"

He smiled, but without humor. "Perhaps the better term would be a disordered personality. There are several categories— hysterical, histrionic, passive-aggressive, and borderline, among others. The terms refer to the self-defeating mechanisms used to defend against the person's world. The problem is that the mechanisms don't work, but they are the only things the person can use." The smile faded out completely. "I cannot tell for sure, but I think that Angel Harwell has a personality disorder."

"In other words, she's nuts."

He shook his head. "No. People with personality disorders can be insane, but mostly they are not psychotic. It's usually a lifelong problem that limits their development and makes them and the people around them miserable."

"But you said Angel was nearly at the genius level. If she's that smart, she should be able to figure things out and make corrections."

He shook his head. "It doesn't work that way, unfortunately. Sometimes we aren't the captains of our souls. Anyway, I'm not completely sure about Angel. You see I can't really diagnose accurately when the person is trying to hide something from me, especially if what's being concealed may be the main cause of the way she acts and thinks."

"Why do you say she was hiding something?"

"I've seen it before. It's in the way they answer questions, both written and verbal. Of course, since Angel is so bright, she's better at it than most."

"Do you think she may have killed her father?"

He inhaled, then expelled air through pursed lips. "I'm in no position to answer that, Charley. Some people with personality disorders can be explosively violent. Some have no sense of guilt or regret if they do something antisocial. Angel might possess either of those traits or both of them. I can't tell without learning much more."

"Jesus. Then she may have killed him. Maybe that's what she's trying to hide?"

He shrugged. "I think it's more basic than that."

"What's more basic than knocking off your father?"

"I said I had seen that evasive pattern before. Many times, as a matter of fact. If she did kill him it might even hold the reason for her action."

"What the hell are you trying to tell me?"

"The pattern. It's employed by people who are so profoundly ashamed of something they can't risk anyone else knowing."

"Like what?"

"Incest."

"Holy shit! You mean her old man might have been plugging her and she stabbed him?"

"I'm not saying anything definite, Charley. I don't know what she's hiding. All I'm suggesting is one possible construction. I asked her many questions about her childhood and her relationship with her father. It was like trying to scoop a live fish out of the water with your bare hand. She was masterfully evasive."

"She told me she thought you were a pedophile because you were so interested in her schoolgirl activities."

He smiled, then chuckled. "Angel has an inventive mind. That's something I'm sure she would say." He studied me for a moment before continuing. "I wish I could be more definitive. Of course, I'll put all of this into a written report so whoever testifies at the trial can use the findings, for what they're worth."

He stood up. "I hate to throw you out, but I don't want to be late for my dinner engagement."

He walked me to the door and through the reception room. The receptionist and the patient were both gone.

"Angel is a very complicated person. I don't know what might be lurking under that stoic surface of hers. It might be quite innocent, or it could even be dangerous. But there is something about her that I just can't put my finger on. Whatever it is, I get the feeling it wouldn't be wise to get on her wrong side. Keep a wary eye, Charley."

The thunder boomed just above the building and the building shook a bit. A superstitious person might have considered that an omen.

17

THE PRACTICE OF LAW IS A PEAKS-AND-VALLEYS BUSI-
ness, at least for lone lawyers like myself. I had been in a valley
for a long time, in terms of both work and money. Suddenly I was
experiencing a peak in both.

Robin and Angel were in Florida. Sidney Sherman and his people were digging up rocks of information, and I was waiting for
the doctors and hospitals to send in reports on Angel's past treatment. The Harwell case was managing to speed along without my
doing a thing.

It was just as well. The publicity was bringing in all kinds of
other business. Some good, some bad.

A banker in Port Huron had borrowed a little money from his
place of employment without them knowing about it and the feds
were about to drop the net on him. He wanted Charles Sloan, the
lawyer he had seen on television, to defend him. The retainer was
substantial.

Two brothers ran a chop shop down river near New Baltimore.
Like all successful chop-shop operators they relied on an army of
car thieves to bring in nice new autos at a bargain price. They
would chop up the nice new auto and send out the almost new
parts for resale. Some prime models were worth more apart than
they were in one piece. One of their car thieves, hoping to get a
good deal from the Macomb County prosecutor in another case,
gave them the chop-shop boys on a silver platter. They were out

on bond, but they couldn't think of anyone they wanted to defend them except the famous Charley Sloan. That money was substantial, too.

Mostly, it was criminal defense work coming in, but I picked up some other stuff, too.

Like the little drunk who must have said something really nasty to the bartender at the place where he was drinking. He couldn't remember what he said, but he remembered the bartender leaping over the bar, knocking him down, and kicking the general hell out of him. It must have been some insult. The little guy had one arm in a cast and his broken jaw was wired. I agreed to sue the bartender, who had been arrested for the assault, plus the bar he worked for. The owners had the real money. I took the case on a contingent basis. If we won, I would get one-third of whatever was paid the little man. I figured that could end up as a tidy little sum when the legal smoke cleared.

There were a few others like that, cases where liability was pretty clear and the measure of damages possibly fat. Some went the other way and eventual victory was doubtful, usually for technical legal reasons.

It had been a long dry spell, but it was beginning to look like the old days again.

Of course, I got my share of folks who were worth their weight in trouble.

One woman wanted to sue a boyfriend for transmitting herpes to her during sexual intercourse. But she wasn't exactly sure which boyfriend it was, she had several. She wanted to sue all of them and let them figure it out. I passed on that one.

Some, like Howard Hughes's daughter, were flat-out nuts and had made a career out of bothering lawyers.

Still, I liked being busy again.

Of course, I hadn't yet been tested in a real courtroom battle. Everything so far had been mostly office work, or out talking to witnesses. Even if I couldn't work out pleas or settlements, none of the cases would come up for trial before the Harwell case.

That would be my real test. But the Harwell trial was five weeks away. Like a trip to the dentist, anything five weeks away wasn't worth worrying about.

At least I tried not to worry about it.

In keeping with my new success I needed some new clothes.

My old tailor was among my creditors who had settled for a fraction of what I owed him. Although some years had gone by, I thought he was probably still angry so I decided not to call him. God knows where he might put the zippers.

I had been buying cheap stuff off the rack, and damn little of that. But I knew I'd need some summer suits for the Harwell trial in August.

I wondered what Mark Evola would wear. Sometimes it was wise to dress down for the benefit of a jury.

Old Harry Boyd, a courtroom star of my youth, had amassed more money than an Arab oil mogul, yet he always wore a ill-fitting old suit when trying a jury case. Harvard Harry, the name lawyers called him, liked to stand before a jury and sorrowfully confess that he wasn't very good as a lawyer but he was the best his poor client could afford. Harry, of course, charged on a scale that would have made Bonnie and Clyde sick with envy. Juries liked him. They were impressed by this plain honest man standing before them in his worn, ill-fitting clothing, telling the pure simple truth in his halting, uncultured voice.

Harry, who could speak four languages, made out like the bandit he was.

So, the selection of what to wear before a jury was not always a simple thing.

Harry might be able to get away with a "man of the people" approach, but I knew it wouldn't work for me.

So, I tossed my business to a local tailor who almost kissed my hand in gratitude when I paid him. I now possessed three very nice conservative summer suits, together with some expensive shirts and muted ties. I could never match Mark Evola, who looked like a Brooks Brothers ad even in running pants, but I wouldn't appear to be a bum off the street either.

I bought some new shoes. Not Gucci, but better than my round-heeled old ones.

I was ready, at least on the outside. The inside would perhaps take more than a tailor to get ready.

It had been a slow morning except for Mrs. Johnson.

If Mrs. Johnson had been a piece of cloth, you would have thrown her away. She was that worn out. A small, thin black woman who looked eighty but was only fifty. She worked nights as part of the local school's cleaning crew.

She had nine children. Make that eight; one had just died. A boy of seventeen. He had crashed a friend's car, injuring himself. The police took him to a local hospital. She had seen him there. He looked scraped up a bit, but otherwise all right, except for a fractured kneecap that would require surgery. They wheeled him into the operating room, but he had not come out alive. The doctors told the family he had died of heart failure. He was young, athletic, and although he was often in minor trouble, his mother loved him dearly.

For so young a man death seemed impossible. She wondered if the doctors might have killed him.

Mrs. Johnson was a quiet woman, the stoic kind who usually accepted the harsh realities of fate. But this time she couldn't accept what she had been told, not without proof.

She offered nothing more than suspicion. The doctors had been very nice, very sympathetic, but she had to know if they had caused her son's death. It was a question she had to have answered.

It was obvious she wasn't interested in money. I could see that in her eyes.

"I'll look into it," I told her. "I'll get a copy of the autopsy report. They do an autopsy when someone dies in surgery. Have you seen the report?"

She shook her head. "No."

"I'll get that for starters. Then, if that's questionable, I'll do some additional investigation."

She pulled a wallet out of her small purse. It was almost as worn as its owner. She carefully extracted a small packet of bills.

"How much will this cost?" she asked.

"I'll tell you what, if I find something that suggests a lawsuit and you want to go ahead with it, I'll handle the case for a percentage of what you might get. But until then, there'll be no charge."

"Are you sure?" She sounded suspicious. It was a tough world and Mrs. Johnson was accustomed to having to pay for whatever she got.

"I'm sure."

I escorted her out of the office and told her I'd get in touch in a few days.

Doing things for free was one perk of a lawyer practicing alone. In a firm, especially a large firm catering to business clients, doing something on the cuff meant a visit from the managing partner, and possible death by strangulation if the amount lost was large.

Sidney Sherman called. He was as cheerful as ever but there was an underlying note of anxiety in his voice.

"I got some copies of Angel Harwell's school records and some other stuff," he said. "I'll fax them to you."

"I don't have a fax machine, Sidney."

"Hey, how about entering this century, Charley. Everybody has a fax."

"I'm an exception. Send it to me by express mail. You didn't call just for that. What's up?"

"Did you get a copy of the prenuptial agreement from Robin Harwell?"

"Not yet," I said.

"Well, we can get one, but it's going to cost."

"How much?"

"A couple thousand."

"What the hell are you going to do, bribe somebody?"

He sighed. "Charley, you really don't want an answer to that, do you? I mean, not in this age of electronic technology, and especially over a phone."

"I told you I'm not agreeing to anything illegal, Sidney." I said that automatically, just in case someone was listening. "What's the problem down there?"

"The Florida lawyer. Harrison Harwell's divorce lawyer. He's pissed. I suppose he could see the yellow brick road stretching before him when this millionaire walked in and gave him the biggest divorce case of his career. Instant riches. Then the guy died. I think he's taking it personally. He won't give up the files, or even let anyone have a peek."

"Is the money for him?"

"No." The word was snapped out quietly, without explanation. Obviously Sidney's people had found someone in the lawyer's office who knew how to use a copy machine, but only for pay, and lots of it.

"Maybe if it would help if I contacted the lawyer," I said.

"I doubt it. This guy has dug in his heels. Nothing is going to be shown unless there's a court order. He's adamant about it."

"Maybe I should keep after Robin Harwell to get it."

"This, ah, arrangement we have down there includes the court pleadings that were going to be filed. It might be wise to know what's in them, Charley. You don't want any nasty surprises at trial."

"You have the money I gave you," I said. "It's up to you how to spend it. I must insist that nothing illegal or unethical be done."

"Nice point," he said, chuckling. "Okay, Charley, I'll go ahead."

He paused, then spoke again. "I suppose you want my people to continue digging into Angel's background?"

"Absolutely. And her late father's, too."

"The meter's running, you know."

"I know. Keep at it anyway."

"It's your funeral."

"I hope not."

My list of things to do was growing, not only in the Harwell case, but generally.

Suddenly I had been thrust into a busy law practice. Sidney was right, I had to get the proper tools to do the job.

I had called a temporary secretarial service and discovered that their girls no longer typed, at least not on typewriters. The world had turned and everything was done on word-processing machines now. The ladies had been trained for a variety of machines, none of which I was familiar with. All the computer terms sounded to me like an entirely different language.

If I was going to have a secretary I would have to update my equipment. And get a fax machine.

Pickeral Point had no place that rents business equipment so I went to Port Huron.

The man I talked to had apparently been trained as a used-car salesman. He was all teeth and good cheer. He pretended to have great knowledge of computers, but I soon discovered he knew

234

very little. However, we cut a deal. I rented a computer, complete with every software program necessary to run an office; a printer, which he said was so good that I could print a newspaper or a book on it if I wanted; plus a fax machine and a copier. My new best friend gave me a deal he said he wouldn't even give his mother. I got everything for six months at a price that would have ransomed two or three kings, along with the opportunity to buy the equipment at the end of the six-month lease for a figure my friend said would get him arrested if it got out. It would have, but for unarmed robbery.

He had seen me on television so he took my check without protest and loaded everything into my car. When he saw the car I think he had second thoughts about the check, but by that time it was too late.

I took everything back to my office. I found out that I couldn't begin to make the computer work, although it buzzed with authority and little lights went on. The same thing happened with the printer. The little how-to books supplied defied human understanding. But the fax machine apparently worked.

I sent a fax note to my new friend in Port Huron as a test and he sent one back with a list of other things I could rent at equally wonderful prices. He knew a sucker when he saw one. My friends at the telephone company informed me they would install a fax line for a reasonable charge. Until then my present arrangement would do nicely. I could turn on the fax when I needed it. I flipped the little button that returned my line to normal telephone operation.

At last, I was in business.

Now I could offer someone a job without shame. Well, at least not too much shame. Everything else in the office was a bit shabby. The new equipment looked very much out of place.

I didn't look out of place, however, and that bothered me just a little.

As he was required to do by law, Mark Evola had sent me a list of the witnesses the prosecution planned to call in the Harwell case.

I was over visiting a new client at the jail, a man who had punched up his wife when he had come home unexpectedly. She had greeted him naked, which he said was unusual, and he had wondered why until he caught a glimpse of her equally naked lover diving out the bedroom window. The fists flew then. I expected the wife would probably drop the charge eventually, given the circumstances.

After the jail I dropped by Evola's office a short walk away.

As usual, I admired Evola's ladies and would have been happy to sit in the reception area and ogle but Evola came out at once. Also, as usual, Evola fussed over me like a returning hero, his standard greeting for everyone except people he had indicted.

"Sit down, Charley! Hey, I'm excited about trying this thing, aren't you?" It was as if we were going on a camping trip together.

"I take it then that you won't drop the charges?"

He laughed, his nice professional politician laugh, too long and too loud. "You are a funny man. I like someone with a good sense of humor."

He sat behind his desk, grinning at me.

I took the list of witnesses from my briefcase.

"I got the list of your witnesses in the Harwell case here, Mark. Some I know. Some I don't. I'd like to go over them with you if you don't mind."

"Of course. I'm here to serve."

"Morgan and Maguire. Them I know."

He nodded. "Our crack homicide team. They talked to the witnesses and Angel."

"As did you."

The grin got wider. "In their presence. Also, they can testify to their investigation at the scene of the murder."

"Who is Ned Bentley?"

"A uniformed officer. Bentley and Ralph Harris, who is also on the list, are Pickeral Point policemen. Alex Cramer and John Joffrey, who are there too, are Kerry County deputies. They all answered the run that night." He leaned back in his chair. "You know how it goes, Charley, we have to list everyone who was there. Those cops talked to the family and servants and saw the body."

"Did any of them talk to Angel?"

He nodded. "Bentley and Harris. They went to her room and found her hiding."

"Hiding, my ass. She was on her bed."

"Covered in her dead father's blood, Charley." The grin became even broader. "Shocking, eh?"

"Come on, Mark, don't get cute. I presume they asked her about the blood?"

"That, and the dead man with a knife sticking in him. They inquired about little things like that."

"And?"

"She said she did it and would do it again if she had the chance." Then he laughed. "Not really. She was putting on her madwoman act at that point. Little Ophelia, driven insane by grief."

"Did they read her her rights?"

"Hey, they might be Pickeral Point cops but even they know enough to do that."

"I see Dennis Bernard listed here, and his wife, along with some of the other Harwell servants. What's the purpose of that?"

"It's the law, Charley. I have to list everyone who was present when it happened. The old res gestae rule. A prosecutor can't pick and choose. I have to include everything that happened. They were there, so I have to call them, or at least list them. Of course, Bernard and his wife also identified the body as being Harrison Harwell, so they will have to testify to that."

"I see Robin Harwell listed. Did she make the identification too?"

He shook his head. "Actually, we didn't use her for that. We didn't need her, considering we had the Bernards to do the job. I always hate to show a butchered corpse to a new widow. They seem to get so upset."

"If she isn't going to be an identification witness, why do you have her listed?"

"Res gestae again. She was there so I have to show her as a witness. Of course, I realize she's in a delicate position since we're trying to nail her stepdaughter for murder, but those are the rules. Look, Charley, I'll be frank. Mrs. Harwell didn't say anything we feel is essential to the case. I'll let you waive her appearance if you want. I'm a reasonable guy. I'll do the same for most of the servants too, although I want to keep a couple in just to show how the house was and who was there before the murder."

Theresa Hernandez was also listed. I didn't want her on the stand. "Whatever," I said casually. "Probably the Bernards would fulfill anything you need for that purpose. Unless something comes up between then and now, I'll waive the rest of the servants."

"All except Theresa Hernandez," he said, smiling. He knew.

"What's she going to testify to?"

He shrugged. "Nothing much. She's no one you should worry about."

I pretended I didn't know any better. If she showed up, she might be as deadly to my case as a cobra bite.

"I see listed my favorite pathologist, Ernesto Rey."

"He will testify to the cause of death, Charley. I have to show that or I don't have a case. You were awfully mean to him at the examination. He's not a bad little guy. Let him get on and get off. His testimony will just be routine anyway."

Rey was one of the keys to my defense of suicide. Asking me to let up on him would be like asking a hungry cat to give up a fish.

It was my turn to shrug. "I've taken my best shot with him anyway. I'll ask a few questions just to let the jury know I'm awake, but other than that Rey should have no problems with me."

He nodded as if he believed me. He didn't.

"Who is Bently Jenkins?"

"He's new up here. An evidence technician. He'll testify to the blood on the knife. Things like that."

"And the blood on my client's clothing?"

He shrugged. "Oh yeah, that too." He said it as if it wasn't important. We both knew better.

"Herbert Ames?"

Evola chuckled. "Otherwise known as Dirty Herbert. He was the deputy who filmed your lovely client making her lovely confession. It's routine to list him, as you know. Odd duck. The cops say he shoots private porno as a hobby, although that's only a rumor. I don't know about that, but he always does a nice professional job for us. His official title is evidence technician."

"I want to talk to him."

238

"Why? All he did was run the camera."

"Several times."

Evola sighed. "I thought that was all behind us."

"We still have the Walker hearing on the admissibility of Angel's statement. I may call him myself then."

He looked disappointed in me, as if I had just confessed to drowning small animals.

"I don't see the point."

He saw the point perfectly. Dirty Herbert could testify to the several versions of the alleged confession. He might even say why the other tape had been erased.

"Humor me, Mark. It's that or I get the court to order it."

"It might be a problem. He's on vacation."

"Isn't it funny how cops always seem to take vacations when defense attorneys want to talk to them? It's five weeks until trial. How long do you guys give for vacation? Or has he got you on one of his porno flicks?"

Evola's smile was broad but not quite as quick. "Shame on you, Charley. Okay, if you want him I'll get him for you. How about a couple days before the Walker hearing? He'll be back by then."

"Whatever. But if I don't get to talk to him I'll raise holy hell, Mark."

"So would I if I were in your boots. I'll have him for you, Charley. Don't fret about it."

It was one of those promises. Evola wasn't going to give up an inch, not if it was important.

"Who is Milo Zeck?"

"Who?"

"Milo Zeck."

He looked up at the ceiling as if trying to recall the name, then he looked at me. "Oh yeah, him. He's a cop."

"Here?"

"All cops look alike to me, Charley."

"Come on, Mark. Who is he?"

The leer was the kind you see on cartoon characters just before they smash their enemy into bits.

"A cop," he said. "A Florida cop."

"Just passing through and wanted the experience of testifying in a Michigan murder case?"

He laughed. "Close. But a little more than that."

"Quit playing games. Who is this guy and how are you going to use him?"

Evola looked at me. I thought I saw pity. "He's a detective down there. Your little Angel got her pretty little ass into some trouble a while back. He'll testify to that."

"Jesus, how can he? Are we tossing out the rules of evidence here? You can't prove a crime by showing another crime. You know that."

"There are exceptions," he said. "You can use it to show a common scheme, plan, or design, for instance."

"That's absurd in this case."

He was no longer smiling. "Is it? Angel tried to kill daddy once before. She missed that time. She succeeded up here. We can show intent, Charley. We can show a plan to kill dear old dad. That's how we will offer Detective Zeck's testimony."

It was almost impossible to appear calm, but I tried. "Is this a joke?"

Evola shook his head. "I'm afraid not."

"I demand to talk to this cop, to take his statement."

"Feel free. You can hop down to Florida or you can wait until he gets up here. If you like, I'll have him flown in a day early just for you. It will cost the county extra, but, like I said, I'm a reasonable guy."

"What do you mean, she tried to kill her father before?"

Evola shook his head slowly. "Morgan and Maguire talked to the guy. She tried to kill papa before. That's about all I know."

"You mean, that's all you're going to tell me."

He held up his hands as if showing his innocence. "Charley, would I do a thing like that?

Like it or not. I would have to go to Florida.

I GOT the autopsy report on the Johnson boy. Blood work showed he had enough cocaine in him the night he died to keep Bogota prosperous for a year.

Despite his youth, he was a long-time user and it had taken a silent toll. His young heart was damaged beyond repair, but it didn't show on the tests they did prior to surgery. No one could reasonably have expected a heart so young in a body so strong to be in such bad shape.

240

In a way, he had killed himself.

I drove out to see his mother. She lived with assorted grand-children and relatives in a small house in a section near I-94, a section that was almost exclusively black.

The house was neat and perfumed with the odor of rich cooking.

I told her that I had seen the report and talked with the doctors. The last was a lie. I said he had a rare heart ailment that no one could have discovered, a defect that caused him to die during surgery. I said the doctors told me he would have died soon anyway, given the condition.

It seemed to satisfy her. I didn't tell her about the drugs. There was no point to it. She offered me money and when I turned it down she made me accept a pie.

The pie was good. It was one of my more satisfying fees.

18

I AWOKE IN THE MIDDLE OF THE NIGHT. THAT DAY I
had moved to my new apartment and for a moment I didn't know
where I was. Then I remembered.

A nightmare had jolted me awake, but I had no clear memory
of it.

What I did have was a nagging urge to drink. I could think of
nothing else.

Sleep was out of the question. I put on the light and got up.
Sometimes when the need comes it helps to eat, even if you
aren't hungry. I made a sandwich in the kitchen and poured a
glass of milk.

The choices on television, even with cable, aren't terribly interesting at three in the morning.

Every time I flipped to a movie I seemed to come in at the
middle of a drinking scene. Everyone looked so happy; they paid
little attention to the full glasses in front of them. But I did. I was
riveted on those drinks, so I kept flipping the channels.

I caught a nature program in progress. Some scrawny woman
with haunted eyes was explaining why she had spent her life
studying baboons. The baboons scampered about in the background. Although she obviously adored them, the creatures regarded her indifferently. They didn't give a damn about her,
although they were clearly the center of her existence.

Love is often that way. Even among nonbaboons.

I turned off the television and tried to review the events of my day. Something had triggered the sudden need and I wanted to know what it was so I could make sure it wouldn't happen again.

The day had been a busy one for me, with two motions in cases before Judge Mulhern. But they had been routine matters. No stress, no challenge.

The main stress in the day had come with the afternoon mail. I had requested reports of treatment from doctors and hospitals that had treated Angel Harwell. Three of them had come in. The medical reports were more confusing than helpful. To lay a foundation to keep Angel's damaging statement out of evidence I would need some nice clear medical evidence. What I got was not clear or nice.

A decision would have to be made soon. If I used the medical evidence to show Angel was emotionally fragile Evola might turn it around and convince the jury she was just the kind of nut who would kill someone. It was going to be a gamble at best, and perhaps my subconscious fondly remembered how I used to blunt the pain and worry over risky decisions. To drink, or not to drink, that might have caused one hell of a mental conflict, and conflicts, they say, are the seeds of nightmares.

It made sense. I finished the milk and went back to bed.

I lay there in the dark, trying to make myself calm. The damn Harwell case was getting to me. Fear, like a faint odor, was beginning to seep into my mind. Sleep came, but only in tormented naps.

I CALLED Bob Williams early, before he left home. He sounded grumpy, but so would most people at that hour. Irritation quickly turned to interest when I said I had some of Angel's medical history in hand. I asked if he could explain the reports to me.

Angel was a puzzle and he wanted to find the key that would give him the answer. The reports were at my office. He said he would drop by on his way to the hospital. I didn't have time to shower or shave. I threw on some clothes and arrived at my office just moments before he did.

"You look terrible," he said, studying me with a professional eye.

"I didn't sleep well."

"Let's see what you've got." He settled his massive bulk into one of my old chairs.

He took a few minutes to read the reports. There were hospital charts with entries in what looked like unreadable handwriting. But it didn't seem to bother him. Finally, he looked up.

"So, what's your problem?" he asked.

"I think that's self-evident. She was in three different places. Each set of doctors came up with a different diagnosis. Which one is correct?"

He lay the reports on my desk. "Interesting, this girl. I think you can disregard the first diagnosis from the New York hospital. That was probably done to get her temporarily committed."

"They said she might be schizophrenic."

He nodded. "Maybe she was then. She had just turned eighteen. Adolescents sometimes seem that way. Psychiatrists know that. We treat what we see, but we are aware it may be only a passing phase."

"They say she was hearing voices. That's not quite the same thing as getting pimples."

"Maybe it is, in a way. Anyhow, they put down what she told them and what they saw. You'll notice that when they sent her to the place in Florida, they thought it was an adjustment disorder. I don't see any reference to voices when she was a patient there."

"What's an adjustment disorder?"

He shrugged. "Just what it says. Something traumatic happens or a person is going through a rough phase. They can't adjust to it emotionally. Perhaps they go into a depression or are nearly paralyzed by anxiety. Most of the time, with treatment, or even without, the thing straightens itself out. And, sadly, sometimes it doesn't. I also see they think she may have an Electra complex."

"What's that?"

"The opposite of the Oedipus complex, where little boys want to sleep with mama and think daddy is in the way. Electra is when a little girl wants to go to bed with daddy and it's mama who is in the way. I don't see the basis for their conclusion. Anyway, it's an interesting theory."

"That last place, the other Florida hospital, says she has a personality disorder," I said. "That agrees with what you thought originally."

244

He nodded slowly. "Maybe. But they think it's a hysterical disorder. I disagree, but maybe when they saw her it was exactly that. We can't tell, of course." He tapped the reports with one huge finger. "Many of these records have been altered."

"Oh? How can you tell?"

"You can when you've been a psychiatrist as long as I have. Some of the treatment notes, the usual stuff we do after talking with a patient, are missing from the record. Most of them, as a matter of fact."

"I could raise hell about it and make them produce what's missing."

"I doubt if that's possible, frankly. This was done some time ago, unless I miss my guess. Someone insisted that something be deleted." He pulled out the New York reports. "See, there are some references here to family discord. Believe me, that would have been developed, but there are no notes by the treating doctors."

"What are you telling me? Can you bribe a hospital?"

"You can't. Too many people. However, if you ask the treating physician to delete certain things from treatment records, he will if the reason is good enough."

"Isn't that unethical?"

He shook his head. "No. Doctors don't enjoy the same protection as lawyers and priests. You should know that. Oh, some courts will say it's the same, that a patient's statements are privileged communications, but others, many others, say they are merely confidential and will compel doctors to testify to what their patients told them. A doctor has to keep what is told him confidential—that is, he can't tell anyone voluntarily or he can get sued. But he can often be compelled to tell under oath in court."

"So?"

"Charley, psychiatrists are keenly aware of that little legality. When people tell us things they think it will go with us to the grave. If they thought otherwise, they wouldn't talk about anything but the weather. We try to protect them in various ways."

"Like altering records?"

He nodded. "Sometimes. At least the official records. The patient or the family may even request that harmful material be excluded. If there's a good reason, it might be done. It depends."

"On what?"

"Many things. Like health insurance, for instance. If a patient is paying through a health plan and certain things are required to qualify, those records are sent and can't really be altered later. However, if the person is what we call a direct pay, we possess the only records and editing them is no problem. As I say, it's done when it's in the patient's best interest."

"What's your idea of a good reason?"

"Let's say that you're a congressman and you get depressed to the extent that you're contemplating suicide. You realize you need treatment, but if it gets out, for whatever reason, your mental health will become an issue in the next campaign. So you ask the doctor to keep any harmful details out of the treatment notes, perhaps even keep them under a false name."

"Is that done?"

He came close to smiling. "Did you get anything on Angel from Buckingham Hospital yet?"

"No. Why?"

"Buckingham has a program for public officials and others who need psychiatric treatment but who cannot risk that becoming known. It's all private-pay stuff and the patient is given another identity, like someone joining the French Foreign Legion. Any inquiries, court or otherwise, will get the same response—they never heard of the person." He shrugged. "If Angel Harwell was enrolled under that program while a patient, you'll get nothing from them."

"Even with her request for release of information?"

"Not unless she supplies her secret identity, which is probably impossible."

"Why?"

He did smile. "Simple. They never tell the patient. She'd have no way of knowing."

"All this sounds like you people should burn incense and wear clerical costumes, complete with masks. It's like something out of the Middle Ages."

"Charley, if the law treated us the same as you lawyers or religious people, we wouldn't have to resort to such tactics."

246

"But it is the same."

He shook his head. "Remember the guy that blew up his boss in California, the one who was engaged to that movie star?"

"Yeah, I read about it."

"Well, he confessed doing it to his psychologist. The psychologist told his girlfriend, who blabbed to someone who blabbed to someone else, and the psychologist was forced on the witness stand to tell what had been told him. Remember that? The bomber was convicted."

"That's up on appeal."

He got up. "Perhaps. According to what I read, the judge in that case thought the statement could be admitted because it had been told to a third person. An exception to some rule, he called it. That seems to be stretching things to me, but you lawyers are very inventive people when you really want to be. When a doctor like myself reads something like that, he knows he must be very careful to protect his patient."

"Angel's school records were also altered," I said.

He shrugged. "Probably for the same reason."

"Like what?"

"Who knows? Maybe that's what Angel is concealing. I told you what I suspected."

"Have you ever altered your records?"

"Sometimes. If there's a good reason."

"Doesn't that bother you?"

"No. I treat sick people, I don't judge them." He chuckled. "If I did, I might strangle a number of them."

"What about justice?"

He walked to the door. "I leave that to lawyers. Or God. Either way, it's a pretty dicey concept."

I DIDN'T want to go to Florida.

But someone had to talk to the Florida cop. His information might be nothing but fluff, harmless gossip that was inadmissible anyway. But it could be something else and the cop might turn out to be Evola's chief card, his ace. There was only one way to find out.

And there was Angel's Florida psychologist. I had sent him a

247

release-of-information form but so far had received nothing back. I had to talk to him.

Down there I could nose among the neighbors down on Sheridan Key. They might come up with something to bolster my suicide theory. It was worth a try.

Also, the days were passing swiftly and I had to prepare Angel for the courtroom. Robin, too. It is a technique lawyers call polishing the witness. It is more art than science and I consider myself pretty good at it.

I called Sheridan Key. A maid answered and I waited for a very long time before Robin finally came on the line.

"Hello, Charley." On hearing my voice, she sounded pleasant enough but not overly enthusiastic.

"Robin, I need to come down there and do a few things. Is any time better than another?"

"What things?" she asked.

"The prosecutor is calling one of your local cops as a witness. I need to talk to him. A couple of things like that."

She hesitated. "Well, I suppose one time is as good as another. Will you be staying with us?"

"Would it be better if I stayed at a hotel?"

Again there was a significant pause, as if she was thinking that over carefully. Then she spoke. "It would probably be more convenient for you if you stayed here."

"I don't wish to impose."

"Don't be silly, Charley. We have plenty of room. When would you come down?"

"How about tomorrow? I can only stay for three days. I have some court appearances up here that can't be adjourned." That wasn't entirely true. I did have some court dates but they were routine and easily rescheduled. This was to be a working visit and I needed to establish that right at the start.

"Do you know your flight number and arrival time? I can have one of our people pick you up."

"I wanted to check with you before I arranged all that. I'll rent a car at the airport. Just tell me how to get to your place."

I took notes as she gave detailed directions.

"Is there anything you need done here before you arrive?"

"I don't think so."

"When you know what time your plane gets in, give us a call."
She paused. "Angel will be so pleased that you're coming."
"And you?"
Again a pause. "I would think that would be obvious."
Maybe it was, and maybe it wasn't. I would soon find out.

DESPITE my dreadful credit history a bank in Delaware had recently offered me a credit card, albeit at ridiculously high interest rates. Apparently they had sent the mailing to every lawyer in the country. I had filled out the application thinking I didn't have a chance of being accepted. To my surprise I got the card, practically by return mail. I tried it a couple of times to make sure it worked. It did. After that, I just kept it in case I ever needed it.

I used the card with a local travel agent and charged the tickets, full fare since it was short notice. I would add the tickets to the growing list of Harwell case expenses. If it had been my own money I would have flown tourist. It wasn't, so I chose first class. There was no problem getting a flight to Sarasota. Not too many people were rushing off to steamy Florida in the middle of summer.

A car would be ready for me when I arrived. The travel agent said the rent-a-car people were pathetically grateful for my business during the off season. I could have any kind of car I wanted, any kind. At very reasonable rates.

I ordered a Cadillac.

I almost couldn't remember when I had last flown first class or had been behind the wheel of a Cadillac. I had almost forgotten what that kind of life was like.

ON the flight down I was the only passenger in first class. Part of the allure of paying the extra money is the free drinks. The stewardess, a pretty girl, thin but pleasant, so young she looked like she belonged in high school, kept trying to push drinks at me as if she was being paid by the ounce.

Habit is an odd thing. I hadn't flown much since my troubles, and when I did, it was always in the cheap seats.

Prior to that, I went first class as if it were a tenet of my religion. When I boarded in those days, I would insist on a drink, a double, even before we took off. They do that for you in first class. Then, as they winged me through the skies, I used to consume more alcohol than the plane did fuel. Some people were nervous in airplanes, but in those circumstances any alcoholic would love to fly.

Habit, as Pavlov's dog would agree, is a very powerful thing. I spent every minute wishing for something I couldn't have.

I was damn glad when we touched down in Sarasota. The direct flight from Detroit had been just over two hours, which is a long time to be salivating.

It had been warm in Detroit. Here it was hot. Very hot. There was no wind. The humid air lay on the place like wet slime. Sweat began to pop out on me before I even got down the ramp from the plane.

It was just like the tropics, except you didn't have to go through customs.

I had to sign all kinds of forms at the rent-a-car desk, but the Cadillac was waiting. Parked out in the sun the gleaming car was as hot as anything could get without bursting into flames. However, the air conditioner pumped cold air in minutes and by the time I was ready to drive out of the small airport it was beginning to cool very nicely.

Palm trees. For some reason the sight of palm trees always surprises me. And there were plenty of them.

I drove through the town of Sarasota, which in different parts looked either like a transplanted part of the Midwest, all malls and gas stations, or like something out of a 1938 Humphrey Bogart movie, with ancient Florida houses built for coolness in the sun, the kind of places that whisper of dark Southern secrets. The stuff of Faulkner or Tennessee Williams.

Sarasota has a history. Once it was the winter home of Mr. Ringling's circus. Signs for various circus exhibits remind the visitor of those days. It's an exotic place. Even the boats in the town's harbor, each worth a fortune, seem somehow sinister, like props in a spy movie.

I followed Robin's directions and turned right at the light she had described. The Cadillac was now chilly, but it felt good. I drove on a two-lane road past flat fields that alternated with clumps of jungle. I passed a number of subdivisions, places with houses built into the greenery, places where Tarzan would have felt quite at home.

Robin's directions had been very accurate. I approached the bridge she had described, a short concrete span that led into Sheridan Key. A fisherman lounged on the bridge, watching several lines he had put into the water. A huge gray pelican, with an eye like an ancient god, perched on the rail and watched the fisherman. Man and bird were motionless, intent on what they were doing. Both ignored my Cadillac as it rumbled past.

The bridge seemed to end in an enormous clump of jungle, and then the road turned. What lay around that bend looked like a border crossing, complete with gate and guard. Above the gate, a small sign proclaimed: SHERIDAN KEY, A PRIVATE COMMUNITY. The word PRIVATE seemed to stick out, although it was the same size as the other lettering.

The small, gaily painted gatehouse could have been borrowed from the road company of an old musical comedy. But there was nothing comical about the uniformed guard who emerged.

Middle-age spread caused his belly to lap over his gun belt but there was muscle beneath the straining uniform fabric around his shoulders. He wore a military-type cap pulled down to the rim of his reflecting sunglasses.

His skin was the color of rare roast beef and marbled with little purple veins that had ruptured in the surface of his sun-soaked nose and meaty cheeks. A world-class drinker, by the looks of him.

I hit the switch and my electric window glided down. The warm air came through like a soft slap.

"Yes, sir. Can I help you?" The words were polite but his challenging tone bordered on hostile.

"My name is Sloan," I said, smiling. "I'm here to see Mrs. Harwell."

He studied me for a moment, even glancing into the back of the Cadillac, then he spoke. "Charles Sloan?"

"That's me."

There was no sudden change, but now that he had identified me he became immediately respectful. He was the kind who was either at your feet or at your throat. "You're expected, Mr. Sloan. You can go on through. The Harwell place is about a half-mile up the road, on the Gulf side. The name is out front, sir. You can't miss it."

He returned to the little gatehouse, did something with a control, and the striped gate rose smoothly.

Sheridan Key was surprisingly narrow, just a spit of land traversed by a winding road. On one side was the Gulf of Mexico, on the other a large bay. The shoreline houses on each side of the road were almost hidden by palms, flowers, and other greenery, but I could see glimpses of them. It was not a place for poor people.

The houses were small palaces, each set on an acre or two of land. The twisted road was very narrow at places and I worried about meeting another car, but the place seemed almost deserted.

At points along the way huge boulders retrieved from the Gulf lined the roadway. I thought the road was probably a nightmare to drive at night.

There was an exotic, foreign feel about Sheridan Key. The island was so narrow and low it seemed that one good-sized wave from the Gulf might wash the whole thing away. The island had a make-believe quality, like a movie set.

Each jungle estate had a small metal sign at the mouth of each driveway. Nothing much, just a name. I saw HARWELL, and turned into the drive.

The house and grounds were hidden from the road by enormous tropical hedges so thick even a small bird wouldn't have been able to penetrate them.

The Harwell estate was a compound of three very large, low-slung buildings with matching red tile roofs. If they had had thatched roofs they would have looked like something out of the South Seas.

The main house, which seemed as long as a football field, was set near the water. Beyond the house, the Gulf of Mexico, picture-postcard perfect, was shimmering and green, with tiny white cloud banks forming on the distant horizon. The two other structures in the compound were a huge garage and what looked like an apartment motel. I assumed the servants lived there.

I parked the Cadillac.

"Mr. Sloan?"

The athletic young man hurried toward me. He was dressed in white shorts and a blue shirt. His grin showed perfect white

252

teeth, their whiteness exaggerated by contrast with his milk-chocolate skin.

"The ladies are out by the pool. I'll take you to them."

He opened the back door and I followed. The place was something out of the pages of an architecture magazine, all tile and sunshine. There seemed to be a view of the Gulf from every window.

The house had been built in horseshoe shape with an enormous outdoor pool in the center, to give the illusion that the pool was an extension of the Gulf. The young man opened the door and I stepped out of the air conditioning. The slight breeze off the water carried the tangy odor of the Gulf and the heady fragrance of exotic flowers.

Robin and Angel were laying on beach chairs watching me.

I noted again the striking similarities despite the difference in age. Both bodies glistened with oil.

"Hello, Charley," Robin said, smiling. "We have spare suits in the house if you'd like to join us."

She looked over at Angel. "Honey, put your top on. You don't want to embarrass Charley."

Except for a small bit of cloth, more of a patch, below her navel, Angel was naked. She didn't smile, nor did she seem flustered. She sighed, sat up, and slowly donned the top, a couple of other patches.

"Better?" She looked up at me.

"Sit down, Charley." Robin nodded at a beach chair. "Good trip down?"

"Fine."

There were some boats far out in the Gulf. I watched two pelicans gracefully glide past on huge outstretched wings searching the water for whatever it is pelicans eat.

Soft recorded music was being piped out to the pool area. It sounded Hawaiian.

"Tough way to live," I said.

Robin laughed. "If you force yourself, you can get used to it. Can we offer you something to drink? One nice cold beer wouldn't hurt, would it?"

"I'll pass."

"You said something about a policeman down here," Robin said. "What's that all about?"

"I intend to find out. Have you ever been arrested down here, Angel?"

"What do you mean?" she asked.

"Have you ever been picked up by the police here? For anything?"

"Once," she said.

"What happened?"

Robin cut her off. "That wasn't an arrest, Charley. Harrison had the police take Angel to a hospital here."

"I stayed three days," Angel volunteered. "That was as long as they could hold me legally. At least that's what I was told. They were nice about it. Some aren't, you know."

"Why did the police take you?"

"Daddy," she answered.

"He called them?"

She nodded. "Yes. He was drunk."

"The police have been here several times," Robin said. "Harrison could get very loud and abusive. He frightened the servants. They were the ones who usually called the police."

"How come they took you, Angel, and not your father?"

"They should have taken him," she said. "He was the one who was out of control."

"Why did they take you then?"

"Because of what he told them," she replied.

"And what was that?"

"He said I had tried to kill him."

Robin interjected quickly. "Things got rather tense. Harrison got cut on the arm."

"Did you try to kill him, Angel?"

"That time?"

"Yes."

She looked out at the Gulf, then spoke. "Oh, I suppose I did."

254

19

MILO ZECK DIDN'T LOOK LIKE A COP.

We met at a small bar just outside of Sarasota. I had followed his directions and found it easily enough. I had hoped it would be an exotic tropical place but it wasn't. The saloon could have been moved to New Jersey and no one would have noticed a difference. It was air-conditioned to the point of frost.

I tended to avoid bars for obvious reasons but sometimes I couldn't gracefully. This was one of the times.

Zeck was tall and skinny. About forty, he wore wire-rim glasses and a rumpled seersucker suit, but no tie. Sandy-haired and fair-skinned, he could easily have been an accountant or a bank clerk. We sat at a table in the back of the place.

I had a Coke and he drank bourbon, straight up. He had just finished his shift and the bourbon, he told me, was his way of rewarding himself for getting through another day. I was familiar with that kind of reward.

We talked about Michigan. He had never been there and looked forward to coming up as a witness.

I had anticipated hostility but his attitude seemed quite the opposite. You would have thought he was my witness.

"I got you something," he said, handing me an envelope from inside his coat. "We believe in cooperation down here."

The papers were copies of official police reports. The subject of the first report was Angel Harwell and the incident that had led to her being taken to a local mental hospital. It was written in standard terse police language that seemed to be universal. The officer had answered a disturbance call at the Harwells. Harrison Harwell had been cut on his left forearm. He told them his daughter had done it, that she had tried to kill him with a knife. The daughter, the policeman was told, had a history of mental illness. Harrison Harwell declined to press criminal charges but asked the officer to take Angel to a small private mental hospital in the area. Harwell told the officer he would seek medical help himself for the substantial cut. There was no reference to what had caused the trouble between parent and child. Angel had struggled and the officer had used handcuffs to restrain her while conveying her to the hospital. The medical people had been alerted and were waiting when the police car got there. The report laconically described Angel Harwell as hysterical. It was signed in several places by the officer, Milo Zeck, and countersigned by his watch commander.

The other three incident reports concerned additional police contacts at the Harwell place. All had occurred before the cutting and each had been described as a family disturbance, but with no details. Each time Milo Zeck had been one of the policemen responding.

"Thanks," I said. "What were those other incidents about?"

Zeck grinned, sipped his bourbon, then spoke. "Family-trouble runs, just like it says. Every time old man Harwell got a snootful he thought he was John Wayne and started raising major hell. We'd run out there and calm him down. That sort of thing happens a lot out on Sheridan Key. From my point of view rich people aren't that different from poor. They drink, screw around, go nuts, everything, just like us poor folks. We handle them a bit different, the rich."

"How so?"

He gulped down the drink. I tried not to stare. He signaled the bartender to bring another.

"I'll bet it's the same the world over," Zeck said. "Those people out on Sheridan Key contribute to the local politicians, local charities, and so forth. They pay a lot of taxes. We're instructed to handle them with kid gloves. Don't misunderstand, we do our job, but we're very polite, maybe even sensitive about how we do it. Anyway, I think I spend half my duty time talking to some drunken millionaire who has just blackened his wife's eye."

"How about Harwell's daughter? Outside of the cutting incident, was she involved in the other troubles?"

He smiled his gratitude at the bartender as the fresh drink was delivered. I bolted down my Coke and asked for another.

"Once. That was the first time I ever saw her. When we went out there as usual to cool her father down. She was yelling and stuff, but her mother dragged her into the house while we talked to Harwell. She seemed out of control then, but not as much as that time I carted her off to the hospital. Both times I thought she might have been on chemicals, having a bad trip or something. It happens. There's probably more cocaine on the Key than in Bolivia. Anyway, the time I took her to the hospital I had to wrestle her into the car. I remember thinking she was a hell of a lot stronger than she looked." His laugh ended in a snort. "Man, she kicked the hell out of me until I slapped some cuffs on her ankles. I was working alone that day, so it was tough. She was biting, spitting, kicking, every damn thing."

"What did she say?"

"Do you know a cop from up your way named Morgan? An older guy, a detective."

"I know him."

"He was down here. He asked me the same thing. He had one of those little hand-held tape recorders with him."

"What did Angel say, if you remember?"

"Oh, I remember. It's a long drive to the hospital when you got a screwball thrashing around in the backseat. I remember it real good. She was as pissed as a hornet and stayed like that until I dumped her off with the orderlies."

"What did she say?" I repeated.

He sighed and sipped the whiskey. "Mostly, she was screaming, but not out of fear or anything like that. She must have really hated her father. Everything was directed at him. Well, almost everything. I came in for a fair share of abuse on that ride. Like I say, from my point of view, she was either nuts or sky high on something."

"Go on."

"You won't like it."

"Try me."

"She kept repeating, over and over, usually at the top of her lungs, that she was going to kill her father."

He sipped again. Then he chuckled. "Man, she knew dirty words that even I hadn't heard before. Her language was kind of colorful, but it all came out to the same thing. She said she was going to cut his heart out." He paused, looking away. "As a matter of fact, those were her exact words."

"That's when Morgan turned on his tape recorder?"

He smiled. "Yeah."

"You've been very helpful and I appreciate it." It was time to get out of there. "Of course, there are some very good legal reasons to prevent your testimony at trial."

He nodded. "Yeah. It would be the same down here. Unless you got a very friendly judge, of course. All things are possible then."

He looked at me. "Can I ask a favor?"

"Depends."

"I know you have to object to what they want me to say. I understand that. But maybe you could hold off until I'm up there? See, it's a free trip for me, kind of a vacation. I'd like to see Michigan. How about it?"

"I can't object until they call you, not effectively. Unless something changes, you'll get your trip."

"Sure you won't have a real drink? I'll buy the round."

I stood up. "Thanks, no. I may give you a call before the trial." I left money for the bourbon and the Cokes.

He nodded. "She's good looking, that Angel. You, ah, getting anything besides your fee?" It was said as a joke, the locker-room kind.

"I learned a long time ago not to mess with clients."

He nodded again. "Yeah, especially that one. She's nuts. You might end up like daddy." He smiled. "I'll see you up there. Maybe we can have a few drinks, okay?"

He grinned and raised his glass in a parting salute.

I CALLED Angel's psychologist and to my surprise he said he would see me. No hassle, no fuss about fitting me into a busy schedule. He just told me to come right over Things in Florida

258

seemed to go so much more smoothly. I wondered if it was the climate.

It was getting toward the end of day when I arrived, and I was the only one in the waiting room. Besides a potted plant that looked like it might eat anything that got too close, there was nothing exotic about the Florida office; it was spartan and businesslike. There were a few placid prints hung on the walls and three diplomas. I took a closer look at the diplomas.

Alphonse Germain had popped out of Rutgers some twenty years before with bachelor and master's degrees. Then a Connecticut college a few years later had awarded him a doctorate in philosophy. There was also a framed certificate proclaiming that he had completed a psychology residency at a New York hospital.

Dr. Germain came out of his office, escorting a lady patient to the door, his hand on her elbow as if it were a tiller. She was a stout, middle-aged woman who looked at him with adoration and longing. As soon as she was out the door he offered me his hand.

Milo Zeck hadn't looked like a cop and Dr. Germain didn't look like a psychologist. If anything, he resembled Steve McQueen, although he was a little shorter. Fifty maybe, his smooth face suggested that a plastic surgeon might have taken a few tucks here and there.

"Al Germain," he said grinning. His brown hair had been permed and cut to increase the McQueen illusion. Tan and lean, he wore a thick gold chain at his neck. His silk shirt was worn open, displaying the gold against his graying chest hair and sundarkened skin.

His grip was strong, probably from hours of tennis.

"Cm'on in," he said, escorting me into his office, holding my elbow just as he had his stout lady patient's.

His office was as spartan as the reception room. Germain sat down behind the uncluttered desk and indicated I should take a chair opposite. There was a black leather couch, but it was against one wall and didn't look like it was used for business, at least not his doctor business.

"How's Angel?" he asked.

"I thought you might be able to tell me."

He smiled. The teeth were perfect and gleaming white. "Angel's no longer a patient of mine. Didn't she tell you?"

"No."

He nodded. "We ended the therapy a couple of months ago."

"You did, or did she?"

"She did, frankly. She got the idea I was somehow conspiring with her father. Under those conditions additional therapy would have been pointless. In this business you have to have the trust of the patient, otherwise it's impossible to make any progress."

"Who paid your bills?"

He shrugged. "Her father did."

"Maybe she had a point, eh?"

He didn't appear offended. "Some people are covered by medical insurance. Some aren't, especially if therapy's long-term. It's not unusual to have a family pay for someone. It helps them all in the long run."

"I assume you received the release form I sent? The one Angel signed?"

"Oh yeah, I got it. There's a problem. That's why I didn't respond."

"What's that?"

"All I have in the way of records on Angel are diary entries and paid bills."

"Didn't you keep notes?"

He shrugged. "Sure. But when she discontinued therapy I got rid of them."

"Did you store them?"

"No. I destroyed them."

"Isn't that unusual?"

He shrugged. "That's how I do it." He smiled that open self-assured smile people have when they're lying.

I'd get back to the records when he wasn't quite so ready for the questions. "How did Angel come to be a patient of yours?"

"There had been some trouble out on the Key. A family dispute that turned physical. She ended up at a splendid little hospital here. She promised to accept therapy on an outpatient basis and the hospital recommended me."

"I received the hospital's records," I said. "They said they treated her for a personality disorder."

"She was only in there for a few days, but that was their diagnosis."

260

"You don't agree?"

"Not entirely. Angel is a complicated young lady."

"You do know she's charged with her father's death?"

He laughed. "Everyone knows unless they've been in a space capsule. The case has been splashed all over the papers down here and I've followed it on television. I've seen you on the tube, as a matter of fact."

"Do you think she did it?"

The smile died. "How would I know?"

"Therapists usually have a basis for that kind of an opinion."

He studied me for a moment, as if I had suddenly become visible and he was seeing me for the first time and didn't like what he saw.

"Look, I'm not going to testify, if that's what you're after."

"I'm not, at least not now. But what's your problem?"

"In my business it's not good to get on the stand and repeat what the patient told you in confidence."

"Even if the patient asks you to do so?"

He looked away. "She wouldn't."

"Why not?"

"Hey, she spent most of the sessions here telling me how much she hated her father. Did you know him?"

"No."

"He was a piece of work." He chuckled. "The original tight asshole, to use a slightly unprofessional phrase. The guy was a walking bundle of anger."

"Did he hate Angel?"

"He wasn't my patient, but I don't think he hated her or loved her, frankly. She was his daughter and he thought of her as a possession, like his car or house. Also, this guy lived by rules, ironclad rigid rules. I see a lot of guys like that here. That kind of inflexibility makes rich men out of people like me. Anyway, if you put me on the stand, I'd have to say Angel told me she was going to kill her old man. I don't think you want that, right?"

I nodded. "It could hurt."

"Hurt? Hell, it could kill."

"What was in your notes that made you decide to destroy them?"

"They were just notes to myself, that's all. There was nothing special."

"Did you destroy them after she was arrested?"

He eyed me warily. "Before."

"How often did you see Angel when you were treating her?"

"Once a week, for an hour. That's standard, unless there's an emergency. Why?"

"I've been sent a number of records by her doctors and hospitals. Most of them have been edited. Yours aren't the only notes missing."

"So?"

"The experts I have reviewing the medical reports say it looks like someone went through and deleted much of what Angel said."

"It's probably just a coincidence. It happens."

"Did anyone tell you to destroy the treatment notes?"

"That's a rather nasty question considering how cooperative I've been."

"Did they?"

"Of course not."

"Did she ever tell you she was sexually abused by her father?"

"What she told me is confidential."

"You have her signed release. I'm entitled to know."

"Incest? I don't think that was ever mentioned."

"I think you're lying."

"Look, Mr. Sloan, I have other things to do. When you see Angel tell her Al says hello."

"I could depose you, make you answer questions under oath, you do know that?"

He nodded slowly. "Sure you could. Under oath, like you say. I don't know much about legal procedure but I understand that you'd have to let the other side have a crack at me, too. Right?"

"So?"

"If you do, I've got to tell the truth. Angel said she would kill her father. That's something I can't lie about."

"I just might take that risk."

"It's up to you." He stood up. But there was no apparent anger. "Say, if you do see Angel, will you tell her something for me."

262

"What?"

A sly Steve McQueen smile spread across his tan features. "Tell her I think she should get another lawyer."

THERE was a new guard on the entrance gate to Sheridan Key, almost a twin of the first one, although a bit thinner and a lot less booze-ravaged. I identified myself as before and he let me pass.

The young black man who had greeted me when I first arrived took me through the Harwell house again. I could hear music coming from the pool area. This time it sounded like live music.

As if reading my mind, my guide grinned. "There's a cocktail party out by the pool. It's our turn tonight."

"Turn?"

"Each night, except Sunday, there's a cocktail party. The people who live out here on the Key take turns hosting it."

"Is it mandatory to attend if you live down here?"

He laughed. "Oh no. But most people show up for an hour or so. It's a way for them to stay in touch with their neighbors."

"Sounds a little like the British colonies in Kenya or India in the old days."

He chuckled, glancing down at his own black skin. "Not all that different when you come to think of it." He grinned. "Sahib."

It was very hot and even the slight breeze off the Gulf didn't help much. I could see a flock of people standing around the pool area as we approached. Most of the women, all ages but mostly razor thin, wore frilly summer dresses. The men, gray-haired or bald, most of them portly, were decked out in slacks or walking shorts. Everybody held a glass.

A three-piece combo, guitar, base, and electric keyboard, softly played a lilting Cole Porter melody. The three middle-aged musicians were the only ones wearing coats. As they played they stared off into space as if to assure the people present that whatever happened, none of it would be seen or reported.

Robin hurried over to me.

"Everyone's dying to meet you."

"This is quite a party. How long does it last?"

She smiled. "That depends on how much fun we have. Sometimes it breaks up before dinner. Sometimes it goes on into the wee hours of the morning. It just depends on the mood."

"I need to talk to Angel."

"Later, Charley. Let loose a bit. Look around you. Palm trees, the Gulf of Mexico, lovely ladies, music. You must admit, this beats Detroit."

She did have a point.

"Let me get you a drink."

"Not right now. Thanks."

"Let me introduce you around." She took my arm in the same fashion as Dr. Germain had. Perhaps it was a Florida custom.

Robin was good at it. We managed to meet everyone, more than thirty people, in less than an hour. The people at the party became for me a montage of smiling faces and insolent eyes. Apparently, I was considered a minor celebrity, thanks to national television coverage. These people, all of them very rich, seemed interested but not impressed. They could buy and sell me and they knew it. I tried to remember the names but it was impossible.

By the time we had worked our way through the people my shirt was plastered to my skin. I gratefully gulped down a large iced tea brought by one of the maids.

"Did any of these people know Harrison well?" I asked Robin.

She looked around at the group as if trying to make up her mind. "I think he may have slept with that dreadful Madge Foster over there. The blowzy redhead. Of course, damn few men here haven't. Madge is almost a rite of passage with this crowd."

"It doesn't sound as if that made you wildly jealous."

She smiled. "By the time it happened, I didn't care one way or the other. Of course, as I told you, Harrison was in a kind of perpetual heat. He considered himself a bull, bellow and all. I thought age might finally slow him a bit but it didn't."

"How about the men here? Anyone a special buddy of his?"

"A friend?"

"Even rich people have them."

She laughed. "Not Harrison. Most people here considered him a son of a bitch. Harrison had to compete at everything he did, and his main social ploy was putting others down. He was good at it, but that ability doesn't win many close admirers." She paused. "If anyone here could be considered a friend, it might be Willoby Johnson."

"Which one is he? I'm afraid all the names became a jumble as you whirled me around out there."

"Willoby, everyone calls him Willy, is the short stocky man with the colorful shirt, the bald fellow next to the tall woman. She's his wife, his fourth wife."

"Scrawny but beautiful."

"If you read women's magazines you'd recognize her. She was a top model before she married Willy."

"There must be something wildly compelling about a beer belly and baldness."

She nodded. "There is, when the belly is connected to a fortune worth over a hundred million."

"True love."

"There's a lot of true love like that out here on the Key."

"Like yours?" I regretted saying it as soon as it escaped my lips.

She smiled but I thought I saw pain in her eyes. "Ours was a genuine love match, at first." She sighed. "It faded quickly, but in the beginning it was like something out of a storybook."

"I'm sorry I said that."

She looked away. "I have always preferred honesty, Charley, even if it hurts. Don't worry about it."

"I think I'll have a talk with rich Willy."

The combo played a familiar old tango as I walked toward the Johnsons. It was hard not to dance over. Also, caught in the mood of the soft, pulsating music, the sea, and the palms, I felt an urge to forget everything else, get a real drink, and just kick back and enjoy life. It only lasted for the distance it took to reach my bald-and-bellied target.

"Are you enjoying yourself, Mr. Sloan?" Mrs. Johnson was tall enough to play basketball for the Detroit Pistons. She looked down at me with green eyes that would have been beautiful except for the calculating quality I saw there.

"It's a working trip for me," I answered.

I looked down at her husband. A few more pounds and he could be the basketball. His eyes I recognized. I had seen that kind of eyes in every bar and saloon I had ever spent time in. He was already having a hard time focusing. His wife's eyes were calculating, his were hostile.

"Mr. Johnson, I understand Harrison Harwell and you were close friends."

"We played golf," he growled, "until I couldn't tolerate his cheating. It was the same at cards. He couldn't stand to lose. He was a dishonest, mouthy bastard. I didn't like his father, either."

I thought he would make a touching witness.

"Oh, Harrison wasn't so bad, Willy," his wife said. "If you got past the bluster, he could be charming."

"You only say that because he was trying to fuck you," he responded indifferently, as if the subject had become boring.

"He was like that with everyone, not just me," she replied, also indifferently.

"My experts think he may have committed suicide," I said. "You knew him. Does that seem possible?"

"No," she said.

"Yes," he said, almost at the same time.

She glanced down at her husband. I thought I saw disgust, but just for a second. Then she smiled. "Harrison had too much life in him for anything like that," she said. "Oh, he had his faults, we all do. But he would be the last person to even think about suicide."

"The prick was going to lose his fucking boat business," he snapped with authority. "That would put him over the edge. Jesus, he couldn't stand to lose at anything. That business was his whole life. Suicide makes a lot of sense to me. Full of life?" He looked up at his wife, his watery eyes narrowing. "Harrison was full of shit."

"What are Angel's chances?" his wife asked me, deftly changing the subject.

"Good, I hope. Of course, a jury might see things differently. We'll find out soon enough."

"Do you plan to plead insanity?" she asked.

"No."

"Angel's nuts," her husband said. "But then, none of the Harwells were ever wired too tight."

"Robin's nice," his wife said.

"She's not a Harwell. Not by blood."

"Will you be staying here long, Mr. Sloan?" she asked.

"A day or two. It depends."

266

"We're having a few people over tonight. Why don't you come? We're just three places down. You can walk it. I think I can promise you a good time, Mr. Sloan."

"Jesus, Wanda, first that young boat boy, now this. What the hell's wrong with you? This guy's nothing but a lawyer, for Christ's sake."

She smiled. "Here on the Key my husband is considered something of a wit. Amusing, don't you think? Can we expect you?"

"Thanks, but I have work to do. It's been nice talking to you."

The combo was playing a Hawaiian tune as I retraced my steps.

Milo Zeck was right. The rich, in some ways, aren't all that different.

Robin was talking with a couple I had met but whose names I couldn't remember.

"Where's Angel?" I asked.

"She's down by the shore," she said. "She doesn't like these parties very much." She smiled. "Were the Johnson's any help?"

"Like holes in a boat."

I went to find Angel.

SHE was perched on a boulder near the water, one knee drawn up so that it served as a support for her chin, the other leg extended straight down, her toes buried in sand. She stared out at the gentle Gulf.

Angel was dwarfed in a huge loose shirt worn over walking shorts. She looked like a little girl.

Faint music drifted down from the party near the pool.

"Hi," I said as I came up to her.

She didn't move an inch, her eyes fixed on the water. "Not much of a party, Charley?"

"Depends on your mood, I suppose. Robin says you aren't thrilled by these things."

"I've known those people up there most of my life. Toads have more personality. They're all so full of alcohol and judgment, although God knows most of them have committed enough twisted sins to write a new Bible." She paused. "Did you like them?"

I settled myself on a smaller boulder near hers.

"I didn't spend enough time to find out. But today I did talk to

267

the cop who arrested you down here, the time you cut your father. Tell me about that."

"I prefer to forget things like that."

"I wish you could, but the prosecutor is calling the cop as a witness against you, so I have to know what happened."

"If I cut Daddy once, I would cut him twice; I suppose that's the reasoning."

"More or less. What happened?"

For a moment I thought she wasn't going to answer. She just continued to stare at the water. Then she spoke. "We had an argument, my father and I. Things escalated. He began to knock me around. He was drinking." She looked over at me. "He was always drinking. I was afraid he was going to kill me, he was that angry. Very violent. I grabbed a knife off a table and held it in front of me, to keep him away. He was so mad he didn't even see it. He swung at me and cut himself."

"What was the fight about?"

She returned her gaze to the Gulf. "I don't remember, there was always something."

"The policeman said you were out of control."

She sighed. "Anyone would be."

"What do you mean?"

"My father went berserk when he saw he was bleeding. He told me he was going to have me put away for good. I thought he meant it. My father called the police. That cop didn't even give me a chance to tell my side."

"He seemed like a fair man to me."

"Maybe he is, but that's all anyone has to hear—she's a former mental patient. It's like having some hideous warning tattooed on your forehead."

She looked again at me. "Have you ever been locked up, Charley?"

"A few times, I'm sorry to say."

"I can't stand it."

"No one's very fond of it, Angel."

"I've been in four hospitals, and once in that awful jail until you rescued me. When they close and lock a door I feel like I'm drowning. I can't breath. Anyway, I believed my father, I thought he would arrange it so I could never get out."

She sighed. "I did what anyone would do in that circumstance, I tried to keep from going. That policeman believed everything my father said. There was no mercy, no doubt, no nothing. He was very mean to me."

"Angel, you said four hospitals. I know about three. Were you ever in Buckingham Hospital in Michigan?"

She nodded. "Yes."

"Recently?"

"A couple of months ago, something like that. I was in there for almost three weeks. Robin got me out, thank God."

"I heard something about you being in a violent ward there. True?"

"Thanks to my father, yes."

"What happened?"

"I know it sounds like a broken record, but he started knocking me around again. I tried to fight back. He told the doctors I was violent. Everyone always believed my father."

"A knife again?"

"No. Nothing. I was just trying to keep from being hit."

"Were the police called?"

"No. He had everything set up. Some orderlies from the hospital came." She paused, looking again at the water. "They used canvas restraints. It was awful."

"If you had that much trouble at home, why did you stay?"

She snorted. "I did leave once. I have the money my mother left for me now, but not then, so I had to find someplace to make a living. I went to New York. You already know what happened there. He came after me and I ended up in that hospital. Nobody ever left my father, not without terrible things happening to her. God knows, he told me that often enough. I was a prisoner. A long leash maybe, but a prisoner nevertheless."

"Why didn't Robin help?"

"She did. But she was a prisoner too." She sighed again. "If it hadn't been for Robin I never would have survived."

"Angel, maybe you can help me. What medical records I've been able to get from the your doctors and the hospitals have all been altered. Anything that showed what caused you to need treatment has been deleted. Why, do you suppose? And who did it?"

She looked surprised, or I thought she did. Then she nodded slowly. "My father did, obviously," she said. "It was all in there, what he did to me. He knew. It was his goddamned pride. I'm sure he arranged that anything that might reflect on him was removed. He was a powerful man. He knew how to do things like that."

"Angel, one of the doctors I had you talk to thinks you fit a familiar pattern."

"I'll bet."

"He says the pattern resembles someone who has been the victim of incest."

I hoped for a reaction of some kind, but there was none.

"Even if that happened, so what?"

"It could help explain what happened."

She turned and stared at me. "Charley, I didn't kill my father. But I don't think you really believe that."

"Whether I believe you isn't important. What a jury will believe is. I need to know about you and your father."

"My relationship with my father was strange no matter how you look at it. I don't want to think about it, much less talk about it. I'm sorry, but that's the way it is."

"Did you tell the doctors, about the relationship?"

She nodded. "Yes. I suppose that's why my father had some records removed."

"Was it incest, Angel?"

"It doesn't matter anymore, no matter what it was."

"I have to know."

"Why?"

"It might help me defend you."

"No it wouldn't," she said.

I decided not to press it now. There was time enough later.

Angel watched the Gulf for a few moments, then she turned and fixed those cool blue eyes on me. "I can't go to jail, Charley."

"That's why I'm here, Angel. We're doing everything to see that doesn't happen."

"Charley, I know what would happen to me if I'm convicted. Even the few days I spent in the jail taught me that. I wouldn't last. I couldn't."

"As I say, we're—"

270

"I won't go to prison." The words were spoken softly, but with surprising intensity.

"Let's not even think about that, Angel. We'll—"

"No!" Her eyes had widened, although that was the only visible indication of emotion. "You don't understand. I won't go." She turned away and stared at the Gulf. "I can't. If I'm convicted I'll make sure they can't lock me up. Never. Never!"

"Like what? Kill yourself? Look, I know how you feel, but let's walk this road together, one step at a time. Don't think about giving up."

She stood suddenly, then stretched. "I trust you, Charley. I haven't trusted many people in my life. I know you're doing everything you can for me." Her tone once again was completely calm.

Angel brushed off her bottom. She looked down at me, patted my head, and then headed back toward the house. "Just so you know," she said as she walked away, "I will never be locked up again. It won't happen, no matter what your court may do."

I sat there. It was my turn to stare out at the water.

She meant exactly what she had said. I sensed that.

I wished I had never taken the damn case.

20

THE WONDERFUL COOPERATION I WAS ENJOYING IN
Florida ended with my phone call to Harrison Harwell's divorce
lawyer. His reaction would have been more appropriate if I had
been selling small children into prostitution. There was enough
ice in his voice to freeze Miami.

It was only after I threatened, wheedled, pleaded, and begged
that he agreed to give me ten minutes, and that only if I hurried
over at once since he was going to fit me in between clients.

So I hurried.

The place was enough to make Donald Trump sob with envy.
Not huge, but sinfully luxurious. The law firm owned and occupied a very large, almost new building, mostly tinted glass, two
stories high and very long. The architect had designed it to create
the illusion that the sleek glass structure had blossomed there,
magically, all by itself, a natural outcropping among the lush tropical trees and flowers that bordered the place. There was ample
parking for customers in the front, with staff parking in the rear. I
drove back there just to take a look. Judging from the cars, the
lawyers either did a lucrative business or the firm was a front for a
Mercedes dealership.

I was escorted by a charming young woman, prim in appearance, her good figure concealed in a power suit, and so polite
you could slide on it. She took me to the office of Alexander
Cameron.

272

A little rooster of a man, Cameron was wearing a monogrammed shirt and a dainty bow tie. His rusty hair was graying and I guessed him to be on the near side of seventy. His eyes had the hard look of a born fighter.

"You have ten minutes, Mr. Sloan," he said, ignoring my extended hand. He sat down behind his desk and waited.

"Nice place," I said. "All from divorce business?"

The eyes narrowed. "We are a general litigation firm. Divorce is not our main practice. You now have nine minutes."

I laughed. "Okay, I'll get right to it. As you know, I represent Angel Harwell. Angel will go to trial for second-degree murder in roughly a month. Frankly, I believe I can prove that Harrison Harwell took his own life. That's why I'm here. To find all I can about him."

One eyebrow had gone up. "Suicide? Are you serious?"

"Very."

"That's ridiculous."

"Why?"

"Did you know him?" he asked.

"No."

He leaned back in his chair. I thought he seemed slightly less hostile. "Mr. Harwell was a client. I didn't know him socially, but I spent quite some time with him in connection with legal matters. He never impressed me as someone who might commit suicide."

Despite himself, he smiled. "Murder, yes. Suicide, never. I've read about the case. I rather doubt you'll succeed with a suicide theory, frankly. But I suppose you have to come up with some kind of defense, no matter how far-fetched."

"Harwell was planning to file for divorce, I understand?"

"I'm not going to answer any of your questions if you plan to call me as a witness."

"There's no reason to call you."

He chuckled. "There better not be." He shifted in his chair slightly, getting more comfortable.

"Have you ever defended in a murder case before, Mr. Sloan?"

"Yes."

"Often?"

"Often enough."

He smiled. "I have been defense counsel in three murder cases here in Florida. I won one, got one reduced to manslaughter by the jury, and lost one. The case I lost, the man was executed."

"That must have been tough to take."

He chuckled again. "Not really. I did my best, perhaps more than I should have. He was a murderous animal. I grew to hate the man. I did not tear out my hair when the state of Florida ended his miserable existence.

"Don't mistake me, Sloan. I had a job to do and I did it. It was one of those cases that couldn't be won. I am a professional, I went flat out for the rotten son of a bitch. Whether I liked him or not had nothing to do with the quality or vigor of the defense."

"Do you do much criminal work?"

"Some. I am a trial lawyer, Mr. Sloan. That's why Harrison Harwell retained me. He anticipated some nasty litigation. Nasty litigation is my specialty.

"Divorce, I assume?"

He hesitated, then nodded.

"But nothing was filed, I understand. If the divorce case was ready to go, why not?"

Cameron studied me for a moment, then spoke. "I suppose there's no harm in telling you. Any lawyer could figure it out."

"I'm slow. I can use the help."

"Harwell's boat company was in the process of being sold. I assume you know that?"

"Yes."

"The sale itself was being handled by a firm up in Detroit. If we had filed the case before the sale was completed, Mrs. Harwell's lawyers might have been able to freeze the sale proceeds. All that money would be tied up until the divorce was litigated. If we waited until after the sale we could shelter that money before filing the action. There are ways, as we both know. It seemed an excellent strategy at the time. Now, I regret that we waited."

"Why?"

"Making everything public might have prevented his murder."

"Suicide," I said.

He smiled. "Let's settle on death, shall we?"

"Go on," I said.

Cameron shook his head. "There's no point to it.'

"Harrison Harwell is dead. The client privilege died with him. You're free to tell me."

He smiled coldly. "Not as far as I'm concerned."

"Did you know Mrs. Harwell, or Angel?"

"Only what Harrison told me."

"Surely, you can tell me this? Was there a prenuptial agreement?"

He stood up. "The meter has run, Mr. Sloan. Your ten minutes are up."

"Look—"

"I'm sorry. I have a client waiting."

I walked to his door and stopped. "Listen, we're both in the same business. Couldn't you just let me take a quick peek at the file? I'd look at it right here. Someone could watch me. No copies, no notes, just a look. How about it?"

He smiled. "That comes under the heading of nice try, Mr. Sloan. As it is, I've told you more than I intended to. It's been interesting talking with you." The smile became a grin, almost a leer. "I plan to follow your case. It doesn't sound as if you have much of a chance. Do they have the death penalty in Michigan?"

"No."

"Pity," he said.

THE morning air that had been so fresh and clear was turning warm and humid by the time I drove back to Sheridan Key.

Robin, wrapped in a robe, was up, sitting outside, watching the Gulf and sipping coffee. Angel, she told me, wasn't up yet.

A maid brought coffee for me.

"So, Charley, are things down here working out as you expected?"

"I'm finding more problems than solutions. Did you ever find a copy of the prenuptial agreement?"

"I looked high and low," she said. "I'm beginning to think Harrison took it."

"Why?"

"God knows."

"I just talked to his lawyer down here, Alexander Cameron. Do you know him?"

"I've heard of him. He's in the newspapers quite a lot. I've never met the man. I wasn't aware that Harrison even knew him."

"Cameron had drafted a divorce suit. It was to be filed after the boat company was sold."

"I told you Harrison would never have filed for divorce," she said firmly, sipping her coffee.

"How do you know?"

She reached over and patted my hand. "Charley, can't you relax? You worry far too much. Funny, I don't remember you as a worrier. Anyway, Harrison was always threatening divorce. Oh, he would sometimes go to the trouble of getting a lawyer, but it was always just bluster. He never went through with it. There were too many little girlfriends waiting for him. Marriage was his shield and protection, but he was forever shouting that he was going to do it."

"Judging from what I can find out, the trouble out here was increasing. Correct?"

"I told you that. Sometimes it was almost unbearable."

"Why didn't you leave?"

She smiled and looked out at the water. "First, someone had to protect Angel. Second, I've grown used to living in this fashion. I'm being quite candid. If I had left Harrison, I would be leaving all this too." She gestured at the house and pool. "Mainly, though, I stayed for Angel's sake."

"To protect her?"

"Yes."

"From what? Incest?"

She didn't register surprise, but merely looked at me for a moment before answering.

"Angel was ten years old before I came into her life,' she said quietly. "That might have happened before I came. I really don't know. It might even be the root cause of Angel's problems."

She paused, then looked away. "Whether that happened or didn't, it wasn't a happy relationship. The only thing Angel ever got from her father was abuse, either mental or physical. That's why I had to be here."

"She's twenty-one, Robin. Why didn't she leave?"

Robin sighed. "She did, as you know, and she ended up in a mental hospital for her efforts. After that she was afraid to leave." She paused. "And there was another reason."

"What?"

She smiled slightly. "Angel thought she was my protection, too. Harrison didn't much care whom he abused. I caught my fair share." She again looked out at the Gulf, her eyes following a gull. "It wasn't, I admit, the ideal happy home."

I waited to hear more but she merely sipped her coffee, indicating the subject was closed.

"Robin, I'm going to need some more money. I'm bringing in some experts. I'll want them to talk with Angel before the Walker hearing. And they'll be staying over since they'll be testifying at both the hearing and the trial a week later. We pay their air fare, hotel, and expenses, plus their fee. It adds up."

"Submit a bill, Charley. You'll have what you need."

Robin leaned back, allowing the robe to open enough that the top of one breast was visible. "Are you still planning on going back tomorrow?"

"Yes. I have a lot of work to do. Mostly on Angel's case."

She looked away. "I really regret we haven't had a chance to be together, Charley. Things keep getting in the way somehow. Maybe, if you stayed over a couple of days—"

"That's a pretty powerful argument to stay, Robin. But I really have to get back."

"Eventually, we'll work this out, you and I." She finished her coffee. "Well, what's the rest of the day like for you?"

"I have to see a few people down here. I thought I might just wander around the Key now before it gets too hot. Maybe talk to some of your neighbors."

"Use the beach, Charley. It's the main highway down here for all of us. You walk along and talk to whomever you see. Only be careful."

"Dogs?"

She laughed. "Worse, women. Not all the maneaters swim out there in the Gulf. A couple of them lounge by their pools and look for victims."

"Well, in that case, I better get going right away."

She chuckled. "If you don't come back, we'll send out a search party.

"Another caution, Charley. Real, this time." Suddenly she was no longer smiling. Her face was solemn. "Gossip is a way of life on the Key. Don't believe everything you hear."

I WALKED the beach. It looked like white sand but it wasn't. It was the crushed remains of ten billion shelled sea creatures broken into sandlike particles, but they were sharp and brittle. I was glad I was wearing shoes.

There was no wind. The Gulf was as peaceful as shimmering green silk, an illusion disturbed only by the passage of an occasional boat in the distance. The sun dominated a cloudless blue sky, baking everything below.

Sheridan Key was a place of Spanish palaces. The huge palms and tropical growth up by the road hid the fortresses of wealth from view, but the beach provided an unobstructed look. In the old days pirates would have come ashore and sacked them. I walked slowly, feeling the sweat trickle down my back.

"Well, look who's here."

Her voice floated down from the lip of an olympic-sized pool. She was stretched out on a deck chair beneath an enormous striped awning. When I squinted up at her I thought for a moment that she was wearing only sunglasses.

Squinting a bit harder I saw a band of fabric around her chest with a matching band at her hips.

"Do come up, Mr. Sloan. I'm lonely and bored. I don't mind being lonely, but being bored is dreadful."

I crunched off the beach and up to the pool. I didn't recognize her at first, then I got a closer look. Her legs seemed to go on forever, so long and shapely they seemed almost unbelievable. The rest of her wasn't bad either, except she was so flat-chested that the thin fabric bathing suit top was hardly needed. I thought she looked even better out of clothes than in.

"Mrs. Johnson," I said. "I'm flattered you remembered me."

"A beautiful man like you? Who wouldn't." She laughed.

I laughed too. It was a ridiculous statement.

"Is Mr. Johnson around?"

"Willoby Johnson, owner of half the world, told me he is playing golf today."

"Good weather for it."

She took off her sunglasses and smiled. "He must play extremely skillfully. He spends hours at it but never gets tan."

"Some people have been known to have their best rounds in the bar."

"Speaking of bar, would you like a drink, Mr. Sloan?"

"Just water. By the way, everyone calls me Charley."

"Rosa!" Her voice, suddenly powerful, seemed to echo off the waters of the Gulf.

A young woman in jeans and tank top appeared.

"Rosa, bring Mr. Sloan some ice water. Oh, and a margarita for me."

The girl smiled and disappeared.

"A lovely girl," she said. "Out here on the Key we tend to steal each other's servants. Rosa used to work for Patricia Barkley, the shipping Barkleys, until I stole her away. Money seduces, Charley, and Willoby's money allows me all kinds of juicy seductions. It's so much different here than Cleveland."

"Cleveland?"

She giggled. "I was the tallest girl in Cleveland, or at least in my high school. There, on the banks of Lake Erie, I was considered something of a freak. When I moved to New York I found that what was freakish in Cleveland was fashionable in Gotham. I became a model. The gay designers loved my long bones. From there I went to Paris, met Willoby Johnson, one of the richest men in the world, unhorsed my predecessor, became the fourth Mrs. Willoby Johnson, and ended up here in Sheridan Key."

"A love story."

She snorted. "Sure, just like in the storybooks, with one small exception. Willy isn't playing golf, Charley. He's in a dreadful little apartment in Bradenton, being whipped by a chubby young man decked out in leather. He goes twice a week."

"C'mon."

"It's true. Poor old Willy is as twisted as a pretzel. It's the only way he can get his little pecker up anymore. I used to do it. You know, pretend to hurt him, the usual S-and-M crap, but I tired of it. I'm the one who lined up the chubby little specialist, although Willy doesn't know it."

The maid brought the drinks. I sipped mine to make sure it was just water. It was.

She came away from the margarita with a green-lined lip. Her tongue, a pink snake, provocatively licked it off. "Other than that small variation on a theme, this is an ideal existence. Willy isn't half bad. He's in the bag most of the time, but out here that's almost expected. He's harmless."

She looked at me. "Tell me, Charley, do you like to fuck?"

"Why don't you dress up in leather and find out."

Her laugh echoed off the water.

"Mrs. Johnson—"

"My real name is Wanda. I didn't like it, so I changed it in New York to CiCi. There's a lot of Wandas in Cleveland but damn few CiCis. I prefer it."

"CiCi, I'm down here trying to build a defense for Angel Harwell. Frankly, how do you figure the situation?"

"Do I think Angel killed her father? Perhaps she did. She's an odd duck, that Angel. She's like a ghost. You see her flitting around, but there's little chance for conversation. So I have no real way of knowing." She smiled. "You're her lawyer. You tell me. Did she do it?"

"I don't think she did. As I told you last night, I believe that Harrison Harwell may have killed himself."

She seemed genuinely interested. "You really mean it, don't you?"

"Did you know him well?"

"Not as well as he wanted me to, but I knew him as well as anyone else here on the Key. We are, as you saw last night, one happy band of brothers down here. More or less."

"I take it he made a pass at you?"

She sighed. "I'd have been offended if he hadn't. There's three sports down here, tennis, golf, and screwing. Frankly, I think when you men get old and fat you slow down in all three." She smiled. "I suppose that's why they have senior leagues, eh? And then, some still talk a good game but can't even play anymore. But I understand that wasn't Harrison's problem."

"What was the gossip?"

"You aren't a hairdresser on the side, are you Charley?"

"No."

"They just love to hear all the juicy stuff too. Anyway, Harrison tried to lay every woman he met. A kind of backroom Tarzan. He did everything but beat on his chest and thump the ground. I thought him amusing, but most people here thought he was a horse's ass. Anyway, our aging Tarzan made a specialty of pronging the little Hispanic women who worked as household staff. The joke here was that he had a boat and a full-time boat captain to bring them in and take them back."

"What was the effect on his wife?"

She snorted. "Robin? She didn't care. I think she may have even endorsed the arrangement. Just as I approve of Willy's little twice weekly so-called golf games."

"Are you sure? I understand the police were called there several times."

"That was Tarzan. Harrison was the kind who loved to beat on women. There are a few just like him down here. He'd get drunk and take after Robin or Angel. More mouth than fist, like so many drunks."

"What about Angel?"

"I hardly know her. And that's unusual down here. We are rather inbred and if someone has a pimple on his ass it becomes a topic of mutual concern. But Angel never mixed in."

"Maybe she's shy?"

She snorted again. "Harrison was convinced she was crazy. Something about her really got under his skin, although we never really knew why. Of course, she was never around down here until a few years ago."

"Oh?"

"When her mother died Harrison shipped her off to some fancy school in Europe. Of course, at that time I hadn't even met Willy and didn't know this place or these people even existed. It was a Swiss school, I hear. She finished school in this country. Quite a bright girl, they tell me. But Angel didn't go on to college. When she began living here full-time, that's when the fireworks really started. There was some dynamic between father and daughter. What it was I never really knew."

"What about Robin? How well do you know her?"

She smiled. "Tell me, where are you from again?"

"Detroit, a few miles north of there now."

"I've never been to Detroit but I'll bet it's a lot like Cleveland.

Escape while you can, Charley. Robin did. So did almost every woman down here. We, all of us, are numericals."

"Numericals?"

She laughed. "I'm a number four. Robin is a number two, a rather rare thing on Sheridan Key. It's the number wife you are to the millionaire of your dreams. We are like a sorority. Robin and I are friends. Not close maybe, but friends. Of course, she's managed to win the big prize."

"And that is?"

"To outlive your rich old husband. It can get dicey, Charley. For instance, Willy may decide to dump me for some young thing who loves to play crack the whip. I would get what I bargained for in the prenuptial agreement but the whip lady would become number five and maybe end up with it all."

She stretched, writhing like a boa constrictor, one segment at a time; her moving body seemed to go on forever. "Anyway, Robin, although only a number two, has won it all. Still, she had to put up with a lot. Ten year's worth. But she can now do whatever she wants with the rest of her life, and in a style Cleopatra would have killed for."

She studied the empty margarita glass. "Life is a contest and Robin has grabbed the brass ring."

She sat up enough to reach over and stroke my arm. "Are you sweet on her, Charley? I do notice a little note in your voice when you speak her name. Is that why I don't stand a chance?"

I laughed. "We knew each other as kids. That's all."

"Why don't you marry her and move down here? That would be a novelty, having a man as a number two." She batted her long eyelashes. "Think about it. You'd like it here. Everyone is discreet. You could sneak over and we could play all kinds of delicious games."

"Like crack the whip?"

She grinned. "If that's what you like, sure. Everything goes down here."

I TALKED to some other people on the Key. I got the impression that they knew a great deal more than they were willing to tell me. Some were charming about it, some weren't.

When I got back I questioned the members of the Harwell's

282

local staff. Again, they were polite but very guarded in what they said. That was natural, given the circumstances. Loose lips can sink jobs. Still, it seemed to me that their careful reserve went beyond even that.

The sun was near the horizon by the time I finished up. A swimsuit had been provided in my room so I took a nice solitary swim in the beautiful pool, mostly floating or paddling on my back and enjoying the warm air and the cloudless tropic sky. CiCi Johnson had inspired the thoughts I was having. Being a kept husband, living in such magic splendor, enjoying this tropical paradise, might not be the worst fate imaginable. It was kind of fun to think about.

After the swim I showered and dressed. Then I had one of the servants take me to Harrison Harwell's office.

It was a carbon copy of the one at Pickeral Point, down to the smallest detail, including the identical photos on the wall and the little statue of a Japanese warrior on the desk.

Both swords, exactly the same as those in Pickeral Point, hung behind the desk.

I slid the small sword from its scabbard. It was a beautiful thing, as much a work of fine art as an implement of war. I tentatively fingered the blade. It was so sharp a person could literally shave with it.

Or kill. I put it back.

The expensive state-of-the-art stereo was an exact duplicate of the one in Michigan. There was a tape ready to play so I pressed the button.

The small room filled with Japanese music, very beautiful, played slowly and mournfully. I didn't know if they had funeral dirges, in Japan, but to my ear it sounded like one.

I snapped it off.

Somehow the Tarzan that CiCi Johnson had described didn't seem to fit with this room or the music.

I felt sad. And it wasn't only because of the tape.

DINNER, with just the three of us, was strained, like three strangers sharing a table. The conversation was formal and touched topics that were universally neutral.

Even when I brought up my conversations with their neigh-

283

bors, editing some of what CiCi had told me, there was no more than polite interest.

Coffee was served, and then after-dinner drinks. The lure of sweet rum, and the mental ease it promised, whispered to my consciousness, inspired by the tropic night. But I stayed with the coffee.

"What happens now, Charley?" Robin asked.

"I go back home and start preparing for trial."

Angel studied me. "Which means?"

"Basically, we have two trials. First, there's the Walker hearing on the admission of your statement, Angel. I'll be using several doctors as witnesses. I have to prepare them. We have to show that what the police did, the way they questioned you for hours, amounted to mental and emotional duress so that the statement wasn't voluntary."

"Is that it," Angel asked, "just doctors?"

"Not exactly. The prosecution will put the cops on the stad to show you did everything of your own free will. There's no jury on this one, just the judge. He decides whether they can use the statement against you at trial."

"What happens if he says they can?" Angel asked.

"He might not. Nothing's sure. I think I can make a hell of a case to keep it out. If he does exclude it, that damages their case against you. Maybe not fatally, but significantly."

"And if he keeps it in, what then?" Robin asked.

I shrugged. "It makes things more difficult. I can still attack the so-called confession at trial, basically using the same witnesses, but that brings in things I'd rather a jury not look at."

"Like what?" Angel asked.

"Your treatment records. That kind of thing can go either way in a case like this. But if your statement gets in, we have to challenge it. There's no choice. How we do it will depend on the circumstances. Jury trials, for that matter any trial, take unexpected shifts as they go along. You have to adjust to those shifts as they happen. You try to plan for everything that could happen, but nothing ever quite goes the way you expect."

"Will I have to testify?" Angel asked.

"If we keep the statement out, probably not. If we don't, that's a judgment we'll have to make at the time. A good prosecutor can make Mother Theresa look like Jesse James on the stand. It's always a gamble. We'll just have to wait to see if it's worth it."

"I wish it would all just go away," Angel said.

"Me too," I responded. "But it won't."

"You've done a lot of work on it now, Charley," Robin said. "What do you think of the chances now?"

"Good." I said it, but I didn't really mean it.

"I will not go to prison," Angel said, her tone as quietly determined as it had been before, perhaps even more.

"It's my job to see that you don't," I replied.

"We have every confidence in you, Charley," Robin said. I wondered if she really meant it.

I COULDN'T sleep. I left the windows open in my bedroom. The air was warm but I wanted to listen to the soft sounds of the tropical night and the whisper of the Gulf.

I must have dozed off because I didn't hear her come in. I became aware of her naked body, cool and supple, as she slid in next to me in the bed.

Her hand slid slowly down from my chest, moving with sensuous slowness past my stomach. I felt her lips on the side of my neck and then her teeth as she bit me softly and painlessly.

"It's been a while," I whispered, reaching for her.

She said nothing. Her hand did all the communicating necessary.

"Oh, Robin," I sighed as I turned.

There was some moonlight, enough to see that it wasn't Robin.

"Surprise, Charley," Angel said.

She was as naked as I was.

I pulled away.

"Don't be like that."

I almost laughed at myself. It was a scene out of a farce. I jumped out of bed and turned on the bedside lamp.

She lay there, watching me, knowing the effect she was having. "Are you gay, Charley?"

"No, Angel. But this just won't work."

"Why not?"

"Look, in a few short weeks I have to defend you for murder. I have to be objective. That sounds silly to you. It even sounds silly

285

to me. But it's true nevertheless. If I'm to do a job for you, a good job, I can't be emotionally involved."

She sat up slowly. Again expressionless. "Are you sure?"

"I'm sure."

She stood up. She was magnificent, physically perfect.

That Mona Lisa smile played briefly on her lips. "You'll think about this, Charley, you will. And you'll regret it. This chance won't come again. Are you really sure?"

"Good night, Angel."

"Dream of me, Charley," she said.

And then she was gone.

21

EVERYTHING WAS GOING MUCH TOO FAST.

I had forgotten how much detail work was necessary in a major case. The troubling memories of my short stay in Florida receded as I threw myself into preparing for trial. There seemed to be a thousand things to do.

The days flew by, imitating the hands of a clock that showed the passage of time in old movies, or so it seemed to me.

And I had my own problems. I needed office help, but getting it hadn't been easy. I thought for a while that I was working my way through every secretary the temporary service had on its list.

The first woman they sent me, a middle-aged matron testing returning to work as if she were dipping a tentative toe into a murky pool, suffered from a terrible telephone addiction. She couldn't stay away from the thing no matter how much other work had to be done. She had a thousand friends to chat up. I called the service, when I finally pried the phone away for a minute, and had them send another candidate.

The next, a skinny little woman, eyed me as if I was about to rip the clothes off her. My simplest request paralyzed her with wide-eyed fear. She went after one day.

The third was a young man who frequently broke into tears for no apparent reason. The fourth was a stocky woman with a mashed nose and a golden front tooth who had arms like tree trunks and who I thought might rip my clothes off and perform despicable acts on me.

The fifth, Donna Massey, was a former medical secretary, fiftyish, who worked with quiet competence and who could spell. She was available only for part-time work, just the mornings, but I grabbed her like a life ring.

Sidney Sherman's people continued digging, providing information that sometimes seemed more confusing than helpful. Sidney informed me that the deal for the copy of the prenuptial agreement was about to bear fruit, the kind of fruit that blooms only in the dark of the moon.

The money I requested had been sent from Florida. It was sufficient to finance the fees and expenses of the expert witnesses who had agreed to appear.

The Harwell trial was just over the horizon now and I began to resent the intrusion of the routine tasks I had to do for my growing stock of other clients. I tended to think of trips to the courthouse, insurance claims, and the other mundane duties of a practicing lawyer as annoying interference with my work on the big case. I'm sure my other clients didn't see it quite that way.

The Harwell trial was becoming almost an obsession, a troubling obsession. Sometimes, in the middle of the night, I would be jolted awake by the vivid realization of what was at stake.

Lawyers try to stay objective about clients. Emotions can fatally flaw judgment. A lawyer tries to see things as they really are. "Try" is the operative word, at least where Angel Harwell was concerned.

She remained an enigma, but if we lost the case I didn't doubt that she would kill herself. I had seen that icy resolve in those strange eyes. That put another chip in the game, a chip I wasn't so sure I could handle

I wasn't sure Angel was innocent. I wasn't sure she was guilty. But I was sure that I didn't want to consider the consequences of a loss.

When I wasn't thinking about Angel, I was thinking about myself. My own situation wasn't all that different. A matter of life or death too, but in a different way. If I won, I'd be on top again, something that became more important to me as each day went by. I liked having money again. But what I really liked was the respect. I had almost forgotten the tangy feel of that.

I was a lawyer. That probably meant more to me than it should.

If I lost the Harwell case, that would be taken away forever. I was sure about that.

SIDNEY Sherman had called before he came up. He said he didn't want to make the trip and find out I wasn't in. He tried to hide it but I could tell he was excited about something.

He made it up to Pickeral Point in less than an hour.

"Charley, you got money now," he said as he entered my office. "When are you going to get yourself a secretary?"

"I got one. She only works in the mornings."

Sidney sat down and grinned. "Only the mornings? Big deal. If you look like a success, you are a success. People don't trust a lawyer who looks like he's about to go on welfare. If you look like a bum, you are a bum."

"Who said that?"

"My mother. A very wise woman. Speaking of cheap, how come you're not using a shadow jury on this case? Belleman and Swartz use a shadow jury on each and every trial. They're big guns, Charley. They represent some very big corporations. They should know what they're doing."

"But they don't, Sidney, that's why they set up a play jury and go through a play trial. Most of the Belleman Swartz lawyers can't find the courthouse, let alone try a real jury case. Shadow juries are for amateurs."

"Hey, these guys make more money than professional athletes. I wouldn't call that amateur."

"I do. If you put in some wunderkind from Harvard to try a big case, somebody whose sole contact with trials is watching reruns of *Perry Mason*, you do need play juries and play judges. And the client needs real prayer."

Sidney shook his head. "They must think it works, Charley?"

"You can't duplicate a jury. One set of twelve doesn't mean that another set will see things the same way. Sidney, you've worked with Morgan and Maguire. They're as good on the witness stand as it's possible to get. Give them one tiny opening and they rip your guts out. Tell me, Sidney, where are you going to get an actor who can match Morgan or Maguire?"

"You might have a point," he said, although his tone indicated I hadn't really convinced him. He patted his very expensive briefcase. "Anyway, after much intrigue and packets of money I have for you the Harwell divorce file, intact, as promised. That attorney down in Florida is really angry at the survivors. God knows why. Anyway, one of his staff wasn't so picky and was a bit more greedy."

He opened the case and extracted a thick file.

"Have you read it, Sidney?"

He grinned. "Of course. I wasn't going to pay out that kind of dough unless I knew we were getting the real thing."

Sidney extracted a leather packet. "This was to be his new will. He was scheduled to sign it when the divorce papers were served. They weren't and he didn't."

"What does it say?"

"You won't like it."

"Probably not, but go ahead."

"Harrison Harwell was going to leave almost everything to a trust to take care of Angel, but only if she accepted medical treatment. And that was to be decided by trustees he selected. If she didn't do what they said, the corpus of the trust was to be paid over to a named charity."

"Cruel. She'd be a prisoner for life."

Sidney nodded, then reached into the briefcase and came up with a stack of papers. "I got the divorce pleadings, the ones they were going to file. It's standard language. They base the divorce on that old standby, irreconcilable differences. There are no details given."

"What about the prenuptial agreement?"

"We got that." He smiled as he extracted the envelope and handed it to me. "It's all signed and legally correct. The happy Harwells entered into it a day before they were married. Romantic, eh? I took the liberty of having a Florida lawyer take a peek at the thing. He says it would have been enforceable. Florida says the terms of those things are binding in the event of a divorce."

"I'll read it," I said, "but give me a quick sketch of what's in it."

He nodded. "If that divorce had been filed and had gone through, Robin Harwell would have received a mere one hundred thousand dollars. In other words, in relation to what Harwell had, peanuts."

"She agreed to that?"

290

"Yeah, ten years ago, before they got married. I suppose she would have agreed to anything to set the hook. Women can be like that."

"What about death?"

"The agreement says that's to be covered by will or operation of law. The Florida guy says that's a little unusual down there. Usually, who gets what if someone cools is spelled out. But not this time."

Sidney took out some more papers from the briefcase. "To give you some idea of what all this means, I had accountants do a rough estimate of what's in Harwell's estate."

"So?"

"Without burdening you with details, it is a lot less than it was, but with the real estate and everything, it comes to just over twenty million. We got a copy of the existing will. When everything shakes out, my people estimate that the widow will get a clean eight million, the daughter the rest. In case you didn't do well in arithmetic, Charley, eight million is one hell of a lot more than one hundred thousand."

"So?"

"Ain't it fortunate for mom that daddy died."

"Are you still trying to tell me the widow did it?"

He shrugged. "Also, daddy's death was a big financial break for the kid."

"She has the money her mother left in trust."

One eyebrow went quickly up. "It isn't much, Charley, at least not the way these people live. If you're used to butlers and maids, twenty thousand is lunch money."

"That's it, twenty thousand a year?"

He nodded. "I thought I told you. I guess I didn't."

He sighed and sat back, then spoke. "Let me state the obvious, Charley. If papa had lived and everything had gone through—the will, the divorce—little Angel would have been in one hell of a financial mess. Twenty large won't buy much of a lifestyle in these times. She'd get only what daddy would give her while he was alive, and nothing after his death unless she checked into a convenient nut house. Now, in comparison, she is sitting very pretty indeed. In other words, pal, if the prosecutor ever gets his claws on all this, he could use it to burn the fanny off your lovely little Angel. It's what we in the trade call a motive."

"Only if she knew, and she probably didn't. Is there any indication anyone else knows about the proposed will?"

Sidney shook his head. "They might know about the divorce, but you have to steal the file to find the will."

"You worry too much, Sidney. The prosecutor up here doesn t have the smarts to dig up something like this."

"Charley, you aren't back on the sauce, are you? What about Morgan and Maguire? Jesus, they could find Jimmy Hoffa if they put their minds to it. How come you don't think they would go after this?"

"Because they think they have a perfect case."

"Maybe they do."

"THE issue is simple enough," I said. "The cops kept at Angel Harwell for hours, taking statement after statement until she finally told them something they would settle for. They didn't use a real rubber hose, but it amounted to the same thing. She had just found her father's bloody body. She was in shock, anyone would have been. Plus, she has a history of being emotionally fragile."

"I trust they informed her of her legal rights?" Dr. Henry Foreman had driven up for lunch and a conference with me. He was Detroit's leading forensic psychiatrist, an expert who seemed to be a witness in every major civil or criminal trial where mental capacity was an issue. He had become well known and usually ended up doing more television than Johnny Carson.

"They gave Angel her rights. The usual mechanical words, yes. But their actions—"

"She knew she could call a halt to the questioning any time?" He buttered a roll.

"Whose side are you going to be on here?"

"Yours, but that doesn't answer the question." Dr. Foreman was a proven dynamite witness, a tall, dignified man with friendly eyes and a firm professional manner. Juries loved him. "I read Bob Williams's report and I reviewed the psychological profile done on Miss Harwell. She isn't exactly retarded, is she?"

"No, but—"

He held up the roll as if signaling for silence. "So, you have a

292

young woman with extraordinary intelligence who is informed repeatedly that she doesn't have to answer any more questions, and yet she does, over and over again for hours." He bit the roll, chewed for a moment as if judging its quality, then continued. "The basic question is, why would she do such a thing, wouldn't you say?"

"I don't understand."

Those friendly eyes regarded me for a moment. "Anyone that smart would have asked for a lawyer, at the very least. After the first round of questions, an intelligent person would have pointed out that everything had been answered once and politely refused to continue."

"Maybe I should consider getting a different expert witness?"

He smiled, ignoring the question. "So, why didn't she choose to exercise any of her legal options? A normal person, with even average intelligence, would have done so. The answer, Mr. Sloan, was that she was so intimidated, so frightened, so paralyzed mentally, that she couldn't think straight. In other words, she was incapable of resisting, and finally fabricated the answer they repeatedly suggested by their questions. The popular term for that is brainwashing."

"Maybe I'll stick with you after all."

He nodded. "That would be wise. You do understand that I have to interview Miss Harwell before I testify." He finished the roll and washed it down with coffee. "I can testify without making a one-on-one examination, but that's frowned upon by my fellow psychiatrists. Also, having seen her will take away an obvious line of attack upon me by the other side."

"That will be no problem. Angel is scheduled to come up here two days before the hearing."

"Good. I can see her at her convenience. It won t take long. An hour at the most. Also, I'd like to see the tape of this so-called confession. I've read the transcript, but I think I can punch up my testimony a bit if I refer to the tape itself. Make points about certain mannerisms, manner of speech, reactions or the lack of them, that sort of thing."

"Okay. Anything else?"

"I understand I'm to testify at the Walker hearing, but will you need me at the trial itself?"

"That depends. If I can get the statement thrown out, that ends the need for psychiatric evidence. If not, I'll have to attack the statement's validity, this time in front of the jury. If that happens, I'd need you again. Any problem with that?"

"No. Actually, August is a very slow month for me. I can easily work my schedule around. Tell me, will you be using any other psychiatrists?"

"I'm planning on calling the one who did the testing, but no one else."

"No treating psychiatrists?"

"So far I haven't exactly been overwhelmed with cooperation from her treating sources. Even if I could get somebody here it might be dangerous. It could open the door to things I might not want known."

"How serious are you, Mr. Sloan, that the death was suicide?"

"Very serious."

He nodded. "Suicide, as you probably know, is a great risk with patients who are seriously depressed. The treatment of depression is one of my main fields of expertise. Would you want me to go into that at the Walker hearing?"

"No. The prosecution probably thinks I'm only going to raise suicide as a smoke screen. There's no reason to alert them that it will be a main defense. I'm going to save that until the trial."

"You might want to use me in that capacity then."

We were served the main course. Dr. Foreman attacked his fish with gusto. "Tell me," he said between bites, "what do you think of Miss Harwell's chances?"

"If we keep the statement out, pretty good."

"And if not?"

"Not good."

"Is there any chance of a plea bargain?"

"The prosecutor plans to ride the publicity to a higher political mountain."

He touched his lips with his napkin. "I know of course that a Walker hearing determines whether a defendant's statement is voluntary or not. But I've always wondered about the name, Walker. A judge, I presume?"

"No. A defendant. Lee Dell Walker had a record of robbery. He was arrested for killing a merchant in a robbery. He confessed. He didn't want to leave witnesses. He was convicted by a jury."

"So?"

"The Supreme Court said the issue of his statement had to be determined before trial. That's how the hearing got its name."

"And Walker was retried and acquitted?"

I shook my head. "No. A judge ruled the confession voluntary and another jury convicted him again."

"And he went to prison."

"No. The Supreme Court let him out again. The prosecutor gave up."

"So Mr. Walker was convicted twice of first-degree murder and was never punished?"

I nodded.

"Does it ever strike you, Mr. Sloan, that our legal machinery sometimes leaves a great deal to be desired?"

"Walker didn't think so."

Dr. Foreman seemed to mull that over for a moment, then he spoke. "Is there any gag order regarding this trial, as far as the lawyers and witnesses anyway?"

"Not so far."

He smiled broadly. "Oh good. When I testified in the Roscommon murder trial last year I ended up on *Good Morning America*."

"Do you like that, Doctor? Being in the public spotlight?"

Dr. Foreman sighed. "I see it as a public service. A way to carry the message of good mental health." He took another bite. "Besides, it's better than sex."

I thought he was kidding, but I wasn't sure.

THE judge ruled on my motion. A technicality had freed my client.

"You came close this time," I said to my client. "You had better give some real thought to quitting the booze."

He shrugged. "I have a few now and then. It relaxes me. There's no harm in that. I can handle it."

I put my papers and notes back in my briefcase. The arresting officer sat a few chairs away, glaring at me, still angry.

"You're going to kill someone or yourself if you get shitfaced and then drive." I snapped the briefcase closed and looked at my client.

He was almost forty, a nice-looking man, a little beefy, the father of three with a good office job in a Port Huron manufacturing company. The problem was that he couldn't handle the stuff.

The cop got up, shot me one more dirty look, and then stomped out of the nearly empty courtroom.

"You're pretty good," my client said. "I should have had you for those other cases."

He had been convicted twice of driving while impaired. His license had been suspended the second time for two months.

"You were drunk. That cop knows it. And you know it," I said. "The policeman made an error in the way he handled the breathalyzer results. It was a technical mistake. The judge had no choice. He had to dismiss the case. You won't get that lucky again."

He snorted. "Luck had nothing to do with it. Hell, I got me an expensive lawyer and I walked." He laughed. "It's the American way, eh? Come on, I'll buy you a drink."

"I don't drink. I found out I couldn't handle it."

"So that's it. I should have known. You know the saying, there's nothing worse than a reformed drunk." He grinned but there was a nasty edge to his words.

"I think you should take up horseback riding."

"What do you mean?"

It was my turn to smile. "Unless you change your ways, you won't be driving a car for long."

I left the courtroom, looking smug, but I really wished I could have joined him for a drink in some nice air-conditioned bar, someplace quiet and far from the courts. Someplace where I wouldn't have to think about Angel Harwell.

Time was running out. Angel and Robin were scheduled to fly in The Walker hearing was only two days away and there was so much still to do.

A drink would have been just right.

LIKE flights of geese in the spring, the newspeople were honking back to Pickeral Point.

Donna, my new part-time secretary, got a little round-eyed

talking on the telephone to producers who dropped the names of Dan Rather, Ted Koppel, and some of her favorite talk-show hosts.

Summer was slow. The diplomats and generals were all on vacation. A nice juicy murder trial was the answer to a network news-hawk's prayer.

I was already on the bad side of Judge Theodore Brown, so I continued to duck requests for interviews to avoid incurring further displeasure.

But Mark Evola felt no such restrictions. It was becoming difficult to find a newspaper or magazine that didn't have an article about him and his view of the legal system. If he was spending any time preparing for trial it wasn't apparent. He was digging into the publicity hill like a miner who had discovered gold but knew it wouldn't last forever.

I hadn't been ignored. A television camera crew had taken footage of the outside of my office while a reporter talked into a microphone. They were nervy people, coming up the stairs and trying to push their way in and force an impromptu interview.

I stayed in my inner office while Donna repulsed the invaders. She was polite but firm. I was impressed.

The telephone messages were becoming numerous, piling up until they were thick as a book. I called my other clients back. I suspected that most of the calls were just people who needed to become a small part of the Harwell circus. Something to tell relatives and friends—"I just talked to my lawyer, he's Angel Harwell's lawyer, you know"—a chance to shine in a vicarious spotlight.

I did return one telephone call from Dan Conroy, my friend on the *Detroit News*.

We went through the usual little conversational dance, exchanging jokes and barbs, then Conroy got down to business.

"I've done a personality profile on you, Charley. The paper wants to run it tomorrow."

"What do you mean, profile? You didn't interview me."

"No, not formally. This is just a little biography. My editor wants to get a picture. We have some shots from the last hearing when you got the charge reduced, but he wants one, a studio head-shot, to match the one we have of your opponent."

297

"What the hell are you talking about?"

"We're going to make this a full-page thing. One side a picture of Evola and a matching article, the other side you and the piece I've done."

"Dan, can you hold it off? Tomorrow is Tuesday. The Walker hearing's scheduled for Wednesday. This judge is the kind who only likes publicity about himself. He might get sore."

"So what?"

"I have a client to protect."

"You're news, Charley. You have to get used to that. Sorry, but my editors are hot to run this."

"How about making it a three-way thing, Dan. Give the judge a picture and an article. That would take the sting out."

"The page is all laid out, Charley. What about the picture? I can have one of our photographers there in an hour."

"No dice."

There was a pause. Then a chuckle. "By the way, Evola isn't so shy. He did give an interview. He said some interesting things about you."

"Like what?"

"Well, in fairness, I sort of baited him into what he said."

"Go on."

"He said you have a reputation as a trickster. He expects you to try a dozen different underhanded things to try to win."

"Dan, are you trying to bait me into replying?"

"A little, yeah. What about the trickster business?"

"I'm not going to reply. What did he say? Exactly?"

"Don't be cheap. Buy a paper tomorrow and read it for yourself. Oh, by the way, I think I did pretty good by you. There's a couple of things in the article you won't like, but overall it's not bad."

He paused. When he spoke again his tone had changed. It seemed to have an almost wistful quality. "Charley, I know you've been through a lot. Maybe this time your luck will change. Anyway, I want you to know I'll be rooting for you." Then, slightly softer, "no matter that happens."

He hung up before I could ask what he meant.

It was getting late. Angel and Robin should have arrived so I called the Harwell place.

Dennis Bernard answered. "They're not here," he said when I asked.

"What do you mean? Didn't you pick them up at the airport?"

"Mrs. Harwell called. She was concerned about the media people. They're such pests. She thought they might even have found out what flight they'd be on. So she changed her plans."

"What!"

"Mr. Sloan, we are under a state of siege here again. Those television people are waiting out in the street, just like before. The Harwell plant security people are back, too."

"Where are Mrs. Harwell and Robin?"

"I really don't know. They may fly in tonight, perhaps tomorrow. I suspect they're staying the night in Atlanta. That's where they were to change planes."

"C'mon, Bernard. Don't give me that crap. Where are they?" I tried not to be angry, but I was. Very angry.

"I'm sorry, Mr. Sloan. I swear to you, this time I haven't the foggiest idea where they might be."

I thought he was lying, but if he was, he was doing a very credible job.

And, there was no point in shouting at him. He was only the messenger.

"Bernard, do these women know what will happen if they fail to show up?"

"I presume they do, sir."

There was no point to continuing. "Look, if they call in, or if you should know where they are, tell them I have to talk with them immediately. You have my home phone number?"

"Yes, sir." Then he added. "Don't worry, Mr. Sloan, they'll be here."

"I'm not the one whose being charged with murder, Bernard. Angel should be the one who is worried. Not me."

I hung up. So much for careful planning.

I thought about the pint of brandy in the desk. I got out of there before I did something about it.

22

I FOUND IT REMARKABLE. THE ANGER SMOLDERING
in me somehow replaced the usual urge to drink when I felt
stressed. Tuesday morning came and went and they still hadn't
shown up.

Dr. Henry Foreman was staying at the Pickeral Point Inn, waiting to interview Angel. I kept him advised of the situation. He
didn't seem upset in the least. Of course, his career wasn't at risk.

If Angel didn't show up, Judge Brown wouldn't just raise hell,
he would demand a human sacrifice. Someone would have to be
punished, and I knew just who that someone would be.

Ever since I was little boy, when things got really nasty in my
life my favorite fantasy was always one of escape.

I sat in my office and stared out at the river. There wasn't a
great deal of money left in my account, not after paying out all
the expenses and front money required by the experts, but there
was enough to buy a one-way ticket to some faraway place, maybe
Mexico. There was still enough to live modestly there for at least
a couple of months. I could almost conjure up a quiet beach,
tropic skies, and the tangy taste of tequila. But drinking fantasies
are dangerous for alcoholics; they tend to come true. I changed
that part of my daydream to a soft drink.

Reality has no part in a pleasant fantasy. The dream of escape
withered and died

As usual, Donna, my secretary, had departed at noon. A few
minutes before one o'clock the phone rang.

It was Dennis Bernard.

"Mrs. Harwell just called," he said. "They did stay overnight in Atlanta."

"Where are they now?"

"At Metro. They just arrived."

"Detroit? Both of them?"

"Yes."

I felt my muscles relax. I hadn't realized how tense I had become.

"Are you going to pick them up, Bernard?"

"No. Mrs. Harwell thought the newspaper people might follow me. They'll come by cab. I would think they'd be here in an hour or so."

"I'll get Dr. Foreman. We'll be over there before they arrive."

"I don't know, Mr. Sloan. They may be tired from the trip. Perhaps you should let them call you."

"Bernard, if we don't take care of business, Angel will get a really nice rest in a place with bars and guards. I'll be there in an hour."

There was a pause. "As you wish," he said, his tone disapproving.

I hung up. Relief replaced anger. It was like getting a last-minute reprieve. Mexico would have to wait.

IT had been an anxiety-producing evening, but only for me. Before coming home Robin and Angel had stopped off to do some shopping. For someone who threatened to do away with herself if convicted, Angel wasn't exhibiting much heart-stopping fear over what might happen to her in court.

After they finally arrived, I sat through Angel's session with Dr. Foreman. At first Angel seemed almost amused, but that eventually slipped into boredom. By the time they were through, Angel's hostility was overt, her clipped answers icy and arrogant. The doctor, although straining to keep a cool professional attitude, finally reacted, and his questions were beginning to sound hostile too when he finally called it quits.

"Interesting piece of work, that," he said of Angel as I walked him out.

"Well, besides not falling madly in love with her, what is your assessment?"

He smiled. "Doctor Williams is quite right in his diagnosis. She suffers from a pronounced personality disorder. I would classify it as mixed, several types of disorders manifesting various levels of problems."

"If I put you on the stand tomorrow, what can I expect?"

"I trust you observed her low tolerance for interrogation? It would have been the same that night with the police. They only had to keep at it. Although she might not show it, eventually she'd become annoyed and say anything to get it all over with, no matter what the consequences might be for her. That kind of thoughtless and irresponsible behavior is often a hallmark of a personality disorder."

"Was she insane when they questioned her?"

"No. She knew what she was doing. The problem is that because of the disorder, her way of responding is different than normal. But she would think her response logical even if it obviously wasn't."

"If the prosecutor asks you—"

He held up his hand. "Please, Mr. Sloan. This is my line of work, isn't it? Have no fear. In my opinion the statement she gave that night was not voluntary. Believe me, I can make that stick." He paused. "Are you planning to put her on the stand?"

"No."

"Very wise. A person like Angel is liable to say anything if she thinks it will serve the purpose of the moment. She is a bit too erratic to be reliable."

Dennis Bernard drove the doctor back to the Inn. I spent what remained of the evening in an attempt to instruct Angel and Robin on the proper way to act in the courtroom and in public.

They remained as cool as the ice cubes in their drinks. Angel's attitude would have been more appropriate if she'd only been a spectator. It was as if what was going to happen in the morning had no connection with their lives.

Back at my apartment, my mind filled with the terrible things that might happen in the morning. High overhead, heat lightning caused distant rumbling thunder, echoing the Japanese funeral music that kept replaying in my memory.

I PUSHED my way through the crowd of reporters and cameramen waiting outside the courthouse and through another mass of newspeople in the hall and made my way to Judge Brown's second-floor courtroom.

Every seat was filled. People were talking and laughing like an audience waiting for the opening of a play. Actually, that wasn't far off the mark. An American criminal trial usually includes all the dramatic elements—love, hate, lust, greed, good versus evil. It's a flesh-and-blood movie with everything except the popcorn.

Angel and Robin had not yet arrived. I tried not to think about that.

But Evola was there, surrounded with several of his assistants and the policemen who would testify. For the first time since the case had begun I thought he looked nervous. I found that reassuring.

He had cause to worry. If I was successful and the statement was thrown out, Evola's chance of success would be considerably diminished. And if he lost this case his dream of a golden political future would sink right along with it.

If I lost, it would be even worse for me. Not to mention Angel. Today was going to be a big day for everybody.

I walked over. Morgan and Maguire smiled. There was no nervousness evident in either veteran policeman. They reminded me of two tigers who were about to feast on a fat antelope.

"Good morning, Charley." This time Evola's smile was only at half power. "Are you ready to go?"

"You bet," I said. "I will be calling several doctors to give opinions on my client's mental state the night she was arrested." I took the copies I had made of Angel's medical records from my briefcase and handed them to him. "These are reports of previous treatment and the psychological tests done in preparation for this hearing."

"Jesus Christ," he snarled. "These things are as thick as a book. What the hell is this? We don't have time to look through all this now. What kind of bullshit is this! I'm going to object if you try to introduce any of this crap."

I was pleased that he was as jumpy as I was. It made me feel much better.

"Relax, Mark. This is part of what the doctors used to form their opinions. I'm not offering any of it as an exhibit. I just thought it should be available to you. In fairness."

"Fairness, my ass! If you wanted to be fair you could have gotten this to us days ago, and you know it. I don't like this, Charley, not a bit."

"It's a hell of a lot more honest than trying to conceal the other statements my client made. Where are they? You have a hell of a nerve yelling about being fair. I want those statements, Mark, and I want them now."

I preferred being angry to being nervous. It felt better.

"I'm not concealing anything," he said, his irritation evaporating before my anger. "They weren't kept. It's as simple that, Charley."

"Simple? We'll see how simple it is." I walked away.

There was a rising ripple of noise as the court officers escorted Robin and Angel into the courtroom. Robin took a front-row seat. I was annoyed to see Nate Golden with her. His glance at me was the kind you might see at executions—stern, cold, and unforgiving.

Angel came up and sat behind me at the counsel table.

"Glad you could make it," I whispered.

She stared at me with those expressionless eyes, then she spoke. "You worry too much, Charley."

The clerk rapped the gavel and Judge Theodore Brown came stalking from his chambers, his black robe fluttering as he quickly moved up to the bench.

"This matter is a Walker hearing into the admissibility of a statement made by the defendant Angel Harwell, which the prosecution plans to offer as part of their main case." Judge Brown snapped the words with such staccato force that the courtroom was cowed into complete silence. That seemed to please him. He almost smiled.

"Okay, let's get this over with. Mr. Sloan, you're the one making the objection. What's your position?"

I glanced at Angel. She looked back, displaying only mild interest. I wished I could look as calm and self-controlled.

I got up and walked to a point just in front of the bench. The words came surprisingly easily. I was making two arguments, one to the judge, and the other to the media. Same words, different targets. I couldn't see how it was affecting the reporters present but I was looking right up at the judge. His was the standard stern judicial mask employed in such situations.

I didn't do badly. In fact, I thought any reasonable person listening would have to agree with what I said. And maybe that would have been true if it had ended right there.

But then Evola got his turn to speak. Unfortunately, he didn't do badly either.

So it would be up to the witnesses.

The first four were easy enough for both sides. They were the two uniformed Pickeral Point cops and the two uniformed Kerry County officers.

Evola dwelled on the fact that Angel had been given her rights every time the officers talked to her. I made sure each witness established how long Angel had been held and questioned before her alleged confession, but my main emphasis was that she had not even hinted to any of the officers that she had been responsible for her father's death. Each cop, when he was excused, almost skipped out of the courtroom in exaltation. Traffic cases they knew, murder cases they didn't.

The prosecutor called Morgan first. Evola's nervousness had departed, and he seemed to draw emotional strength with each succeeding witness. Morgan sat in the witness chair, as saintly and good as anyone's benign grandfather. But I saw those tiger eyes and I knew he was waiting for me to make some small misjudgment, just enough to let him quickly snake in something poisonous.

So I was very careful. I worded my questions so tightly that it would have been impossible to slip anything extra into the answer. I asked him for his notes, the ones made when Angel gave her first statement.

"I didn't keep them." He spoke with quiet assurance.

"But you did make notes of what she said, correct?"

"Yes, but I—"

"Just answer the question please," I said quickly. "What happened to those notes?"

"I destroyed them."

"Did you burn them?"

"No."

"Did you give them to someone else to destroy?"

"I tore them up and threw them in a wastepaper basket."

"Why?"

God! As soon as I had blurted out that one-word question I knew I had given him his opening.

"After she confessed to murdering her father, I didn't need them anymore."

Morgan's face remained calm and kindly, but those tiger eyes gleamed with satisfaction.

I knew that if I tried to repair it, Morgan would use the attempt to chew some more with those tiger jaws, so I ignored it and kept after him about the number of statements Angel had given that night, taking him minute by minute through each of the interrogations.

The testimony of his partner, Maguire, was almost identical, although I remembered not to ask him any open-ended questions. Evola dwelled on how many times Angel had been told that she didn't have to answer questions and that she had a right to an attorney.

Evola was building toward introducing the taped statement, and I could hear the murmur of interest in the courtroom as he called Herbert Ames, the county evidence technician who had run the video camera that night.

I had never seen Ames before. Evola had kept making excuses so I couldn't get the opportunity.

Now I could see why he had kept him hidden away. Herbert Ames did not have the look of a tiger. He resembled a lamb. I damn near began to salivate.

Ames was a gawky man in an ill-fitting winter suit. His eyes, already widened by fear, seemed even larger through his thick glasses. His sleeves and trousers were too short for his long arms and legs. His response to the oath was barely audible.

Evola merely asked his name, his occupation, and whether he had taken the tape to be placed in evidence against Angel Harwell. That was it, nothing more. Evola treated Ames as no more than a functionary called to satisfy evidenciary procedure. He did it a bit too quickly to be convincing.

I walked over to the far side of the courtroom so the television camera could get a better angle. Nothing might happen, but if something did, it could be the kind of dramatic spot that would play well on the nation's news programs.

"I understand they call you Dirty Herbert, is that true?"

"Objection!" Evola screamed.

Before I could reply, the judge barked in a low, dangerous voice, "Sustained."

But sustained or not, the question had had the desired effect.

He seemed to shrink back in the witness chair. I took a few steps closer.

"Herbert, have you ever used the county camera for any work not connected with official business? You know, home movies, girls, that kind of thing?"

Evola's objection was followed by the judge's growling admonishment to stick to the matter at hand.

Poor Herbert. His lower lip had developed a slight twitch.

"That night when you taped Miss Harwell, who called you to come into the police station?"

He hesitated for a moment. "I'm not sure. I think it was Detective Maguire."

"About what time was that, roughly?"

"It was late."

"How late?"

His eyes darted over to the prosecutor as if seeking a clue as to what he should say. Then he looked again at me. "I was in bed. Sleeping," he added.

"What time was it?"

"I don't remember."

"Didn't you look at the clock when the call woke you?"

"I probably did. Yeah, I guess I did."

"And what time was it?"

"I'm not sure."

"Tell us where the big hand was, Herbert."

The laughter from the crowd was mixed with Evola's objection and another warning from the judge.

Two red spots of embarrassed color blossomed on Ames's white cheeks. "The time was just past three o'clock, I think."

"And you got dressed and drove over there, is that right?"

"Yes."

"How long did that take?"

"Not long. A half-hour maybe."

"Did you set up the camera when you got there?"

"Yeah."

"Did you tape the statement from Miss Harwell as soon as that was done?"

"A few minutes later, I guess. Not long."

I walked two steps closer. He watched with apprehension, the way a bird watches an approaching snake.

"How many statements did you tape that night?"

"Just Miss Harwell's."

"One tape only?"

His eyes bobbed around for a minute as if seeking an escape route.

"Two tapes," he said in a near whisper.

"Pardon me?"

"Two tapes," he repeated, a bit louder. "We took two statements from her."

"What happened, Herbert? Trouble with your camera? Or did you maybe botch the first take?"

"No." He seemed indignant at the mere suggestion.

"Did you tape them one right after another?"

He shook his head. "No. There was a break between them. Maybe a half an hour, maybe longer."

"What happened during that break?"

He shrugged. "I don't know. I wasn't there." He sounded very relieved at being able to make that answer.

"Why weren't you there?"

"They asked me to step out of the room. You know, have a cigarette or something."

"Who asked you?"

He paused, took a breath, and then answered. "Mr. Evola."

"What did he say?"

"Objection," Evola said. "This has no bearing on—"

"Overruled," the judge said. "Go on."

"Well, what did he say, Herbert?"

"He wanted to talk to Miss Harwell some more, he said. Just him and the detectives."

"Morgan and Maguire?"

"Yes. So I went out in the hall and had a cigarette. You aren't supposed to smoke there but no one was around so I thought it wouldn't make any difference."

"And when they called you back in they made the second tape, is that right?"

"Yes."

I walked a bit closer. "Herbert, what happened to the first tape you made? That first statement Miss Harwell gave in front of your camera?"

"I erased it."

"Is that usual?"

"No. We usually keep them, at least until after a trial, if there is one."

"Why didn't you keep this one?"

He looked away from me. "Because we made the second one." His voice was so low it was almost inaudible.

"That wasn't the reason, Herbert, and you know it. Why did you erase the first tape?"

"Mr. Evola told me to do it." He spoke so quickly the words ran together.

"Did he say why?"

Herbert Ames looked over at the judge. "He said he didn't want some smartass lawyer getting his hands on it."

"Why was that?"

He half-smiled. "Oh, on that first one she denied everything. You know, she said she was innocent."

"And that's when they asked you to step out of the room?"

"Yeah."

I just stood there, for effect. In the old courtrooms the wall clocks used to tick, at times a very dramatic sound. This clock was electric, just a low buzz, but the effect was the same.

When I thought I had milked the moment for everything I could get I turned to Evola, who sat grim-faced at the counsel table.

"Have you no shame?" I snapped, knowing my outraged face was the only thing the camera at the back of the courtroom could catch.

What I provoked was another sharp warning from the judge, but it was well worth it.

Evola made a speech, denying any wrongdoing. Then he played the tape on the screen set up for that purpose.

Then it was my turn.

My line of attack was simple enough. I would show that Angel had been treated in the past for emotional illness and was fragile at best. I would show that she finally cracked under police pressure and after six steady hours of questioning gave a statement in a desperate attempt to end the torment.

I had already set up the time and circumstances through Evola's witnesses. Herbert Ames, a gift from the gods, had established the suspicion that perhaps Evola and company were not completely trustworthy. Now I had to show that Angel was not firing on all pistons that night and that the police had taken advantage of her weak emotional condition and the horror of seeing her bloody father.

A confession, or even a questionable statement, must be given voluntarily if it is to be admitted into evidence. Anything less leads back to the rack and thumbscrews.

I was surprised that Evola let the psychologist who had given Angel the tests get off so lightly. Evola hit on Angel's high intelligence but not much else. A faint warning signal began ringing in my mind.

Dr. Monroe Gishman was an international authority on brainwashing techniques. He was a consultant to our State Department and to Amnesty International. As they say, he wrote the book on the subject. Not a best seller on the *New York Times* list, but it earned the doctor a nice annual income on sales to universities.

Dr. Gishman was my witness and Dr. Gishman didn't come cheap. First, there was his fee. It probably could have ransomed a hundred political captives held throughout the world. And there were his expenses. Dr. Gishman did not go tourist.

I think it was the amount of money wasted that bothered me the most.

I called Dr. Gishman and began the questions to qualify him as an expert on brainwashing.

Evola objected. I had expected that. I even had a number of leading cases supporting my view to argue to the judge.

Leading cases or not, Judge Brown ruled against me, saying that so far the evidence did not establish a case for brainwashing, at least not the kind where an expert like Dr. Gishman was required.

I didn't think Dr. Gishman was all that upset by the ruling. He had been paid in full. He grinned at me and waved as he made his way out of the courtroom.

But losing a battle did not mean losing the war.

"I call Dr. Henry Foreman," I announced.

There was a stir among the spectators as Dr. Foreman made his way to the stand.

He came forward, exuding serene self-confidence. Tall, gray, and wise, Dr. Foreman radiated a calm stability.

I led him through the qualifications. Evola objected, but this time he lost. Dr. Foreman would be permitted to testify as to Angel's background and her state of mind on the night her father died.

Like those other expert witnesses, Maguire and Morgan, Dr. Foreman possessed the quick mind of a courtroom tiger.

Actually, he was so good I had very little to do.

In a calm, authoritative voice, Dr. Foreman took all of us back to that night. He described what it was like for Angel, a frightened, shocked girl whose emotional flaws worked against her, flaws that made her do things that would have otherwise been unthinkable for one with such a fine mind.

Hell, he convinced me. But I wasn't the important one. I watched Judge Brown. Again, the judicial mask was firmly in place, although at times I thought I saw sympathy.

Finally, I was satisfied. I turned the doctor over to Evola.

Evola got up. He had my medical reports in hand.

He smiled, the full smile, at Dr. Foreman.

"Sir, this morning the attorney for Miss Harwell gave me a number of reports, which he said represented the past treatment afforded his client for, well, emotional or mental reasons. Let me show you them."

He handed the papers to Dr. Foreman, who briefly thumbed through them.

"Do you recognize them, sir?"

"I do."

"And, as you testified, I trust these were the reports of past treatment that you relied on, in part, in making your assessment of Miss Harwell's mental state."

"Yes. They seem to be the same reports."

"When you studied them, did you find anything odd about them, Doctor?"

"Odd? In what way?"

Evola smiled, even wider. "Like missing pages, for instance?"

I was waiting for Foreman to knock him into next week, but that didn't happen.

"I would estimate that perhaps a third to a half of the pages are missing," he said.

"Is that odd, do you think?"

"Very."

The word was like a spear through my heart. I knew what was coming.

"Did you delete the pages, Doctor?"

"No."

"Do you know who did?"

"No."

"Could it have been the treatment sources?"

Foreman nodded. "Possibly."

"Someone else?"

"That's possible too. I have no way of knowing, to be frank."

"We appreciate your honesty, Doctor. Could it even have been Mr. Sloan?"

"I doubt that."

"But, could it have been?"

"I suppose so. Yes."

Evola dropped the package of reports on the floor, as if they were no more than garbage, then he looked up at the judge.

"If the court please, this witness testified that his assessment was done, in part, on the basis of past medical history. I have no reason to doubt the doctor's honesty. However, someone has doctored the records, no pun intended. I submit that since that is the case, this witness's testimony must be stricken, since it is predicated on a false assumption. I make that motion, now."

"If the court please," I said, getting to my feet, "there is no basis for—"

"Did you alter or make deletions from these records, Mr. Sloan?" the judge asked in an almost friendly tone. That was my first indication that all was not well.

"No sir, I did not!"

"But somebody did, would you agree to that?"

"Your honor, why that was done I have no idea, however—"

"But it was done, you agree?"

312

"Yes. But—"

The judge's face was friendly, but his eyes were hostile.

"Like you, Mr. Sloan, I have no idea who altered those records. Or why. Apparently, no one does. But they were altered. And, Doctor Foreman's testimony was indeed based in part upon those records. Therefore, I find his testimony, albeit offered with the best of intentions, as faulty as the data upon which it was based. The prosecutor's motion to strike the doctor's testimony is granted."

I argued long and hard. I put on the best show I could and still stay out of jail. It didn't do any good.

"Do you have any other witnesses to offer, Mr. Sloan," the judge asked after I had exhausted myself in a fruitless effort.

"No."

"Mr. Evola?"

"I have a rebuttal witness," he said.

If he had jumped up stark naked, I couldn't have been more surprised.

"The people would like to call Doctor Evelen Skomski to the stand."

It was like the slow opening of a nightmare.

Dr. Skomski was a bit chunky but otherwise an attractive young woman who worked as an emergency-room physician at the local hospital. The police had taken Angel there for an examination to make sure the blood all over her wasn't from any wound on her body.

The doctor, who responded to Evola's questions about training, had taken some psychiatric courses in order to better handle the crazies brought in to her emergency room.

Did she talk to Angel?

She did.

Was Angel Harwell hurt or injured in any way?

She wasn't.

Was she incoherent or did she manifest any sign of emotional or mental illness that night?

She did not.

Did she answer all questions in a logical and normal way?

She did.

Was she mentally competent?

I objected, of course, saying that the doctor wasn't qualified to make that diagnosis. It didn't do any good. The judge took the answer.

Angel, said the doctor, was cool, calm, and knew exactly what was going on.

Evola smiled to the doctor, to the judge, and then to the television camera. Then he turned the doctor over to me.

It was like being thrown a snake. What the hell was I supposed to do with it?

"Doctor, when did you first know you might become a witness in this matter?"

"That night. The night I examined her. Mr. Evola talked to me about being a witness."

I raised my hands as if to heaven. "That figures," I said. I hoped my tone implied bribes, corruption, and perversion.

Okay, it was a cheap shot. I admit it. And worse, it didn't work.

Judge Brown let things calm down a bit before he spoke. His was the deep sepulchrul tone of a hangman. He looked directly out at the camera.

"I have given careful consideration to all the evidence. I find that the statement given by the defendant, Angel Harwell, was voluntarily made."

He managed a frosty smile. "That does not, of course, bar you from raising the question before the jury at trial, Mr. Sloan."

The clerk cracked the gavel and Brown hurried from the bench before I could even object.

We, Angel and myself, were in a great deal of trouble. Very serious trouble.

"GET rid of this goddamned drunk."

Good old Nate Golden. That was his rather loud advice to Robin and Angel after the judge's decision. He was playing the same song. But his words seemed to echo in my mind. Maybe he was right.

But I had no time to reflect.

I worked through most of the night preparing an emergency appeal to Michigan's Court of Appeals. Donna came in, at three times her usual pay, and typed up what was necessary.

Although I had had no sleep, I shaved and showered, changed my clothes, and headed for Detroit with my paperwork.

314

A panel was sitting on other matters and a few phone calls established their jurisdiction to hear the appeal.

Three judges, and I knew them all. I felt pretty good. One was a friend from a long time ago, a nice even-tempered man who I considered a very good lawyer. The other two I knew, but not well. They had been trial judges and I had had cases before them. If they weren't friends, at least they weren't enemies.

It was an emergency appeal. There would be no argument, just a behind-closed-doors meeting of the three judges to decide if my plea had merit.

So I waited.

Unless you are a drinker there isn't much you can do in downtown Detroit on a weekday.

There are no movies open, at least not the kind any sensible person would risk going to. The big stores are now just a memory.

There is the river, so I took a walk. It is nice there but the homeless were out in force, with staring eyes and outstretched hands. And always, downtown, there is an underlying feeling of danger.

The mayor goes about in a bomb- and bulletproof car that could survive an atomic hit. He travels with a small army of policemen who have machine-guns with extra clips. He says the city is absolutely safe. Some people suspect he may occasionally stretch the truth. Whether he does or doesn't, the feeling of danger is there.

I went back to the court's offices and sat around, trying to fight off sleep. At four that afternoon a clerk came out and gave me the result. The three judges, even my old pal, had turned down the emergency appeal.

Angel Harwell would go on trial for murder as planned.

I don't know how many bars I passed on the way back to Pickeral Point. For once in my life I didn't even notice.

23

DONNA, MY PART-TIME SECRETARY, WAS BECOMING A
rich woman.

I needed her to come in for hours of night work as I prepared
the pleading necessary to bring a motion for a change of venue. It
had to be done fast. She was a nice little woman, this former
medical secretary, but I caught the glint of a rapacious pirate in
her eye when she set the rate she would charge per hour.

Asking for a change of venue is basically asking to transfer the
case to some other place, preferably far, far away.

If Angel's statement had been tossed out things might have
been different. Now things were desperate and I had to make the
motion. I would argue to Judge Brown that Angel couldn't get a
fair trial in Pickeral Point because of the deluge of publicity about
the case. And that was probably true, although because of the
extensive national television coverage, even shepherds in Wyo-
ming probably had formed an opinion based on what they saw.

Still, I had to make the motion, although the chance that
Brown would grant it was nonexistent. Judges usually like to stay
home. If I lost the motion and the case, the failure to move the
trial would be one of the main cornerstones of the appeal. Of
course, some other attorney would be handling the case then. If I
lost the jury trial, I knew that I would no longer be Angel Harwell's lawyer.

Judge Brown heard my change-of-venue motion on Friday afternoon. The throng of media people had thinned a bit since many of the national people had snuck away for a long weekend before the trial's scheduled start on Monday.

I didn't expect to win, and I didn't.

Brown chose to play genial judge, his courtroom manner kind, even friendly. But I was up close and I could see his eyes. Friendship and kindness stopped somewhere around the bridge of his nose.

Later, on the steps of the courthouse, I made a nice speech to the cameras. Abe Lincoln couldn't have done it better. I told them that while I personally loved the press, television, and the First Amendment, the case was being tried in the media and not in the court, and that poor little Angel was facing the impossible situation of trying to get a jury of twelve people who hadn't already made up their minds.

I thought the argument was good. Later, when I saw the clip on the televised news, it sounded good.

The horror, for Angel and for myself, was that it was also very truo.

THERE wasn't enough time in the weekend to do everything. I had to get ready. I had to review everything, talk again to witnesses I planned to call, and try to work out several game plans for the trial, each based on possible eventualities. I still made it a point to visit Angel and Robin on both Saturday and Sunday nights.

I didn't stay long either time. The visits were chiefly for morale purposes, although I did have a few last-minute details that needed clarification.

I sensed a definite change at the Harwell house.

Angel, I thought, was even more distant, as if she resented having to go through a trial and somehow held me responsible. She wasn't hostile, just more remote. I wondered if she regretted now that she had insisted I be her lawyer.

Robin's attitude was even more puzzling. She was nervous, but that I could understand, given the circumstances. The change was evident in small things. She avoided eye contact with me and although she was polite, I sensed a coolness I hadn't experienced

317

before. I thought perhaps Nate Golden had finally persuaded her that I was a mistake.

And maybe I was.

Of course, the Harwell house was once more under siege by the army of media, and that sort of thing could make anyone nervous. They were camped out on the street. The security men guarded the driveway entrance; otherwise they would have invaded. I don't know what the waiting crowd of media people thought might happen. Perhaps they figured Godot might finally show up. Whatever their expectations, the camp-out was boring and they were doing a little drinking while waiting. Each time I drove by I was greeted by catcalls or cheers. The later the hour the louder and more boisterous the noise.

On Sunday night I found the atmosphere at the Harwell House even more tense. Like the people out at the gate, Robin had been drinking and was a little tipsy. If Angel had been matching her drink for drink, she didn't show it. But she was on edge and that did show. When she spoke her words were clipped and icy.

"Run it by us again, Charley," Robin said as I was getting ready to leave. "What happens now?"

I had told both of them what to expect numerous times, but they were understandably nervous and edgy so I took the time to do it again.

"Tomorrow morning we'll start picking the jury. Depending on how it goes, that should take one or two days, maybe longer. When we finally get a jury, it will be fourteen people. Two of them will be excused at the end of the trial and the remaining twelve will make the ultimate decision."

"Why should picking a jury take so long?" Angel asked.

"Usually it doesn't, but this time I have to really dig to see if they've made up their minds about you before hearing the evidence. They've all heard about the case, obviously but I'll try to come up with people who I think will keep an open mind. That's what will take the time."

"Do you think you can find people like that?" Robin asked, "after everything that's been on television and in the papers?"

"I'll try."

"Then what happens, after you get the jury?" Angel was staring out at the river.

318

I had covered it all before, many times. I was nervous too, but I found the patience to explain it all again.

"Angel, the prosecutor goes first. He has the burden of proof. He puts on his witnesses and I cross-examine. When he's done, it's our turn."

"And how long will that take, the prosecution's part of the case?" Robin asked.

"That depends on how I do with the witnesses. Sometimes things go faster than expected, sometimes they take a lot longer. My guess is two days, maybe three for the prosecution's case.

"And how long for us?"

"As long as it takes. You know the witnesses I'm going to call and what they're going to say. Again, barring major surprises, it should take a day, maybe two, maybe three."

"Will you put me on the stand?" Angel asked.

"At this moment, I'd say probably not. But if it's necessary and you think you can handle it, we might."

"And then you lawyers argue to the jury, is that the way it goes?" Robin's words were slurred slightly, but I heard an under-tone of hostility.

"Yeah, that's the way it goes. Figure a day, day and a half for that. Then the judge gives the jury his instructions as to the law the jury must apply. Then it's up to them. His instructions should take about an hour. After that, there is no way to guess how long the jury might take to reach a verdict."

"Tonight, if you had to bet, what are my chances?" Angel turned and this time stared at me.

"Good. If things go the way they should, your chances are very good." I didn't feel that confident but sometimes stark truth can be unnecessarily cruel.

"Can you do this, Charley?" Robin asked sternly. "Handle this whole trial?"

"It's a little late to ask that, isn't it? Yes, I can handle it."

"Would you feel more secure if another lawyer came in and helped you?"

"What's your point, Robin?"

"Well, it's just that sometimes two heads are better than one. Nate Golden suggested that—"

"I've gone this far with Charley, I'll go the rest of the way with

319

him." Angel's word's were brave but I thought they lacked the full measure of her previous determination.

"Another lawyer coming in now would be dangerous," I said. "It would be like two drivers trying to steer a brakeless truck down a hill. I wouldn't advise it."

Robin said nothing. She turned away and looked out at the dark river. Angel also fell silent. It was time to go.

"This will be a lot easier than it sounds," I said as I left.

Of course, I was lying.

TRIAL. The word has many meanings.

It can be the examination of fact and law before a judicial tribunal. The Harwell case would be exactly that.

It could also, according to the dictionary, be a state of suffering, distress, or pain. *The People* versus *Harwell* was that too.

At least it was for me.

I had tried well over a hundred jury cases, some big, some small. I had literally looked into the eyes of over a thousand jurors. Before, in the old days, I approached a trial with a certain elan, partly whiskey-inspired, the kind of romantic spirit I like to think the old World War I fighter pilots possessed—just wrap that white silk scarf around your throat, pull on the goggles, and fly up to do or die. Smiling, confident, ready.

This time it was different, very different.

I awoke and found I existed in a vacuum of emotion.

Every movement was mechanical. I shaved and showered and dressed. My reaction, I thought, was probably like how a person feels on the way to the hospital for a major operation.

Alia acta est, as Caesar used to say, according to the nuns. It was the only Latin I remembered. The die is cast.

I was not smiling or confident this time.

But I was ready.

A stranger who came to the courthouse this morning would have thought the circus was in town. It was that kind of eager crowd and that kind of excited atmosphere. Everything but the elephants.

The morning began with stern warnings from Judge Brown.

This time, none were directed at me.

The first was aimed at the reporters and cameramen. The

judge, his eyes narrowed to the point of closing, snapped off the rules with quick, simple precision. Any media person stepping over the line would find instant accommodation in Pickeral Point's beautiful new jail. No one in the crowded courtroom doubted that he meant exactly what he said.

His second lecture was directed to the bank of nearly one hundred potential jurors assembled. They were told what would be expected of them and what they might anticipate if selected. His words were carefully chosen and on paper would read like a nice kindly lesson in civics. However, with the growling verbal spin he gave each word it was more like a declaration of war. I wasn't a potential juror but he scared even me.

The judge then directed his menacing attention to Evola and me, asking if there were any motions to be made before jury selection began.

I had debated making a motion that all the witnesses be sequestered, that is, kept out of the courtroom, until it was their turn to testify. It was a tactic that often paid handsomely, since one witness might give an entirely different version of something another witness testified to, not knowing what the other person had said. The jury often disbelieved both because of the conflict. However, it was a sword that could cut both ways. I didn't want that to happen to my witnesses, either. It would be all witnesses or none. So I did nothing.

Evola was probably thinking along those lines, too. Each of us stood in turn and declared we were ready for trial.

The judge gave the assembled jury candidates the oath.

We were off and running.

"You told Mr. Evola that you have three children, Mrs. Harris. What are their ages?"

Mrs. Harris, according to the report I had received from Sidney Sherman, was fifty-five years old, a widow who worked as a store clerk. Sidney's people had discreetly looked up as much information as they could on each member of the panel, being careful not to go far enough to be accused of interfering with jury selection.

Mrs. Harris was a small woman whose stark white hair, worn pulled back, made her look much older than she actually was. She

321

sat in the seat assigned to her in the jury box, along with thirteen other potential candidates.

"My oldest daughter is thirty-four. My son is thirty, and my other daughter is twenty-one."

"The same age as Angel Harwell?"

"Yes."

I watched to see if there was any reaction to the mention of Angel's name. None was apparent.

"When Mr. Evola asked you, you said you had followed the case on telvision and in the newspapers but that you had not formed an opinion as to guilt or innocence, is that right?"

"Yes." She said it rather proudly.

I smiled. "The case has really become the talk of the town, hasn't it, Mrs. Harris?"

She smiled back, but warily. "Yes, I suppose you could say that."

"I assume you've talked to your family about the case, perhaps even your neighbors and friends?"

She paused, the smile fading. "Like you say, there's been a lot of talk."

"Have you ever expressed an opinion to anyone, say anyone at work, about Angel Harwell's innocence or guilt?"

Mrs. Harris tried to conceal her blossoming anxiety.

"No," she said, hesitating for a telltale second.

She was lying, of course. She knew it. I knew it. Evola knew it. But it was a human kind of lie. It was impossible to live in Pickeral Point and not discuss whether little Angel had really knocked off her old man. Opinions were part of that process.

It was my job to see if she harbored any real bias toward Angel despite her declaration that she did not.

"You told Mr. Evola you aren't related to anyone in this case, correct?"

"That's right."

"Have you ever talked to any of the Harwells?"

She shook her head. "I never talked to any of them. I would occasionally see Mr. Harwell around here. And his father, but I never talked to them."

"Was any member of your family ever friendly with the Harwells?"

322

"No."

I thought the answer was a little too fast and a little too definite.

"Did you or any member of your family ever work for the Harwell boat company?"

She nodded slowly. "My brother."

"Does he still work for the company?"

"No." Again the answer was a little quick.

"He left the company?"

"He was fired."

Suddenly she assumed the face of a good poker player. I couldn't read anything from her bland expression.

"Did you agree with that at the time?"

She shook her head. "No. It was unfair, quite unfair."

I waited for just a moment, then asked, "Who fired him?"

"Harrison Harwell."

There was a bustle of whispers in the packed courtroom, silenced by the judge's stern stare.

"Do you have any resentment about that?"

"I resented it at the time. I don't now."

That was another human lie. The problem was whether she held it against any Harwell, which would be very bad for us. Or did she hate Harrison Harwell so much that his death would seem like simple justice? That would have been very bad for Evola.

I walked to my chair and sat down. Selecting jurors is like a poker game. You make the other side bet if you can. There are only two ways to have a juror excused: peremptory, meaning no reason needed, and cause, meaning a very good reason needed. I could have used one of my peremptory challenges—I had twenty of them since it was a life sentence case—and she would be gone. I could have also challenged her for cause, but it wouldn't stick since her answers, lies or not, didn't reveal any overt prejudice. Challenges for cause could be made without limit, except the cause had to be demonstrated and it had to be pretty strong.

If I passed, it would be up to Evola. He couldn't establish cause either, and he, as prosecutor, had only fifteen peremptory challenges. Making the other side spend its challenges was all part of the game.

The comparison between jury selection and poker was inaccurate. This time it was more like Russian roulette. Any juror might be the fatal bullet, the one who would persuade the others to go against you.

But it was time to twirl the cylinder and pull the trigger.

"Pass the juror for cause," I said to the judge.

Evola held a short whispered conversation with Morgan to get his advice, then stood up. "The People will excuse Mrs. Harris," he said in a friendly tone, as if he was doing her a nice little favor.

Jurors were always sensitive to how lawyers treated fellow candidates. No lawyer wanted to seem vicious, for obvious reasons.

Mrs. Harris, looking more resentful than relieved, got up and eased her way past the other candidates and out of the jury box. The clerk called a replacement, who came up and took her seat.

Then it began again.

Any one of them might be that fatal bullet.

It went by like a speeding train. I had tried my best.

Fourteen, eight men and six women, had been selected. I looked over at Angel and wondered if she realized just how important these fourteen people would be in her life. At the end of the trial, they would rule like Roman emperors, either thumbs up or thumbs down. Lions would not devour the loser. We were more civilized, although in a way the result would be much the same.

The fourteen of them were given the final oath.

The judge directed the other members of the panel, those not selected, leave the courtroom. Their still-warm seats were instantly filled by newspeople.

It was almost five o'clock. I expected the judge to knock off for the day.

"Mr. Evola," he said, "do you want to make your opening statement now, or wait until the morning?"

"I'm ready now, Judge." He stood up. "I shall be brief."

"Brevity is the soul of wit," the judge said, a rare smile on his lips as if he had thought it up all on his own. "Please proceed."

An opening statement is like a menu. A lawyer isn't supposed to do any arguing. The idea is just to state the case you expect to prove. Of course, any lawyer worth his salt tries to slip in a little venom here and there.

324

Evola really didn't need to. And, he was brief.

He stood in front of the jury and waited until he had their absolute attention. Then he held one of his big long-fingered hands up in front of him.

"The people will prove the following," he said, taking hold of his thumb. "Harrison Harwell and his daughter on the night of June fourth engaged in a nasty, screaming dog-dirty verbal fight."

"Objection," I snapped, rising in pretended outrage. "This is argumentative, prejudicial, and basically unfair, and Mr. Evola knows it is."

"So is your objection," the judge growled. "Both of you cut this kind of business out right now. Sustained. Stick to matters of proof, Mr. Prosecutor."

Evola nodded but was unruffled. "They had a fight," he said, gesturing with that long thumb. "Then, later, Harrison Harwell was found dead, a long knife thrust into his chest, clean into the heart." He held his forefinger, showing he had just stated another essential element of his case.

With each succeeding finger he made another point, adding that Angel had been found covered in her father's blood, that her fingerprints were found on the blood-soaked handle of the knife, and, last finger, she had said she thought she might have been responsible for her father's death. He called that a confession.

He held those long extended fingers before the jury, then he slowly closed them into a huge fist.

"When you put it all together," he said slowly, "it proves beyond all reasonable doubt that Angel Harwell murdered her father. And the People will ask you for justice. We will ask you to find her guilty of that cruel, unnatural murder."

He was done. It was pretty good.

The judge glanced at his watch. "Well, it's late and—"

I jumped up. I couldn't let the jury go home for the night with Evola's words echoing in their ears. Evola had planned just that.

"If the court please," I said. "I do not choose to reserve my opening statement until after the people rest. I wish to make it now."

"Mr. Sloan, the hour is late. First thing in the—"

"Your honor, Mr. Evola has misstated the case and the evidence, and it would be manifestly unfair if I was deprived of a

325

chance to talk to the jury after what I consider to be a very prejudicial and unfair statement."

I heard Evola jump up behind me and object.

"Mr. Sloan, you know better than to use such reckless language," the judge snapped. "I will not sit here and let you people
run wild in my courtroom. You will—"

"Judge, I apologize, but please let me make my opening statement. I, too, will be brief."

He scowled. I think if the television camera hadn't been re-
cording everything he would have banged the gavel and sent everyone home.

But, as the protesters used to shout, the whole world was
watching.

"Go on," he growled. "But make it short."

EVOLA had used his hand like a blackboard. The jury would remember those long fingers. It was an effective device. So effective, I thought I had better use it myself.

My hand is small compared to that of the former basketball
star, and my fingers are sort of stubby, but they would have to do.

I held out my hand, imitating Evola. "This is our side of
things."

I saw a couple of the jurors smile.

"Fathers and daughter argue. If that's become a felony, then
many of us, probably most of us, are guilty. Angel Harwell and
her father had an argument that night. Nothing more, a normal
family spat. We will show you just that."

"This is the big finger," I said, wiggling my index finger.

One of the jurors snickered. Smiles were good, snickers meant
I was going too far.

"Harrison Harwell was indeed found with a Japanese ceremonial short sword stuck in his chest. We will show you that Harrison Harwell's business had collapsed. We will show that
everything he had ever valued in life was crashing around him.
We will show you that he went home that night an embittered
man. We will show you that he planned suicide, even talked
about it. We will show you that Harrison Harwell, a man who all
his life had imitated Japanese warrior values, that night performed the ritual suicide of a samurai. We will show you this was
no murder. We will show you he committed suicide."

326

I held that finger aloft as if it had taken on a life of its own. There were no snickers this time.

"We will show you that Angel Harwell discovered her father's bloody body after he killed himself. We will show you that she tried to pull the grotesque sword from his chest, but could not. We will show you that she is as fragile as she is beautiful. She was deeply in shock at the horrible sight."

I was working my other fingers, just as Evola had. "Finally, we'll demonstrate that the so-called confession came after she had been mentally abused for hours and brainwashed, and although she continuously denied hurting her father they kept after her until she gave them something one might expect from a brutalized prisoner."

"Objection," Evola shouted. "This is argument, pure and simple, and it's also baloney."

"I will sustain the objection, and I will caution you both to conduct yourselves like lawyers. I will begin to keep a scorecard, gentlemen, and I will note the number of times my orders are disregarded. At the conclusion of this trial, you will both be held accountable. I trust I make myself clear?"

I thought that responding would weaken the effect of my words, so I continued as if I hadn't heard him.

"We will show that the prosecution has manufactured a case."

I had worked my way through my last finger. It was time for my fist. I held it up and waited for dramatic effect before I continued. I took a step closer to the jury so I could lower my voice a bit, also for effect.

"You had to walk past literally hundreds of reporters and camera operators to get into this courtroom this morning," I said, holding my fist up. "This is international news. It produces headlines all over the world, as I'm sure you know.

"So if my client is innocent, why charge murder?"

I waited for just a second.

"For fame, for fortune, God knows what. This is a trumped-up charge and we will show you—"

Evola was up and shouting, but I continued.

"Angel Harwell is innocent, absolutely innocent!"

The judge banged his gavel, and I could feel his eyes on me as I walked back to the counsel table.

"You've just earned a few points on my scorecard, Mr. Sloan," he said. "I instruct the jury to ignore everything but the facts they will hear from the witness stand." He looked at me for a moment, then said, "You may not remember all this, Mr. Sloan, but I shall."

The gavel rapped again.

"We are adjourned until nine tomorrow morning,' the judge said. "And when I say nine o'clock, I mean nine o'clock."

He stomped off the bench. Then the court officer escorted the jury out of the courtroom.

I sat down and turned to Angel. "Well, what did you think?"

"Sort of cornball, weren't you?"

24

POOR EVOLA, THEY IGNORED HIM COMPLETELY. I was the story. If I had produced Elvis in person, alive and well, I wouldn't have gotten any more media attention.

As I stood on the courthouse steps I couldn't begin to count the number of cameras pointed at me or the forest of microphones clustered just in front of my face.

And mouths, there were a lot of those, too. All shouting questions, all of the voices melding together in a kind of chaotic chant. Except for the distinctive voice of a French newsman who was so excited he was shouting his questions in French, which amused me.

I couldn't look amused, however. That was the wrong image to project. I was trying one lawsuit inside. And I was trying another out here in the public eye. The one out here would intrude on the other, no matter how many cautions might be given by the judge, so what I said and the way I said it were of real importance.

It was the suicide claim that got them.

It was Monday, the summer news was slow, and suddenly they got the gift of a lead story, not only for the television news, but one that would command dramatic headlines in all the world's newspapers. It was a lot sexier than the drought in Kansas.

Looking as coolly outraged as I could I told the world that the charges against Angel Harwell had been trumped up by ambitious public officials. A suicide, a family tragedy, had been perverted into a murder charge. I was careful not to say too much since I knew Evola's people would be listening and I didn't want to telegraph any of the punches I intended to throw later in the courtroom.

I thanked them, ignored the continuous shouted questions, and pushed my way through to the parking lot, driving away in my battered old car.

Back at my empty office my energy level dropped to zero as I felt the emotional letdown from the hectic events of the day. The mail contained nothing of importance. The answering machine blinked with messages but I didn't feel like listening.

I was tired. It had been a long day, climaxing in a flurry of expended energy. In the quiet of my office, thoughts of failure began to creep into my mind. Like Sandburg's fog, they came on cat feet.

Maybe Angel had been right, maybe I had been cornball. Maybe I had been cornball right from the beginning. It had been a long time since I had faced a jury.

I needed a drink. This time it was more an intellectual urge than a physical one. I began to rationalize what a drink would do for me. It would raise my flagging spirits. It would relax me, and I needed that badly. It would restore me and I would be able to think clearly. One drink, maybe two. It couldn't hurt.

If only I could be that persuasive with the jury.

One or two drinks wouldn't hurt me, they would destroy me. That didn't make me want them any less.

I DROVE home, took a shower, and tossed down several root beers, pretending they were something stronger.

Although I really didn't feel like talking to anyone, especially about the case, I called the Harwell house. It had been a very long day for Angel, too. I thought she might need some encouragement.

I asked for Angel but Robin came to the phone.

"Charley, are you all right?"

"I'm fine."

"Nate Golden worries that you might start drinking again."

He wasn't alone.

"Tell him I'm touched by his thoughtful concern."

"Don't be difficult, Charley. He's only trying to be helpful."

"Yeah, the way Hitler was helpful to the Jews. How's Angel doing?"

"All right. She's sleeping now. All this is very taxing, as you can imagine."

"I'm home," I said. "If Angel wakes up and wants to talk she can call me here."

"Charley, I'm very worried. About the case."

"In what way?"

"I think we should have another lawyer come in. I'm sorry, I know I'm the one who got you involved in all this, but I really think this isn't going very well. In the beginning you wanted us to get someone else, and now I think you were right. Nate says that he can have someone up here tomorrow morning to take over, if that's agreeable."

"Is that what Angel wants?"

"No. But I think we have to do what is right for her. I'm sure you agree. We never should have pushed you into this."

"Did Golden tell you what would happen if you try to substitute lawyers now that the case is underway?"

"He said several things might happen."

"I'll tell you what is the most probable. A new lawyer would need time to prepare. The court, if substitution was permitted, would declare a mistrial and this would all have to be done over again, right from scratch."

"But much later, according to Nate. Months, he said. And he said we would probably get another judge, a better one."

"And do you think all that would really benefit Angel?" I asked.

"Nate thinks he might be able to work out something, a plea or something, if he had more time."

"Time would only give the prosecution an opportunity to fine-tune their case now that they know the line of defense. What you suggest would only damage Angel's chances. I'm not withdrawing, Robin. If Angel wants to fire me that's up to her. Until then I'm her lawyer. And if the select committee out there, you and Nate, feel otherwise, that's just too goddamned bad."

I slammed the phone down.

I told myself I shouldn't even think about what she said. Tomorrow was an important day, the first real day of trial, and I needed to be relaxed and calm.

That fog seemed thicker now. I didn't get much sleep.

THE media army was again out in force. Just getting into the courtroom was like running a gauntlet. But I made it.

When I got there I didn't know what to expect.

Angel was there, seated at the counsel table. I looked around, wondering if another trial lawyer might be there, my replacement, looking on me with pity or triumph. I didn't see anyone who matched that description. But Nate Golden was there, scowling as usual, with Robin, who avoided eye contact.

"Are you okay?" I asked Angel.

She nodded. "Yes."

I debated asking if she would prefer another lawyer. It was probably the fair thing to do, given the circumstances. But if she did get another attorney at this point, I was doomed. The judge and the bar association under the guidance of Nate Golden would dive on me like hawks. Unfair or not, I didn't ask her.

The judge stalked out of his chambers at nine o'clock precisely. The jury was brought in, and we began.

My old mentor, Gabriel Aaron, said trying a lawsuit is like telling a story in a theater. The lawyer is the playwright, but he cannot invent his characters—they already exist, and the lawyer is stuck with them. The play is written by fate and the lawyer must craft his story in a logical sequence by using witnesses, who function as actors. He must also obey the rules of evidence and traditions of the court. He tells the story to a small select audience, all seated in the jury box. If the story is told well, the lawyer wins. If not . . .

Also out front during this judicial production is another lawyer-playwright, who is going to do everything possible to screw up the drama being presented.

There are easier ways to make a living. But in this case, at least the beginning, everything began very smoothly and proceeded with surprising speed.

Evola marched the witnesses to the stand, and I was surprised at how quickly and skillfully he drew the necessary facts from each of them. He was a much better workman than I had anticipated. As if things weren't already bad enough.

The uniformed officers began the story with that pleasant June evening when they had been called to the Harwell house. They briefly described what they saw and what time they saw it. Evola had a large drawing of Harwell's office, a diagram with the outline of a body drawn in red. It was reasonably accurate and I thought I could use it later myself, so I made no objection when he offered it as an exhibit.

Each of the uniformed officers admitted to me that Angel had denied stabbing her father. I established the time when Angel was first taken into custody to show just how long she had been held and questioned.

So far, no fireworks from either side. I thought the media people looked disappointed. A few seemed outright bored.

Dennis Bernard and his wife testified that they had identified the body as being that of Harrison Harwell. They were just procedural witnesses, really. But they provided the first skirmish in our little legal war.

I asked if either had heard a verbal fight between father and daughter that night. They hadn't, although they were at home then.

They both admitted that from time to time there were spats between father and daughter. Nothing unusual, they said in answer to my questions.

Evola attacked with vigor. I threw him off by objecting. I said he couldn't cross-examine his own witnesses. He got angry at that and lost it for a minute. I thought the jury looked entertained. The judge ruled, as I expected, that since Evola had to call the identification witnesses he was allowed wide latitude.

Evola couldn't shake the Bernards, although he tried. It was a very small victory, but I gloated anyway.

Evola thought I'd be the one to explode when he called the police photographer to the stand. In a murder case, the cops take dozens of gory photographs, the bloodier the better. And in color. Every prosecutor tries to introduce the photos, usually wearing a saintly expression such as you might find on old, kindly preachers. This kind of photo can so inflame a jury they are eager to

333

punish someone. Ah, and there's the defendant, just sitting there. It's so convenient.

Defense lawyers are equally predictable. They demand the jury be excused, then they go into an emotional tirade about how the pictures will poison the minds of the jury and deny their client a fair trial. It's accepted practice to toss in the Constitution, the Magna Carta, and the Code of Hammurabi if things really look bad.

The whole procedure is as predictable as an old morality play. You know exactly what each actor will say and do. But this time, I didn't follow the script.

I looked at the photos as if I was seeing them for the first time. Taken at different angles, they showed Harrison Harwell lying on his back, his shirt all bloody, his eyes open and staring. The short sword stuck obscenely out of his chest. It was the kind of thing that makes you look quickly away. There were other photos, taken on the autopsy table. In those the body had been stripped of clothing.

Evola waited, mentally preparing for the fight.

I didn't ask that the jury be excused, which was my first surprise.

"People's proposed exhibit two," I said to the judge in a voice loud enough to be heard by the media people, "consists of ten numbered photographs. I have no objection to photos numbered one through six, taken of the deceased at the Harwell house. However, photos seven through ten were obviously taken just prior to autopsy. The body is without clothing and I see no legal reason to show the jury those pictures. The others are quite horrible enough, and they should serve Mr. Evola's main purpose, which is obviously to poison and inflame the juror's minds."

Even the judge looked surprised. I had caught Evola flat-footed. He stammered for a moment, trying to figure what I was up to so he could effectively respond.

"Okay," he said finally. "We'll move to introduce only photos one through six and withdraw the others."

"If the court please," I said. "The practice is to show the jury the photographs at this point. I respectfully ask that the jury not view the photos until Dr. Rey testifies."

"They should see them now," Evola said quickly. He wondered what I was up to.

The judge scowled. "Dr. Rey is your next witness, is he not?" Evola nodded. "Yes."

"I see no problem in holding off until then," the judge said. "People's exhibit number two, six photographs, numbered one through six, is admitted."

He looked at his watch. "Well, it's almost noon. This is probably a good time to take a break. We will begin again at one-thirty precisely."

The clerk banged the gavel, and I went back to the counsel table.

"What was that all about?" Angel asked.

"I plan to use those photos with our expert witnesses to show it was suicide."

She looked at me, then glanced back at Robin. As usual, it was almost impossible to tell what she was thinking. When her eyes returned to me, she said nothing.

Angel left with Robin and Nate Golden to have lunch.

I could guess who the subject of their conversation would be.

My lunch consisted of a candy bar out of the machine and a quick conference with my two experts, Dr. Henry Foreman and Dr. Hans Voltz.

They were being paid to attend and observe, but both were as enthusiastic as two playgoers bubbling with enthusiasm at intermission.

From my point of view they looked distinguished, and both spoke with the gentle certainty of men who knew what they were doing. I would have bought a used car from either one. They had become friends and had dined together.

I listened as Dr. Foreman, the psychiatrist, told me of his study of the life of Harrison Harwell and how he was convinced the death was suicide.

Dr. Voltz, the pathologist, gave me a short lecture on Japanese culture and weapons. He supported Dr. Foreman's position and added physical findings to show the knife wound was self-inflicted.

I listened to them, trying to hear them as a juror would. It sounded good, very good. If they perfected their act, they might even be able to take it on the road.

I could make an excellent case for suicide. Max Webster would testify to suicidal intent. Dr. Foreman would provide a convincing psychological profile showing that Harwell was suicidal. And Voltz would take care of the physical possibilities and the Japanese honor code that Harrison Harwell loved so much.

The little cat feet of fear seemed to retreat a bit.

I was ready for Dr. Ernesto Rey, the dapper, diminutive, lady-loving pathologist who had done the autopsy on Harwell. Of course, I knew that Dr. Rey was also ready for me.

Evola would have had the doctor memorize the transcript of the testimony he gave at the examination, and then Evola would have quizzed him carefully. Catching a witness making conflicting statements under oath was like scoring a Superbowl touchdown or the winning goal in a World Cup soccer match. Lawyers were careful to make sure that didn't happen to their witnesses. At least they tried.

So Dr. Rey was primed and ready. But, to my advantage, he was also wary of me since I always seemed to have great luck with him on cross-examination. That concern would translate into a slightly less than authoritative manner, which might give me a little edge.

Evola took him through the autopsy, giving special emphasis to the old scar on Harwell's left arm, but he didn't develop it further. I supposed he hoped I wouldn't notice. Evola then got the short sword into evidence with no objection from me, and even got the doctor to say again that the cause of death was homicide, not suicide.

The beautiful short sword was shown to the jury. Then it lay on the counsel table, a silent witness to what had happened that night.

Evola next gave the jury the photographs of the body. It took a while as the jury members passed them along from one to another. The men tried to show no reaction. Several of the women turned away and quickly passed the pictures on. When they had all had a chance to see the photos, Evola continued.

Ernesto seemed to gain confidence as he went along, especially

336

since I wasn't objecting very much. I suppose he thought this time he was going to get a free ride.

When it came time to cross-examine, I gently questioned him about how he arrived at his conclusion that the death was caused by someone else. He was ready for that, as I knew he would be. Apparently his fear had ebbed, because he started to elaborate on his answers, trying to stick it into me deeper each time. He didn't win with me often, and enthusiasm replaced his normal caution.

Which is exactly what I had hoped for.

Sidney Sherman's detectives had done a very good job. Now it would pay off.

"Doctor, are you saying that this kind of wound could never be self-administered?"

"It's very unlikely," he said. His chocolate eyes gleamed with satisfaction. "I would say, quite impossible really."

"Doctor, have you, as a pathologist, ever had a suicide case with a similar wound?"

He smiled, almost in pity. "No, Mr. Sloan, I have never seen a self-inflicted wound like Mr. Harwell's."

"And you do a lot of autopsies, right?"

"Several hundred a year." He assumed a pleased and satisfied expression. He was a workman proud of his production.

"And you never saw a wound like this and ruled it a suicide?"

"Never." He exuded quiet confidence.

"I guess you'd be pretty sure about something like that, Doctor, wouldn't you?"

He nodded, but the little knowing smile was fading. "I'm sure, yes."

"Do you see many suicides up in this area—Pickeral Point, Port Huron, Marine City?"

"Unfortunately, yes."

I walked back to the counsel table as if accepting defeat, then I stopped, pretended to think of something, and turned.

"People commit suicide for any number of reasons. Is that a fair statement?"

He nodded. "Oh, yes. It ranges from pain caused by an incurable disease to getting a bad mark at school."

"As a pathologist, I take it you've made a study of suicide, not only its physical indications, but also the reasons people do it?"

"Oh, yes."

"Have you ever had a case where a man killed himself because of a business failure?"

"I've had many cases, Mr. Sloan." He was relaxing. "As I say, it's regrettable, but people sometimes take their lives over trivial problems. Sometimes even over the loss of a job or bankruptcy, that sort of thing."

"But they don't do it by stabbing themselves in the stomach, is that your testimony?"

"Essentially, yes."

"Do you recall doing an autopsy on Marvin Michaels last September?"

Those little eyes widened in horror. He knew he had stepped into a trap.

"No, I don't."

"You didn't do it, or you don't remember it?"

"I don't remember."

"Let me show you your autopsy report and see if that doesn't refresh your recollection."

Evola objected. The jury was excused and we argued. Unfortunately, I had lost the element of surprise since I had to disclose the reason I brought up the deceased Marvin Michaels. He had stabbed himself in the stomach and Dr. Rey had certified it as a suicide.

The judge reluctantly allowed me to continue and the jury was brought back in.

Sidney Sherman's people had gone over the autopsy reports in the area for the past five years, thousands of them, culling out those done by Dr. Rey. Suicides got preference. It was a sad report. People knocked themselves off in a variety of ways, some mundane, some exotic. Most did not stab themselves in the stomach. We found two who had, both within the past year. One was Marvin Michaels, an eighty-four-year-old man living with his abusive daughter. He had no other means at hand, apparently, so he used a kitchen knife. It did the job. The other was a young man, an AIDS victim. Apparently, he had decided to hack off the member that had caused his sad problem, but stabbed a little

338

high and bled to death. Dr. Ernesto Rey had certified both deaths as suicide.

Fortunately for my purpose, no suicide note had been left by either man, just as there was no suicide note from Harwell.

Ernesto Rey was in agony. He tried to repair his previous testimony, but I wouldn't let him wiggle off. Finally, after I worked him over a bit with the second suicide, he caved in and said suicide by a knife in the belly wasn't all that uncommon after all. Evola's face was a stoic mask but I presumed he would have a few unkind things to say to the doctor in private.

I wish all witnesses were like Ernesto. But they aren't. Bently Jenkins, the evidence technician, was on and off the stand in minutes. He merely testified that the blood of the deceased and that found on Angel's clothing matched. And he identified the bloody prints on the short sword as belonging to Angel.

Evola called Morgan but the judge intervened and adjourned for the day. It was almost five o'clock.

I was surprised. I hadn't even noticed the passage of time.

MILO Zeck, the Florida cop, was decked out in a new cream-colored summer suit. He was seated in the spectators' section. He grinned as he worked his way forward through the mass of people leaving the courtroom.

"Hey, Mr. Sloan," he said, pumping my hand. "You're pretty good. You had that poor little doctor roasting in his own juices. I'm glad we don't have to worry about facing you down home."

"Good trip here?"

"Oh, great. Real nice. Say, we'll have to wait on that drink though. The prosecutor said he didn't want me talking to anybody connected with the case. Maybe when it's all over you and I can step out and hoist a few."

"I assume they're still planning on calling you as a witness?"

He nodded. "The prosecutor here said you probably would be able to keep me off now. But he wants me to stick around. He said they might be able to use me as a rebuttal witness."

He grinned even wider. "Say, every day I'm here is like a paid vacation for me."

Zeck asked about restaurants and night life, then he left.

I looked around and Angel had gone too. So had Robin and Nate Golden.

Dr. Hans Voltz, my expert pathologist, had been in attendance all through Ernesto Rey's testimony, as I had requested.

"What did you think?" I asked him.

"He's probably a very good doctor, but he makes a terrible witness. I thought you handled him quite well."

"Evola will use his testimony and findings when he questions you. You heard what he said. Will any of what you've heard cause you any problems?"

He smiled in a superior way. "Heavens no. I shall use all of it to our advantage. I almost pity your friend, the prosecutor. He'll discover what it is to match wits with a real expert."

"Pride, they say, goes before a fall."

"Not this time." The smile became arrogant. "Don't worry. Just leave everything to me."

I wonder why I wasn't wildly enthusiastic.

ANGEL called almost the minute I stepped into my office. "Charley, are you planning on coming over here?"

"I'm going to review some stuff for tomorrow and then I'll drop over," I said.

"I don't know if that's such a good idea," Angel replied. "Nate Golden is here. Robin and he want me to fire you as my lawyer. I think it might be best if you stayed away tonight."

"Angel, do you still want me to defend you?"

I didn't breathe until she answered.

"I guess so. According to Golden if I did ask you to step aside we might have to go through all this court business again."

"That's probably right." Judges usually refuse a defendant's request to change lawyers at the trial stage, unless there was a very good reason. Judge Brown, however, would jump at the chance to bump me—he had made that clear enough. I didn't inform her of that little nuance. Self-destruction, career or otherwise, was something I wasn't particularly fond of.

"Besides, Charley, I'm tired," Angel said. "I don't do anything but sit there all day but I still come home whipped."

"It's the strain. That's normal enough, Angel."

"Anyway, I'm going to have a few drinks and then hop into bed unless there's something you want me to do."

"No. Just keep your spirits up, Angel. We're doing very well so far."

There was a pause, and then she spoke. "I'll have to take your word for that, Charley," she said and then hung up.

My total food intake for the day had been a morning cup of coffee and an afternoon candy bar. But the feeling that gripped my stomach wasn't hunger. It was fear.

And those cat feet were becoming heavier and louder.

I wanted some relief from the terrible tension building within me. I was walking a very high wire with no net. I wanted to get down. But I didn't know how.

25

BACK IN THE COURTROOM IN THE MORNING I TRIED
to force myself to relax, but it was impossible. Too much was at
stake.

Morgan and Maguire, the two detectives, testified. I was as
careful with each of them as if I was reaching into a barrel of
cobras. I did establish that Angel had been questioned nonstop
for hours and that she denied committing any crime until the very
last statement.

Evola then called Milo Zeck. I asked that the jury be excused.
After they were out of earshot the war began.

Evola said he would prove through Zeck that Angel had tried to
kill her father once before. I knew his main target wasn't the
judge but the army of reporters in the courtroom. So we held a
minitrial right there. Officially I won. The judge would not allow
Zeck's testimony, saying that the state couldn't prove one crime
by alleging another. Unofficially, Evola was the true winner. The
story of a previous alleged attempt would be the day's sensation.

The jury was called back in, but before another witness could
be called the judge announced a short lunch break.

My lunch again consisted of a candy bar while I reviewed the
cases I planned to cite to the judge to keep Angel's statement out.

Then the afternoon session began.

Evola tried to get the videotape in without calling Herbert
Ames, the technician I had barbecued at the Walker hearing. I
didn't let him.

Ames, who had been present during Dr. Rey's slow torture yesterday, was now in a state of near-collapse. The judge had to keep prodding him to keep his voice up.

He was almost as good for us as he had been at the Walker hearing. The jury got the point. Angel wouldn't crack until the last. It sounded as if Evola and the cops had sent Ames out of the room so they could work her over, then called him back.

Evola then tried to introduce the tape. I demanded the right to call the witnesses I had used at the Walker hearing to challenge it. Judge Brown listened carefully to my arguments. Then he ruled.

It was like getting my legs chopped off. He would allow me to present witnesses as to Angel's mental state that night, but only as part of the defense case later. He would not allow a trial within a trial, he said.

It was a devastating ruling and I tried to enlarge my legal argument. I told the judge that the jury wouldn't be able to judge the statement fairly unless they had heard my experts before they viewed the tape.

He smiled and said that he understood but disagreed. There was nothing I could do.

It was getting late and I didn't want the jury to see the taped statement as the last thing of the day. But Evola did, and he won again.

The statement seemed worse each time I saw it. Angel, unemotional, poised, calm, sure of herself, said she thought she might have been responsible for her father's death. She coolly explained her prints on the knife, saying she had tried to pull it out but couldn't.

She was so calm, so cold. The courtroom remained quiet even after the tape had run. The video had enormous impact.

The judge cracked the gavel, the sharp sound echoing in the silence. We were adjourned for the day.

"IT didn't go well, did it Charley?" Robin's remark was more of a statement than a question.

We were sitting again in the long glass atrium. Although it was just after nine, it was getting dark. The days were becoming shorter. But the nearly ninety-degree heat outside held no hint of

343

an approaching autumn. Inside everything was pleasantly air-conditioned, not too cool, not too warm, just right.

Angel had been swimming and her long black hair was still wet, her body wrapped in a long, lush towel. Robin had changed into shorts and a blazing red T-shirt. They were dressed for a picnic but the mood was more funereal than festive.

"The video statement hurt us," I said. "But I expected that. Our experts on brainwashing should be able to turn that around when they testify. We'll see."

Robin looked at me, then spoke again. "Do you really think so?" Her tone indicated that she did not.

They were already drinking by the time I had arrived. I had stopped at the office, talked by phone with several of my witnesses, and then prepared for the start of our case in the morning. I hadn't eaten. I didn't feel like it. I had gulped down the orange juice Robin gave me when I arrived.

"You have to look at things from the viewpoint of the jury," I said. "They'll tend to credit what they saw on that videotape, unless we give them a reason not to. Our experts should provide that, give them a basis for suspecting that maybe the statement was made under duress. But everything hangs on the question of suicide. If the jury accepts even the possibility of suicide, they'll be convinced the statement was forced by an ambitious prosecutor. It's kind of a one-two punch."

That seemed to catch Angel's interest. "Do you think they'll do that, accept the death as a suicide?"

"We're going to present a strong case, Angel. If they aren't totally convinced, the shadow of a doubt should be sufficient."

"Let me freshen that for you, Charley." Robin took my glass and walked the length of the room to the small bar at the other end.

"Suicide and a forced statement." Angel spoke as if she was talking about someone else's case. "It sounds too simple to me. If I were a juror, I'd be suspicious of anything so basic."

"Believe me, the less complicated the better. A jury becomes a kind of basic beast, even if it's made up of twelve Albert Einsteins. There's a chemistry that takes place, a sort of meltdown into a single primitive intelligence that demands things be kept simple. Trial lawyers know that. One basic idea, well pitched,

344

over and over, is the most effective tactic there is." I took the orange juice from Robin and slugged half of it down.

"Unfortunately, Evola knows that, too. He's been doing a good job keeping things very basic. So will we. We don't have to prove it was suicide, we just have to show that it might have been. If we do that, we win."

I was beginning to feel relaxed, comfortable. It was peaceful here, sitting and watching the river.

Then Mary Beth Needham came to call.

Angel got me another orange juice and I tried to find a politic way to caution Robin and Angel to watch what they said in front of Needham, since she was now sitting next to me.

But I really didn't have to worry. Oddly, the little blonde writer chose not to talk about the case itself. She dished up some juicy tidbits she had dug up about Mark Evola's private life. I already knew about that but she presented everything in a witty, bitchy way that amused me.

I realized I was gotting drunk along about the fourth glass of orange juice.

"Robin, what's in this?" I held up the nearly empty glass.

"A little vodka, Charley. You knew that. You needed something to relax you. We don't want our lord protector having a nervous breakdown in the middle of the trial. It won't hurt, Charley. Just this once."

I hadn't tasted it, I thought, but maybe I did. But whether I knew or not, I liked the feeling. Hell, I loved the feeling. I felt better than I had since the case began, perhaps a lot longer than that.

I looked at my glass. "You might be right."

Mary Beth Needham frowned. "Charley, this isn't such a good idea, drinking."

I shrugged. "I've had more vodka in my time than Stalin. A couple more won't hurt."

"We can have a nice little party," Robin said, taking my glass again for a refill.

"But I have to get going soon," I said. "Big day tomorrow."

I saw the alarm in Needham's eyes. I was so happy, I wondered why she wasn't. Everything was just swell.

"Charley," she said, her voice low and urgent, "you're an alcoholic. You shouldn't be doing this."

"Listen, I—" My words came out slightly slurred.

I stood up, and to my surprise found my balance wasn't quite right.

"I've got to go."

"I'll drive you, Charley," Needham said.

I shook my head. "No. Thanks."

"You shouldn't drive." Her voice was strained.

I waved as I weaved my way out. "I'm not going to drive. I'm going to walk."

IT was dark out when I left the Harwell house. My car was there. The keys were in it—no thief in his right mind would steal it. I felt pretty good. I reconsidered my decision not to drive. I'd just motor over to some quaint local bar, have a nightcap, and then get a good night's sleep.

Besides, I argued with myself, the media folks were probably still waiting out at the entrance. If I walked they would insist on getting a statement. Also, my apartment was two miles away. It would be inconvenient to walk.

But I was still unsteady and I wondered just how much vodka I had consumed. Probably not much, but my body wasn't accustomed to alcohol anymore.

I looked at my old Ford. Suddenly it seemed to be a symbol for what had become of my life. I wanted another drink, very badly, but I no longer wanted to be like my car, a rusting wreck, barely functioning, noticed by no one. So I went on walking.

The guards at the entrance were surprised to see me.

"Walking is good for the mind," I said, answering the question before it was asked. "Where is everybody?"

There were no television trucks, no cars full of reporters.

"They took off. I guess they figured the show was over for the night. You okay, Mr. Sloan?"

"Never better. Good night."

I walked along the shoulder of the road. It was dark and it was dangerous. The road consisted of two narrow lanes, and despite that, cars whizzed by like racers heading for the checkered flag. The side of the road was rough gravel. I stumbled several times, tripping on small rocks.

346

The lore of Alcoholics Anonymous is full of horror stories of men and women who take that one unsuspecting sip of alcohol and find themselves seized by an uncontrollable urge to drink, followed by a downward spiral into degradation. In A.A., they called it a slip. I wasn't like that. No, I wanted to continue drinking, but it was only for the relaxation of it, for the companionship of fellow drinkers, for the ease provided by a few civilized cocktails.

Sure.

I was walking faster, trying to breathe deeply and force my body to throw off the effect of the vodka. I stumbled again and almost fell.

And it was then that the scout car pulled up behind me.

There was an officer behind the flashlight but I couldn't make out his face behind the light.

"Hey, are you okay?"

"I'm fine," I said, trying not to slur my words. "I'm just taking a little walk."

"You're Mr. Sloan, the lawyer, right?"

I smiled. "Yes."

"Have you been drinking a bit, Mr. Sloan?"

"No."

"It's dangerous out here, Mr. Sloan. There isn't much room between you and the traffic. How about we drive you home?"

"I'm not drunk."

"Why don't we give you a lift anyway? We don't want you to get hurt."

"I'm just walking to help me think. I'm trying the Harwell murder case and tomorrow's going to be a big day."

"I'm sure it is, Mr. Sloan. But you can't try it if you're an asphalt pancake, can you? Come on, get in the car. We'll take you home."

They were both young and respectful. They took me to my apartment and waited until they saw me go in.

The sense of elation the vodka had inspired had passed and now the dark cloud of depression began to descend.

Along with the depression came the fear.

I fixed a frozen dinner in the microwave, hoping food might help counter the effects of the vodka.

A frozen dinner fixed in the microwave is no big deal, so I

347

gulped it down. After I did that, I just sat there, staring at the little plastic plate.

It was garbage now. Just something to be tossed away.

Like me, maybe.

And then I cried.

It was mild, but it had been so long that I had forgotten what a hangover was like. I had forgotten the nasty ache behind the eyes, the nausea, the dry mouth. W. C. Fields, a gin addict, said he felt sorry for nondrinkers because when they woke up in the morning that was as good as they were going to feel for the rest of the day.

I would feel better later, I knew that from experience.

Someone had returned my car to my apartment. I presumed it was Bernard. I drove to the courthouse.

"The judge wants to see you," The clerk said as soon as I had pushed my way through the mob clustered at the back of the courtroom. "Just you."

I followed him into the judge's chambers. Judge Brown was already in his robe, seated behind his desk. The clerk left us alone.

"Sloan, I believe I told you my views on drunks and what would happen if you started drinking during the course of this trial?"

"Yes."

I was standing. He looked up at me over the rim of his little half glasses. "The police arrested you last night for being drunk."

"No."

"I've been told they did."

"I wasn't arrested."

"But you were drinking?"

"No."

He stared at me. "All drunks are liars. I presume you know that?"

I tried to smile. I hope the expression didn't look as forced as it felt. "I've known a few who bent the truth now and then."

"I've requested information from the police on this incident," he said. "If you were drunk I'll declare a mistrial on the basis that Angel Harwell isn't getting adequate legal representation."

348

"If you do that, jeopardy will have attached and she can't be tried again. As you know."

His mouth had become a short angry line. "You're wrong. A defendant is entitled to adequate counsel under the Sixth Amendment of the Constitution. If you had a heart attack or some other physical disability and couldn't continue there'd be no problem with trying the case again."

"That's different."

"I don't think so. A drunk lawyer is at least as dangerous as a sick one."

"Judge—"

"I'll have the police report later today and I will use it, Mr. Sloan, either when this case is done or when I feel I must remove you." He paused. "I'm not your enemy, Mr. Sloan. You are."

He looked down at some papers in front of him. "I know about drunks, Sloan. My father was a drunk. I hate drunks. They ruin everything they touch." His eyes remained fixed on the papers before him. "That's not going to happen here, I assure you. Now, get out."

Evola came forward as I came out of chambers.

"What was that all about?" He was concerned. In an ongoing trial it was most unusual for a judge to talk to one of the attorneys alone.

"I bribed the judge," I said. "Maybe if you go in there fast he'll split with you."

Evola hadn't been smiling much, but this time his grin looked genuine.

"You better bribe the jury too, Charley, because otherwise I'm going to beat your ass."

Angel had come in and was seated at the counsel table. Robin was in the first row, as usual, but this time Nate Golden wasn't with her. I didn't know if that was bad or good.

"Mark, are you about ready to rest your case?" I asked.

"Yes, but we can't find Theresa Hernandez," he said. "We've tried everything. The Puerto Rico police even tried to find her for us. She's taken off."

"Come on, Mark, it's your duty to produce all the res gestae witnesses. I'll raise hell about it on the record if you don't."

"Morgan thinks you're responsible, Charley. Little Theresa

would have hurt you pretty bad. Morgan thinks you've got her hidden away somewhere so she can't testify."

"That's bullshit and you know it."

He shrugged. "I don't know it, Charley. Morgan says you used to have a reputation for this sort of thing. He said you were known in the Detroit courts as a trickster. True?"

"I've never hid a witness, then or now. I'm going to raise hell that the girl isn't here."

I was, but only for show. I was absolutely delighted she wasn't. Theresa could have brought the whole case crashing around us. I suspected that Robin had a hand in helping her disappear, but I didn't know that and I didn't want to know.

"There are two res gestae witnesses, Charley. There's Robin Harwell, too."

"I thought you weren't going call her? I told you I'd waive on her."

"That was then, Charley. This is now. Maybe Mrs. Harwell can throw a little light on the father-daughter relationship, you think? Maybe she even knows how her husband came by that scar on his arm."

His smile was still there, but it had become challenging.

"Suppose I waive on both?"

"Sorry, Charley."

I walked back to the counsel table. Angel looked up at me.

"That was a terrible thing you did last night," I said.

"It relaxed you," she said calmly. "You liked it."

She watched Evola walk toward the front of the courtroom. "What happens now?"

"He's going to call Robin," I said. "He'll try to use her to get in the Florida stabbing."

"Can he do that?"

"Maybe. I'll do my best to keep it out."

The courtroom whispers rose excitedly as Evola called Robin Harwell to the witness stand. She looked terrific, a nicely dressed, very attractive woman, a lady in every way.

She was sworn and then sat down. I noticed that Evola was listening to Morgan's intense whispers. Morgan had that tiger look again.

"What is your name please?" Evola asked.

350

"Robin Harwell."

"And you are the widow of Harrison Harwell?"

"Yes."

"Mrs. Harwell, I realize that all this is extremely painful but I shall be asking you questions about your late husband that are not intended to be embarrassing, but are merely an effort to get to the truth."

I jumped up. "That's a speech, not a question. I object."

"Sustained," the judge said, sounding bored.

"Mrs. Harwell, were you at home here in Pickeral Point the night that your husband died?"

She paused, then spoke in a soft but firm voice. "I respectfully refuse to answer that question on constitutional grounds."

I thought I had imagined the answer.

"Pardon me?" Evola was as surprised as I was, and showed it.

Robin looked determined. "I said that on advice of counsel, I respectfully refuse to answer your question on the grounds that it may tend to degrade or incriminate me. I'm invoking the protections of the Fifth Amendment."

I was stunned, and so was everyone else. I looked at Robin. For an instant I vividly recalled the image of the young girl I had loved as a kid. But I also recalled the woman who had made such passionate animal love the night before her husband's funeral. This seemed to be still another, different woman.

Evola was red-faced and shouting. "This is a rotten, underhanded attempt to mislead the jury, nothing else."

I thought he might physically attack me, but he pointed. "And this miserable excuse for a lawyer knows it! I demand—"

The judge's gavel cracked like a rifle shot. "The jury is excused," he said, his voice low and angry. "And the jury will disregard everything they just heard."

They seemed slow to troop out, disappointed they weren't going to be able see what was about to happen. No one moved or spoke until the jury was gone.

Then Judge Brown looked at me, gesturing with the gavel still in his hand.

"Mr. Sloan, this appears to be an extremely serious breach of ethics. There is no possible way you could be unaware of that."

"I had no idea that Mrs. Harwell would claim constitutional

privilege," I said. "I offered to waive her production as a res gestae witness."

"That's was a fake," Evola exclaimed. "He planned this whole drama."

"What did you expect to do, Mr. Sloan?" The judge's voice was full of anger. "Ask her if she killed her husband and have her then plead the Fifth Amendment? Did you possibly think I'd allow you to mislead the jury with a slimy trick like that?"

"I assure you I had nothing of the sort in mind."

He didn't have to call me a liar. His eyes did that.

"The judge looked at Robin. "Mrs. Harwell, you said you were refusing on the advice of counsel. Did Mr. Sloan so advise you?"

It was like being beneath the guillotine, waiting for the fatal blade to drop. If Robin answered yes, the judge would declare a mistrial and throw me in jail for a couple of months, something he would easily be able to make stick. Obstruction of justice and contempt of court for starters. When I came out I would no longer be a lawyer. Nate Golden would see to that.

Robin turned to the judge. "I respectfully decline to answer that on the same constitutional grounds."

I felt faint. I had escaped the blade. I was in trouble, but I wasn't dead. Not yet

"Mrs. Harwell," the judge continued in a surprisingly gentle tone. "The constitutional privilege against self-incrimination extends only to yourself. If your refusal is for your own protection, that's one thing. However, if the refusal is designed to protect someone else, that's another. For instance, you cannot refuse to answer if it's to protect the defendant, your stepdaughter. You can only refuse for your own protection. Do you understand that?"

"Yes."

"And is this for your own protection?"

If a pin dropped it would have sounded like thunder—the courtroom was that quiet.

She looked straight ahead. "I respectfully refuse to answer on the grounds that—"

"That's enough," the judge snapped. "Get her out of here."

Robin left the stand. But the judge wasn't through.

"I will take all of this under advisement, Mr. Sloan. When this trial is concluded, I will decide then what to do about you."

"He's poisoned this trial," Evola almost yelled. "The jury knows what the Fifth Amendment means. They've seen this kind of thing on television. They'll think Robin Harwell is the murderer. That's why Sloan staged this whole thing. This is nothing but a rotten underhanded trick to create the fiction that someone else committed the murder. It is something that can't be cured."

"I don't agree," the judge said. "I will instruct the jury to disregard this entire episode. They are intelligent people. I think they'll be able to read between the lines." He pointed the gavel at me. "You were lucky this time, Mr. Sloan, but I warn you now, if you refer to this sorry business in questions, in argument, or in any other way, you will be in automatic contempt and I will deal with you swiftly and to the full extent of my powers. Do you understand, sir?"

I nodded. "Yes."

The judge studied me for a moment, his eyes burning with fury. "Bring them back in," he said to the officer.

Evola stepped over to me, his face still flushed. "You're a rotten son of a bitch," he said in a hoarse angry whisper. "That was a shyster trick and it didn't work. You're going to lose your license over this. I'll see to that. They warned me about you. I should have listened. The gloves are off, asshole."

"Why did she do that?" I whispered to Angel.

"I don't know," she said. "She loves me. She was trying to help."

"Well, maybe she did," I said. "And maybe she didn't."

Evola made a speech about the missing maid, accusing me of hiding her.

For the record I protested, but I got the impression that not a person in the courtroom believed me.

The jury was brought back and listened to the judge's stern warning to strike from their minds everything they had just heard from Robin Harwell.

Evola, his face still pink with rage, stood up, glared at me, and then said, "The People rest!"

26

THE JUDGE WASN'T ABOUT TO GIVE ME TIME TO PRE-
pare. He was as furious as Evola. So I began our case at once.

I opened with the doctors I had used at the Walker hearing.
Evola was better prepared this time, although he did no significant damage.

Of course, opening up the files on Angel's mental problems was
like jumping on very thin ice. If you jumped a little too hard you
could go right through. It was extremely dangerous, but I had no
other choice. I wanted the jury to believe she was emotionally
fragile and unable to think correctly when she finally caved in and
gave them that final videotaped statement.

My problem was that they might not stop there. They might go
a step or two beyond and decide she was just nuts enough to stick
a sword right through dear old dad.

All life is a gamble, they say. This time it was Angel's. And in a
different way, mine.

Since Evola had worked the witnesses in the previous hearing,
he knew what he wanted to ask and he knew their probable answers. So did I. We went through the doctors, one after another.
It went much faster than I expected.

Dr. Henry Foreman was good, very good. Evola tried to keep
out any testimony about Harrison Harwell's mental state, but I
got most of it in. Enough at least to give the jury a basis for what
was coming.

We moved so quickly we were soon up to my trump card, Dr. Voltz. It was going too fast. I didn't want the jury to get the idea that our case sped by because it wasn't substantial.

I called Max Webster as a witness to set the stage for the doctor's testimony.

Webster, who looked even older, came forward. I quickly reviewed his many years with the Harwell company and his present position as head of security at the plant. He spoke of his long friendship with Harrison Harwell. Webster told again how Harwell had talked of suicide that last night when they were alone at the boat factory, the night he died.

Evola asked only a few questions. It was obvious that Webster was telling the truth. That made him dangerous, so Evola let him go as quickly as possible.

Then I called Dr. Hans Voltz to the stand.

Voltz came forward, looking like one of God's senior angels.

I walked to a point in the courtroom where both Voltz and I would have to raise our voices to be heard clearly. It was a good tactic because it would help emphasize his important testimony.

The case, I thought, would stand or fall on the suicide issue, and Voltz was our main card.

"Your name?"

"Hans Voltz."

"You are a doctor, licensed to practice medicine?"

"I am."

Evola stood and said he would waive the doctor's qualifications. It sounded like a very polite act on his part but it was a maneuver to keep the doctor's impressive history from the jury. I thanked him equally politely, but declined his kind offer.

We spent fifteen minutes as Dr. Voltz spelled out his education, degrees, and training. Finally, we got to work.

He was as good as they said, maybe better.

There are witnesses, and then there are *witnesses*. Dr. Voltz was definitely a *witness*. Even the judge seemed to hang on every word. When Evola kept objecting, a tactic to try to throw the doctor off stride, the judge finally told Evola to sit down and shut up.

Dr. Voltz took the short sword taken from the Harwell's body and used it to give a fascinating lecture on Japanese culture, tracing the weapon from its samurai origin to present times. I watched the jury. They were as riveted as the judge.

And I glanced from time to time at Evola. He looked, as the saying goes, like a five-pound bird laying a ten-pound egg.

Dr. Voltz explained in his friendly, learned way that the short sword, called a tanto, was the traditional weapon used for suicide by the samurai. He vividly described the ceremony of hari-kari. He even explained that in the old days it was customary to have a friend standing by so that, after stabbing oneself, the friend could lop off one's head with the long sword, called a tachi. The doctor joked that because of a shortage of good swordsmen, the practice had fallen into disuse. No one laughed, but everyone smiled.

And I was able to use the gory photographs to good effect. The doctor, lecturing to the jury, pointed to the significance of the placement of the sword, saying it showed the blade had been thrust in and up by the dead man. Then he went into the many causes of suicide, why people did it and how people did it. Then he related everything he had said as it related to Harrison Harwell.

It was suicide, he said. It could have been nothing else.

I don't know about the jury, but I believed him.

I didn't envy Mark Evola. Cross-examination of someone as sharp as Dr. Voltz was an almost impossible job.

Evola came at him in different ways.

"How could a man cut into himself like that?"

The doctor explained that the sword was designed to do just that. The blade had entered just below the sternum bone, a center mass of thick bone that acted as a shield to the heart, and then the blade sliced up and in.

"That would have taken a great deal of force, wouldn't it?" Evola asked.

The kindly old doctor shook his head. No. There was a muscle wall to be penetrated. That would have required only normal strength. Then the blade would have gone through the internal organs as if they were butter, slicing up into the heart. Blood would have followed the blade, squirting for a short time, seconds, while the heart still pumped. That explained why there had been so much blood.

Evola tried several attacks, and each of them failed.

I tried to hide my elation. We were going to win the god-damned case!

Evola walked slowly back toward his seat, the picture of defeat.

He turned, in a sort of swan song, looking for some graceful way to get off the stage. "Is that sword really that sharp, that a man could easily drive it into his stomach and into his heart?"

"Absolutely."

"How about coming out?"

"I don't understand?"

"Would a person have any trouble pulling that sword out?"

Dr. Voltz smiled. "None whatsoever."

"Even a woman?"

Voltz beamed. "Even a child."

"So if someone said she tried to pull that sword out and couldn't, would she be lying?"

I felt frozen. Time stopped. I couldn't breathe. Angel, in explaining why her fingerprints were found, had said in all her statements that she had gripped the sword handle and tried to pull it out, but couldn't.

Voltz hesitated. I think he finally realized the implications of what he had just said.

"I repeat," Evola said slowly, drawing out the words. "If someone said that, would that person be lying?"

The courtroom was stunningly quiet.

"Yes."

We were going to lose the goddamned case!

"We'll break here for lunch," the judge said, looking over at me with a smile. But his eyes could not have been more cold.

ANGEL seemed absolutely unconcerned. "We're in trouble, aren't we?" The question was without emotion, as though she were inquiring about the score of an uninteresting game.

I wondered how frank I could be. On the other hand, there was no point in sugar-coating things at this point.

"Yes," I said. "It's not over until the fat lady sings, but this is a very bad break. The suicide issue is still in play, but the business about pulling out the knife hurts."

"I really didn't pull, you know," Angel said.

I turned so I could look directly at her. "You said you did."

357

She shrugged. "I was going to pull it out," she said evenly. "I did take hold of the handle, then I froze. His eyes were wide open and staring. He was dead. I ran away. I panicked, I admit it."

Angel's calm was unnerving. It was like she was talking about a flower arrangement. Again, there was a strange absence of emotion, any emotion.

"I'll try to work that in somehow."

"How?" Angel asked. "Will you have me testify?"

The jury would be as shocked as I was by her calm, her stillness, her unconcerned manner. There was something unsettling about it. Perhaps even frightening.

"I don't think it's a good idea," I replied.

"I want to testify, Charley."

"Oh yeah? What are you going to do? Take the Fifth too? Jesus, that would really put the capper on things."

"I want to tell my story."

"It's too dangerous."

"We've lost the case, Charley, in case you haven't noticed. My only chance is up on that witness stand."

"Look, don't panic, Angel. We haven't even gone over what I might ask, or Evola."

"I want to testify. I demand that you put me on the stand."

"It's your funeral."

"That's exactly what it is, Charley."

"Well, let's talk about it at lunch."

"No. When I come back I will testify."

She got up and left in the company of the Harwell security people, without even a backward glance. I noticed Robin had already gone.

There was no point in following. I obviously wasn't welcome.

I just sat there. I had no appetite. Why even think about lunch?

The courtroom was now almost deserted. I looked around. It was nice. Courtrooms were always nice.

This would probably be my last time in one.

PEOPLE began to come back and the courtroom was again jammed. Angel returned. I noted that Robin wasn't with her.

358

"I'm ready," she said.

"Look, I'll ask for a few minutes. We have to talk this over."

"The time for talking is over," she replied coolly. "Let's just get this over with."

I nodded.

The judge came out and everyone stood. He rapped the gavel, but I remained standing. He looked at me.

"Mr. Sloan," he said, as if my name were a bad word, "are you ready to proceed?"

I paused, the way you might before diving into dark and dangerous waters.

"I call Angel Harwell to the stand."

ANGEL had a story to tell.

She told it in a quiet, straightforward manner, her expression unchanged as she serenely related a history that rivaled anything in fiction, even very dark fiction.

Her lack of emotion gave even more punch to the powerful story she told.

I occasionally asked a question but it really wasn't necessary. She didn't need my help.

She told of her life after her mother died, of being sent away to school, missing her mother's affection and feeling cast out by her father.

Angel seemed to be looking at a point in the back of the courtroom, a point that only she could see. In the hushed room, her steady voice was the only sound that could be heard.

She had returned to live with her father and stepmother. At first everything was better. Her father was still distant but her stepmother made up for that, giving her attention and support. But as Angel developed into a woman she found herself confronted at long last by attention from her father, but not the kind she wanted.

It was a dark history, a story of rape, incest, and physical abuse. I noticed one of the women on the jury wiping away tears.

According to Angel she didn't tell anyone because she was ashamed and she was afraid to leave since she was a minor and had no money. Her mother had set up a small trust fund, but she wouldn't receive any income until she was twenty-one. Her father's drinking accelerated and he became increasingly abusive toward her stepmother. Angel said she felt she had to stay to protect Robin since Robin tried always to protect her.

Angel, her eyes fixed steadily on that same distant point, said that despite everything, she still loved her father. But she feared him and what he might do. When she reached eighteen she finally summoned up the courage to leave, but her father followed her to New York, accused her of being a prostitute, and persuaded a court there to commit her. It was the first time she had ever seen the inside of a mental hospital.

Angel told the jury she believed that her father could have her committed whenever he chose. He said he could. And he had carried out that threat more than once when there had been trouble at their home. She told the jury of the time in Florida when he attacked her in a drunken rage.

She believed then that he really meant to kill her. She had grabbed a kitchen knife and held it before her to try to keep him away. He cut himself trying to grab her. The police came but he wasn't arrested, she said. She was once again taken to a mental hospital, just as he had promised.

Hers was a story that had the simple but powerful ring of truth, every word.

Then Angel got to what happened the night her father died. She said that she had argued again with her father that night. He was losing his business, drinking more and getting worse, much worse. She was going to leave this time. So was Robin. The quarrel ended when Angel ran from his den. Later, out of fear of what he might do to her, she went back to apologize and found him dead. She felt responsible. She had placed her hands on the knife intending to get it out but didn't try because he was obviously dead. In shock over what had happened, she ran to her bedroom, where the police found her.

I knew which parts of her story Evola might attack, so I took her gently back over that ground, covering anything that I thought needed more explanation as preparation for what was to come.

The power had come not only from what she said, but equally from the way she said it. I shouldn't have worried. The lack of emotion had served only to underscore the horror.

360

I looked at the jury. You can tell, you know, sometimes. You can read on their faces what they're thinking. This was one of the rare times. They believed.

"You may take the witness," I said to Evola.

He was still angry and that rage was affecting his judgment. He came at Angel like a pit bull, shouting his questions, his voice full of ridicule and disdain.

It was the wrong tactic.

Angel was a young woman who had been greatly damaged by what had happened to her in life. She replied evenly in the same unemotional way, never reacting to his disbelief.

I didn't object. It was going too well.

Evola became really nasty, shooting short, cutting questions at her, hoping to provoke anger. She answered as calmly before, but two little tears began a slow trip down her perfect cheeks. Just as they had the first day I had seen her. No emotion, just the tears.

It was absolute dynamite.

Frustrated, Evola stood closer to her, almost yelling in her face. All he got for his trouble was her firm dignity and those silent tears.

I stood up and waited, looking directly at her.

Angel Harwell looked directly at me.

Finally, in a voice just above a whisper but loud enough for the jury to hear, I asked, "Angel, did you kill your father?"

"No."

The courtroom was absolutely quiet.

"The defense rests," I said.

EVOLA said he had rebuttal witnesses.

He called the young woman emergency doctor who had testified at the Walker hearing. I had noticed her sitting in the courtroom while Angel was testifying.

Evola asked her to describe how cool and calm Angel had been that night.

Then it was my turn.

There are various avenues of attack. Some work with witnesses who you think are lying. Some work with witnesses who you think are probably telling the truth. I thought the doctor was truthful.

361

"Doctor," I said, beginning my cross-examination, "you were present here this afternoon when Angel Harwell testified, is that not so?"

"Yes."

"Today, on the stand, did you think she was about the same as she was the night in the hospital when you examined her?"

"Yes."

"And you thought her manner unusual that night, given the circumstances, correct?"

"Yes."

"Having seen her today, on the stand, looking back, do you still think her manner that night unnatural?"

"No."

"That is how she is, isn't it, no matter the pressure, no matter the circumstances?"

"I believe that's so."

"Thank you, Doctor."

Evola knew better than to try to repair her testimony. He tried again to put Milo Zeck on the stand. And, once more, he failed.

"Is that it, Mr. Evola?" the judge asked.

"The People rest."

The judge turned his cold eyes my way.

"The defense rests," I said.

The judge consulted his watch. "It's almost quitting time. We will begin at nine o'clock sharp as usual. I want the attorneys here a half-hour before so we can review any request relating to the charge. Then both of you gentlemen should be prepared to make your final arguments. Any problems?"

I shook my head.

"No problems," Evola said.

"Good," the judge said, allowing a small smile. "If all goes well, ladies and gentlemen of the jury, you may have this case by to-morrow night."

He hesitated, then spoke again, this time in a commanding tone. "I am going to order all the attorneys and the people who have appeared as witnesses, all police officers, and anyone else connected with this case not to discuss any aspect of this matter with"—he smiled coldly—"anyone connected with the press or other media."

He stood up and the clerk rapped the gavel. "All stand," the clerk barked as the judge hurried toward his chambers.

Then the gavel rapped again. "This court stands adjourned until tomorrow morning."

ANGEL, circled by a ring of security men, fled the courtroom before I could talk to her.

I was instantly surrounded by reporters, all snapping questions.

"You heard what the judge said." I raised my voice above the din to be heard. "As you know, I am a champion of truth, justice, and the American way, but if I talk to you they will send my well-intentioned ass to jail. I'm sure you don't want that to happen."

They didn't care, and they let me know it. A couple of the reporters shouted questions about a courtroom trick. Others yelled something about slick lawyers and questionable ethics. I pretended to pay no attention.

I pushed my way out of the courtroom and was immediately surrounded outside by television cameras and people with microphones demanding I give a statement as they followed me down the stairs and out the door. I repeated my act, smiling all the while, and finally managed to get to my car and drive away.

I drove to my office.

I locked the door after me in case any newspeople were in pursuit. Then just sat there for a few minutes.

If I ever needed a drink, this was the time. But I had one more day to go. One more day.

Then, I just might do it.

AFTER a few minutes of watching the river I began to relax.

I called the Harwell house and Dennis Bernard answered.

"Bernard, I'd like to speak to Angel."

"Mr. Sloan, I've been instructed to tell you that phone calls are not being accepted."

"Why?"

"I'm not entirely sure of the reason."

"Okay. I'll be over there in ten minutes."

"Mr. Sloan, that wouldn't be wise." I could hear the embarrassment in his voice. "I'm afraid you aren't welcome at the moment.

The gate guards have been instructed to turn you away if you do come over."

"Jesus, what's going on over there?"

"Mr. Sloan, all I can tell you is what I've been told to say."

"Am I fired as Angel's lawyer?"

"Not that I know of."

"Tell her to get on the goddamned phone. Now!"

I heard him draw in a long breath. "Please, Mr. Sloan."

"Okay, Bernard. I won't put you in the middle. Tell those two wonderful women I'll see them in court in the morning. Tell them to pray that I'll be good. Got that?"

"I'll say a prayer, Mr. Sloan, if that counts."

"It counts, Bernard. Thanks."

I was angry. But there wasn't anything I could do. I could go out and get stone drunk. It would serve them right if I didn't show up in the morning. The idea was stupid and juvenile and I recognized it as just another manufactured excuse to drink.

It was Thursday night, the regular meeting of the Club. I looked at my watch. I could make the drive to Detroit. I had the time. Then I decided against it. I would use the evening to prepare my final argument.

I should have gone to the meeting.

I STARTED my preparation.

I'm a good workman. I know what has to be done. If I was a bricklayer I would build one hell of a good wall. It might not have the flying buttresses of Notre Dame or the reach of Chicago's Trade Tower, but it would be a good wall.

I made an outline of all the testimony heard by the jury. There was a lot of detail. I began to make a diagram of the more important points. But I couldn't find a theme, a framework suitable for getting everything in. There seemed to be too much to cover.

A pizza delivery boy brought me a double cheese, double sausage dinner, complete with giant soft drink. It helped, but not all that much. My wall wasn't getting built.

I put the argument aside and worked some on what instructions I might ask the judge to give.

Judges, most of them, worked from a form book of printed instructions. Some had memorized them, some just went ahead and read the damn things to the jury. Attorneys can request additional charges, statements by the judge to the jury about the law, but the judge doesn't have to give them if he thinks them improper.

I tried to anticipate what Evola might request. That was the easy part. I could anticipate with some certainty, judging from the direction of his questions during the trial, and I had a number of standard objections at hand for anything damaging he might want. But I couldn't get a grip on anything specific that I might want the judge to tell the jury. Again, I couldn't seem to get focused.

The pizza was gone, as was the cola.

I tried once more to draw up the main points of what I might say to the jury. Nothing effective would come.

There was that little bottle of brandy hidden in the desk. I wondered if a few drinks might release the genie of creativity. That was what they call dangerous thinking. I got up and went home.

I had no idea of what I might say to the jury. I slept, but it wasn't a restful sleep. In my dreams buildings fell on me, and I swam in a sea of snakes. I was relieved when morning finally came.

EVOLA wanted the judge to instruct the jury that they could find Angel guilty of manslaughter. He wanted to give them a compromise verdict in case they had trouble with the main charge of murder. I cited my cases opposing it. The judge said he would instruct the jury that they had only two possible verdicts, guilty as charged and not guilty.

So far, so good.

Evola then wanted an instruction that they could find Angel guilty but mentally ill. I fought hard on that one. I had the cases, but that really didn't mean much given the judge's attitude toward me. Judge Brown seemed to mull it over. Then, to my relief, he said he would not include that as a possible verdict.

Evola asked for some other special instructions, some harmful, some not. In the end, I knew the judge's decisions would do Angel no major harm.

Then the judicial eyes turned to me. "Well, Sloan, let's hear it. What do you want?"

"Nothing special, just the standard instructions, the ones in the manual."

He looked at me with suspicion. "I have to give them anyway, according to law. Nothing else?"

"No, sir."

"All right. I think we're ready to go then, gentlemen."

Both Evola and I stood up.

"Sloan," the judge said sharply.

"Yes?"

"I haven't forgotten, in case you were wondering. We will be meeting, you and I, as soon as the jury brings in its verdict."

"Judge, I—"

He waved his hand to silence me. "Let's go," he said.

Evola turned to me as we walked out of chambers. "Just so you know, your ass is grass up here in Pickeral Point, no matter what happens. You're a slimy little prick, Sloan. If the judge does decide to hang you I want to be the one who gets to tie the fucking rope. Understand?"

"Are you angry?"

He didn't see the humor in it. Neither did I, actually.

Angel was sitting at the counsel table.

"How come you wouldn't talk to me last night?" I whispered.

She looked at me, but said nothing.

The gavel sounded and the judge came out.

27

MAYBE EVOLA WOULD GET ELECTED TO CONGRESS,
or even the White House. His argument to the jury was the kind
of dramatic, riveting speech that earned those kind of jobs.

He was good. Very good.

He started with the outstretched hand, just as he had in his
opening argument. He reviewed the testimony witness by witness. Sometimes you lose a jury by doing that. They get bored.
But not this time. He did it as dramatically as any actor. The
jurors paid close attention to his every word.

I listened and made notes as he picked apart my defense of
suicide. He picked apart everything else, too. And then he began
demonstrating the strength of his case.

Evola's theme was pretty simple, really. Harrison Harwell had
been stabbed through the heart. Angel's fingerprints were on the
murder weapon. She had confessed that she was responsible for
his death. Evola said that the only thing lacking was a videotape
of the actual killing.

But they didn't need that, he told them.

Then he started on Angel, although he was careful not to go too
far. He went over her long history of emotional problems. He
said that the previous wounding in Florida had been a preview of
what finally happened; that everything in evidence showed a
homicidal pattern of behavior.

Evola, knowing it was almost lunch time, stretched things out but finished on a high note, telling the jury that Harrison Harwell cried to them from his grave for justice. He demanded they bring in a verdict of guilty. It was the kind of performance that would have drawn a standing ovation if given in a theater.

Evola's demand for justice seemed to echo in the packed courtroom.

I had been watching the jury during his argument. To my dismay several of them nodded in silent agreement with some of the points he made. One even nodded when he asked for the guilty verdict.

The judge again consulted his watch. He knew what time it was. The gesture was for the jury's benefit.

"It's almost lunch time, Mr. Sloan. We'll take a break and—"

"I respectfully ask that I be allowed to make my argument now," I said.

He looked at me, startled. "I think you may want some time to prepare."

"I've had sufficient time."

"There's no point to beginning, and then taking a break."

I didn't feel like smiling but I made myself do it. "I won't be long," I said. "I will finish before we break for lunch."

"You're kidding," the judge said, then instantly regretted the words. "Well, whatever. If that's what you want. Go ahead."

I looked at Angel. Again, there was no expression, none that I could read. Her icy blue eyes were fixed on mine. I wondered what she might be thinking.

I STOOD before the jury. I really didn't know what I was going to say. But whatever came out had to be fast, and organized. A rambling history of the case would just lose them.

They had seen Angel's performance. If they believed her, we would win. If they didn't, we would lose. It was as simple as that.

I briefly covered the points Evola had raised. The jurors were paying as close attention to me as they had to him. I told them that Angel was innocent. That her father's death was a suicide, not murder.

It went quickly enough, perhaps too quickly. But I could think of no other way to do it.

"It boils down to this," I told them. "The prosecution must

prove every element beyond a reasonable doubt. That's not just lawyers' words, that's what you must find. The judge will tell you that is exactly what the law demands.

"Did Harrison Harwell kill himself? You heard the proofs. He was depressed, he talked of suicide the night he died. His life was crumbling around him, his personal life as well as his business life. Did he kill himself?"

I waited, making eye contact with each of them.

"I think he did, but I don't really know," I said.

I could hear the stirring in the courtroom.

"Was he the terrible person his daughter described? He was a drunk, perhaps a child abuser, many things. But was he what she said he was?"

I waited. Then, "I think he was, but I don't honestly know. Not to a moral certainty." I said it in the same tone of voice, just a shade louder.

"Did somebody else kill him?"

Now I was dancing on the edge of the judge's warning, but I didn't care anymore.

I waited. "I don't know," I raised my voice again slightly as I said it.

"Did Angel Harwell kill her father?" I damn near shouted the question.

"I don't know!" I did shout the answer. It echoed.

Then I waited, knowing that the courtroom was stunned into silence. Several of the jurors were wide-eyed.

"Frankly, I don't know," I said in a whisper. "Ladies and gentlemen, I have perhaps more information than you do, and if I don't know, how can you know?"

I waited again. Some of the jurors looked distinctly uncomfortable. "And if you don't know, then that is what they call a reasonable doubt."

Again I waited, but only for a second. "If there is even a shadow of doubt about the basic facts in your mind, it is your sworn duty to acquit."

I decided to use the old Tom Chawke close. "Yours is a decision where there can be no room for a guess," I said. "Yours is a decision from which there is no appeal. There can be no room for a mistake, if justice is to be done."

Tom Chawke, a legendary trial lawyer, had practiced his magic before my time, but they said he had been great. He often used the same closing. It worked for him. I prayed it would work for me.

I stepped back a bit and looked again at each of them. "Ladies and gentlemen, if I make a mistake, it will be a mistake of law, and a higher court can correct it. If my skilled opponent, Mr. Evola, makes a mistake, it will be a mistake of law, and a higher court can correct it."

I was raising my voice just a little on every phrase.

"Even if the learned judge makes a mistake, it, too, will be a mistake of law, and a higher court can correct it!"

I took a step toward them. "But if you make a mistake, it is a mistake of fact, and no court in this land can correct that."

I took a step closer. I was damn near in the jury box. "If you make a mistake," I said my voice rising, "no one can correct it. If you make a mistake," I dropped my voice to a hoarse whisper and pointed at Angel, "Angel Harwell will unjustly walk the hard floor of a prison cell for time eternal!"

I looked from one face to another. No one looked away. I returned to my seat, the squeak of my shoes the only sound.

"We take an hour's break for lunch," the judge said.

Then it was nothing but sound, or so it seemed.

I turned to talk to Angel, but she was gone.

I DON'T know about the jury, but I was filled with doubt. I had violated a prime rule of defense lawyers, to even hint that there is the remotest possibility that a client might be guilty. It had been risky but it seemed like the only thing to do. The case against Angel, when everything was boiled down to basics, was strong. The only thing that would save her was her own performance and the doubt about her guilt it might have raised.

I was too nervous to eat, not even my usual candy bar. I just sat in the courtroom and waited.

People began trickling back and everyone was in place when Angel came back, precisely at one-thirty.

I didn't get a chance to talk to Angel. Evola made his rebuttal argument. The prosecutor, who had the greater burden of proof, always got two shots at the jury. This speech was shorter, but it was almost as good. Unfortunately.

Then the judge immediately began his instructions. He was direct and forceful as he followed the exact language in the book. I was listening to see whether he shaded the instructions to favor either side. I didn't think he did.

I listened especially closely as he covered reasonable doubt. "A reasonable doubt," he said, "is a fair doubt, growing out of the testimony, the lack of testimony, or the unsatisfactory nature of the testimony. It is not a mere imaginary or possible doubt, but a fair doubt based on reason and common sense. It is such a doubt as to leave your minds, after a careful examination of the evidence, in the condition that you cannot say you have an abiding conviction amounting to a moral certainty of the truth of the charge made against the defendant." He went on, but that was the important part as far as I was concerned.

I watched the jury. They seemed as emotionless as Angel, their faces set as they listened with strict attention to everything the judge said.

And then he was finished. The two excess jurors were excused and the remaining twelve went off to the jury room to decide the case.

"Well, that's it," I said to Angel.

She nodded as she stood up. "Do I have to stay here?"

"No. But I have to know where you'll be. If they reach a verdict you will have to come back and be present for that."

"I'll be at the house," she said, standing. She turned to leave with Robin, then looked back at me.

"Oh, by the way, Charley, you're fired."

She was gone before I could even reply.

I just sat there for a moment. When I stood up I was once again surrounded by the media, but the judge's warning still applied. I heard the shouted questions and I forced a smile, but I didn't answer.

I told the clerk where I'd be and then I drove to my office. The first thing I did was call the Harwell house.

Nothing had changed, Bernard told me. My phone calls and, for that matter, myself, weren't welcome.

He apologized and said he still didn't know the reason for his instructions.

So I sat there and watched the river. I had done everything I could. All that remained was to wait for the verdict.

I assumed the judge would keep the jury working until late at night. It was the usual practice. He had told them that if no verdict was reached he would have them work through the weekend.

The betting would be on a Monday or Tuesday verdict. Longer might mean a hung jury and a mistrial. Quicker would mean they had no major problems with the decision. That could be very bad for the defense. A quick verdict usually meant a victory for the prosecution.

I was about to call the court at eight o'clock and tell them they could reach me at home, but the phone rang as I was reaching for it.

It was the court clerk. They had a verdict.

It was very quick. Too quick. That didn't bode well for Angel.

I called and spoke again to Bernard. He said Angel and Robin would leave for court right away.

If the verdict was guilty . . .

I couldn't allow myself to think about what would happen then. I suppose I should have been thinking of Angel. But I really was thinking of myself.

I GOT there quickly.

But when I arrived the media people had already jammed themselves into every available courtroom seat. I don't know how they got there so fast, but they did. They appeared as eager and as tense as a fight crowd awaiting the main event. The sense of suspense was almost physical.

Evola was sitting there with Morgan and Maguire. If he was eager or excited, he didn't show it. His face was calm, but his jaw was rigid, the only visible indication of his anxiety.

Angel hadn't yet arrived. We all waited for her.

Evola caught my eye as I sat opposite him at the counsel table. There was no smile. "Whatever happens, Sloan, your ass is grass."

"I'll keep that good thought," I replied.

Noise in the courtroom behind us indicated that Angel had arrived. She came in followed by Robin, the security men, and Nate Golden.

Robin Harwell looked worried. Nate Golden looked worried. Angel Harwell appeared entirely unconcerned.

She nodded to me, but said nothing. A court officer escorted her to the empty prisoners' box on the opposite side of the courtroom from the jury box.

I walked over. It is customary for a lawyer to stand next to his client when the verdict is announced.

"Are you okay?" I asked.

She gazed at me impassively, then said, "I'm fine." If she felt the slightest fear or any other emotion, it wasn't evident. She could have been waiting for a bus.

"They didn't take long," I said, to make conversation. She didn't reply.

The judge came out, took his accustomed place, and nodded to the court officer. The jury trooped out, following the court officer in single file. They formed a semicircle in front of the judge's bench.

The judge remained standing.

The clerk voiced the traditional question. "Ladies and gentlemen of the jury, have you reached a verdict? And if so, who will speak for you?"

The first juror in the semicircle, a woman, said in an unnaturally loud voice, "We have reached a verdict, and I will speak."

"What is your verdict?" the judge asked.

It was so quiet, it was as if time had stopped.

And then she spoke.

"We find the defendant not guilty."

THE courtroom erupted. No cheering, no boos, just noise. None of the spectators really cared about the result. They were just excited about getting the story.

Angel was formally discharged by the judge and before I could say anything except warn her not to talk to anyone, sne was engulfed in a tidal wave of her security people and reporters.

I got caught in my own wave. I was facing a wall of screaming voices, opened mouths. Some hand behind shoved me forward, others pulled. It was like being caught in a riot.

I was jostled along until I ended up at a stand in the hall where the news services had set up banks of microphones in front of a small podium. The television lights were blinding and I squinted out at the bank of cameras set back of the mob of newspeople. It was a madhouse. I hoped the security men had been able to spirit Angel away.

As I tried to adjust my eyes to the lights I wondered if the trial would have received such frantic attention if it had happened at any other time of the year. August was usually a lousy month for news. People went on vacations and the world slowed. They damn near closed up Paris every August. But if you had to put on a news show or get out a newspaper you just couldn't shrug and say nothing happened. You had to find something or get another job.

Which was why all these people were shouting at me. Nothing else interesting was happening. We were the show du jour.

I held up one hand and smiled. "One at a time please," I said as calmly as I could.

It didn't help. They continued to try to outshout each other. One deep bass voice rose above the others like a clap of thunder.

"Did the verdict surprise you, Charley?" he yelled.

"This was a complicated case," I said. "There are people who criticize the American criminal justice system." I tried looking as pontifical as I possibly could. "And, admittedly, there are things that could stand some fine tuning. However, while our system is not absolutely perfect, it does the job. In my opinion, the verdict here tonight clearly demonstrates that our system still works. That didn't surprise me."

I didn't pause or I would have been interrupted.

"Harrison Harwell's tragic death was suicide, not murder. I believe the verdict of not guilty validates that position." I said it as if I meant it. I had once. But I wasn't so sure anymore. "That is not to say that this wasn't a difficult case for everyone concerned."

I went on quickly. "I want to thank each member of the jury. They listened carefully to all the testimony and they did their job with diligence and intelligence." That was true enough. "And I want to thank Judge Brown, who was both wise and impartial." That was stretching things a bit, but I still had to face Brown's wrath, and although the victory would rob him of the ability to do me any significant harm, I thought a few kind words might save me from anything more serious than a nasty scolding.

"Are you happy with the outcome?" some idiot yelled.

Everybody laughed.

I nodded solemnly. "I think you could safely say that."

"Did you really think you would win?" one of the disembodied voices demanded.

"I prayed that we would. I was convinced that Angel Harwell was innocent. I had trust in our system of justice."

"Is that why you pulled all that stuff?"

I tried to peer into the lights to see who had asked the question.

"Hey, Charley!" Another voice spoke. "The prosecutor said you're unethical, that you cheated to win. Is that true?"

"I put in the very best case I could," I said evenly. "Everything I did was fair and ethical."

I was surprised at the laughter.

"Ethical, like in having the widow take the Fifth Amendment, Charley?" someone called out, the tone sly and deriding. "Or how about the brainwashing doctors? Charley, you did everything but admit to the killing yourself."

It was no time to show anger, although I felt it. I tried to smile. "I believe in a vigorous defense, if that's what you mean."

I didn't like the laughter. It wasn't nice responsive laughter. It was more of a disbelieving snicker. It was the kind of sound people might have made if Jesse James got up and said he had never robbed a bank.

"What's Angel going to do now?" a woman called out.

"She'll get on with her life. This has all been a horrible nightmare for her."

"Is she really nuts, Charley, or was that just another one of your special effects?"

Laughter again.

"Angel Harwell had, like many of us, some emotional difficulty during a very stormy and sad adolescence. From her father's tragic death through this trial, she has been in a crucible that could break anyone, but she has survived." I tried to look mildly offended. "There have been no tricks, by the way."

More laughter.

"Evola says he's going to complain to the bar association about you. He called you a shyster," someone snapped. "Aren't you afraid they might jerk your license?"

"No." I smiled to show confidence. Actually, I was pretty sure of that answer. Winning can cure many ills, including charges of incompetence. Nothing succeeds like success. If I had lost, they would have absolutely nailed me, but winning was my shield, it was my proof of competence.

But I didn't like the implication of their questions, or the tell-tale laughter. Their perception would show up on television and be reported in detail in the papers. If I came out with a reputation as an unprincipled courtroom trickster, it might be good for getting business—anyone who is guilty of anything wants a lawyer who can beat the rap, fool the jury, buy the judge—but it can be fatal in court. Judges and other lawyers shun someone with that reputation as they might a leper. And eventually, that reputation invites defeat and disgrace.

I had just won a great courtroom victory. I had done it fairly and ethically, but that didn't count. I was being tagged by the world's press as an unscrupulous trickster.

I could just imagine what Evola would say when he followed me for his turn before the microphones.

"Now that you're king of the hill are you going to move back to Detroit, Charley?"

The question was followed by snickers.

I shook my head. "No. Look, this case is over. I'm going back to doing what I did before, just practicing law, nothing more. I'm just a small-town lawyer."

They erupted into explosive laughter. Maybe I should have gone into standup comedy.

I stepped away from the microphones and pushed my way through the newspeople, being careful to keep smiling. I heard Evola's voice as he started his news conference. I couldn't hear his words, but I recognized his tone.

Outrage.

I MADE it out to the parking lot alone. The media were now focused on Mark Evola.

As I climbed into my car I jumped back. Someone was seated in the passenger's side.

"Jesus, don't you ever lock your car, Charley?"

I recognized the voice before I could see her in the dim light.

"Who would want to steal it?" I said to Mary Beth Needham. "I'm sorry if I startled you, Charley, but I wanted to have the chance to talk to you alone for a minute. I thought your car was probably my best bet." Her cigarette glowed in the dark as she inhaled.

"Actually, I should be very angry with you," she said.

"Why?"

"Winning that case may have ruined my chance for a best seller. People love to read the juicy details when there has been a conviction. An acquittal, unless it proves someone else did it, isn't very sexy. And a suicide, if that's what it was, is just sad. People can get sad on their own, they don't have to buy books to do it."

I laughed. "Sorry."

She blew some smoke at me. "Well, despite my own little disappointment, I did want you to know I thought you did a splendid job."

"Thanks."

"How do you feel, Charley? I mean, how do you really feel?"

"Elated doesn't quite catch it."

"I've done quite a bit of research about you," she said.

"I know."

"You're good with juries."

"It's the system, not me."

"Whatever, you're back on top of the world."

I laughed. "Did you ever see the movie *White Heat* with James Cagney?"

"I probably did."

"You remind me of Cagney's exit line. He's on top of a huge gasoline tank and surrounded by cops. He's important once more, the top gangster. He's crazy but he's ecstatic. He yells 'Top of the world, Ma,' just before he fires his pistol into the tank and blows everything up. I feel a little like that. Top of the world, Ma."

She studied me in the dim light. "I don't know if I'd want to equate success with self-destruction. But to each his own."

She reached over and kissed me on the cheek and then slipped out the car.

"Good-bye, Charley," she called out as she walked away. "If I ever kill anybody you'll be the first person I'll call."

28

THERE WAS ONLY ONE TELEVISION TRUCK IN FRONT of the Harwell place. The crew waved to me as if I were an old friend.

I wondered if the two guards would let me through. There were no welcoming smiles but I was waved on in.

Dennis Bernard met me at the door.

"Congratulations, Mr. Sloan."

"Thanks, Bernard."

There seemed to be a lot of activity. Members of the household staff were busily scurrying about.

"What's going on?"

"We're packing up," he said, smiling. "Everyone is going back to Florida tonight."

"Pretty sudden, isn't it?"

He didn't reply, just smiled and then indicated that I should follow him, once again leading me toward the atrium.

They were both there, alone, sitting in the same two chairs drawn up together. Robin looked tired but Angel was as fresh and relaxed as if nothing had happened.

"Well, hail the conquering hero." Robin raised her glass in salute.

Angel merely nodded.

"Get Mr. Sloan a drink, Bernard." Robin paused. "No liquor, just orange juice or something. Right, Charley?"

"I'll pass, thanks." I remembered the taste of vodka and how wonderful it made me feel, at least for a while. Maybe I would drink, later. But I had other things to do first.

I sat in a chair opposite them. "Bernard says you're going back to Florida tonight."

"Yes." Robin nodded. "I told the realtor to wait a week and then put this place up for sale. He thinks we may get a million, although the market is soft. But these river-front places, he said, are still hot."

"You've had it appraised by a realtor?"

Robin nodded. "Last week."

"So this is it then, no more Pickeral Point?"

Angel's laugh was more of a snort.

Robin smiled. "We bid fond adieu as of tonight. Both of us need a vacation, Charley. We were thinking of a cruise, maybe Alaska. It's not too cold yet. It should be quite wonderful this time of year."

"Robin, could I talk to Angel in private? Just for a few minutes."

Robin looked concerned. She glanced at Angel. I could sense she hoped that Angel would object.

Angel shrugged. "Why not?"

Robin nodded. "I have a dozen things I should be doing anyway."

She got up and ran her hand over Angel's head, stroking her gently. She smiled at me and left.

Angel sipped her drink. "Well? What is it, Charley? Money?"

"I'll send a final bill."

She smiled that peculiar little Mona Lisa smile. "Well then, what did you want to talk to me about?"

"Several things, Angel. First, I'm sorry you didn't trust me enough to tell me in the beginning about the sexual abuse by your father."

The little smile faded. "What difference would it have made?"

"If I had known, there might have been a chance to get the prosecutor to drop the charge, or failing that, knock it down to at least manslaughter."

"He would have been sympathetic then, is that what you're saying? Everyone understands child abuse, don't they, Charley?"

I nodded. "Yes. That's why you should have told me. I presume that's what was deleted from those treatment records. Your father arranged that, didn't he?"

She nodded. "He arranged to have the records altered. Anyway, it's done now, everything is water over the dam."

"You still should have told me."

"Maybe I should have. What else did you want to discuss?"

"May I be frank?"

The little Mona Lisa smile came back. "Please."

"Angel, suppose your father's death wasn't a suicide?"

"So?"

"If you didn't kill him, then who did?"

She shrugged. "That's rather irrelevant now, isn't it?"

"Maybe not. I'm thinking about your safety."

"Oh? Why?"

"Because if your father was murdered and you didn't do it, I hate to say it, but the logical candidate is Robin."

"I suppose this all comes out of that Fifth Amendment business in court. She was trying to draw suspicion to herself. That doesn't mean she did anything, Charley. She only refused to testify to try and help me."

"Maybe yes, maybe no."

"Charley, relax. Robin didn't do it."

"How do you know that, for certain?"

"I would think that would be obvious."

"What do you mean?"

"I did it, Charley."

The little Mona Lisa smile remained.

"I wouldn't make jokes like that, Angel."

"What a sweet, trusting man you are, Charley. Robin said you were but I really didn't believe her completely. I don't think most lawyers are, do you? Do you want a drink now, Charley? You look a little pale."

"Cm'on, Angel. This is too serious for this kind of thing."

"It wasn't planned, if that's what you're thinking." She sighed and sipped from her glass. "I didn't go to his study with the idea of hurting him. Things just got out of hand. We were screaming at each other, the sword was hanging there. I grabbed it and stabbed him. It sort of just happened."

"If you thought he was going to try to rape you, you had a right to defend yourself."

"Rape?"

"You testified he had raped you before."

Angel laughed. It was an odd sound, humorless, like small, silver bells, only they were bells that sounded slightly out of sync.

"Oh, Charley. He never touched me. Not sexually. He would have die first."

"But you testified—"

"Frankly, I lied. Not a pretty thing to do perhaps, but human. It saved my neck. Look, I read. So many people have been abused as children. I wasn't. But even those who haven't been have empathy for anyone who was. That jury was no different. That's why I said what I did."

"If it wasn't true, why would your father have those records altered?"

She shook her head slowly. "You really don't have a clue, do you?"

"What the hell are you talking about, Angel?"

Her ice-blue eyes were fixed on mine as she again sipped. I thought she seemed to be enjoying my discomfort.

"Charley, my father was an ass, a stereotypical macho man. You saw all those photos he had of himself in uniform. The big war hero. The closest he ever got to combat was watching John Wayne movies. But that didn't matter, he embraced the macho image with a passion. My grandfather was like that, only with him it was real. He really was a tough son of a bitch. My poor father pretended to be, fucking any little thing who would let him, shooting little animals, drinking straight whiskey, playing poker with elderly boys just like himself, all that supermale bullshit."

She laughed. Again I heard that odd discordant sound of bells. I said nothing.

Then she continued. "How did you see your parents, Charley? Big heroes to you, were they? Ma, the perfect housekeeper. Pa, quiet and wise?"

"They were both drunks, frankly."

She laughed, this time a little louder.

"See! Things often aren't the way they seem, or the way we

might want them to be. So many people pretend to be what they aren't. My father was like that."

"And you stabbed him for that?"

"No."

"Then why, Angel?"

The little smile faded.

"I told you, I was angry. Besides, this time I think he was really going to do it."

"Do what?"

"Kick us both out. He couldn't bring himself to do it before. He was too afraid, afraid everything would be made public."

"I'm not getting this."

She sighed. "Actually, we really didn't want to leave. My trust money had kicked in, but it wouldn't be much. Robin had signed that awful prenuptial agreement. One hundred thousand wouldn't last long, Charley, at least not the way we like to live. It would have been a disaster if he had carried through with his threat."

"So you killed him."

She shook her head. "No, not just like that. It just happened. I admit I had thought about it, but it wasn't planned."

"Angel, are you all right? Maybe all this is something you're inventing. You've been under one hell of a lot of stress."

The little smile came back. "I'm not lying now, Charley. Oh, I'm pretty good at it, I think. They say I'm smart. Maybe that's true. I do seem to be able to see things others don't. It's like I'm always one step ahead of everyone else. It's always been that way. Like that jury, even you. The judge. I knew what all of you wanted and I gave it to you."

"Jesus!"

"Don't take it so hard. You did a much better job than either Robin or I thought you would. Really, that's the truth. Of course, we hadn't planned it that way."

"What do you mean?"

"They had a pretty good case on me, wouldn't you say? You were right about that so-called confession, by the way. I don't know why I let them get away with that. I finally just got pissed off. I really didn't think what I said was harmful, I just wanted to get them out of my hair. It was impulsive. I do things like that sometimes. Charley, that shows that even I can make a mistake."

She finished her drink. "I didn't even think about my hand prints on that damn sword. Christ, it all happened so fast. I was truly in shock or I would have done something about it. He was all blood, and very dead. I wasn't thinking, and I did run. I admit it, I'm human, like everyone else."

"Are you?"

"Don't be bitter, Charley." She stood up. "I'm going to have another. Sure I can't fix you one?"

I shook my head. Angel walked to the bar and made herself a fresh drink and then returned. She looked so normal, so beautiful, so wholesome.

"I'm sincerely sorry we tried to set you up, Charley. You must realize we were desperate. We thought that if I was convicted we could get a new trial on the grounds that you were incompetent."

She sipped the drink and smiled. "Nate Golden was sort of a coach there, although he didn't realize it. If I got convicted, he thought I could get a new trial because of you. If that happened, time would go by, Judge Brown would have retired, and Nate thought he could then work out a plea so I wouldn't have to serve even one day. That's why we tried to get you drunk the other night, to show you weren't competent. We knew you had been in trouble, that's why I insisted you stay on as my lawyer. We would have lost our ace if someone else took over. It was cruel to do that to you, I know. But you can't blame us, really, given what was at stake."

"Angel, what kind of a game is this you're playing? Not a word of this is true."

"It is, though."

"If it were, then why would your father go to the trouble to have the treatment records altered? He abused you and he didn't want anyone to know, that's why. There's no reason to lie about it now."

She nodded slowly. "You're right about that. There is no reason to lie, is there? I've been acquitted. I couldn't be tried again even if I took out an ad."

"So tell me the truth."

"I am." She sipped her drink.

"I don't believe any of this."

She sighed. "Charley, my father lived in some kind of macho dream world. When it happened, he couldn't handle it."

"What happened?"

She laughed. "You really don't know, do you?"

"You're lying again, Angel."

"I was a perfect little girl, Charley, did you know that? Skinny, but perfect. Pretty, too, after I got past the gawky stage. When I came home to live I blossomed physically."

"That's when your father came after you."

She laughed, that peculiar bell sound. "I told you. He would have killed himself first. According to him, no real man would even think of doing anything like that. No. I grew out of the ugly duckling stage and became a swan. Robin saw that."

"So?"

"So. So, we became lovers. Affection became attraction, and then love."

"You're lying, Angel."

She smiled. "That shocks you, doesn't it? How much you sound like father. It's true, Charley. It happens, you know. Robin and I fell in love, deeply in love. At first, it wasn't physical, but then it was."

She sighed. "Of course, we didn't flaunt it. But eventually he found out. Can you imagine what John Wayne would have done in those circumstances? He would have sent the daughter to a mental hospital and he would have beat hell out of his wife, the evil stepmother. At least that's what my father thought, and that's what he did."

"Why no divorce, if all this is true?"

"Because he didn't want it known. Macho men are like that, Charley. He didn't want his pals on the golf course snickering behind his back. He couldn't stand the thought of being the joke at the weekly poker game. So he kept trying to break it up, but he couldn't risk divorce."

Angel laughed. "And all of that, the song of lesbian love, was what he had deleted from those medical records. He paid a lot of money to cut out any reference to the horrible fact that his kid and his wife were lovers. It wasn't an oedipal situation, no son was screwing his mother. It wasn't even an Electra thing, no daughter wanting to fuck dear old dad. In his mind, our situation

~was far worse. To him, it proved he couldn't hack it as a man, as a husband or as a father. It was killing him."

"And it did."

She nodded. "How perceptive. When you think about it, he was the ultimate cause of his own death."

Robin had come in, but I hadn't noticed her until now.

"You heard?" I asked.

She nodded.

"True?" I asked.

Robin smiled sadly. "Yes. I'm sorry, Charley."

"You should be."

"I mean, about what we almost did to you. But we were desperate. You have to understand that."

She sat down next to Angel. They kissed. It was indeed a kiss of lovers.

Angel looked at me. "Does that offend you, Charley, to see us kiss like that?"

"No. Sexual preference is sexual preference. I'm not bothered by it. Never have been. But there is one thing I don't understand."

"What's that?" Robin smiled.

"Why the roll in the hay with me, Robin? I can understand that you prefer women. But why did you make love to me here the night before the funeral?"

Robin shrugged, but I wasn't watching her. It was Angel I saw, although Robin didn't see the reaction. For a fleeting second, the mask fell away and Angel's jealous face was alive with flaming anger, a kind of horrific madness. It was fleeting but it was frightening.

Robin colored slightly. "Well, that little episode was a combination of worry and liquor. I needed someone to hold me, Charley. You were closest."

Angel's mask was firmly back in place.

"Okay, that figures. But what about you, Angel? Why did you throw yourself at me? I mean, given everything."

Robin's head snapped around. Her mouth tightened. Jealousy was directed the other way. But it was a normal kind of response. Angel's hadn't been.

"I wanted you to stay on the case, Charley. I wanted to keep you interested," Angel said evenly.

I stood up. I began walking out but I stopped at the atrium door.

"You beat the legal system," I said.

"No, Charley," Angel replied. "You did."

I shrugged. "Well, you know the old wheeze, murder will out."

Angel laughed.

"You feel pretty sure about things do you, Angel? Good idea, wasn't it, this incompetent attorney defense? It was Robin's idea, right? You're smart, you figured it out. If things went wrong and it didn't work Robin had nothing to lose. You'd be in prison and she'd have all the money. Does that give you a lot of confidence in your lady love? Justice has a strange way of being done eventually, official or not."

"A sermon, Charley?" Robin smiled.

I shook my head. "More of a prediction. You girls are about to go traveling together, a murderous Gertrude Stein and a homicidal Alice B. Toklas, from my point of view."

Robin laughed.

"In a while, maybe a day, maybe a year, one of you is going to make the other one very jealous, or very angry. You are dangerous people. If I were either of you I'd always sleep with one eye open. One of you, eventually, is going to kill the other."

Angel cocked an eyebrow. "That's nonsense," she said.

"Maybe. We'll see." I looked at each of them for a moment. "You deserve each other," I said.

Robin stroked Angel's hair. "We think we do."

I FELT sickened.

Angel Harwell wasn't the first guilty person I had gotten off, but none of them had been quite like her. There had been reasons for the others, excuses, perhaps not fully legal, but human at least. None of the others had coolly manipulated the legal system and done it with such arrogance and disdain.

I had shot my mouth off about the criminal justice system. It would play on the world's television screens, and it would look sincere. It had been then. It wasn't anymore.

Poor Harrison Harwell. He tried to match his daddy, but he

never could. He wanted to go to war, but he couldn't. He wanted to equal John Wayne, but he couldn't do that either. He was a poor flawed man, like the rest of us, condemned to exist within the limitations set by his own weaknesses and fate.

And he was dead, murdered.

Who would speak for Harrison Harwell? Mark Evola had asked that of the jury. It sure wasn't me. I had managed to get his killer off, scot fucking free. So much for my wonderful system of justice.

I drove back toward my office. Fury soon gave way to depression. Even if I had lost, Nate Golden would have manipulated the system and achieved almost the same result. Of course, then I would have been ruined. My ticket would have been pulled.

Now I was a very successful lawyer, albeit a slightly shady one, at least in public opinion. I would again make money, at least for a while. But for what? To be John Wayne? It didn't do much for Harrison Harwell.

I could think of no reason not to drink. No one depended on me. There was no point in continuing to struggle against myself. At least alcohol had a kind of anesthetic value for a while.

There was that bottle of brandy back in the desk, the hidden compartment. And if that didn't work, there was the gun.

And if it came to that, who would come to the funeral? Not many, just the Club. But first I would drink.

I pulled up into the parking lot. The clouds obscured the moon so that darkness was almost total. At the top of the outside stairs, there was a light, enough so I could see to climb. By the side of my office door, I saw a figure sitting. As I approached, the figure stood up.

If he was a robber, what could he get? My wallet? It held about fifty bucks and an unsigned check. My life? Hell, that wasn't worth two bits.

"What do you want?" I demanded as I got closer.

"Mr. Sloan? Mr. Charles Sloan?" The voice was feminine.

I thought she might be a reporter, one who just wouldn't give up.

"Get out of here," I said. "Everything is all over."

"I don't have any other place to go." The voice was almost a whisper.

"So? What's that to me?" I was close enough to see her now

under the naked light at the top of the stairs. She was young, a trifle stout, and she had a conspicuous skin problem. She had a hiker's knapsack and nothing else.

She started to turn away, but stopped. "Look, I'm embarrassed about this, but could you make me a loan? I'll pay you back."

I recognized the voice. It was the young woman who had left the messages but no name on my answering machine. "Do I know you?"

She again started to walk down the stairs.

"Hold on. Who are you?"

"It makes no difference."

"It might. Who are you?"

"My name's Lisa."

"Lisa who?"

"Different names. It depends on who Mother was married to at the moment. She tells me it was Sloan originally. I don't remember, but that's what she says."

"You're Lisa? You're my daughter?"

"That's what Mother says."

I opened the office door and flipped on the lights. "C'mon in."

She followed me in and looked around.

"Not much, eh?"

"Well, it has possibilities," she said. "Whose name is on the door?"

"He's dead. I took the office over. I have to have that changed."

"Nice man?"

"I didn't know him. How come you're here and not in California with your mother?"

She took off the worn knapsack and sat down. She could be pretty if she tried. She was someone who the beauty experts would say needed a lot of work.

"Look, if you can let me have a hundred bucks, even fifty, I'll be on my way. I'll pay you back as soon as I get a job."

"Where?"

"I don't know. Wherever I end up, I suppose."

"How come you're not with your mother?"

"You won't lend me the money if I tell you."

"Try me."

388

She sighed. "I was in a treatment center, the twenty-eight-days bit. I snorted a little coke now and then, a little meth, too, but alcohol was the main problem."

"A drunk?"

She nodded slowly. "Yes."

"Did you run out on the program?"

"No. I finished."

"And then what happened?"

"I went home, but mother and her newest husband didn't want me around anymore. She gave me a couple hundred dollars and told me I was on my own."

She shrugged. "I guess I am. I used the money to live on and to get here. It's gone now. I know I shouldn't have come to you, not after all these years, but I really don't know what to do. I've just about played out my string."

"How old are you now, Lisa? Nineteen?"

"Yes." She seemed shocked that I knew.

"How about school?"

"I've graduated from high school. And I had one year of college."

"Good grades?"

She nodded. "Yes, when I was sober enough to get there."

"Is your mother still a drunk?"

She seemed defensive. "I suppose you could say that."

"Well, you come by it honestly. A predictable by-product of the gene pool," I said. "I'm a drunk, too. Did she tell you that?"

"She never talked about you much."

"I'm in A.A."

Her eyes widened. "So am I. I started at the hospital."

"What are your plans?"

"I don't know. I thought maybe I could get a job in New York maybe."

She was putting up a brave front, but I could hear the uncertainty in her voice and see the fear in her eyes.

"Would you want to stay with me for a few days? I have a two-bedroom apartment."

"No wife?"

"I've had a couple since your mother, none now. Do you know how to run a word processor, by any chance?"

"I do. I'm pretty good."

"Want to work for me, until you find something else?"

"I don't know. Do you think we'd get along?"

"We'd have to find that out, wouldn't we?"

She smiled shyly. "I guess we would." She studied me for a moment. "I saw something on television in the bus station, about a lawyer, a famous one, a Charles Sloan. Is that you?"

"Don't pay any attention to that, Lisa. It's all show business, just show business."

She grinned. "I'm impressed."

"Okay, here's the rules. I'm a recovering alcoholic. If you are too, swell. But if you have to snort a little coke or sip a little gin, our arrangement is over. Any trouble with that?"

The grin became wider. "None."

"I go to an A.A. meeting every Thursday, sometimes more often. You can come with me or not as you choose. Okay?"

I thought I saw the beginning of tears.

"Hungry?"

"Yes."

"There's a couple of places still open. How about dinner?"

"Thank you."

Then she hesitated. "What should I call you? Every time mother married somebody I had to call him 'dad.'"

"How about Charley? Just about everybody calls me that."

"Charley." She said it as if testing the sound of it. "It's okay with me, Charley, if it's okay with you."

"Good. Look, go out to the car, okay? It's the only one down there, an old Ford. I have a chore to take care of. But I'll be right there."

"Sure." I thought she looked happy.

I waited until she closed the door. I took out the secret door, fished out the bottle of brandy and the gun. I wrapped them in a cloth, weighted it down with a heavy stapler, and closed up. I skipped down the steps, picked my way to the river, and threw it in.

Swiftly, the dark waters closed over the small, weighted package. I stayed there for a moment.

It was a new beginning.

For a while, at least, someone needed me.

I was whistling as I got back to the old Ford.

And I was hungry. Really hungry.